CRITICAL ACCLAIM FOR THE WORKS OF JAMES RADA, JR.

Saving Shallmar

"But Saving Shallmar's Christmas story is a tale of compassion and charity, and the will to help fellow human beings not only survive, but also be ready to spring into action when a new opportunity presents itself. Bittersweet yet heartwarming, Saving Shallmar is a wonderful Christmas season story for readers of all ages and backgrounds, highly recommended."

- Small Press Bookwatch

Battlefield Angels

"Rada describes women religious who selflessly performed life-saving work in often miserable conditions and thereby gained the admiration and respect of countless contemporaries. In so doing, Rada offers an appealing narrative and an entry point into the wealth of sources kept by the sisters."

- Catholic News Service

Canawlers

"A powerful, thoughtful and fascinating historical novel, Canawlers documents author James Rada, Jr. as a writer of considerable and deftly expressed storytelling talent."

- Midwest Book Review

Between Rail and River

"The book is an enjoyable, clean family read, with characters young and old for a broad-based appeal to both teens and adults. Between Rail and River also provides a unique, regional appeal, as it teaches about a particular group of people, ordinary working 'canawlers' in a story that goes beyond the usual coverage of life during the Civil War."

- *Historical Fiction Review*

Canawlers

"James Rada, of Cumberland, has written a historical novel for high-schoolers and adults, which relates the adventures, hardships and ultimate tragedy of a family of boaters on the C&O Canal. ... The tale moves quickly and should hold the attention of readers looking for an imaginative adventure set on the canal at a critical time in history."

- *Along the Towpath*

Beyond the Battlefield

"Tales of these and other topics await the reader of Rada's interesting book. You will never think of Gettysburg as just a battle site again."

- *Pennsylvania Magazine*

"These are the untold stories of Gettysburg. They are the stories of the people, places and events that happened in and around Gettysburg outside of the famous Civil War battle, and in many cases they are just as interesting as the Battle of Gettysburg."

- *Gettysburg Times*

CANAWLERS

James Rada, Jr.

LEGACY
PUBLISHING
A division of AIM Publishing Group

OTHER BOOKS BY JAMES RADA, JR.

Non-Fiction:

Battlefield Angels: The Daughters of Charity Work as Civil War Nurses

Looking Back: True Stories of Mountain Maryland

Looking Back II: More True Stories of Mountain Maryland

Saving Shallmar: Christmas Spirit in a Coal Town

When the Babe Came to Town: George Herman Ruth's Small-Town Baseball Games

Fiction:

Beast

Between Rail and River

Canawlers

Kachina (e-book)

Kuskurza (e-book)

Lock Ready

Logan's Fire

My Little Angel

The Race (e-book)

The Rain Man

October Mourning

To Amy,
who shares my life day by day and
who traveled the canal with me to discover its beauty.

CANAWLERS

Published by Legacy Press, a division of AIM Publishing Group.
Cumberland, Maryland.
Copyright © 2001 by James Rada, Jr.
All rights reserved.
Printed in the United States of America.
Fourth Edition: January 2015.

Library of Congress Control Number: 2001119274

Cover photo courtesy of the National Park Service.

LEGACY
PUBLISHING
315 Oak Lane ● Gettysburg, Pennsylvania 17325

1

THE COMING SEASON
MARCH 1862

The *Freeman* rested on dry land like a striped bass gasping for air after being cast ashore by receding spring floods. Only it was no flood that had grounded the canal boat. It sat where it had been floating when the Chesapeake and Ohio Canal had been drained at the end of the season late last January. Now it was the middle of March and the *Freeman* looked like a rotting hulk frozen in the dirt and clay of the canal bed.

Hugh Fitzgerald stood on the bank opposite the towpath side pf the canal, staring at the boat...*his* boat. Ninety-two feet long and made of Georgia pine from back when Georgia had still been part of the Union and trade between the states had been open. Hugh loved the familiar sight of the squarish hull and curved hatch covers. The *Freeman* was more his home than his house in Sharpsburg.

Seeing the boat stirred feelings of roaming in his soul. Hugh had checked the *Freeman* every week since the canal had been drained, braving the freezing winter temperatures just to touch her hull and sit near the small pot-belly stove in the family cabin and smoke a pipe. He would read the newspaper and imagine that the deck under his feet was rolling gently in the lazy current of a full canal. The trips were as much for getting out from under Alice's feet as for making sure nothing had happened to the canal boat, and hence, his livelihood. Now that the opening of the canal season was drawing closer, Hugh studied his canal boat with a critical eye to see what needed to be done to get the *Freeman* in shape for the coming season.

He hesitated only momentarily when he saw the length of rope dangling out of the hay room window between the closed shutters. He would not be relaxing today. He had company waiting for him aboard. Hugh sighed and wondered how much longer such secrecy would have to continue before this grand country came to her senses.

"You do what's right as long as it is right, lad," his father would have told him.

And continue doing it he would. Hugh wasn't sure he could live with himself if he didn't.

1

Soon, he would be on the move again, up and down the edge of the Potomac River between Cumberland, Maryland, and Washington City. Being on the move again would take the edge off the tension that built up within him over the winter to move and be doing something other than caring for his canal mules.

Hugh picketed Seamus, one of his four canal mules near the edge of the canal. Seamus usually pulled the boat, but today he was serving as Hugh's mount. Hugh tossed the leather reins around a branch of a maple sapling. It wasn't a sturdy picket, but that was all the Kentucky mule needed to keep from wandering. He patted the thick gray fur on Seamus's neck and the thick-chested mule shifted his weight forward vying for more attention.

"Feeling the need to take a long walk, Seamus?" Hugh asked.

He'd owned this mule for five years. Seamus was broken to the harness and enjoyed the long months of walking the 185-mile-long towpath once a week. Hugh's four mules had spent most of the winter in the Fitzgerald barn, except for when George or Hugh took them out to ride or to exercise them. With the mules stabled near his home, Hugh was able to make sure that they were well cared for.

Too many times he had seen canal mules that had spent the winter months being taken care of by someone other than their owner. A farmer with extra stalls in his barn just didn't care for what he considered non-productive animals as well as he did his own animals. When it came time to pull the canal boats to Cumberland, those mules were scrawny, sick-looking beasts that were shades of their normal selves. They pulled with less power, lengthening the time it took to make a run up and down the canal. They also slowed other traffic on the canal, particularly at the Paw Paw Tunnel or the narrow paths across the aqueducts.

Hugh depended too much on his mules to allow them to be mistreated or ignored during the winter months. He had purchased a lot in Sharpsburg not far from the house three years ago, and he and George had built the four-stall barn for the mules to stay in during the winter months when the canal was shut down.

Hugh scrabbled sideways down the seven-foot-high steeply sloped bank to the canal bed. The bed was firm, still hard frozen from the winter cold, but at least water was no longer freezing overnight. He walked across the canal bed to the *Freeman*.

He looked first to where the boat sat fastened hard to the canal bed by frozen mud. The ice wasn't thick. Some fire-warmed rocks around the bottom of the boat would begin to break the ice's hold on the *Freeman* without damaging the hull. The rest would come when the water rushed in from the feeder lock to flood the canal and float the hundreds of canal boats within its banks.

Hugh touched the wooden hull, letting his fingers slide into a gap between the boards of Georgia pine. It wasn't too wide. The gap would close up somewhat once the boards became soaked with water within the next month. Even so, he would still need to caulk the gaps with hemp and tar to seal the boat from any leaks. Then when the wet wood swelled, it would tightly seal the gaps.

Hugh walked a few feet farther, letting his hand trace the shape of the hull. The *Freeman* had a good shape. She was a good boat and had served him well over the years.

He paused and dug his fingernail into the wood to pull a chip of white paint off the hull. She would need a new paint job this season, too. Best to do it now while the hull was easy to get to and the paint would have time dry since the canal was still empty. He and George would have to come out tomorrow and begin painting the boat.

Hugh turned away from the boat and pulled out his pipe. He tamped down some tobacco from his pouch in the bowl and lit it with a match. He smiled with his first puff of the rich Maryland tobacco and continued his inspection of the *Freeman*'s hull.

He and George could have the *Freeman* in shape in no time. With the mules looking fit and strong and the hull sparkling white with a new coat of paint, they'd be an impressive site walking into Cumberland for their first load of coal this season. The hull certainly wouldn't be white after a couple of loads of coal with the dust rising with each ton sliding down the chutes into the cargo holds, though.

"White or black, the *Freeman*'s the same underneath," he muttered softly. Too bad this country, which was so fine in so many ways, couldn't understand that point.

Clamping down on his pipe with his teeth, Hugh scrambled up the steep sides of the canal bed onto the seven-foot-wide towpath. He stood up and dusted the dirt from his pants legs. The knees were looking threadbare. He'd have to have Alice patch them before too long.

He walked to the far side of the towpath and kicked aside the brush that hid his fall board. As the lifted the ribbed plank off the ground and propped it against a sycamore tree, he could tell that the fall board hadn't wintered the weather as well as the *Freeman*. He'd have to replace it this season. The last thing he wanted was for it to break while one of the mules was crossing between the boat and towpath and dump the beast into the water. Still, there were plenty of places to buy a new plank along the canal. He didn't need a new one right away. He'd wait until he was coming back up the canal from Georgetown with money jingling in his pocket.

Awkward as it was working alone, Hugh walked the plank across the towpath and lowered it until one end touched the race plank on the *Freeman*. The fall board dropped the last two feet with a thud because its length made it too awkward to handle alone.

He straightened up, rubbing his lower back as he did. It would be a fine thing to start off the season with a poor back.

You're just getting old, Hugh, me boy.

Old?

He'd never considered himself old before, but he was nearing forty years old. George was sixteen, old enough to captain his own boat. Elizabeth was fifteen and Thomas was eight. And Alice...

Hugh smiled.

Alice would forever be sixteen, no matter what the calendar said. Sixteen and lovely just like the day he first saw her in Cumberland walking out of the dress shop on Baltimore Street. She'd been carrying an armful of gingham fabric. Her green eyes had seemed to glow, and when those eyes had turned to look at him, they had held his attention and his heart. He'd been enchanted with her ever since.

Hugh walked across the fall board and onto the narrow race plank, the walkway that ran fore to aft on both sides of the canal boat. He walked toward the family cabin at the rear of the boat so that he could open the windows and doors and give it a good airing out, seeing as how it had been closed up all winter. He also figured it was time to meet his guest.

As he reached for the doorknob, he heard the clicking sound of a hammer being pulled back on a rifle and froze in place. A thousand possibilities ran through Hugh's mind, and too many ended with him getting a bullet in his back.

"You'd better come down off that boat now, before I knock you off with a bullet."

Hugh raised his hands above his head and turned around slowly. Solomon Greenfield was standing on the towpath with his old single-shot rifle pointed at Hugh.

Solomon was a good twenty years older than Hugh. He had a

bald head that seemed pointed at the top. His brown eyes were narrow and they appeared to be slits. Solomon was always squinting because he didn't like wearing his spectacles. He had been tending the locks along this stretch of the Chesapeake and Ohio Canal since it had opened in 1839, moving his family between Lock 31 and Lock 42 at various times in his career. Of course, now Solomon wasn't much more than a level walker while his son, Clay, and two grandsons tended the Shepherdstown Lock at Bridgeport. Solomon and his wife lived in a small cabin in Bridgeport while Clay's family lived in the four-room brick lock house about three miles south of here.

"Solomon, it's me. Hugh Fitzgerald," Hugh said calmly, though he made sure to keep his hands in the air.

"Fitzgerald?" Solomon's voice cracked like a whip.

"Put on your glasses and see for yourself."

Solomon hesitated a moment. Then his frown slipped into a wide smile that showed three missing teeth on the right side where a mule had kicked him seventeen years ago. He lowered the rifle so the butt rested on the ground next to his foot. Then he reached inside his shirt pocket and pulled out a pair of wire-frame glasses and slipped them over his ears.

"Well, I reckon it would have to be you, Fitzgerald. A squatter or one of those soldier boys wouldn't know about my glasses."

Hugh hesitated, wondering how much he could say without betraying his intentions.

"Have you had trouble with them this winter? Squatters and soldiers, I mean, not your glasses," Hugh asked.

Solomon turned his head to the side and spat a wad of dark chewing tobacco into the canal bed.

"A little. Been some Yanks and Rebs hiding out, trying to avoid the fighting. I caught one on Dermott O'Neill's boat back in November, right after they drained the canal. The man was a deserter, but he had a pistol so I let him go his way peaceably. Since then, I've been checking the boats as I walk the towpath, and I always carry my rifle." He lifted the rifle by the blue-metal barrel and tapped the butt against the ground to emphasize his point.

That surprised Hugh since the last he had heard was that the Union had pushed the Rebels back to Winchester after the Rebels hadn't been able to destroy Dam No. 5 from the Virginia side of the Potomac River. Following that foiled sabotage, the U.S. Army had assumed military supervision of the canal since it was a main transportation route, and unlike the Baltimore and Ohio Railroad, it was all within Union territory. The army presence calmed things somewhat, but it might have also been the oncoming winter that calmed things down.

"Just the one deserter?"

Solomon shook his head. "I've seen the signs of squatters here and about. Ashes in the stoves in the family cabins, pried-open doors and rabbit bones and the like. I don't know whether they saw me comin' or I just plain missed them, but they had been there."

Hugh nodded that he understood.

Part of Solomon's duties as a level walker was to patrol the towpath in his district and check for breaks and potential breaks in the canal and report them to the superintendent whose house was on mile 74.

The lock house where his son lived was down near Lock 38, across the river from Shepherdstown, Virginia. Until last year, there had been a covered bridge that brought people across the river into Bridgeport. Clay had run a good side business selling fresh fish he caught in a net he set in the canal until the bridge had been burned by the Confederates as a symbol of the South cutting its ties with the North. It certainly couldn't make the Greenfields feel too comfortable knowing how strong the Confederate feeling ran just a short distance away from their home and workplace. For that matter, Confederate sympathy probably ran strong in Bridgeport, too.

"How does the canal look?" Hugh asked as he waved Solomon on board the *Freeman*.

The lockkeeper walked across the fall board as he spoke. "My section looks fine. I trapped six beavers that were building dams. Not only did I get their pelts, I kept them from making a mess of the banks. I can't say much about the rest of the canal, but the company man said it's looking pretty good. The Rebs blew up one of the aqueducts out east somewhere, but it's already repaired. We'll be ready to start the season."

"Good to hear it."

"Of course, Dam 5 needs some work, but it's holding for now. Not sure how long it will last, though, if General Jackson and his boys keep hammering away at it."

Dam 5 spanned the river above Williamsport. Stonewall Jackson had launched repeated attacks either directed at the dam or at Union soldiers nearby and the attacks had caused some breeching of the dam.

Hugh opened the door and entered the family cabin. It was spotless. He hoped Solomon didn't notice the cleanliness of a room that was supposed to have been vacant for months.

The war was going to make working the canal dangerous this season. What with the Rebs and Union fighting each other and the canal being on the southern border of a border state, there was bound to be trouble; a lot more trouble than just some deserters using empty canal boats to hide out in for a few days. Eventually, the Rebs, as strong as they were, were going to swarm across the Potomac River. If they did that, Hugh doubted there would be much left of the C&O Canal. The Rebs wanted to shut it down, seeing as how it was a major source of coal for Washington City.

"What was the company man doing out this way?" Hugh asked as what Solomon had said sunk in.

"He's riding up to Cumberland and tellin' the superintendent and lockkeepers along the way to get ready. War or no war, the politicians want to eat and stay warm. There's food and coal that needs to be shipped down east, and he means for the canal to be the way it gets there. He said that by now the canal should be open south of Harpers Ferry. They would have opened up the guard lock there a few days back, but I haven't been down that way to check it out for myself."

"Did he say when the boats would be able to get up to Cumberland?" Cumberland was where the coal was mined from the Alleghenies. Cumberland and Williamsport, that is. Williamsport was closer to Sharpsburg, but Hugh always liked his first run of the season to be a full run so that he could get a nice pay off in Georgetown. After the winter, there were too many things his family needed, and it was nice to be able to buy a lot of them on their first trip down east. He could make the shorter runs the closer it got to the time the Canal Company would drain the canal for the winter.

"He passed through here yesterday and said the canal would open in a week as soon as he could get to Cumberland," Solomon said.

Hugh nodded. That meant he would have to get started today. It would take a full day to scrape the flaking paint off the hull and decks and another two days to paint them both. Alice, Elizabeth, and Thomas could take care of getting the family cabin and the mule shed ready for the season, checking the mule harnesses and stocking the hay house for the first trip.

"Guess I'd better get started getting the *Freeman* ready if I want her to float when the water fills the ditch up," Hugh said, slapping a hand against the wall of the family cabin.

He walked forward along the race plank, checking the fourteen hatch covers for cracks that would let in water. The curved covers arched between the race planks covering the huge cargo hold, which took up most of the space on the boat.

"You know," Solomon Greenfield said from behind Hugh. "It's a bad time to have a boat named that. It doesn't sound right."

Hugh straightened up and dusted off his knees. "Named what? *Freeman?*"

Solomon spit another wad of tobacco over the side of the boat and nodded. "With a name like that, people will take you for a Yankee."

Hugh put his fists on his hips and said, "So? What are you trying to say, Solomon? This is a Union state, after all."

Solomon met his stare without backing down. "Just barely, especially here," he said stamping his foot on the race plank.

Hugh nodded sharply. "Barely's enough. More so, I am a Yankee. When I was a lad, my father taught me that this country was an Irishman's best chance of freedom for getting out from under the thumb of the landowners. He came here from Galway with nothing more than a promise from the Canal Company, and he died a free man in Sharpsburg with property and money."

"Your father died a poor carpenter as I recall."

"He might not have had much more than he would have had in Galway, but he died a free man. To him, that was more important than a chest full of gold," Hugh snapped. He didn't like hearing his father's sacrifices trivialized by someone who took his freedom for granted.

Solomon walked across the fall board back onto the towpath. The board held his weight without too much of a complaint.

Solomon held up his hands to stop Hugh. "Don't get angry with me, you dumb Mick. I'm just tellin' you how things stand. Open your eyes and ears and pay attention to what's going on around you. You can hear the same things I've heard."

Hugh bit down on his pipe to keep from yelling at the older man.

How could he not have heard? Even before there had been a war, men had been arguing up a storm about where states' rights ended and federal rights began. And just because Sharpsburg sat above the Potomac didn't mean that it was heavily Union in its sympathies.

When loyal Unionists had raised a United States flag in the town square, someone stole the rope. When another Union flag was raised, the pole was set afire. The war was pitting neighbor against neighbor.

"Well, how do you stand?" Hugh asked.

"I stand for my family first, then my property, then Bridgeport. If anything's left over after that, I'll stand for Maryland. Maryland may sit above the river, but if Stuart, Jackson, Johnston, or any of the Confederate generals were to come across the river, I'd welcome them and feed them and send them on their way as quickly as I could. I wouldn't lift a hand against them if they left my family and my property alone. I'm no soldier, and I'm no fool, either," Solomon said defiantly.

"That sounds like a coward's way."

"And what would you have me do?" Solomon snapped. "Face down the entire Confederate Army with nothing but my single shot? That's a dead man's way."

Hugh harumphed, but he wasn't sure what he would do if he came upon the Rebels crossing the Potomac. Would he be true to his beliefs or true to his family?

Solomon waved a finger in his face. "Scoff if you want, boy, but I value my life and my family's lives, and if that means I have to sing Dixie while saluting the Stars and Stripes to keep two armies from squashing me like a worm, I'll do it and you will, too."

Solomon turned and stalked off down the towpath. Hugh watched him go. He could hear the old man mumbling as he continued the argument with himself. Hugh hadn't meant to offend the lockkeeper, but Hugh was a man who stood on his principles. He had grown up hearing his father's tales of how Hugh's grandfather had groveled to the landowner, Rory DeBurgh, just for the privilege of surviving on his own labors. Shane Fitzgerald had not been able to live like a slave and had taught his children not to live like that, either.

Still, there was a war going on. So far, it hadn't made its way across the Potomac, though it had come close a time or two, but how long could the Federals hold the Confederacy back? The Rebels were just plain better soldiers as much as Hugh hated to admit it.

And even if the Southern army never crossed the Potomac, Southern sentiment had come across the river, seeing as how Virginia was just a stone's throw across the river. Hagerstown, Boonsboro, Sharpsburg, Keedysville; they were all split with supporters for the Rebels and the Union. Hugh supposed it was the same for the border towns in Virginia.

Hugh wondered if it would be safe to leave Alice and Elizabeth behind in Sharpsburg this season. Alice had been hinting all winter that perhaps she and Elizabeth would stay in Sharpsburg instead of riding in the boat with Hugh and the boys. Alice thought that Elizabeth was getting too old to be spending three-quarters of her life on the canal. Up until now, Hugh had just played dense whenever Alice mentioned it since he hadn't made up his mind about the subject.

When he was sure that Solomon was gone, Hugh walked back to the family cabin. Solomon was a good man, but Hugh wasn't going to trust him with his secrets, especially after Solomon had expressed his Confederate sympathies so strongly.

Hugh stepped into the family cabin and closed the door behind him. The small room was twelve feet square. He rapped lightly on the door to the pantry. It was a low-ceiling room under the tiller deck that Alice used to store supplies.

"You can come out now. I saw your signal and I own this boat," Hugh said.

There was no response. Hugh didn't intend on opening the door to the pantry, though. It might get him shot if his guest was armed.

Hugh scratched his chin and wondered if he should sit down at the table and smoke his pipe while he waited out his visitor.

"You need to come out sometime, friend. If I had wanted to hurt you, I could have already shot you through the door," Hugh said.

After a moment the low door swung open. A black hand pushed it open and vanished back into the darkness. Hugh found himself staring at a young slave girl who was so black that he almost couldn't see her in the shadows in the pantry. She was sitting in the back of the hiding area under the cockpit.

"I didn't take nothin', sir," she said as her voice quavered.

Hugh smiled, hoping it would ease her tension.

"I didn't say you did. In fact, this cabin looks cleaner than it has all winter," he said.

The girl smiled. "I used to be a house slave in Raleigh."

Hugh waved the girl out of the cockpit. To his surprise, she scooted out with a sleeping baby in one arm. She stood up in front of him with her eyes lowered. She looked no older than Elizabeth did, but her life had already been much harder and different.

He held out a chair for her. "Sit down, girl. You're not in any trouble…at least not from me."

"A man helped me and my baby across the river and told me to wait here. He told me to hang the rope out the window and someone would come to help me," the young slave told him.

10

Hugh nodded. "That's me. Now that I know you're here, I'll come back for you tonight and bring you into Sharpsburg. There's another man in town who will take you up north into Pennsylvania. They'll move you north into Canada."

The girl nodded.

Did she know where the places were that he was talking about? Or had she been kept ignorant of the places that meant freedom to a slave?

"What's your name, girl?" Hugh asked.

"Ruth."

"And your baby's name?"

"Naomi. My master named us for holy ladies."

Her master obviously hadn't had much respect for "holy ladies" since he had named his slaves after them. The man probably would argue that he was converting his slaves to the gospel by giving them Christian names. Hugh had heard that argument before, but he didn't remember Jesus Christ ever converting anyone to enslave them, only to free them.

"Do you have a husband, Ruth?"

She nodded vigorously and sniffled. "He ran away with us. When the overseer set the hounds after us, we got separated. He led the dogs away from Naomi and me, but he never came back."

She sounded sad, but she didn't cry. She must have been used to such sadness in her life. Hugh had seen too many people like her. Only in giving up all hope of living free had they been willing to gamble their lives and escape to the north.

One of the reasons he helped escaping slaves along the Underground Railroad was because he knew what slavery could do to a person and also what freedom could do. His father hadn't been called a slave, but his life hadn't been his to control just as this girl's life hadn't been in her control.

"You just stay here and keep on doing what you've been doing. I'll come back tonight. If you hear anybody come aboard, you hide like you just were. I'll call you by name when I come back."

She nodded.

Hugh nodded back. Then he turned and left the family cabin. He walked across the fall board and pulled it back into the brush once he was on the towpath. Ruth wouldn't need to get off the boat until he returned tonight.

He clenched his teeth down on his pipe and scrambled down the side of the bank onto the canal bed. Although he was careful, he nearly fell. It wouldn't do to damage the bank now. If Solomon Greenfield saw the bank torn up near the *Freeman*, he would be sure that Hugh had done it out of spite for their earlier argument.

Hugh paused in the middle of his crossing and looked up the empty canal trench. In a few more days, it would be filled with water over his head. Then his life would begin again. During the winter, he got tired of sitting in his house most of the day. If the times had been reversed, and he had to spend three months on the canal and nine months in Sharpsburg, he would have died long before now.

He shook his head and finished crossing the canal and climbed up the other bank where Seamus patiently waited for him, munching on the leaves of the tree. Hugh figured he and the mule were a lot alike and not just in their mule-headed stubbornness (what Alice would have said) either. No, both of them were a part of the canal somehow. Seamus could no more survive being a farm mule than Hugh would last being a farmer.

As he mounted Seamus for the ride back along the hard-packed Boonsboro Pike into Sharpsburg, Hugh wondered if he was really a free man, as his boat proclaimed, or if he was a servant not to a land-owing earl, but to the land itself. And if he gave himself freely, was it really slavery?

How much Fitzgerald blood had been shed to dig this 185-mile-long ditch? His Uncle John had died of the cholera epidemic that swept through the canal diggers in 1832. His Uncle Dermot had lost an arm digging out the Paw Paw Tunnel when some black powder exploded while he was tamping it down. His own father had had multiple scars, not only from fights with railroaders but from fights with Irish Prods and Germans. He also had cousins who had died or been hurt in those skirmishes.

They'd all died or given their blood for hard work and little pay. All because they believed in a dream of being free and escaping the Great Hunger in Ireland. Some had died with not much more than they would have had back in Ireland, but it had been a life of their own choosing.

The Catholic priest in Hagerstown had said Hugh's Uncle John's last words were, "No one owns my soul but me, and I give it freely to God."

That was what being free meant: owning your own life and choosing what that life would be.

For Hugh Fitzgerald, that life was to be a canal-boat captain on the Chesapeake and Ohio Canal, a "canawler."

2

KEEPING THE FAITH

MARCH 1862

Alice Fitzgerald laid the sock she was knitting aside and stood up from the straight-back chair to stretch her back. She wasn't sure how long she had been sitting in the hard wooden chair, but the March chill had crept into the air, which in turn had crept into her bones.

"Are you all right, Mama?" Elizabeth, her fifteen-year-old daughter, asked her.

Alice smiled. "I'm fine, but if I'm going to keep working in this cool air, I need something to keep me warm. I'll put some water on the stove to boil and make a cup of tea. Would you like a cup?"

Elizabeth nodded. "Yes, thank you."

They were knitting socks and scarves for the men in town who were going off to war. Although winter was over, the socks would still keep soldiers' feet from blistering in ill-filling shoes. Women in Sharpsburg had been keeping busy through the winter doing the same thing. Quilting circles had turned into knitting circles. Unfortunately, not all of the women were knitting socks and scarves for Union soldiers. Some of these socks and scarves would find their way across the Potomac River to Confederate soldiers.

To Alice, that seemed like treason. If you lived in a country, you supported its troops in war. That might be the way things worked in other towns, but in Sharpsburg, at least, town ties were stronger than national ties. Most everyone in town had taken a stand one way or another in the war and most everyone else knew those positions. It had led to some tensions between families, of course, but by and large, life went on as it had before the war.

Alice filled the teapot with water from the bucket and set it on the hot stove. Then she pulled the pile of gray fabric out of her sewing basket and set in on the large kitchen table.

After she was finished this pair of socks, she was going to measure Thomas for a new Sunday suit. Her youngest son seemed to grow an inch a week. He was also a lot harder on his clothes than George had been at that age. Alice suspected Thomas set out to be particularly destructive to his best clothes so that he wouldn't have to wear them.

Elizabeth giggled and lowered her head.

Alice looked at her and asked, "What's so funny?"

"If certain people saw you right now, they would think you were making uniforms for the Rebels," Elizabeth told her.

Alice's hand jerked back from the cloth as if it had bitten her. She realized that it was an unreasonable reaction, but she had never thought about the cloth being Confederate colors.

She shook her head, chiding her foolishness, and said, "That's because it's probably the same material they are using, but better it go to a Sunday suit than to a Confederate uniform."

Alice had very strong feelings about this war. For this country to survive, Americans had to find a way to work together. They had to stop thinking of themselves as Marylanders, Virginians, New Yorkers, Pennsylvanians, and North Carolinians and start thinking of themselves as Americans. It was the United States that had won its freedom from England, united in purpose, not loosely banded together by need as the Confederacy represented. The South called their fight a second war for independence, but Alice saw it only as a war of destruction; not only of lives but of this country.

"Theresa said the fighting will be starting again soon now that spring is here," Elizabeth said.

"As long as it stays away from us," Alice said quickly.

"Will it? General Jackson's army is in Northern Virginia."

Alice stared out the south-facing window. Just a short distance away was the Potomac River, the dividing line between two feuding lands.

"The river is patrolled. General Jackson couldn't bring his men across," Alice said.

"It's not patrolled well, though. You know as well as I do that people in this town slip regularly across to smuggle things to the Rebels. Why else would some of the women be knitting socks and scarves for the Rebels unless they knew they could get them to the soldiers?"

Elizabeth had a point. She wasn't stupid, but she had overlooked one thing. "An army's a lot larger than a smuggler. The Union patrols might miss a person or two, but would they miss a 20,000-man army?" Alice asked her.

Elizabeth finished the blue sock she was working on and handed it to her mother for her approval. Alice took it, stuck her hand inside it to spread out the folds, and inspected her daughter's work. Elizabeth had done an excellent job. Her daughter knew how to knit, sew, and cook. That had never been the problem. Elizabeth was a lady or at least she could be if she chose to be. The problem was that she didn't choose to be a lady unless Alice forced her into it.

Elizabeth was a free spirit. She had grown up on the canal working on the *Freeman*, and it was the skills she learned to run a canal boat that she seemed to call her own more than the ones Alice wanted her to exhibit. Elizabeth could steer a boat, shovel coal, work a lock, and drive mules. They were useful skills, true, but a canaller was not a lady. How often did a lady have cause to use such skills?

Alice found herself asking that question more and more lately.

Her daughter was fifteen years old. She had taken on a woman's body this past year and had begun to turn the heads of the young men in town. Yet, she seemed unaffected by the changes. She had long, strawberry blond hair that she preferred keeping tucked up under a cap rather than showing it off. She still played like a boy, roughhousing with Thomas. She was more likely to punch a boy than to accept a compliment from him.

Now that it was nearly time to begin working the canal again, those unladylike attitudes would become more apparent. Canallers, sailors and railroaders would surround Elizabeth. How could she become a lady with those examples?

"Bobby told me that there's going to be a new regiment forming up in Hagerstown. He's going to join them when it forms." Hagerstown was the nearest city to Sharpsburg, but it was twelve miles to the north. "Do you think the army will take George?"

The thought chilled Alice. She couldn't bear the idea that George might be swept up into the madness down south. Her son wasn't a soldier. He was a canaller, and he was needed to help keep the *Freeman* operating during the season. At least that was the excuse Alice hoped would keep her oldest son out of the war.

"I pray not," Alice said quietly.

"Why? Don't you believe in the Union cause?"

Alice shot her daughter a sharp look. How dare Elizabeth question her mother's loyalty to her country! The girl had no idea of the ways that Alice supported the beliefs of the Union.

"Of course, I believe in the Union, but George is more useful here than as cannon fodder," Alice said.

Not that George would be safer on the canal, but at least, he wouldn't be looking for trouble. It would have to come to him.

"Do you want your brother to be drafted?" Alice asked harshly.

Elizabeth shook her head quickly. "Of course not, but I think he would look so handsome in a Union uniform." Her voice sounded dreamy as if she were picturing George in her mind.

Alice sighed. Now Elizabeth chose to act like a young girl and over an issue like this!

"Those blue uniforms don't look pretty when they're red with blood," Alice said.

Elizabeth blinked quickly as the thought sunk in. Then she frowned and said, "I guess not, but someone will die. A lot of boys in town are joining the army. Some are even going to Baltimore to join the navy. If they're not joining the Union, then they're sneaking across the river to join the Rebels. How many of them will die?"

Alice shook her head. The boys in town had grown up playing soldier. Now they would be fighting each other for real, and worse, they would be killing and dying for real.

"I don't know. It depends on where they are sent," Alice told her.

"But some of them won't come back, will they?" Elizabeth asked.

Alice nodded and watched as her daughter frowned. Elizabeth picked up her knitting needles and then let them drop to the table.

"They're going to die, and all I can do is knit socks for them," Elizabeth said.

"We do what we can," Alice said.

"I wish I could knit something that would protect them, maybe thick sweaters that would stop bullets as well as the cold."

"I wish I could make them see a peaceful way to solve this."

All the men Alice loved would be facing danger on the canal this year. The Confederates had already attempted to destroy the canal. What if they went after canallers next? Was that someplace Alice wanted her daughter? The war affected many people, not just those who fought in it.

3

NIGHTMARES

MARCH 1862

When Lieutenant David Windover saw the incoming artillery shell, he thought he was watching death coming for him. The round shell spun slowly as if passing through water rather than air. The whistling usually caused by artillery shells was drawn out so that it sounded like the moan of a dying man.

David clenched his eyes shut and pressed his body flat against the ground as if he thought that he could sink into the ground like water from a light rainfall. The shell hit the frozen ground and exploded, sounding like thunder, lightning, and all of Hell's fury combined. A few pieces of shrapnel whistled overhead and one small burning piece even fell on his back, but David refused to raise his head into the line of fire. Then came a shower of dirt thrown up by the explosion that rained down on him, smothering the fire that had started on his coat from the burning shrapnel.

David tried to slow his rapid breathing. He was going to die here.

He chanced to glance ahead of his position. He saw the Union infantry advancing behind the initial rain of cannon fire.

"Charge!" General Jackson ordered. He sat high and straight on his horse, unafraid of anyone or anything. The order was echoed down the line through the chain of command. The bugles repeated the order in their own staccato way, making the order to charge death sound almost melodic. It was like the Pied Piper leading all of the rats out of Ireland to their deaths.

Only David was one of the rats.

He pushed himself to his knees, holding his rifle in his hands. His hands trembled until he clenched the rifle so hard that his knuckles turned white. He surged to his feet with the other members of his company. He reminded himself that he was their lieutenant. It was his job to lead his men. He tilted his head back and let out a loud Rebel yell; the scream of victory. Answering yells filled the air.

He paused to take aim and fire. He felt the rifle buck against his shoulder and saw the puff of smoke, but amid all of the noise of the battle, he couldn't hear the shot. He wasn't even sure if he had hit the man who he had aimed at. The man fell, but it could have been from David's bullet or not. Soldiers were falling all around him, both Union and Confederate men. It was too confusing. All he knew was that he had to keep the Federals back.

Hold the line.

David ran forward, holding his rifle close to his side. A bullet buzzed close by, tugging at his hair. David tried to forget what would have happened if he had been leaning a bit more to the left.

Keep your attention ahead, not to the side.

The acrid smell of gunpowder burned the back of his throat or maybe it was his vomit threatening to explode from his stomach.

The Union Army drew closer. David thrust out blindly at the nearest soldier and felt the point of his bayonet sink into a sergeant's stomach. The man screamed and collapsed forward over David's rifle. David pulled his bayonet free and swung the butt of his rifle up, catching the dying man in the face. The sergeant grunted and fell backwards.

As the sergeant lay on his back, David glanced at the man's face. It had changed. David was staring at himself. He looked around in panic and saw that all of the soldiers around him were corpses with rotting flesh and bodies torn by bullets and artillery pieces. They marched onward, missing arms or even their heads. Those that were missing legs crawled along the uneven ground.

David screamed.

He woke up screaming.

"Be quiet, Windover," Caleb Donnelly said as he kicked David in the thigh.

David opened his eyes and sat up in his cot. He was shaking so fiercely that he was barely able to hold his balance. His blanket had a large wet spot on it from his sweat.

"You make me nervous and you make the men skittish, too," Donnelly said.

David planted his feet in a way that he hoped would be able to maintain his balance and slowly stood up. He walked to the front of the tent that he shared with Donnelly. He dipped his bandanna into a bucket of cold water, wrung it out, and then wiped off his face.

"Nightmare again?" Donnelly asked from behind him.

He dropped back down in how own cot and lay with his hands behind his head.

"What do you think?" David snapped.

His nightmares were coming just about every night, although it had been weeks since the army had seen any fighting. General Thomas J. Jackson's army was now near Romney, Virginia. When the general had withdrawn from Winchester, Virginia, the Union had moved in. The town was becoming like a hot potato that got tossed back and forth between the Union and Confederacy.

"Don't get mad at me, pampered boy. I'm not the one who's proving to everyone with ears that he is unfit to fight," Donnelly said.

David let the cool water run down inside his shirt to cool himself off. "I can fight."

Lieutenant Donnelly snorted. "Maybe, but who would want to follow someone into battle who might fall to his knees screaming with the first shot? You're lucky it hasn't happened so far."

Donnelly was right, but David didn't want to admit it, not to Donnelly or even to himself. However, David wasn't even sure what he would do if he went into battle again. Would he freeze, unable to charge when it was called? Would he collapse into a screaming mass of flesh like Donnelly suggested?

David knew that if he was given the choice, he wouldn't fight, but then neither would just about anyone else in the army. David had a duty to perform, though. He was a Virginian and the son of a plantation owner outside of Charlottesville. If he wanted there to be a plantation to inherit, his father had told him that he would have to fight for his way of life.

Not that David was in line to inherit Grand Vista. David was the disposable son. He had been the one sent to war while David's older brother, Peter, was heir, and Peter was still safe in the main house at Grand Vista.

David had been proud to serve his country, and he had considered it a way to prove himself to his father. Had he only proved himself a coward, though?

But battle hadn't been like David had imagined it would be. Even winning in Manassas hadn't been without its costs. Men had died on both sides of the battle and they always would. David's best friend, Ben Kyle, had been ripped apart by an artillery shell that nearly landed on top of him. All David had found of his friend afterwards had been Ben's right arm, shoulder, and head. The rest of him had been unidentifiable.

Ben had not been the first dead man who David had seen, but he had been the first one to be killed so brutally and the one whom

David suspected was at the root of his nightmares.

"Lieutenant Windover?" a voice asked outside the tent.

"Enter."

A private who looked barely old enough to shave drew back the flap and stepped inside the tent. He saluted David who saluted him back.

"Sir, Colonel Collins wants to see you at his tent."

"Did he say why?" David asked.

The private shook his head. "No, sir."

"You're in trouble," Donnelly said.

David shot him a withering look.

He turned back to the messenger. "Thank you, Private. Tell him I'll be along shortly as soon as I finish dressing."

The young private saluted again and left. David took his gray coat off the hanger and put it on. It was still chilly out, despite the fact that David felt like he was in the middle of summer.

"The colonel is going to transfer you to supply or some other back-end duty. Maybe you'll be a prison camp guard," Donnelly guessed.

David threw the wet bandanna at his tent mate. Donnelly ducked.

"He's not going to transfer me. He can't complain about the way I do my job." David tried to sound confident, but he wondered if Donnelly might not be right. How many people knew about David's bad dreams? Donnelly certainly wouldn't care about keeping David's secrets.

Donnelly shrugged. "Maybe not...at least not right now, but everytime you go to sleep, you show everyone within hearing distance how unfit you are for command."

David knew his nightmares were unsettling. Donnelly had told him that he tossed and turned in his sleep. Sometimes David mumbled, but he always screamed, and his screaming didn't always wake him up.

"What is it with you, Donnelly?" David asked. "It's not as if you would get my men if I were busted. You've got your own men to worry about."

Caleb Donnelly was on his feet in a moment. He poked a finger in David's chest. "That's right! I do have my own men to worry about, and I don't want them to die because you couldn't do your job!"

"Your men aren't under my command."

"No, but my men and your men are under Colonel Collins's

command. What if your men fail because you can't lead? You don't deserve command, Windover. The only reason you have it is because the generals think that since you can order slaves around, you can order real men, too."

"What are you? An abolitionist?" David asked. Abolitionists weren't unheard of in the South, even in the army.

"No, I'm just a farmer from North Carolina who's had to fight Indians to hold what was his. Just like I've worked my way up to lead my men. I've proven that I can hold the line. You had your rank given to you. I've earned mine."

David frowned. "I'll hold the line. I know how to fight. My great-grandfather was with Washington at Monmouth."

Donnelly snorted. "That proves your great-grandfather could fight. What does it say about you?"

David couldn't answer that. He had never been in a war or had to fight to hold his land before last year. He'd never even had to discipline his father's slaves. That had been his brother's job as heir. David had been raised to be a gentleman not a soldier. Of course, he had trained with the saber and rifle when it became apparent that there would be a war between the North and the South, but he was more at home riding on horseback than charging into enemy fire on foot.

"What it says about me," David said, "is that I am able. The ability is within me as it was within my great-grandfather. Perhaps it is buried beneath refinements that you think are worthless, but the ability is there nonetheless and it will come out when it is needed."

Then he turned quickly and left so he would not have to hear Donnelly's retort.

The camp was laid out in long rows of tents. It was a small city that could be moved within a few hours notice. It was a swarm of locusts that descended on the land, ate everything in sight, and left the rest desolate.

With winter just now letting go of the land, food was scarce. People were living on what they had put away last autumn. Now all of that food would be nearly gone and the first crops wouldn't be ready to harvest for months.

It was normally a lean time, but having an army around increased consumption of those rare food stores. The people had been generous, but now they were hoarding their stored food to keep from starving and the army was beginning to commandeer what they needed to keep from starving.

Most of Northern Virginia was no better off than Romney was with both the Union and Confederacy living off the land. So far the war hadn't been carried above the Potomac River.

To go north of the river would change the scope of the war from defensive to offensive. So the soldiers sat and waited and ate while General Johnston, commander of all the Confederate Army, decided what to do. Now the food was beginning to run out. They were getting some supplies in from down south, but unless something was changed soon, they would begin starving. Virginia wasn't prepared to feed the entire Confederate Army.

As David walked down the lane between the officers' tents, some of the soldiers milling around stopped to stare at him. Had they heard him scream in his sleep? Were they wondering the same things as Donnelly had voiced?

It didn't matter at this point. They might feel the same as Caleb Donnelly, but since David wasn't under their command, they couldn't do anything about it. They could only hope that David would hold the line when it came down to it.

With the day unseasonably warm, Colonel Collins was sitting at a portable desk outside of his tent reading dispatches when David stopped in front of him and saluted.

Collins looked up. A lot of people said that he looked like General Grant with wavy brown hair and trimmed beard. David couldn't say. He had never seen the Union general.

"Lieutenant Windover reporting as ordered, sir."

The colonel nodded and said, "At ease, Lieutenant."

David relaxed.

"I have been told that you have traveled extensively in Maryland, Lieutenant."

David hesitated, wondering at the meaning behind the statement. "I suppose, sir. It depends on what you consider extensive. I have family in Frederick and Hagerstown." His mother was originally from Frederick. His mother's sister still lived with her family in Frederick and his mother's brother lived with his family in Hagerstown.

"So you know middle Maryland well?"

What was the colonel getting at?

"Again, I suppose it is relative, sir. I know it as well as any visitor."

Colonel Collins nodded and paused to stare intently as David. "I also hear that you are having trouble adjusting to the rigors of war."

David shifted uneasily under the man's gaze. He wondered

what was about to happen. Maybe Donnelly was right after all. Was David's time in the army about to end?

"Certain elements of it, sir," he said.

Colonel Collins seemed to peer through him. "It is hard, no doubt. I do believe war is God's refiner's fire. If we survive, we will all be the stronger for it."

David just nodded.

"I have a special assignment for you, Lieutenant. I need information about what is going on in Maryland. I need to be able to suggest paths that an army can use for quick travel to General Jackson," the colonel said.

"Are we going to invade?" David asked. He knew he was out of line, but he couldn't hide his astonishment or keep the question out of his mouth. He could understand scouting Winchester, but Maryland? Virginia was supposed to be defending her sovereignty and that of the Confederate States of America, not trying to conquer the Union.

Colonel Collins's expression didn't betray his feelings about the orders. "Perhaps. I need to know if it's feasible. I need to know our options. Northern Virginia can't continue to be the land where the bulk of this war is fought. The general is reluctant to use spies, but I have no reluctance against using scouts."

"Yes, sir, but where do I come in?"

"I want you to go cross the river into Maryland and explore. Find out how heavy the Union patrols along the river are. Find out where the people's loyalties lie. Where are the best fords? How is the grazing? Are fields being prepared for planting? I need options for ways to cross all the way into Pennsylvania at whatever points are feasible. At the least, I would like to identify sympathizers who would be willing to help feed the army."

"What about the C&O Canal then?" David asked.

Colonel Collins's eyebrows arched. "Canal?"

"It runs along the river on the Union side. The boats will be transporting tons of grain, flour, and other crops when it opens up."

Colonel Collins nodded. "I would be interested in learning more about what those boats transport." He paused. "Could the boats be brought across the river?"

David nodded. "At times. There is at least one place I know of where the canal opens into the river for a short distance."

Colonel Collins scratched his beard. "This is the kind of information I need to know about, Lieutenant."

David realized that Jackson was contemplating flanking the Union and squeeze Washington City from the north and south. If Washington fell, so would the Union.

Colonel Collins said, "You're educated, Lieutenant. I was told that you studied as a surveyor for a year. I've also been told you have your share of common sense. Both of those skills can be put to use with this assignment. I want you to take two men to act as your couriers to send me dispatches of the information you gather. You will be in charge of what information is sent."

"You want me to be a spy."

Colonel Collins nodded slowly. "A scout, Lieutenant. Do you have a problem with that?"

"No, sir."

If he were scouting for the army, his job would be to avoid the fighting and to help the army avoid much of the fighting.

"Good. You'll leave the day after tomorrow. You're dismissed."

David snapped his hand to his forehead in a salute. "Yes, sir." He turned to leave, but then he turned back. "Colonel?"

Colonel Collins looked up. "What, Lieutenant?"

"This assignment, does it have anything to do with my problems …the ones you mentioned?"

Colonel Collins pursed his lips. "I can't say that it didn't play a part, but your familiarity with Maryland is more critical. I have other groups looking at other crossing points. You're not the only one I'm sending away if that's what's worrying you."

David nodded. "It was, sir. I know my duty, and I'll do it. No matter what."

"Good, Lieutenant. Then tell me how to get through Maryland with an army intact."

4

PREPARING FOR THE FLOOD
MARCH 1862

Hugh enjoyed the ride into Sharpsburg. Seamus was quick stepping, too. The mule must have realized that the warm weather meant the canal season was drawing near.

It was a pleasant day, now with the weather warm and sunny. Hugh rocked along atop Seamus, letting his body fall into the rhythm of mule's gait. He watched the scenery pass by and smelled wood smoke from cabins that he couldn't see within the forest.

Sharpsburg wasn't a big town, but it was close to the canal and Hugh liked the area. He'd been born in Ireland right before his father had left for America. His father had bought land here to farm and sent for Hugh and his mother two years later. When Hugh had inherited the land, he had sold the small farm for enough money to buy the *Freeman* twelve years ago. He still had ties to Sharpsburg, though, and a love of the low hills and the people. It was his home.

Five roads came together in town, which made it a popular stopover point with travelers. Sharpsburg also had its own fire company and newspaper. Farm families grew wheat, rye, and hay. They also raised sheep, geese, and beef. The farm lanes were well rutted from wagons going to Hagerstown, Harpers Ferry, Bridgeport, Boonsboro and Shepherdstown. Of course, legal trade with Virginia had been cut off for a year so travel on the roads to Harpers Ferry and Shepherdstown stopped at the Potomac.

As he rode down the pike into town, Hugh waved to Thomas playing in the yard. The eight-year old boy was wrestling with a huge mongrel dog named Jed. They rolled around on the ground, creating a huge brown cloud of dust around them. Hugh hoped that Thomas was in his play clothes or he would catch Alice's wrath later. It was hard to tell now. He was that filthy.

"Papa's back! Papa's back!" Thomas yelled when he saw Hugh.

The boy freed himself from under Jed and ran up alongside his father. Jed bounded around Thomas's legs, threatening to trip him up. Seamus turned his head to glance at the brown-haired boy but didn't break his gait.

"Why aren't you stopping?" Thomas asked.

"I have to go to Mr. Laws's Store for some paint," Hugh told his youngest son.

"What are you going to paint, Papa?"

"The *Freeman.*"

Thomas started jumping up and down. He grabbed onto Hugh's leg. "Can I help? Can I help you paint? I'll be extra careful. I promise I will."

Hugh had no intention of letting his rambunctious son lay a paintbrush on the *Freeman*, but he wasn't going to crush Thomas's enthusiasm. More than likely, the boy would have forgotten his request to help in the work by dinner time.

"We'll see," Hugh told him.

"Can I go with you to Mr. Laws's store to help carry the paint?" Thomas asked.

Thomas must be bored if he kept volunteering for work. Of course, whenever Alice wanted him to help with the work around the house, Thomas was nowhere to be found.

Hugh nodded. "Come along then, lad. You can carry some of the paint back home for me."

Thomas jumped high into the air and cheered. As soon as his feet touched back on the ground, he took off running into town. Hugh just grinned and shook his head.

As Hugh followed after him, he saw Thomas change his path toward a group of boys marching out from one of the alleys, pretending they were soldiers. Hugh couldn't tell whether they were playing Union or Rebel soldiers.

"Thomas, come back here," he called.

"But, Papa, I want to play with them," Thomas whined.

"No," he said firmly.

The boys were of varying ages. Hugh recognized all of them and knew their families. If the real war went on long enough, some of those boys might actually become soldiers. Hugh didn't want Thomas becoming used to the idea of being a soldier or shooting other people. Why didn't children ever want to play peacemaker?

Laws's Hardware sat across Main Street from Gunnison's General Store. Michael Laws kept his storefront in top shape just to show off what a good man with the right tools could do. A large covered porch (freshly painted, of course) covered the front of the building. Some of the more-popular tools hung from the porch roof around the edge.

Those that had blades were all shiny and sharp. Hugh stopped to admire the coiled rope that lay on porch, then he moved into the store. He wasn't interested in rope, saws, or nails right now. Just paint.

The store had shelves that ran from floor to ceiling along three of the four walls. All of the shelves were filled with tools, accessories, and other hardware. In front of the shelves was a large U-shaped counter that held some smaller items on it. Barrels of nails and screws, plows, and other bulky items were shoved into the center of the store. A pot-belly stove in the middle of the room stood unused because the day was warm.

Michael Laws was a bald-headed man who said he was only fifty-two, but he looked ten years older. He wore a thick leather apron, a leftover from the days when he had been a blacksmith. Underneath the apron, he wore a white shirt and black pants.

"Morning, Michael," Hugh said as he took his felt hat off. He ran one hand through his thick, light brown hair.

Two men in front of Michael were arguing about the war so he moved away to one end of the counter.

"Lincoln wants to free the slaves," said John Harcourt.

"This isn't a war about slavery. It's about state's rights and defending the Constitution," said Benjamin Twigg.

Hugh was known as pro-Union. He had never hidden that fact, but he didn't want to be known as an abolitionist. It would draw too much attention to himself and the Underground Railroad, attention that he didn't want. Slavery was one issue that Hugh wouldn't speak about; he would simply act, which is more than John Harcourt would do.

Michael disengaged himself from the two men and walked over to Hugh. "Figured you'd be in soon, Hugh," Michael said, casting a glance at Thomas.

Hugh nodded. "I need some paint. Four gallons of white and one gallon each of red and blue."

"I guess that means it's getting close to time for you."

He took four empty gallon cans off a shelf and set them on a counter. At one end of the U-shaped counter, barrels sat on top that contained the various dyes that Michael Laws mixed with his white paint to create colors.

"Solomon said the company man came by yesterday. He said they were opening the guard locks behind him and that the entire canal should be open in a week at the most," Hugh replied.

"Then I guess that means it's open to Harpers Ferry by now." Feeder Lock 3, which diverted water into Guard Lock 3, was located just above Harpers Ferry.

Hugh nodded. He turned as he heard a banging sound. Thomas was pounding on the hardwood floor with a hammer.

"Thomas!" Hugh said sharply. "Put that hammer away before you break something."

"Awww, Papa. I was squashing ants with it."

"Well, if you want to do that, step on them, but put that hammer away," Hugh said.

Thomas nodded. He stood up and laid the hammer back on the shelf behind the counter. Hugh turned back to Michael. The merchant was filling the second can with white paint.

"I have to say, I don't envy you canallers."

Hugh stopped browsing through Michael's selection of knives. "Why's that?" he asked. "Last spring, you were telling me how you wanted to get away from this shop and ride the river for nine months a year."

Michael nodded. "So I did, but that was last year before we got ourselves caught in a full-scale war. I wouldn't want to be caught in crossfire between the Rebs and the Federals on the river or be stuck down in Washington when the Rebs take over that place. It's bad enough being in the crossfire here in town."

Hugh tapped on the counter. "You think that will happen? I mean, the Rebels overrunning Washington City?"

Michael nodded. "Look around for yourself. We lost the opening fight at Sumter, and then went on to lose at Bull Run. We were lucky the Rebs didn't end it there."

"But we won at Shiloh, Fort Henry, and Fort Donelson," Hugh countered.

Fort Henry and Fort Donelson had both fallen to General Grant just last month. Then there was the battle of the two ironclads earlier this month. The *Monitor* had forced the *Virginia*, an ironclad fashioned from the wreckage of the *Merrimac*, a Union frigate, to withdraw. Now the Union controlled the area of Hampton Roads.

Michael made a casual waving motion. "They're out west. The important battles are the ones like Bull Run that shake up the politicians. If the Federals and Rebs were horses in a race, who would you put your money on? President Lincoln's got to be wondering whether he'll be the last president of the United States of America right now."

Hugh suddenly realized that at this time last year there hadn't been a war between the North and South. There hadn't been a reason to fear the coming canal season, though there had been reason enough during the season, especially after the Battle of Bull Run. Tensions in the North had run high with nearly everyone expecting the South to invade the North, which would have brought the Rebel army across the Potomac River and the canal. Hugh had survived fine, though, and he would again this year.

Somehow.

"It's scary, but at least I'll be on the move," Hugh told the shopkeeper.

Michael nodded. "But half the time, you'll be moving right towards the trouble. The Rebs have got to know that the canal boats are taking coal and grain into Washington."

Hugh nodded. "They do. Alexandria used to get enough of it."

That wasn't happening any longer. The Union Army had seized the Alexandria Aqueduct that led from the canal, across the Potomac River, to Alexandria in December. It was going to cause problems this season.

Michael shook a finger at him. "Well, you see there. General Johnston certainly won't take kindly to your efforts. Some of the Rebels used to work on the canal, too. Sooner or later, they are going to want to stop the flow of coal into Washington and freeze the people out during the winter," Michael said.

The merchant made a lot of good points; however, they only served to confuse Hugh all the more. He could leave his family in Sharpsburg, which would leave them to the dangers of a Confederate Army coming across the river. Or, he could take his family along with him floating along the border of the Union and into the main target of the Confederates. How do you make a choice like that?

Michael tapped the lids into place on the cans and pushed them together in front of Hugh. He paid out the cost of the paint and grabbed four of the gallon containers, two in each hand.

"Thomas, get the other two gallons of paint and follow me out front."

The young boy jumped up from the floor and scurried over to the counter. He grunted as he wrapped his arms around the two gallons of paint and picked them up. Michael grinned as Thomas staggered after his father, his shoulders drooping under the weight of the paint.

Hugh was quiet on the ride home. His head was full of conflicting thoughts. Never before had he ever wondered whether he should take his family along with him on the *Freeman* when the canal opened. He needed them to help him keep the canal boat moving, and he would be lonely without them along. He'd miss watching Alice take a turn at the tiller, standing so straight and beautiful as if she was one of those carved women on the prows of a frigate. He'd miss trying to keep a count of the number of different "pets" Thomas tried to adopt from spiders to fawns. He'd miss watching Elizabeth sit on the race plank and dangle her feet in the water when the boat sat low in the water because the holds were full of coal.

Their wooden house sat on the pike near the edge of town. It was a good bit larger than a lockkeeper's house but about average for most of the houses in Sharpsburg. The L-shaped house had two floors with three rooms on each floor. George, Elizabeth, and Thomas had their bedrooms upstairs. The kitchen, the sitting room, and Alice's and his bedroom were downstairs. Porches ran across the front of the house and the back side that made the interior of the L-shape.

"Set the paint on the back porch," Hugh told his son as he dismounted from Seamus. "We'll take them down to the boat later."

"Aw, can't we do it now, Papa?" Thomas pleaded.

Hugh shook his head. "I'm hungry and want to eat supper."

Thomas sighed and trudged around to the side of the house as Hugh tied the mule's reins to one of the front-porch posts.

Hugh stepped inside the front door, and he could hear Alice yelling at Thomas back in the kitchen. The boy hadn't even been home two minutes and he was already into mischief. Hugh sighed and shook his head. Thomas was mischief on the hoof.

"Thomas Jefferson Fitzgerald, you get into this house right away. I told you half an hour ago that I wanted you to try on your Sunday pants so I could let out the hem. Where have you been?" Alice Fitzgerald yelled.

"I had to help Papa get paint for the boat. He needed my help," Thomas quickly explained.

Hugh groaned. So that was why Thomas had been so anxious to help him with his work. Thomas usually avoided work as much as possible. Only an eight-year-old would have thought standing on a chair so his mother could let out the hem of his best pants was more work than hauling two gallons of paint all the way from the center of town.

Hugh walked into the kitchen through the back door and caught the delicious aroma of corn chowder cooking on the stove. Hugh had built the kitchen cabinetry himself the winter they had moved into the house and it still held up well. The table sat in the middle of the room with a calico tablecloth on it. Alice was standing at the back door that led onto the porch, waving Thomas inside.

When she saw Hugh, she pointed to Thomas and said, "Did you take him into town with you?"

Hugh nodded. Before she could say anything, he held up his hands in a surrendering gesture and quickly added, "But I didn't know you had asked him to do something for you. He was playing in the yard when I saw him."

Sighing, Alice put her hands on her hips. "Why does that not surprise me?" She turned to Thomas. "Go change into your pants and come back down here."

"But they're too hot," Thomas whined. He was barefoot and wearing shorts and a light shirt.

"Go!" Alice said sternly.

Thomas stomped off, his feet slapping the wood floor.

"And put your shoes and socks on, too," she said as he left the kitchen.

Thomas groaned loudly as if he had been given a day full of chores to do. Hugh smiled. He sat down at the table.

"We have a pair of guests," he said quietly.

Alice looked up sharply, understanding immediately what he meant. "A pair?"

Hugh held up two fingers. "A mother and child."

Alice sucked in her breath. "A child? How young?"

Hugh shrugged. "A wee babe."

Alice frowned. Hugh knew what she was thinking. A baby didn't know the necessity of silence, and a stray cry could give away the hiding place of runaway slaves. He was worried, too, but if he let it show, it would only worry Alice all the more.

"What are we going to do?" Alice asked.

"I'll bring them in tonight. Joseph Brimhall is coming by in the morning with a couple of barrels of flour for us. I'll let him know he needs to take something out with him."

Brimhall was their connection along the Underground Railroad in Sharpsburg. He also operated alone when Hugh was on the canal.

Alice nodded. "I'll get the basement ready then." She paused. "Since you had to buy paint, I take it that it's almost time to open the canal?"

Hugh nodded. "In a few days. A week at most. The company man

31

is on his way to Cumberland to tell them to open the guard locks."

Alice crossed her arms under her breasts. "Then we need to talk."

That was a bad sign. Hugh had learned years ago that when a woman said, "We need to talk," what she meant was, "I need to talk. You need to agree with me."

Hugh pulled out a chair from the table and sat down. He leaned over the table and dipped himself out a ladleful of water.

"Hugh, use a cup. How can I teach Thomas not to drink from the ladle when he sees you do it?" Alice complained.

"But I was already sitting down." Hugh rolled his eyes and put the ladle back in the bucket.

Alice sighed. She remained standing and looked down at him.

"I don't want Elizabeth to go out with you on the canal this season," Alice said. She spoke quickly, trying to get everything out. It reminded Hugh of when Thomas was spinning a story. "And since she's too young to stay here alone, I'm going to have to stay with her. The canal's no place to raise a daughter."

"I thought that Elizabeth was already raised," Hugh said calmly, though he longed to avoid this moment.

"Well, the canal is no place for your daughter to find a husband. Imagine her marrying a river rat up at Shanty Town." Shanty Town was the seedier area of Cumberland at the canal terminus, and Elizabeth knew as well as Hugh that they avoided it.

"I wouldn't expect her to. She's got more sense than that, Alice. Besides, she doesn't seem to mind the time she spends on the canal."

Alice dropped down into the chair across from her husband. "That's part of the problem, Hugh. She's not our son who can grow up to be a canaller like George and Thomas." Alice always insisted on pronouncing canaller properly, though nearly everyone else on the canal and definitely everyone else in the family said "canawler." "Elizabeth's a young woman. She shouldn't be wanting to spend more of her time with the canal mules than with young men." Alice paused. "Though I do have to admit being with the mules will probably teach her how to handle men."

Hugh laughed in spite of himself. Elizabeth wasn't the only one who was learning about men from mules. Alice came from a canalling family. Her father had run Lock 75 near Cumberland. One of her brothers ran the Indian Head Lock on the canal spur in Washington and her other brother was a canal boat captain.

"If it's a husband you're after for Elizabeth, what's wrong with

Washington or Cumberland? That's where you found me," Hugh said.

Alice patted his arm. "You're from Sharpsburg, not Cumberland."

"I know, but there's plenty of young men...young gentlemen at the towns along the canal for Elizabeth to meet," Hugh said.

Alice shook her head and brushed her blond hair back. "There might be in a few years, but right about now I'd say most of those young men are soldiers."

Hugh nodded. "I understand your concerns, really I do, but I don't agree with them, and I have to tell you the truth: I couldn't stand being away from you for nine months." Alice blushed as he held her hand. "And I can't stay home or we'll be starving come December."

"I'll have to think about it."

Hugh leaned across the table and took her hand in his.

"While you're thinking about that, think about this, too. You'll be saving my life if you come," Hugh told her.

Alice gave him a sideways glance. "How's that?"

"Well, George can't cook and my cooking's worse than canal mud. If you don't come along to feed us, we'll both starve to death."

Alice grabbed a wooden spoon off the table and waved it threateningly in his direction. Hugh just laughed and grabbed her by the arms and kissed her on the lips. What he had meant to be a quick kiss turned out to be much longer.

"You can be the most-exasperating man," Alice said when Hugh let go of her arms.

Hugh winked at her. "But you love me."

"You and George had better get started on the painting now. They'll be no working on the Sabbath for either of you. Either now or during the season."

That surprised Hugh. He was used to running his boat seven days a week from four in the morning until ten at night.

"But we always run seven days a week."

Alice shook her head and gave him a stern look. "Not this year. Not if you want Elizabeth and me to come along with you. That's the deal. We'll be in church on Sunday not on the canal."

Hugh rubbed his chin. He definitely wanted his family together. Since both options had their dangers, he chose the one that would make him happiest, which was to have his family all together. Still, to give up one day a week from his work, well, that was likely to cut four or five trips from his total this season.

"How much bargaining room do I have?"

She frowned at him. "Very little. What do you have in mind?"

"I won't run on Sunday, but I want to be able to start around the clock from four in the morning on Monday until midnight on Saturday night."

Alice thought for a moment and then nodded. Hugh grinned and kissed her again.

She waved him off. "Now you and George go do what you have to do. I'll have Elizabeth bring supper and dinner out to you."

Hugh found George in his room reading his school books. He had little formal schooling and was always behind the rest of his class. George didn't seem to mind, but Hugh did. He always said that knowledge was never wasted, so he insisted George study extra hard when they weren't boating.

"I need you at the boat. We've got to get her ready," Hugh said.

George cheered as he slammed his books shut. For him, his school year was over. He didn't care that he was falling further and further behind others in his class because he only went to school for three or four months a year. How much schooling did you need to be a canal boat captain?

Hugh only had a minimal education himself. He had spent most of his life trying to catch up to others, though. He wasn't going to have that for George. George might grow up to be a canawler, but he didn't have to grow up to be a dumb one.

He'd have to do some of his book learning on the boat this year, whether it be while he was at the tiller or riding on the back of one of the mules. For now, though, there was work to be done.

5

A CANAWLER
ON THE RAILROAD
MARCH 1862

Alice heard Seamus bray lightly somewhere in the night. Why had the mule done that? He was the quietest of the four canal mules, which is why Hugh had chosen to use him tonight. Silence was important. More than important; their freedom depended on it. They didn't want to draw attention to themselves and what they were doing because there were Southern sympathizers in town who would report them to the sheriff.

She lowered the flame in the lantern so that it wouldn't be apparent when she looked out the window. Then she parted the checkered curtain with a brush of her hand. The clouds hid the moon and stars. That, at least, was good. It would help to hide Hugh and the runaway slaves he had gone to retrieve from the *Freeman*.

If this had been during the season, she and Hugh would have simply left the slaves hidden on the canal boat and ferried them up the canal to Hancock, where Maryland was less than a mile wide. Then they would have helped them across the Pennsylvania state line to the next station along the Underground Railroad. As it was, it looked like these two slaves were about a week too early to take that route. The canal was still dry, at least at Sharpsburg, but it wouldn't be that way for much longer. The woman and child would have to go on an alternate route up through Hagerstown and into Greencastle. Eventually, they would make their way to Canada safely where they would be out of the reach of the Fugitive Slave Law.

Alice looked up and down the street. She couldn't see light from any other lanterns. The town was safely asleep, except for her and Hugh. At least she hoped it was so.

She waited anxiously, and eventually, Seamus walked into view as a dark shadow moving against a darker background. Hugh was walking along beside the mule. A black woman sat on Seamus's back, clutching a small bundle to her chest.

Alice sighed with relief just to see that the girl had made it this far.

Partly from worry that Hugh might be seen and partly out of a need to feel useful, Alice hurried out the door to the street. She looked around quickly to make sure that no one else was nearby. She walked up to the woman and reached up for the baby. The mother pulled back, clutching the child even tighter to her breast.

"It's all right. I'm here to help you. I'll just hold the baby until you climb down," Alice explained in a quiet voice.

The slave girl—and she really wasn't much more than a girl, Alice thought—reluctantly handed the baby to Alice. She gently rocked the child as her mother climbed off Seamus and took the baby back.

"Now let's get you both inside before someone sees us." Alice pointed toward the house. To Hugh, she said, "Any problems?"

Hugh shook his head. "Not a one, Love. A bat or something startled Seamus and he brayed a bit. That was all. No people about. I'm going to walk Seamus down to the barn while you get our guests situated."

He gave her a quick kiss on the cheek and turned to walk away. How could he be so calm and casual about this? He acted like he wasn't breaking the law to help the slaves. Alice moved back onto the front porch where the slave girl was waiting for her.

"You're Ruth?" she asked.

The girl nodded. She looked terrified, or it may just have been that the whites of her eyes made her eyes look large against her black skin.

"I'm Alice, and we need to hide you until morning. Someone else will help you go north from here," Alice told her.

Alice opened the door and ushered the pair inside. She cast one last glance up and down the street. Seeing no signs that anyone was watching, she followed the slaves inside and closed the door.

Even inside the house Alice was quiet. She didn't want any of the children discovering what she and Hugh did in the dark of night. What the children didn't know, they couldn't accidentally tell anyone. She led the slave girl and baby through the sitting room to the door under the stairs. She opened the door and waved the young girl inside. Alice stepped in behind the girl and turned up the flame on the lantern.

The short staircase led down to the basement where Alice stored her canned fruits, vegetables, other food stuffs, and runaway slaves. The basement had a hard-packed dirt floor and a low ceiling. Alice set the lantern on stand mounted to the stone wall. The stand had a reflector behind it that helped amplify the light throughout the basement.

Three of the walls had shelves filled with jars filled with various fruits and vegetables. Dried meat was packed in paper and burlap. The fourth wall was filled from two rows of barrels stacked on top of each other so that they reached from floor to ceiling.

Alice walked over to one of the barrels on the bottom row and jiggled it until she was able to pull it free from the rest. Ruth's eyes went wide when the barrel above didn't fall over.

"It's sitting on a board," Alice whispered. "This one is a little shorter than the rest and empty so that we can move it easily. Now go inside."

"Inside?"

Alice nodded. The girl knelt down and looked into the space created by the missing barrel. It opened up a small area behind the barrel wall. There was a pallet in the open area, a bucket of water with a dipper, and some bread and dried food in a burlap bag.

"You'll have to stay in here tonight. Tomorrow, we'll move you elsewhere. You'll have to be quiet. No one can know you're here. That means the baby, too," Alice said. "I'll bring some food down in a bit."

"Yes, ma'am," the girl said.

She crawled into the hole and lay down on the pallet. Ruth kept her arms around her daughter and clutched her protectively to her breast. There wasn't much room to stretch out in the hiding place. It was only five feet long and three feet wide.

"I can't leave you a lantern because the light will show through the cracks between the barrels," Alice explained.

"It's all right," the girl said as if she was trying to calm Alice.

Alice felt a wave of sympathy for the woman, but she also admired the girl's bravery. This girl had made her way north to freedom with a baby. What pains and dangers had she endured to get this far? No danger that Alice was enduring could compare to that.

She patted the girl's hand. "Don't worry. It will get easier from here on."

The girl had escaped her biggest danger. She had left the South. It was much easier to find friendly faces north of the Potomac and it would only get easier as she and her baby moved north toward Canada.

Alice moved back out of the opening and pushed the barrel back into place. Then she smoothed out the scrape marks in the floor that the barrel had made. When she was satisfied Ruth was hidden as well as she could be, Alice picked up the lantern and went back upstairs to wait for Hugh.

She sat at the kitchen table sipping at a cup of water. She couldn't let the fact that Ruth and her daughter were hiding in her basement change her behavior. Hiding slaves in her home or on the *Freeman* always put her on edge. She and Hugh didn't do it often, but it was often enough that Alice worried someone would recognize the guilt in her face.

When Hugh came in the back door, she jumped, but luckily she didn't yell. The last thing she needed now was to wake the children and have to answer their questions. She put her hand on her chest and glared at her husband.

"Is she settled in for the night?" Hugh asked.

Alice nodded. "She's so young. Only a year or two older than Elizabeth."

Hugh nodded as he bent over to kiss Alice on the cheek. "She's a brave girl. No doubt about that."

Hugh walked to the table under the window and cut himself a slice of cherry pie that Alice had made for dinner. He ate it quickly and then wiped his mouth on the back of his sleeve.

"Hugh, please," Alice said.

"It's already dirty. A little cherry juice won't make it worse."

Alice rolled her eyes.

Hugh kissed her on the cheek. "I'm going to bed. Are you coming?"

Alice shook her head. "No, I need to relax."

He patted her shoulder. "I'll try not to wake you in the morning then. With any luck, they'll be on their way north by the time you wake up."

That was doubtful. Mothers rarely slept late. Besides, Alice was an early riser, regardless of how late she went to bed.

When Hugh had gone, Alice closed her eyes and listened to the sounds of the night. The expected calls and shouts from slave hunters were missing. She always expected to be exposed whenever they helped a slave toward freedom. It hadn't happened yet, but it didn't stop her fears.

Maybe it was good to be afraid. It kept her from feeling overconfident about what she was doing. She knew that she was in the right. That was never in doubt. Holding another person as property was never right. Isn't that what the Bible showed through the stories of the Israelites?

Somewhere in the night, Alice thought she heard a baby cry. It was quickly silenced. It must have been Naomi. Ruth was taking good care of her.

What must Ruth be feeling now? Her hard-won freedom now depended on others. What would she do with her freedom when she reached Canada? Another person had controlled Ruth's entire life. What would she do when she could control her own future? That wasn't Alice's worry, though. Giving Ruth the choice did not mean that Alice should try to make choices for her.

This was Alice's second year of working a stop of the Underground Railroad. It had started when Hugh had told Joseph Brimhall about a slave they had helped across the canal and up to Hancock one summer. It had been careless of Hugh to say something, but he had been drinking and the beer had loosened his tongue. Also, he was aware enough to know that Joseph could be trusted. In fact, Joseph could be more than trusted. He had taken Hugh into his confidence and recruited him to the cause of freeing slaves.

Hugh felt more strongly about slavery than Alice did because his family had been close to slaves; first indebted to an Irish landowner and then indebted to the Canal Company that had brought them to America to work. It created a strong sense of freedom that had been bred into Hugh, and he, in turn, had passed it on to his children. He had also awakened the feeling in Alice with his passion when he talked about being free.

Things were different now, though. With the war being fought, and the canal was on the border between the North and the South. If any of the Confederate soldiers caught them helping slaves escape, they would surely be killed. Even the Confederate sympathizers in Sharpsburg would turn them in to the authorities if they knew about the hiding room in the basement.

Remaining firm in her passion was becoming almost as dangerous as slave trying to gain her freedom.

Alice cut a few wedges of cheese and put them on a plate with bread and a slice of pie. Then she carried the plate and a glass of water down to Ruth.

"Thank you, ma'am," Ruth said, taking the food through the hole in the wall of barrels.

"Good luck, child. I probably won't see you in the morning. I probably won't see you ever again, but your success will be in my prayers," Alice said.

"Thank you."

Then Alice pushed the barrel back into place and went upstairs.

Alice walked into the sitting room. She sat down in a rocking chair and pulled her family Bible off the bookshelf. She opened the Bible to the Book of Ruth and began reading. As she did, she calmed down until she felt tired enough to sleep.

When she awoke in the morning, the slaves were gone. She was dressing for church when Hugh came back into the room. Nothing was said of the slaves. Hugh acted as if he hadn't violated the law last night even if it was for a good cause.

Hugh chafed at the bit after church because he couldn't do any work on the *Freeman* that morning. He was always anxious to be on the water, particularly at the beginning of the season.

On Monday morning, Hugh and George were at the canal with the sunrise to begin painting the canal boat. Alice came down later in the morning with Thomas and Elizabeth. The three of them spent the day washing and cleaning the three cabins on the boat to get them ready for the new season.

Hugh and George finished painting on late Tuesday afternoon while Alice packed the family cabin with food and clothes. Wednesday afternoon, Hugh and George brought the mules down from the stable and stocked the hay house with fresh hay for the mules.

When Hugh came out to the boat on Thursday morning, the *Freeman* was floating in six feet of water. The canal was open, and it was time to go to work.

6

THE QUEEN CITY'S BASTARD SON

MARCH 1862

Tony walked down Baltimore Street, trying to look innocent. That was quite a challenge for a ten-year-old boy born and raised in Shanty Town. No matter what he did with his expressions, his eyes still had that Shanty Town hardness that his upbringing had given him. Still, he had his size to help him. He could pass for a boy two or three years younger. He had also washed his face and hands so that he would look more like a child from Cumberland than the brat of Shanty Town. The crowd moved around him, but nothing presented an attractive target for his quick fingers.

The sky was overcast and the wind blustery, but there were still crowds on the street.

Tony paused to look in the large store windows along Baltimore Street at the clothes and tools and foods displayed by the merchants. His stomach rumbled when he saw a fresh-baked cherry pie cooling in the window. He could smell the tangy scent as it wafted through the open door. His stomach tossed, trying to pull him in the direction of the pie.

He wondered if he could run in, grab the pie, and get away.

His fingers were much more nimble than his feet.

Tony shook his head and turned away from the pie. He wouldn't have it today. He looked over the crowd moving back and forth in front of him. Most of the people were adult men who, in general, were not known for their sympathy. Most of the women were either with men or their own children.

If Tony tried for the pie, some adult would stop him and have the sheriff or one of his deputies haul him off to jail. The sheriff would leave Tony sitting in a cell there, asking him his name and where he lived. Tony couldn't tell the sheriff or anyone else his last name. He didn't know it himself. His mother used too many different names, first names as well as last names. Tony wasn't sure if any of them were her real name.

As for where he lived, that could vary, too. It was usually above Carter McKenney's tavern on Wineow Street. At least it would be until someone came looking for his mother, then she would move somewhere else for a week or two.

Taking the pie wouldn't be worth the day's work he'd have to do in order to pay for a pie he wouldn't even get to eat. Tony moved away from the window.

He wanted cash anyway, not food. Food was gone in a few minutes. Cash he could save for his future. Besides, his mother would give him something to eat because she used him to help earn extra money from her "men friends."

His mother was a whore. Though she had never said anything to him about it, he had figured it out on his own by watching and listening to similar ladies talk about their jobs while Tony was in the city jail with them. However, his mother was the only one he knew of who used her son in her business.

His mother took her payment first from the men. Then when her "man friend" dropped his trousers on the floor, Tony was waiting under the bed to remove a few dollars more. Tony never took all of the money out of the wallet because the man would have certainly realized where he lost it, but if it were only a dollar and some change missing, then he might not be so sure where it had been lost. He would just think he had had too many drinks and spent his pay too freely. Tony's mother got the dollars. Tony kept the change. Even his mother didn't know that.

Tony figured he deserved the change. His mother certainly didn't give him any money. He didn't like being quiet while his mother and a stranger bounced around on top of the bed grunting and yelling. He did it because, in helping his mother, she gave him a place to sleep and a little bit of food to eat. She offered to let him sleep on the bed, but he couldn't bring himself to do it, knowing all that happened on the bed.

Sometimes, his mother's men would beat her up when she didn't do what they wanted or if they simply liked to hit women. When this happened, his mother insisted Tony stay silent under the bed. Coming out to try and help her would only get her beaten up worse or so she said.

Tony wasn't so sure, but it was her getting hit, not him.

He was determined to get away from Shanty Town and his mother. He'd thought about jumping the train and riding it to

42

wherever it went. Wherever he went, though, he would need money to survive. Sooner or later, the sheriff would stop considering him a child and Tony would stay in jail or he would grow too big to fit under his mother's bed and she would send him away. Then what would happen to him? If he were to have a future, he would have to create it.

Further down the street, Tony saw an opportunity. A grocer who had been standing next to his fruit cart outside of his store stepped inside the store to conduct business with a well-dressed woman. Tony quickly mixed in with a crowd walking down the street. Because he was short, he was easily lost among the crowd. If anyone saw him, they would assume he was a child of one of the adults nearby.

As Tony walked by the cart, he grabbed two apples, one in each hand, off the end of the cart. He quickly shoved them into the large pockets of his jacket. He stayed with the crowd a few feet past the cart until he could turn down Centre Street.

He saw a middle-aged woman walking toward him. She was well dressed, but she didn't look as if she was so rich that she owned slaves. More importantly, she wasn't with a man who would discourage her sympathy and generosity.

Tony put on his best pitiful look and stepped up to the woman. "Excuse me, ma'am, I'm trying to help my family raise money." He tried to keep his tales as simple as possible. If he added too many details, it was too easy to get tripped up. "Dad gave me a bag of apples to sell, and I've only got these two left." He lifted the two apples out of his pockets. "Won't you help me out?"

The woman looked around. "Where is your family?"

"They're spread out. We're meeting at the train station at noon."

The woman stared at his face as if studying him. "How much are you selling them for?"

"A nickel."

The woman opened her purse and found a nickel. She handed it to Tony and he passed her the apples as he smiled up at her.

"Oh, thank you, ma'am. You're an angel." He had learned early on that part of working the streets was to make the people he sold his stolen goods to feel good about what they were doing. Besides, what did a kind word cost him?

"Aren't you sweet?" she said as she patted him on the head.

The woman walked away and Tony pocketed the nickel. One of these days he would have enough money to go to California. It was said that it was the golden land where a man could get rich picking gold nuggets up off the street instead of out of men's pockets, which he had been known to do.

He headed back toward the Potomac and past the C&O Canal basin. The canal had been full for a day, and the river was running a bit high. Not surprising with all of the rain they had had earlier in the month.

Tony dug the long branch that served as his fishing pole out from its hiding place under some brush by the river. He also took out an old can he had found long ago and added his nickel to his fortune of twenty-three dollars and eight cents. He thought he might take his money to the bank one day and open an account. He had heard that if you let your money sit in a bank, it would grow larger and Tony needed his money to get big and fat.

He planned on being rich someday. When that day came, he wouldn't have to go hungry ever. He wouldn't have to dress in clothes that made people feel sorry for him. Most importantly, he wouldn't have to hide under his mother's bed just to have a place to sleep.

Tony used a broken knife to dig around in the ground until he found a couple worms in the loose soil. He used one to bait his rusty hook and then tossed his line into the Potomac. Finished, he just lay back and waited for the fish to bite.

Tony liked fishing because it was quiet. He could get away from town if he wanted to walk far enough away. He liked being away from the crowds of people in town or the loud brawls in Shanty Town. He could get away from the sounds in his mother's bedroom.

Besides, he could eat what he caught. Many times it tasted better than what his mother fed him. He would bake a bass and then smother it in butter and pepper. He loved it.

Someday he would find a way to be free from this town.

7

TO CUMBERLAND
MARCH 1862

Hugh locked the back door of the house and stepped off the wooden porch. All of the shutters on the windows were closed and the doors were locked. The hiding area in the basement for the runaway slaves had been cleared away when Hugh and George had loaded the barrels of flour onto the *Freeman*.

The house was closed up, at least for now. Sometimes the Fitzgeralds rented their home to new people who wanted to move into Sharpsburg just as John Arnold rented out the vacant stalls in the Fitzgerald barn for Hugh during the spring, summer, and fall.

Hugh mounted Seamus and rode out of town on the pike toward the canal. Alice and the rest of his family were on the *Freeman* waiting to leave. Five other boats had already passed them on their way to Cumberland for their first load of coal. More canawlers called Williamsport and Cumberland home, but some, like Hugh, preferred Sharpsburg and other towns farther east.

There'd be a long line of boats at the Cumberland Basin ahead of them waiting to load their holds with tons of coal. Hugh hoped that a good number of them would opt to make a short run from Williamsport. It would relieve a lot of the congestion at Cumberland.

Hurry up and wait. That's the way things always seemed to be. Hurry to Cumberland to get a good place in the line at the loading basin, then wait for the coal. Hurry down the canal but wait at the locks. Hurry into Georgetown but wait to offload. Georgetown was the worst wait. Sometimes canawlers waited as long there as it took to come down the canal.

Because the canal was already flooded, Hugh had to cross at the foot bridge at Lock 39 and then walk up the towpath until he reached his boat. It was out of his way to use the foot bridge, but he didn't have much of a choice. Seamus didn't like to swim and his shod hoofs would have torn up the wet canal bank going in and out of the water. Solomon Greenfield would have thrown a fit.

Hugh saw Alice and Elizabeth putting up the canvas canopy

over the family cabin as he approached. It would provide some shade from the baking sun. Then he noticed George on the towpath adjusting the harnesses on Jigger and Ocean.

"Where's Thomas?" he asked his oldest son.

George was standing with the mules. As Hugh watched, George sat down and took off his shoes and tossed them onto the cargo hatches on the canal boat. It was less wear and tear on shoes to walk barefoot on the canal. Otherwise, he would wear out his shoes almost as quickly as the mules wore out their shoes. Mule driving toughened up the soles of his feet. George had once stepped on three bees as he walked through a patch of clover and it hadn't even bothered him.

"He started on up the canal following a black snake. I suppose we'll meet him on his way back," George said, smiling. George was like his father, happy to be working again.

Alice called to Hugh from the roof of the family cabin. "Hugh, I don't want him keeping that snake as one of his pets. One of them got in my corn meal last year and nearly scared me to death."

Hugh nodded. "I remember, lass. I'll talk to him about it." He turned to George. "Get 'em ready, son. As soon as I'm at the tiller, let's go."

Hugh walked across the fall board and then pulled it up after him. He went to the rear of the boat just beyond the family cabin and took hold of the tiller.

"Gee haw," George said to the mules and gave a slight tug on the harness.

The two mules started walking, Jigger slightly ahead of Ocean and acting as the lead mule. As the slack was pulled from the tow rope, it raised out of the water dripping wet. Then it tightened. The mules strained for a moment in their harnesses, and the *Freeman* began to float up the canal. They pulled against a two mile per hour current. It wasn't such a hindrance with a light boat, but it would have been if the *Freeman*'s holds were full. Luckily, the current worked with them when the holds were full.

And so it begins, Hugh thought.

Hugh grinned at Alice, and she smiled back. Hugh loved to see that bright smile. He was glad she had come this season. He would have missed her too much if she and Elizabeth had stayed in Sharpsburg.

The canal boat hadn't been moving for too long when Hugh saw Thomas walking down the canal with a black snake wrapped around the boy's forearm.

"Get rid of that now!" Alice yelled from the race plank, waving and pointing at Thomas.

"Aw, Mama! It's only a black snake," Thomas said.

Alice put her hands on her hips and gave her youngest son a stern look. "It's a wild animal, and I won't have it on this boat."

Hugh chuckled. "Thomas is a wild animal, and you let him on the boat," Hugh said.

"But he's my wild animal," she said with a straight face.

Thomas held the black snake up so that they were face to face. "Sorry, snake, I guess you won't be able to go to Georgetown." Then he tossed the long snake off into the grass next to the towpath.

"Papa, we're not too far from the caves. Can I go exploring them?" Thomas asked as he started walking alongside the boat. Killiansburg Cave was about a half a mile south in the limestone bluffs near the river. Thomas always liked to explore around the mouth of the lime-stone caves. Of course, Alice was always worried that the cave roof would collapse on him.

Hugh shook his head. "No, Thomas. You and George just went through them last week."

Thomas kicked at the dirt on the towpath.

"Don't pout," Alice scolded him.

"Can I come aboard?"

Hugh shook his head. "Not right now. We just started, and I want to keep moving. It's still a long way to Cumberland. You can come aboard when we switch mule teams." That would be almost six hours from now.

"Can I ride Jigger?"

"Ask your brother."

George nodded and brushed his brown hair out of his face. "Go ahead."

Thomas cheered and ran up to Jigger. "Hiya, Jigger," he said as he grabbed hold of the thick, padded harness and pulled himself onto the light-gray mule's back. Jigger looked over his shoulder at the eight-year-old boy, but he kept walking.

They made their first change of mule teams at Lock 44 in Williamsport. Hugh laid the fall board out and led Seamus and King Edward out of the mule shed and onto the canal towpath. Hugh hitched the tow rope to the fresh mules as George led Jigger and Ocean onto the canal boat one at a time. There wasn't room along the race plank for the mules to walk side by side.

"Are you going to stay with the mules?" Hugh asked his youngest son.

Thomas nodded. "Can I get a couple of apples first?"

"Be quick about it."

Thomas ran across the fall board and into the family cabin. He came out a few moments later with an apple in his mouth, one in his hand, and a small bag of raisins in the other hand.

When he got back to the mules, Hugh helped his son onto King Edward's back and then walked back onto the *Freeman*.

"Papa, can I steer for awhile?" George asked. He was waiting anxiously next to the tiller, trying to look nonchalant. The boy waned to captain the boat and feel like he was in control.

"Take the tiller and eat some lunch, too," Hugh told him.

Hugh walked to the front of the boat to the mule shed. George had already taken the harnesses off Jigger and Ocean, and they were munching on hay he had brought in from the hay house. Ocean had lived up to his name. The deck beneath him was wet with urine and the shed was beginning to smell of ammonia.

Hugh picked up the bucket in the corner and climbed out the window onto the race plank. Thomas had started the mules walking and the boat was moving away from Lock 44. He waved to Ben Cooper, the lockkeeper, as Hugh dipped the bucket into the canal and filled it. He emptied the bucket inside the mule shed to wash the urine out of the drain hole in the corner.

He climbed back in and spent an hour currying the mules and cleaning their hooves. They had been freshly shod last month so there wasn't much wear on their shoes yet. However, by next month they would need to be reshod while they were waiting in Georgetown or Cumberland. By then, they would have walked up and down the canal four times. He patted the mules on the neck and talked to them quietly as he worked.

When Hugh had finished with the mules, he walked back to the family cabin and got dinner for himself. Alice had cooked up hot biscuits and beef stew with dried beef.

The sun went down an hour later. Thomas lit a lantern on a pole and set it in front of the mules so they could see the towpath. Hugh also lit a lantern with a mirror behind it so that George could see how the canal turned and twisted. He stood for a moment at the front of the boat, enjoying the cool night air and the sounds of the canal. Crickets chirping. Fish jumping. The sound of the boat cutting through the water. An occasional bray from one of the mules.

When he was satisfied, he went into the cabin to catch a few hours sleep before they changed teams at Lock 51. Hugh preferred changing teams at locks since everything came to a standstill anyway while the boat was being raised or lowered through the lock.

As he walked down into the family cabin, Hugh didn't light a lantern for himself. Elizabeth was already asleep on the bottom bunk next to the stateroom; a light blanket pulled up around her shoulders. She knew she would be driving the mules through the night. She was a good girl and a good hand.

Hugh felt his way through the curtain into the stateroom, which was simply a six-foot by six-foot partitioned-off area of the small family cabin. He collapsed into the straw tick laid out on the bed frame and went to sleep within minutes.

He was awakened by the sounds of the brass horn blowing the first few notes of "Red Rover." They were approaching the lock, and George was letting Shane McDermott, the lockkeeper, know they were coming.

Hugh rubbed his eyes and rolled out of bed. He stretched and parted the curtain. Elizabeth had already lit the lantern in the cabin. He took his pocket watch out and checked the time. It was twelve-thirty in the morning. He was going to have to get used to running all night, too.

"Good morning, Papa," she said as he parted the curtain.

Hugh kissed his daughter on the cheek. She was an attractive lass who stood five feet tall, but seemed like a giant when her Irish temper was raised. Still, she would make some lucky boy a fine wife...some day. She could cook, sew, drive a mule team, and plant a garden among other things.

"Good morning, darlin'. Shall we get to work?"

She nodded. "I'll harness Jigger and Ocean while you help the boys lock through."

When Hugh stepped outside onto the race plank, he felt a chill. The night air was still cold, seeing as how it was still March and they were in the mountains. He glanced toward the towpath. He could see the light from Thomas's lantern. He had stopped moving and was probably unhitching the mules.

"Good morning, Papa," George said from behind him.

"Are you going to take her in?"

"I'd like to."

"Is McDermott awake?"

"I'm awake, you Irish owl!" a voice called out of the darkness.

"What are ya doing out at this time of night? I was sleeping like a baby and dreamin' of bonnie lassies servin' me unlimited ale. I asked a red-headed beauty to sit on my lap and when she opened her mouth to answer me, all that came out of her mouth was the sound of that blasted horn of yours."

Hugh laughed. "Best not let Marcy hear about those dreams, Shane. She'll have you sleeping in a tent to tend lock."

"Aye, that's for sure, as if nightrunners like you let me get any sleep."

Hugh tossed a guide rope to Shane who caught it out of the air. Even in the dark, McDermott had sharp eyes.

"Are you going to tie up for the night once you're through?" Shane asked. "Conrad's here, just beyond the lock."

Hugh jumped from the front of the boat onto the lock wall made of granite cut from the same quarry as the granite that built the White House in Washington City. He quickly looped the line around the snubbing post and tightening it to keep the *Freeman* from being damaged by bouncing off the lock walls and to keep the lock walls from being damaged by the canal boat.

"We're going to keep moving. I plan on being in Cumberland tomorrow night. I can talk to Conrad then when he's a dozen boats behind me in the line at the basin," Hugh told the lockkeeper.

"Just keep your eyes open. You'll probably pass a dozen or so others that had the good sense to tie up for the night."

"That's what I'm hoping. I figure I'm well behind the Hancock boaters anyway. Might as well pass the Williamsport boats while I can."

Locking through took about ten minutes. In that time, the boat was raised up eight feet as water flowed into the lock. When the west lock gates were opened, the mule team pulled it out of the lock and George steered it to the bank until it stopped.

Hugh set out the fall board while Elizabeth led Jigger and Ocean onto the towpath. Thomas yawned as he led the team into the mule shed. Hugh felt sorry for the boy. It would take even Thomas, with all of his energy, a few days to get used to the long hours they worked during the season.

Once Thomas was aboard, Hugh pulled up the fall board and walked back to the tiller.

"Whenever you're ready, Elizabeth," Hugh told his daughter.

"In a minute, Papa."

A short time later, he saw the lantern hanging in front of the mules begin to move forward. Hugh settled down and concentrated on keeping the boat from running aground or into other boats. By six o'clock in the morning, they had gone through six more locks and were well into the mountains. By noon, they were a couple of miles past the Paw Paw Tunnel on their way to Oldtown. A good many boats passed them on their way down the canal, sitting low in the water because their holds were full of tons of coal. Those were the Cumberland canawlers who had wintered their boats at the loading basin so they were the first boats to be loaded.

The *Freeman* floated into Cumberland around midnight. As the Fitzgeralds tied up at the end of the line of empty canal boats in the loading basin, Hugh could hear the tinny music and occasional shooting coming from Shanty Town to the east. Downtown Cumberland was toward the west. That's where he and Alice would go tomorrow for some supplies while they waited their turn to fill their holds.

On the other side of the river, he could see the few buildings that made up Ridgeley, Virginia. Last year at this time, he'd gone over there to visit one of his mother's cousins. This year, they were supposed to be mortal enemies.

When Hugh was satisfied that everything was fine on board, he blew out the lantern and went down into the family cabin to go to bed.

8

FILLING HOLDS
MARCH 1862

Hugh woke in the morning to the sound and smell of sausage frying. He sighed and rolled over in bed. The smell was nearly as delicious as eating the sausage. When he stretched out, his feet stuck out through the stateroom curtain in the family room.

"It's about time you woke up, Hugh Fitzgerald," Alice said from inside the cabin.

Hugh parted the curtain with his foot so that he could see Alice. Her brow was sweaty from cooking over the small stove and a lot of her strawberry blond hair lay matted against her forehead.

"What's the rush, lass? I saw the line of boats when we came in last night. We won't be fillin' our holds until this evening some time."

It took about an hour to fill a canal boat's holds with coal and there were more than a few boats ahead of the *Freeman* waiting to fill their holds.

"I'm not talking about that. George keeps pestering me to go into town."

Hugh blinked the sleep out of his eyes.

"Well, let him go with you then. I'll stay here and sleep."

Alice kicked Hugh's foot. "Not Cumberland. I wouldn't be worried about that. He wants to go into Shanty Town."

Shanty Town wasn't a town. It was the waterfront area around the loading basin. Stores along Wineow Street and a few side streets sold food and dry goods, but the more-popular businesses were the taverns and red-light district. It was a place known for its rowdiness because so many of the canawlers spent their free time getting drunk in the taverns since the sale of alcohol was forbidden along the canal. Fights were a greeting in Shanty Town, at least among the men. The women had another way to greet the canawlers.

Hugh sat up and rubbed his neck. It was stiff. He did miss the feather mattress in the house in Sharpsburg.

"The boy must be feeling his oats," Hugh said.

Alice waved her fork in his direction. "The boy's backside will be feeling my wooden spoon if he keeps this up." She paused. "Of all the places to want to go. Shanty Town!"

Hugh nodded. "I'll talk to him."

"I wish you would do it soon before he slips over the side and goes off on his own," Alice warned her husband.

His eyes narrowed slightly. "He knows better than to do that."

"Well, he should know better than to want to go into Shanty Town, either, but he wants to go. It's just not the sort of place for a good Catholic boy." Her voice sounded slightly frantic. She was truly afraid that George would go into Shanty Town.

Hugh swung his legs over the side and pulled on his boots. He tucked his cotton shirt into his pants as he stepped out into the cabin.

"Where are Thomas and Elizabeth?" he asked Alice.

"Thomas is sitting on the mule shed fishing in the basin. Elizabeth is in the hay house reading a book. She brought her school lessons with her."

Though George always worked extra hard at his schooling during the winter, he never brought his lessons with him to work on while they waited to load or unload coal.

Hugh stepped around his wife, but not before he snatched a kiss off of her neck.

"Go on with you now," she said, pushing him toward the door.

Hugh walked up the two stairs to the race plank. George was sitting on top of the family cabin under the canopy.

"So Mama sent you to put a harness on me," George said when he saw his father. Harnesses tied to the top of the family cabin were used on younger children to keep them from falling off the canal boat and drowning in water over their heads.

Privacy was a rare commodity on a boat where the living quarters were cramped and the windows open nearly all of the time. Hugh knew that his son had heard his conversation with Alice.

"Your mother doesn't think you're a baby if that's what you're thinkin'," Hugh said as he lit his pipe and flipped the match over the side.

George sat up. "She won't let me go where I want to go."

"If you saw your brother about to pick up a cottonmouth, what would you do?" It wasn't such a far-fetched idea when Hugh was talking about Thomas.

"I'd tell him to leave it alone."

"And if he ignored you?" Again, with Thomas that wouldn't be unusual.

"I'd pull him back," George said.

Hugh nodded as he listened. "But you'd be keeping him from doing what he wanted."

"Only because he was being stupid!"

Hugh grinned. "Not quite the way I would have said it, but since you did, I'll say it: Your mother and I are stopping you because you're being stupid."

George frowned. "I'm sixteen. I'm a man. I should be able to do what I want."

Hugh put a hand on George's shoulder. "You may be a man in size, son, but the way you're acting now shows that you're still a boy inside that tall body of yours."

George stiffened but he didn't say anything.

"I don't even go into Shanty Town, except right along the basin to get supplies. Further in, you've just got saloons and whorehouses. If you can give me a good reason for needing to go to either of those places, I'll listen," Hugh offered.

George frowned and crossed his arms over his chest. "I just want to see what goes on there. I hear other canawlers talk about it, and I want to be a part of it."

"So you want to try and pick up the cottonmouth just because you heard of someone else who could do it and not be bitten," Hugh said.

George started to say something but instead snapped his mouth shut. He looked out over the muddy water in the canal basin.

"If you're looking for some measure to prove you're a man, don't use Shanty Town," Hugh said.

"Why not?"

"Just look at the kind of men who do use it as a measure of their manhood. Thieves, drunks, and river rats. Is that the kind of man you want to be?"

George lifted his chin and shook his head. "No, sir."

Hugh slapped his son on the shoulder. "Good, and don't worry, George, you'll find a measuring stick to put yourself up against before too long and when you do, you'll be surprised at how well you already measure up."

"Yes, sir."

"Now can you tend the boat this afternoon? Your mother and sister want to go into Cumberland to shop for supplies and some other things. They want me to go along to carry their packages."

George nodded. "I'll take good care of the *Freeman* for you."

"I know you will."

Hugh, Alice, and Elizabeth left the canal boat after eating a hearty breakfast of fried eggs, sausage, and fresh-baked biscuits. A filling meal always put Hugh in a good mood for the rest of the day as well as energizing him for the day's work.

As he helped Alice and Elizabeth onto the dock, Hugh saw a small boy fishing on the edge of the pier with a ball of string and a baited hook. At first, Hugh thought Thomas had left the boat to do his fishing. The boy had skinny arms and legs and an unruly shock of dark-brown hair. Then he noticed that this boy, though he looked a lot like Thomas, was a year or two older.

When the boy saw Hugh staring, he said, "Don't worry, mister. I won't steal anything. I was just trying to catch my breakfast."

The boy stood up. His dirty white shirt hung open and Hugh could easily see the youngster's ribs. How long had it been since the boy had eaten?

"What's your name, son?"

The boy looked at Hugh suspiciously. His blue eyes were those of an adult. "I ain't your son."

"Well, you're someone's son." The boy snorted. It could have been a half-hearted laugh. "Though I'd have to say they're not taking too good a care of you."

The boy puffed out his chest. It only showed his ribs more clearly. "I take care of myself and I do a good job of that."

"Then how come I can tell you how many ribs you have and me standin' all the way over here?" Hugh asked.

The boy's cheeks blushed. He hesitated and said, "Sometimes I forget to eat because I'm so busy."

Hugh nodded, not believing a word that the boy said. "Uh-huh."

Alice tugged on Hugh's sleeve. "We have some biscuits and sausage still from this morning," she whispered in his ear.

He patted her hand and nodded.

The boy pointed to Alice and said, "Is she saying I stole something? Because I didn't. I've just been fishing here all morning."

"Do you get accused of that a lot, boy?" Hugh asked.

"I'm not a boy."

"Well, you never did tell me your name and you don't like me calling you son, so I guess 'boy' will have to do because it's plain you're not a girl."

The boy looked astonished that someone might even consider that he wasn't a boy.

"My name's Tony."

"Do you have a last name, Tony?"

Tony frowned and said, "No."

So the boy was an orphan. That explained his physical condition. He probably wasn't eating much, especially enough for a boy his age.

"Well, Tony, my name is Hugh Fitzgerald. This is my wife, Alice. If you're looking for breakfast, why don't you find my son, George, on my boat and tell him to give you the breakfast leftovers. Then if you'd like to earn two bits, you can picket the mules out here, feed them, and keep an eye on them while I'm away."

Tony's eyes narrowed as he stared at Hugh. "Why?"

"Because I take good care of my mules and they pull true for me."

Tony shook his head. "Not the mules." He tapped his chest. "Why are you hiring me?"

Hugh rubbed his chin. "You said you're an honest man, and you must do good work if you're so busy that you forget to eat."

Tony blushed. "Aw, you know that's all bull."

Hugh nodded. "But you're hungry and need work. I can help."

Tony wound up his fishing line. "Fine. You've got a deal. I'll do a good job for you, too."

"I know you will."

Hugh turned and walked off with his wife and daughter into Cumberland. Hugh wanted to go to the tobacconist on Liberty Street to buy a newspaper and pipe tobacco. Alice and Elizabeth were looking for some suitable material so that Alice could sew Elizabeth a new dress to wear when she went walking in Georgetown.

As they walked along George Street, Hugh could see the Queen City Train Station across the railroad tracks. He scowled at the four-story brick building.

"I'm sure the train station is very frightened, dear," Alice said from beside him. She laughed.

"It's a reflex," he said.

"Don't waste it on a building."

The Baltimore and Ohio Railroad was the canal's biggest competitor and a thorn in the side of the canal directors and canawlers. Both the canal and railroad began building on July 4, 1828, and raced toward Cumberland. Charles Carroll, one of the owners of the railroad, had kept the canal tied up in legal battles to win the right-of-way at Point of Rocks and the right to pass through land he owned. By the time the canal finally opened in Cumberland in

1850, the railroad had already been operating there for eight years. The canal had already lost most of its flour trade to the railroad, or rather, been tricked out of it by trying to work with the railroad.

Now the railroad and the canal fought for the coal business in western Maryland. Because the canal and railroad ran side by side in many areas, railroaders took pleasure in blowing their whistles to spook mules as they passed canal boats. A spooked mule had nearly trampled George three years ago.

When the Fitzgeralds arrived back at the basin a few hours later, Tony was sitting on a hill talking with Thomas as they watched the mules together. The *Freeman* was also much closer to being loaded with its first load of coal for the season.

"Well, it looks like you did a good job of taking care of the mules," Hugh said as he fished a quarter from his pocket and flipped it to Tony. It was more than the job was worth, but Tony looked like he needed a good meal or two to fill out his ribs.

Tony caught the quarter and it disappeared into his pocket. He waved to Thomas as he stood up. Then he walked over and shook Hugh's hand.

"If you ever need more help when you're around this way, Mr. Fitzgerald, look around for me. You know my name and so does most everyone around here. I'm usually down here on the waterfront and I know where everything is. I can get you a good deal on just about anything you might need."

Hugh nodded. "I'll keep that in mind, Tony."

With that, Tony took off running into Shanty Town, probably to the nearest place where he could spend his newly earned money.

"The basin foreman came by and told me to tell you to be ready to take a load by five o'clock, Papa. We'll be after the *Chesapeake Star*," Thomas said.

Hugh pulled his watch from his pocket and checked the time. It was a quarter to four. Once they were loaded, they could still get started before dark. Travelling around the clock had gotten them to Cumberland early enough to beat the first rush of boats to Cumberland.

"Let's get aboard and get the hatch covers off," Hugh told his family.

With two people on each side of the race plank, Hugh, Alice, Elizabeth, and George lifted the hatch covers up and walked sideways down the race plank until they could stack them on the family cabin, hay house or the mule shed.

When they finished, it was a little before five o'clock. Hugh hitched up Seamus and King Edward and had them tow the boat under the coal chutes.

The chutes dumped coal one rail car at a time into the front of the canal boat. As the forward hold filled, the boat tipped forward so that the family cabin at the rear end of the boat rose slightly. Alice had secured everything in the family cabin to keep it from breaking if it fell. The mules moved the boat forward and another thirty tons of coal was dumped into the rear of the boat. The boat leveled out deeper in the water. The boat moved forward again and another thirty tons of coal rumbled into the front hold and then the rear hold to fill them completely.

Coal falling into the holds sounded like a thunderstorm. The black cloud of coal dust that rose into the air reminded Hugh of storm clouds. His family stood yards off to the side to avoid being completely coated with the dust. Alice had shut the windows in the family cabin, but dust would still coat everything inside the cabin so that she would have to spend a day or two cleaning.

The basin foreman checked the holds, judging the weight against what was marked on his manifest. He signed the drayage certificate for 120 tons of coal, payable on arrival in Georgetown.

Now it was time to get to work.

9

NORTH OF THE POTOMAC
MARCH 1862

David sat on the large, round rock a few feet back from the small fire Private Thelen had built. David had thought of building one, but he wasn't sure how to go about it. The slaves always kept the fires going on Grand Vista and privates like Thelen did the job in the army.

He stared into the fire as he sipped his coffee. It was hot and bitter. A speared catfish hung over the fire slowly cooking.

On the other side of the fire, Corporal Tim McLaughlin and Private Jonas Thelen played cards and smoked hand-rolled cigarettes. David stared at them in their filthy butternut uniforms and wondered if they had been the right men to bring on this assignment. They had come highly recommended from Colonel Collins, who had said these two were the best woodsmen in the regiment.

David wondered if the colonel hadn't simply decided to get rid of some useless men, including David.

He still had his nightmares about battle, but so far, neither of his companions had said anything about David's noisy sleep. For their small forbearance, David overlooked their sloppy appearance.

"You'd better stop staring into that fire, Lieutenant," McLaughlin said.

David's attention focused on the corporal.

"What's wrong with looking into the fire?" David asked.

"Look behind you."

David's head jerked around, thinking someone had sneaked up on him. All he saw, though, was darkness and ghost images from the fire.

He looked back at McLaughlin. "What did you want me to see?"

"It's not what I wanted you to see, Lieutenant, it's what you didn't see. Did you see any of the trees when you looked behind you?"

David shook his head.

"Staring at the fire gets your eyes too used to the light. When you look away, you're blinded for a little while," McLaughlin told him.

"Easy way to get yourself killed," Thelen added with a chuckle.

David cursed himself for not knowing better, but then, he had not known any better. He had been raised on a plantation, not in the backwoods of Tennessee. He had never had to hunt or camp out. Of course, Colonel Collins had said Thelen and McLaughlin were good at these types of things. Apparently, the colonel had been correct.

"We're not expecting to cross a Union patrol," David said.

"That don't mean we won't. Until we can find something else to wear, we are rabbits in a field for whatever hawk happens by."

David said, "Well, we'll have to find some clothes soon so we can go into Hagerstown and Frederick."

"Are we going to steal some clothes so we don't look like soldiers?" Thelen asked.

David shook his head. "No. I have some cousins who live nearby. We can get some clothes from them. We won't have to steal them."

McLaughlin cocked an eyebrow at him. "Are you sure they will help us and not turn us in?"

David was shocked at the thought. "They're family."

"They're Yankees."

David shook his head.

"We should blow up some of these bridges that the canal boats and trains use. If we stop the coal they carry from getting into Washington, we'll freeze out the Yankees in the winter."

"We're not here to fight the Yankees by ourselves. We're supposed to find the safest way for our boys to get north. We may be invading the north before too long."

McLaughlin chuckled and nodded. "That's fine, but who's to say we can't cause some damage on our way home? It would make things easier for the colonel."

David waved his hand around the camp. "We don't have any explosives. We aren't here to have the Yankees chasing us back into Virginia. The colonel gave us a mission. We need to accomplish it and get back."

"Get back to what? Our boys are starving across the river while they sit and wait to get on the move," Thelen said sharply.

"Then that's all the more reason to find out what we need and get back quickly so the colonel will know which way to go."

McLaughlin suddenly grabbed the pot of coffee and poured it over the fire, quickly putting it out. The flames sizzled under the fluid and the last thing David saw was a plume of gray smoke wafting up. Then everything was dark.

"Be quiet, you two. I hear a horse," McLaughlin whispered loudly.

David and Thelen immediately stopped talking. David felt more than saw Thelen move away from him. David slid his Navy Colt from its holster and laid it across his lap. Had the Union patrols found them? They had been avoiding towns, but they hadn't taken extraordinary care to conceal themselves.

As David listened, he heard the clopping of horse hooves. It was one, maybe two, horses. Then he heard someone humming. It was a man on horseback. David realized that the man, whoever he was, was drunk.

Then David heard the man grunt as if he'd been hit in the stomach unexpectedly. After that, he was silent.

"It's fine. I got him," McLaughlin said.

"Good going," Thelen said.

"What do you mean you 'got him?'" David asked. He still couldn't see much more than shadows. Ghost flames were dancing in his eyes. McLaughlin had been right about staring into the fire.

"I slit his throat so he won't be singing anymore," McLaughlin said.

Thelen chuckled.

"Why did you do that?" David asked.

"We can't let anyone know where we are, Lieutenant," McLaughlin said.

"That man couldn't have told anyone anything. He was drunk. Even if he had seen us, he wouldn't have remembered us in the morning."

"Hey, Corporal, look at what I found," Thelen said.

McLaughlin laughed. "This man was planning on getting very drunk. We've got ourselves a full bottle of whiskey and a second bottle that's almost full."

A few minutes later, Thelen had another fire going. The light spread out, but the fire brought no warmth to the cold that David felt. He sat on a rock and watched as his two companions passed the whiskey bottles back and forth and got drunk on the dead man's whiskey.

David walked over to where the dead man lay close to their camp. Luckily, David couldn't see the dead man clearly in the shadows. He walked back to the camp site and watched the two soldiers.

Soldiers?

Who was David kidding? They were no more soldiers than David was.

He wasn't staring at soldiers. Despite their uniforms, there was nothing remotely military about McLaughlin and Thelen. They were nothing but ruffians.

What had he gotten himself into? How could the South hope to prevail over the North if they had to lower themselves to the level of the Yankees?

Thelen laughed uproariously at some joke that McLaughlin told him. David didn't hear the joke, which was probably better.

Of course, as loud as they were being anybody within a mile could probably hear them.

Were these men the future of the South?

10

GIVING TO THE CAUSE
MARCH 1862

As the *Freeman* drew closer to Georgetown, Hugh began to wonder at the lack of boats that passed him heading west for another load of coal. He knew that he was making good time by traveling nights, but he also knew that there had been plenty of boats ahead of him that he had seen loaded and heading towards Georgetown. Of course, it was possible, indeed probable, that there was a back up to offload. Many of the cargo ships would be involved in the war, but Hugh hadn't seen any other canal boats. Certainly there must be some boats that had emptied their holds of coal and headed back to Williamsport or Cumberland.

Alice walked out of the family cabin and passed Hugh a thick slice of bread lathered with homemade jam. Hugh took a bite. The bread was still warm and delicious.

"Have you thought about how you are going to introduce Elizabeth to the eligible men of Georgetown?" Hugh asked.

"Some."

"Well, we may be in Georgetown for awhile this trip. I haven't seen any westbound traffic."

Alice frowned. She was a canawler's wife. She knew that a lack of traffic meant that the boats had to be crowding the wharves at Georgetown.

"Remember Grace Sampson?" she asked.

Hugh nodded. Alice loved Grace like a sister. She was married to Congressman Eli Sampson from Pennsylvania.

"I thought that I might ask her to help me find who would be suitable young men for Elizabeth. She probably knows many of them," Alice said.

"Does Elizabeth know that you're husband hunting for her?" Hugh asked. He finished off the bread and licked his fingers.

Alice gave him half a grin and shrugged, "She's not thrilled, but she knows I'm not going to make her marry. I'm just trying to expand her options."

Hugh still wasn't sure how he felt about his wife's idea. Certainly he wanted Elizabeth to find a good husband, but he had an inkling that his idea of good differed from Alice's idea. She wanted a gentleman to marry Elizabeth, someone like Eli Sampson. Hugh just wanted his daughter's future husband to be someone who loved his little girl and took good care of her.

"Options? She's a canawler, Alice. Not just by birth and family, but in her heart. Is she going to be happy if you marry her off to a city boy?" Hugh said.

"A woman's heart will take love over profession any time."

Hugh started to say something along the lines of, "That's my point. She's a canawler. Would she be happy married to a lawyer or a doctor?" Then he saw the look in Alice's eyes and decided that it would be better to keep his mouth shut.

Hugh was immediately suspicious the next day as his family approached the way bill lock, the lock near Georgetown where the canawlers presented their manifests and collected their pay for their loads. Hugh saw a squad of soldiers stationed between the lock and the lock house. Two of them stood up and walked over to the down river swing arms and waited. They carried their rifles with them.

"George," Hugh said quietly. George was napping on top of the family cabin.

George opened his eyes and arched his neck so he could see his father standing behind him.

"What, Pa?"

"Go into the cabin. Don't rush. Get my rifle and wait in my cabin so you can look out the window," Hugh told him.

George sat up quickly. "What's wrong?"

"Nothing…yet. Just do what I say, but don't run."

George looked over toward the lock and saw the soldiers. His eyes widened and he swung his legs over the edge of the cabin.

As he walked near his father to go down the stairs into the family cabin, Geroge said, "They're Union."

"But they are where they shouldn't be."

George nodded and walked down into the cabin. A few moments later, he said, "I'm ready."

"Good boy. Just wait."

The *Freeman* approached the lock and Cole Johnson walked out to the lock. He was a skinny man who was barely bigger around than the swing arm on the lock doors. He glanced at the soldiers and then looked over at Hugh.

"How have you been, Hugh?" Cole asked.

"Got through the winter all right, though I'm glad to be moving again."

Hugh tossed the snubbing line to Cole. Cole grabbed it and looped it around the snubbing post set into the ground near the lock. He snugged the rope around the post but didn't tighten it.

"Where's George? He needs to grab the other line."

Hugh shook his head. "George is busy right now. Why don't you ask one of the soldiers to do it? They're just standing around," he said calmly.

Cole looked over his shoulder at the men in the blue uniforms. "I only wish they were," he said quietly.

"Why are the soldiers here?" Hugh asked.

Cole hesitated a moment and then said, "They're commandeering boats."

"What?" Hugh lost his calm and shouted the word. The soldiers stood up, suddenly alert.

"They're here to escort boats to the wharves where they're holding them until they can decide what they're going to do with them."

"If they don't know what they're going to do with them, then why are they stopping them?" Hugh asked.

Cole shrugged. "Because they can, I guess. The boat captains are fuming, but there's nothing they can do. They've been trying."

Hugh glared at the soldiers. He doubted that his stare would force them to back down, but maybe he could shame them a bit.

"I own this boat and there's nobody that's going to take it from me," Hugh said defiantly.

Alice came out from the family cabin and shaded her eyes as she looked around. She seemed to take in the situation immediately, but she had probably heard most of the conversations through the open door to the cabin and windows.

"I'll get the other snubbing line," she said quietly.

The snubbing lines were needed to brake a canal boat and keep it from crashing into the lock doors. A canal boat was designed to fit snugly into a lock. There was only a few inches clearance on either side. If a canal boat started rocking too much while being raised or lowered, it could damage the canal walls or the lock doors.

Hugh was grateful that Alice didn't mention George. She picked up the snubbing line and looped the coils over her shoulder.

Then she waited on the race plank until the boat was moving into the lock. She jumped onto the lock wall, which was level with the boat, and looped the rope around the snubbing post.

Once the boat was inside the lock, she and Cole pulled on their lines to slow the *Freeman* to a stop. Cole jumped on the east doors and opened the sluice gates with a lock key to let the water out of the lock. The two waiting soldiers moved to climb on board the *Freeman*.

"Whoa! You two off of my boat!" Hugh shouted, waving the soldiers off.

"We can't do that, sir," the corporal said. "Our orders are to escort all incoming boats to the wharf and register them until the government decides what to do with them."

"The government doesn't own this boat and neither does the Canal Company." Hugh stabbed his thumb in his chest. "I paid for it and I decide what to do with it."

The soldier rolled his eyes, and Hugh realized the young man had probably heard this argument many times before.

"Not any longer, sir. Our orders are to appropriate all canal boats."

"Appropriate! Don't you mean steal?"

"You'll be reimbursed for your boat," the young soldier said indignantly.

Hugh snorted. "That would be fine if I was intending to sell the *Freeman*, but this boat earns me my livelihood, boys. Even if you did pay me top dollar, I'd still have to have another boat built, and I'd be out of work for a year while that was going on."

"That might not be a bad thing with the war going on."

Hugh shrugged. "Fine. Then you sell the government your boat. I'm unloading my holds and then heading back to Cumberland for more coal."

The soldiers jumped from the lock wall onto the *Freeman*'s race plank.

"Sir, you don't understand. You don't have a choice," the corporal told him.

Hugh slapped the roof of the family cabin with the palm of his hand. "George." The barrel of the rifle poked out between the curtains in the cabin window. "You don't understand, boys. I do have a choice. I'm not some slave. I'm like the name of my boat. A free man."

The soldiers stopped. They couldn't back off the boat because it was already three feet below the edge of the lock wall and dropping. They lowered their rifles to the deck.

"Now why don't you boys unbuckle those gunbelts and then both of you move over toward the mule shed," Hugh ordered them.

Cole looked down from the lock doors and saw what was happening. "Fitzgerald, are you a fool or is it your dumb Mick blood showing?"

"This is my boat, Johnson. If President Lincoln expects me to support and defend the Union because it's my country, then he ought to expect me to do the same for something more personal like my property," Hugh replied. He yelled so he could be heard over the roar of impounded water rushing out from the lock.

"And what are you going to do with those soldiers? Shoot them?" Johnson yelled.

Hugh stared at the soldiers. They didn't look afraid. "I hope not unless I have to. Until then, I'll just thank them to get off of my boat."

The other soldiers began to appear on the lock walls holding their rifles. When they saw the situation, they raised their rifles to their shoulders and aimed them at Hugh.

"Are you going to start a second war, Fitzgerald?" Cole asked. "Because I think that this is one war that the Union could win fairly easily."

"And what would you do if the government wanted to take your home, Johnson?" Hugh asked him.

"Your boat is not your home!"

"For nine months a year it is, and it's my livelihood, too. So what would you do, Johnson? Would you just give up your home and walk away from all of your work?"

Alice stood on the lock wall looking worried, but she didn't say anything. Thomas stayed with the mules beyond the lock, keeping them quiet and Elizabeth stayed in the cabin with George.

Cole glanced nervously at the soldiers. "No," he admitted. Cole paused. "But I certainly wouldn't get myself killed over it, either," he added.

Hugh stared at Cole. There was wisdom in what the man was saying, but what would happen to his family without the *Freeman*? They could ride the mules back to Sharpsburg and then what? Hugh wasn't a farmer. He never had been. He wouldn't have any money until the government paid him, which could be the end of war. How many merchants would give him credit, not knowing whether they would live through the war, let alone Hugh?

Then Thomas walked up to the lock doors to stand next to

Cole. The young boy looked scared and so did Alice. Hugh hated to see the fear in their expressions.

"You can't win, Fitzgerald," Cole said. "You've got one shot. Once you take it, they'll kill you and George, too."

"Hugh, they're just following orders," Alice added, finally breaking her silence.

He looked up at her. Her eyes were wide and she kept glancing at the rifles. She didn't want him to die. Hugh sighed. He felt his defiance seep out of his body.

"Put the rifle away, George," Hugh said with a sigh.

"Are you sure, Papa?"

Hugh stared at the soldiers. Could he have told George to shoot one of them? Hugh wasn't sure, but he knew he didn't want to risk George's life to find out. It wasn't the soldiers' faults that they have been given bad orders.

"I'm sure. Let's not get ourselves killed," Hugh said.

The rifle barrel disappeared into the cabin and few moments later, George walked out of the cabin empty handed and stood next to Hugh. Hugh put his arm around his son's shoulders. The tension around the lock eased noticeably.

"You did well, George," Hugh told the boy.

"But we'll still lose the boat."

Hugh shrugged, trying to look more unconcerned than he felt. "But we'll keep our lives."

Above them, Alice and Cole opened the lock doors by leaning their weight on the swing arms. The two soldiers on the boat picked up their rifles. They hadn't bothered to undo their gunbelts. The soldiers on the lock walls eyed Hugh suspiciously as if they expected another trick.

Cole tossed the snubbing line onto the boat. It thumped heavily on the cargo hatches as it landed. Alice brought her line with her when she jumped onto the roof of the family cabin and then climbed down to the race plank. She didn't bother to coil the line. She just ran to Hugh and threw her arms around him.

"I'm glad you weren't completely foolish," she said.

He stared at her with pleading in his eyes. "But what do we do now?"

"I have an idea. I'll tell you about it later," she whispered in his ear.

Hugh was doubtful that anything could be done. "Unless it's something that can be done now, I don't think we'll have the time."

"Cole said they're just holding the boats at the wharves. They haven't done anything with them yet," Alice reminded him.

Elizabeth took over the driving with the other mule team and pulled the canal boat out of the lock. The soldiers stood on either side of the hay house, watching Hugh.

Hugh said, "All of that rush to get here and for what? I have to give the *Freeman* away to the cause."

"Just be glad that you're alive, Hugh Fitzgerald," Alice told him. She gave him a hug.

"But for how long? Without a needed trade, they'll draft me into the army for sure and the sad thing is that I'll have to go to be able to send you money."

Alice patted his arm. "Don't give up yet."

The *Freeman* found a spot along the wharf and tied up. He recognized some of the captains as they waved to him. There must have been eighty empty boats tied up and waiting along the wharves on the river.

"See they got you, too," James Gallen called from his boat.

"Welcome to the ex-canawlers club," John Brady, captain of the *Hancock* called.

"And the sad part is that I made my best time getting down here," Hugh called back.

"Didn't we all, and I thought the Union was on our side. I've got a good mind to go join my cousins in Martinsburg," Brady said.

The two soldiers jumped off the *Freeman* and tied it to the wharf. Hugh saw Joseph Partridge, the wharf owner, approaching and he groaned.

"It's not enough for them to take my boat, but Partridge's going to bleed me dry of what I get for this load," Hugh said to Alice.

"We'll manage," she said calmly.

The soldiers intercepted Partridge and obviously told him something that he didn't want to hear. He threw his hands up in the air and began shouting at them. Against his better judgment, Hugh smiled. It seemed like the canawlers weren't the only ones being robbed of their livelihood. Partridge wasn't going to be able to collect dock fees on the commandeered boats, and judging by Partridge's reaction, that must have been most of these boats.

"So what happens now?" Hugh called to the soldiers.

"You wait until the government decides what to do with the boats," one of them told him.

"You mean they are keeping me from working, they are stealing my boat, and they don't know what they want to do with it? Do you think I'm going to take my boat somewhere they can't find it?" Hugh shouted.

The soldier at least had the good sense to look embarrassed. "I just take orders, sir. I don't make them."

Hugh shook his head.

"What was your idea, Alice?" Hugh asked, turning to his wife.

"Grace Sampson."

"What does your friend have to do with this?"

"She's married to a congressman, Hugh. Since it's the government that's holding our boats, then maybe the government can pry it free, too."

Hugh thought for a moment and smiled. He said, "You are a genius, Alice. When can we meet her?"

"We should wash up and put on our Sunday clothes first. I don't want her thinking we are beggars," Alice suggested.

Hugh looked around and shrugged. "Well, I don't have anything else to do right now."

They washed and changed in the family cabin. Hugh felt like he was getting ready for church, but the Sampsons lived among Washington society. Hugh and Alice didn't want to show up on their friends' doorstep looking like beggars.

Hugh left the boat under George's care. Hugh usually didn't wander too far from the wharves in Georgetown. He wasn't comfortable being in big cities. This, however, was a special case. He would do anything to get his boat back.

The Sampsons lived in a three-story brick home on Union Street. Alice stopped walking when she saw the town house and stared at it in awe. The white-shuttered windows were open to allow in the breeze. Bright white curtains flapped in an out of the windows. Beneath the windows were freshly painted flower boxes.

"How rich are the Sampsons?" Hugh asked.

Alice chuckled. "It's not that they're rich. Eli Sampson is a congressman from Pennsylvania. This is the home they stay in when Congress is in session, which apparently is most of the time with the war going on."

"Does Eli know President Lincoln?" Hugh asked.

"I don't know, dear. You can ask him yourself."

The Fitzgeralds walked onto the wide porch and knocked on the oversized front door. The butler, a black man, answered the door. He wore a gray suit, which matched his graying hair. His brown eyes still looked youthful, though, despite his age. Alice wondered if the man was a slave, but Grace and Eli Sampson were from Pennsylvania where anti-slavery sentiment ran strong.

"Hello," Alice said. "Alice and Hugh Fitzgerald to see the Sampsons."

"Yes, ma'am. Come in, please." He waved them into the foyer. "Mrs. Sampson has mentioned you before. My name is Chess. I work for the Sampsons and keep house, so if there's anything you need, you let me know."

Alice looked around the foyer, still impressed by the house, although this was her third time here. Large paintings created by Eli decorated the walls of the house. He was actually quite an excellent painter of country scenes. The broad front staircase ran upward and curved to the second floor. The doors to all of the rooms off the foyer were open to allow the air to circulate through the home.

"Chess is an interesting name," Hugh said. "Is it because you play the game of chess?"

Chess smiled broadly, causing his narrow face to take on a pear shape. "No, sir. Chess is short for Chesapeake. I was born on the banks of the bay in Maryland when my mammy and daddy were still slaves," Chess explained.

He led them through the house to the rear porch where the Sampsons were sitting in cane-backed chairs.

"Alice!" Grace Sampson said, jumping to her feet. She hurried across the porch to hug Alice. Grace was a small woman, about Elizabeth's size, but Elizabeth wasn't full grown yet. She was Alice's age, but when the two of them got together, they both sounded like schoolgirls.

"It's wonderful to see you, Grace. I love your home," Alice said, returning her friend's hug.

Grace laughed. "You always say that. I didn't know that you were in Washington."

"Actually, we're stuck in Washington," Alice said.

"Stuck?"

"Soldiers are commandeering the canal boats as they come into Georgetown."

Grace's eyes widened. "Whatever for?"

"We don't know and the soldiers don't know, either. I was hoping that Eli might be able to help us get our boat back. It's our livelihood," Alice said.

Grace turned to Eli and Abel who were sitting at a table. Eli was a tall, thin man with thinning brown hair.

"Eli, can you help the Fitzgeralds?" Grace asked her husband.

Abel stood up. He was an eighteen-year-old youth who was a few inches taller than when Alice had seen him last year. He had his father's shade of hair and his mother's blue eyes. He was also wearing spectacles.

"I'll leave you all alone to talk," Abel said.

"It's good to see you, Abel. You're growing into a fine man," Hugh said, shaking his head. It had been a couple years since Hugh had seen him.

"It's good to see the both of you, too. Tell Elizabeth, George, and Thomas that I asked after them."

"We certainly will," Alice added quickly. Hugh turned to look at her, but she was staring intently at Abel.

Abel went inside and the four adults sat down at the table.

"Abel certainly looks like a fine young man," Alice said.

Eli nodded. "And hopefully this war will leave him alive to become a fine man."

"Has he joined the army?"

"Not yet, but he wants to. He has his father's desire to preserve the Union. Now that he's turned eighteen, we can't stop him if he chooses to join," Grace said.

"He'd make a fine soldier," Hugh said.

Eli nodded. "Yes, but he is my only child." He paused. "Now you thought that I might be of some help with your problem."

Hugh nodded and leaned forward. "The government took our boat this afternoon."

Eli scowled. He folded his hands together in front of his face. "I had feared that they might carry out their foolish idea."

"You know what's happening?"

Eli shook his head. "Not precisely. The decision was a cabinet-level decision, but I'm not sure which secretary you can blame for it. I know of it because the legality of the action is being debated. That is probably why nothing more has been done yet."

"But why? Why would they do it?"

Eli's tone took on a lecturing, oratory voice that he probably used when he addressed Congress. "Washington now finds itself in a precarious position. We sit right on the border of the Confederate States of America. Many people fear the Confederate navy might sail into the mouth of the Potomac under covering fire from Ar-

72

lington and Alexandria. We are quite vulnerable. A very vocal part of the government wants to make us less so, particularly in light of the fact that we have suffered losses along the eastern front and more precisely at Bull Run. And although the Confederate's iron-clad was forced into a retreat, it is still a threat."

"But how can confiscating canal boats help?" Hugh asked.

"Some will be used to carry supplies to General McClellan's men on the peninsula. That idea I support because the vessels are needed, but can be returned to service once they are done. However, others also want to use the canal boats to create temporary bridges over rivers and make temporary wharfs. Such uses would definitely damage the boats. However, there is also one idea being discussed to sink the boats."

"What?" Hugh nearly shouted.

Eli nodded. "People are scared, Hugh, and when people with power are scared, they do foolish things. In this case, they want, they want to sink the canal boats near the mouth of the river to keep the Confederate Navy out. With all of the bridges to Virginia either burned or heavily guarded, we have then made it very difficult for the Confederacy to bring in their army by foot or ship."

"There's got to be other ships that the government could use."

Eli shook his head. "Any seaworthy boats have been pressed into service as fighting vessels."

Hugh collapsed into a chair. "It's not right, Eli. I'm not a slave to the government. My people came to this country to be free and to own property. Now that trouble shows itself, it looks like this country is not much different from what we left behind in Ireland."

Eli nodded. "Sadly, you're right, my friend. However, it is not the country and its underpinnings that have failed you, but its leaders. I fear that in large measure is why the Southern states have sought to form their own country. They are wrong, though. Running from the problem won't create a better government. We need to elect better leaders; men who honor the Declaration of Independence, the Articles of Confederation and the Constitution."

Hugh said, "I don't disagree with you, Eli, but until that time, I don't want my boat to be sunk. I perform a service for this city that I happen to think is more valuable than using my boat for a blockade."

"I, too, think that."

They were quiet as each person was lost in his or her thoughts.

Finally Eli said, "I believe that I can help you, Hugh, though I still fear that some of the canal boats will eventually be lost. I wish

I could turn the President's Cabinet from this folly, but unfortunately, as our prospects for victory seem dimmer, their desperation becomes greater."

"What can you do?" Hugh asked, trying not to sound anxiou

Eli stood up. "Follow me."

They walked back into the house and Eli led them into the library. Hugh was amazed at the shelves of books. He had never seen so many books in one place. Eli sat down at his roll-top desk and pulled out a piece of paper from the desk drawer. He dipped his pen in to the inkwell and wrote out a letter. When he finished, he passed it to Hugh.

Hugh looked at it and read it out loud: "To Whom It May Concern: Be it known that the canal boat of Mr. Hugh Fitzgerald is not to be appropriated for any government program without Mr. Fitzgerald's permission. Mr. Fitzgerald better serves this country during her time of testing by doing what he does best, which is to supply Washington with food and coal. As such, he is not to be interfered with in his duty to his country. Signed the Honorable Eli Forrest Sampson, Congressman, Pennsylvania."

Hugh looked up. He couldn't believe his luck at having this letter. "Thank you, Eli."

Eli leaned back in his chair and crossed his hands over his stomach. "That was the easy part. Now I need to make sure that the lockkeeper at the way lock and the commander of the company of soldiers at this end of the canal know that this is no forgery."

"How will you do that?"

Eli stood up. "I'll accompany you to the way lock and allow them to witness my signature. Did you ride here?"

Hugh shook his head.

"No matter. I have a carriage. We'll ride out to the lock and take care of business while our wives can remain here and catch up with each other's lives," Eli said.

"Alice?" Hugh asked, turning to his wife.

She put a hand on her arm. "I'll stay here and talk with Grace while you two do what you need to do."

Hugh stood up and kissed her on the cheek.

The Sampsons owned a two-person carriage. Chess harnessed a pair of geldings that would pull the carriage while Eli put the top down.

As they rode toward the way lock, Hugh asked, "Is the war going as badly for the Union as you make it sound?"

Eli sighed. "Only in the minds of men who haven't fought. While the Confederate soldier, in general, is probably a better soldier than those in the Union, the Confederacy doesn't have the capability to fight an extended war. Even now, General McClellan is pressing toward Richmond. His success would end this conflict. If the Union can simply continue without making too large a mistake, the blockade of the South's ports will begin to wear the Confederacy down."

"It sounds as if you want to break their will."

Eli shrugged. "If we must."

"How good a citizen will a man be with a broken will?"

"A better citizen than a dead one. The Southerners are prideful. They will need a broken will if they are to be brought back into the Union," Eli told him.

Hugh nodded thoughtfully. "Aye, you may be right there. The problem there is that we are fighting ourselves. Our generals know each other and so they know each other's strengths and weaknesses."

"If we must break that strong Southern pride for a generation or two to keep the Union together, then that is what we will do." Eli's voice was hard, but it had a sad tone within it. Hugh suspected that the war had forced Eli to go against his gentle nature about different issues.

Eli stopped the carriage in front of the small two-story lock house. The squad of soldiers stationed there had a fire burning and a kettle of soup cooking over it. Eli and Hugh walked over to them.

"Corporal, who's in charge of the soldiers stationed here?" Eli asked.

"Lieutenant Carver."

"Where might I find him?"

The corporal nodded toward the lock house. "He usually eats supper with Mr. Johnson and his wife."

Eli nodded. "That's fine. I need to speak with Mr. Johnson, also."

Eli waved to Hugh and they walked to the lock house. Eli rapped on the door with his gloved hand. A middle-aged woman answered the door.

"Mrs. Johnson?" The woman nodded and Eli handed her his card. "I'm Congressman Eli Sampson of Pennsylvania. I was told that I would be able to speak with your husband and Lieutenant Carver here."

The woman opened the door wider and Hugh saw Cole Johnson. "I'm her husband. Can I help you, Congressman?" Cole said.

"And I'm Lieutenant Carver," said a soldier standing in the middle of the room.

"Good," Eli said.

Eli handed the letter to Cole who read it slowly. The lockkeeper looked up from Eli to Hugh and back again.

"Do you understand it?" Eli asked.

"Yes, but I'm not the one with the guns," Cole said, looking at the lieutenant.

Lieutenant Carver walked over and took the letter from Cole and read it. When he finished he passed it back to Eli. "I have my orders, sir."

Eli refused to take the letter and left Carver holding it. "This countermands your orders in this instance."

"With all due respect, Congressman, you are neither the military nor the commander-in-chief," Lieutenant Carver told him.

Eli sighed. "You are right, Lieutenant. What I am, though, is someone who can still have you busted to private and sent to a duty that might not agree with you as much as this one. Do I make myself clear?"

The lieutenant hesitated momentarily and then snapped to attention. "Yes, Congressman."

Eli turned to Cole. "And I would request that you, sir, put Mr. Fitzgerald's boat to the top of the list of boats to be offloaded. I am sure he will want to get on his way as soon as possible. With the fools I work with ordering boats to be commandeered, the capital city will be awfully short of coal if the weather turns cold again. Perhaps, all the Confederates have to do is save their men and wait for us to kill ourselves."

"I'll get on it right away, Congressman," Cole said.

Eli held up his hand. "Before you do, I want you and Lieutenant Carver to sign this letter as witnesses. I don't want to have to go through this again."

Cole carried the letter over to his desk and signed it at the bottom. Then Carver signed and passed the letter to Eli.

Eli shook Cole's hand. "Thank you, sir."

Then Eli and Hugh walked back to the carriage. As they settled into the seat, Eli said, "I'll leave you with your boat and then have Chess drive Alice back when she is ready. I'm sure that you have things to get in order before Mr. Johnson arranges for a coaster to take on your coal."

"I don't know how to thank you, Eli. I didn't know what I was going to do if they had sunk the *Freeman*," Hugh told him.

"I'm glad that I could help, Hugh, though I doubt few boats will be sunk and they will probably be those of men who wish to get out of the canal trade. Our leaders will come to their senses soon and begin to think."

Hugh was very doubtful about that. "And if they don't?"

Eli cocked his head to the side and looked out across the canal. "If they don't, we will have bigger problems to worry about."

"Like what?"

"Like a new country equal in size to our own just across the river from us."

11

GHOSTS IN THE TUNNEL
MAY 1862

George leaned back against the tiller of the canal boat, easing his weight from one foot to another. The days on the canal had settled into their lazy rhythm now that all of the hectic activity associated with the opening of the canal had worked itself out. In particular, he was glad they hadn't lost three weeks at the wharf in Georgetown waiting with all the boats that had been impounded by the government. Thirty-one boats had actually been filled with rocks, taken to the mouth of the Potomac, and sunk to create a protective barrier against the Confederate navy. More than 100 were taken for use as transports or bridges. George was glad one of them hadn't been the *Freeman*.

The Federal government had formally released any of the canal boats it still held late in April. That meant a lot more boats were back on the canal, though travel on the canal had been intermittent at best since March. This was only the *Freeman*'s fourth trip to Washington this season. The Canal Company had been trying to repair damage to the canal caused by troop movements and floods that had occurred in February.

The days were warm and pleasant, and George was learning to handle the boat better. He'd gotten over his initial discomfort of having control of the boat. He'd even gotten used to running the boat twenty four hours a day. Sometimes he found himself steering the boat in the middle of the night and other times, he might be working in the middle of the day. They were always moving, except for Sundays, of course. His mother saw to that, making sure they attended whatever church was closest.

George liked the responsibility his father trusted him with, though sometimes he had trouble concentrating on his work. He found himself thinking about girls like Becky Crabtree a lot. He was saving the money his father gave him as payment for working on the boat so that he could buy Becky something nice in Georgetown. He just hadn't thought of what it should be yet. He'd bought a razor for himself in Cumberland. He planned to start shaving so that his barely visible beard could toughen up and make him look older.

It was just after seven o'clock at night and the sun was setting. Even in the darkening light, he could see the east entrance to the Paw Paw Tunnel a quarter mile ahead, a small black hole at the base of the canal among the other shadows. The entrance formed the only regular shape, so it was distinguishable among the others.

The Paw Paw Tunnel had taken twelve years to build and the cost and time had almost bankrupted the Canal Company. It had been built to save five miles of canal that would have been required for the canal to follow the Potomac River along the Paw Paw Bends. The tunnel was hand-dug and more than three-fifths of a mile long. George had heard his great-uncle Dermot who had lost his arm building the tunnel say that there were almost six-million bricks used to hold up the mountain above their heads.

"Thomas, can you go light the headlight before we get to the tunnel?" George asked his little brother.

Since the tunnel was so long, canawlers lit red headlights on their stern and white headlights on their bow. The headlights were large square lanterns with reflectors behind the flame so that all the light was cast forward. That way a boat coming into the tunnel would be able to know which direction another boat already in the tunnel was going and whether they could enter the tunnel or needed to wait. That was an important thing because there was no room to turn around inside the tunnel. If two canal boats met inside the tunnel, one of them would have to back out, which meant a lot of wasted time.

Thomas was lying on his stomach, trying to get a large turtle he had adopted to eat a piece of lettuce. Thomas looked around as if he was noticing it was getting dark for the first time.

The young boy stood up and jumped off the roof of the family cabin. He landed on the race plank with a dull "thud."

"Be quiet. Papa's sleeping," George warned him.

"Sorry," he said as he hurried to the front of the boat to light the white lantern that hung in front of the mule shed.

The canal narrowed as it headed into the tunnel. On the towpath, Elizabeth lit her own lantern and lifted the harness ropes over the railing that bordered the towpath as it passed through the tunnel. The top of the wooden railing had been worn smooth by hundreds of tow ropes being dragged across it, but its gentle reminder had kept many a mule from stepping off the towpath and into the canal.

George saw the white glow appear from the headlight and then

Thomas walked back and sat down on the roof of the family cabin again. As the boat entered the tunnel, George peered forward, trying to make sure that another boat wasn't already inside the tunnel and moving west toward Cumberland. He wouldn't want to meet another boat in the middle of the tunnel.

"Woooo!" Thomas tried to say eerily. He listened for the slight echo off the tunnel walls.

"If you ever met a ghost, you'd run screaming to Mama," George said.

"I would not," Thomas said defiantly. "I'd catch it in a jar and toss it in the river. Then the river would take it out to the ocean and over to England or France."

"You would not."

"Would to!" Thomas shouted.

"Then where's your jar?"

"What jar?"

George rolled his eyes. "Your jar for catching a ghost."

Thomas looked around suspiciously. "What ghost?"

"But we're going through the Paw Paw Tunnel," George said.

Thomas's brow wrinkled as he stared at his older brother. "So? We've been through the tunnel lots of times before."

George's mouth dropped open. "Oh, I'm sorry. Never mind."

Thomas stood up and walked over to George. "Never mind? Never mind what?"

"I guess Papa hasn't told you yet because you're too young. After all, he only told me about the ghost last year."

"Told you what? About what ghosts?" Thomas grabbed his brother's arm. "What did he tell you, George? I'm old enough to know."

George forced himself to frown when all he wanted to do was grin. He had Thomas hooked like a fish. Now George would have some fun.

George shook his head and tried to look embarrassed. "No, I shouldn't say anything. Besides, if you ever turned chicken going through the tunnel, Papa would be mad at me, not you. You're a little kid. He'd be mad at me for saying something. You'll have to wait for him to tell you."

"The tunnel's haunted, isn't it?"

They were well inside the tunnel now, and it was dark except for the lantern light and that seemed so far away. The brick ceiling arched overhead and seemed ready to collapse. Spots on the wall dripped water from rain yesterday. The dripping water formed a rhythmic beat as it struck the water in the canal.

George shook his head. "I didn't say that."

Thomas threw his shoulders back proudly. "I'm not dumb, George. I figured it out for myself."

Figured it out wrong.

"So how's it haunted, George?" Thomas asked.

"Well, since you figured it out for yourself, I guess I can tell you the rest of the story. Actually Uncle Dermot is the one who told Papa about all of this when Papa started boating on the canal. He warned Papa to stay out of the Paw Paw Tunnel at night and now here we are," George told him in a serious tone.

"Why shouldn't we be here? We've been through at the tunnel at night before."

"It's not just the night. It has to be a night after a good, soaking rain like the one we had yesterday so the ground's good and wet and water's dripping through the bricks."

Thomas fell quiet as he listened to the water dripping into the canal.

"Why's that so special?" Thomas finally asked.

"Why's that so special?" George said in amazement. "That just goes to show that a little boy like you don't know nothing."

"Doesn't know anything," Thomas said.

"What?"

"You should have said, 'That just goes to show that a little boy like you doesn't know anything'," Thomas corrected him. "You should pay more attention to your school lessons."

Since Thomas was younger, he still had time to study his lessons that their mother gave them during the season.

George didn't like being reminded that he wasn't as smart as other kids his age that didn't work on the canal. Of course, those kids didn't know how to drive mules, lock through a canal boat or steer a boat. George had his life's work laid out before him and it didn't require much book learning.

"Do you want to know how to avoid being killed by the tunnel ghosts or not?" George asked.

"Why does the tunnel need to be dripping?" Thomas asked.

George smiled. "There's quite a few people buried above the tunnel because there's a workers' graveyard up on the mountain filled with the bodies of those who died during the twelve years they were building the Paw Paw Tunnel. Some died in building accidents. Some died in drunken fights, but they're all buried above the canal." George was making this up as he went along. Luckily, Thomas didn't know that the canal worker's cemetery was near Paw Paw and that the ground above the tunnel was too rocky and steep for a graveyard.

Thomas looked at the brick ceiling nervously and moved closer to his brother. George grinned.

"Those bodies decay after awhile. Then that rainwater comes through the ground and carries away small parts into the canal and from there they float down into the Potomac," George told his brother.

"Yuck!" Thomas said.

George put a calming hand on Thomas's shoulder. "That's not the worst part, though. All of the spirits in those bodies are pretty upset that their bodies are being scattered all over the place. I mean, how are they gonna have bodies in Heaven if they are broken up into thousands of pieces and scattered all over the place? So when the rains come, so do the ghosts. They walk through the tunnel trying to find a way to stop their bodies from decaying and falling into the canal."

Thomas straightened up and looked around. "How can you see them?"

"You won't see them in the lantern light. They won't come near that, but you can see them in the dark. They glow like a will o' the wisp. I've heard that if enough of their body gets carried away, they try and find another body to replace it. Jack McBurney got ripped apart in 1851 by two ghosts fighting over him, and Sam Poole got hisself buried alive by a ghost who wanted his body."

"Really?" Thomas asked, his eyes wide.

George nodded. "That's what I've heard."

Thomas hurried forward and turned up the wick on the lantern and increased the light being cast in the tunnel. Then he stayed close to the lantern, sitting on the edge of the mule shed. George laughed.

"George Washington Fitzgerald, if your brother starts having nightmares about the tunnel, guess who's going to have to sit up with him?" his mother said from the doorway of the family cabin.

George hadn't realized that anyone was listening to him weave his tale for Thomas. He should have, though. A canal boat had little privacy.

"Mama, Papa told me ghost stories all of the time when I was Thomas's age."

"Yes, and who do you think sat up with you when you woke up crying at night because you were having nightmares?"

George did remember. It had been his father.

The *Freeman* came out of the tunnel a short time later. Since it was dark outside, too, Thomas stayed near the safety of the lantern's light, but he noticeably relaxed. He lay back on top of the mule shed and put his arm over his eyes.

"Why don't you get the horn ready?" George called to his brother.

They were approaching the odd locks: 66, 64 2/3, and 63 1/3. The reason for the odd numbering of the locks was that the Canal Company had decided to eliminate Lock 65 to save money on their over-budget project when the canal was being built.

The lock house for Lock 66 sat back from the canal. The carpenter shop where the canal gates were manufactured and repaired occupied the lot where a lock house would usually sit next to the lock.

Thomas got the brass horn out of the hay house and blew the first notes of "Red Rover" to let Lucas Crabtree know they were coming. By the time they reached Lock 66, Lucas had the west gates open and George guided the *Freeman* toward the narrow opening. It seemed so much smaller when only the lantern hanging on the front of the boat lighted it. He called for Elizabeth to stop the mules. The lock allowed only three inches of clearance on both sides of the boat so getting into the lock without damaging either the lock walls or the boat was the trickiest part of locking through.

Once the boat moved into the lock, George tossed a rope to Lucas who looped it around the snubbing post to brake the *Freeman* to keep it from crashing into the east lock doors. Lucas kept the rope tight enough to allow the ninety-two-foot-long canal boat to move all the way into the lock while keeping it from damaging the west lock doors.

George jumped out on the river side of the canal. He leaned on the long swing beam to shut one of the west canal doors while Lucas shut the other door on the north side of the canal. They then walked out on top of the massive canal doors and turned the lock keys to shut the sluice valves.

Now the *Freeman* was entirely contained within the 100-foot lock.

Lucas and George walked to the east end of the lock and used the heavy, metal lock keys to open the sluice gates at the bottom of the lock doors so that the water within the lock would drain out. Once the

Freeman was level with the water level outside the east gates, the doors would be opened. It would take about eight minutes. The surge of water being released between locks created the two mile per hour current that helped carry the canal boats to Washington.

As George stood next to the snubbing post playing out rope and watching the *Freeman* sink below the lock walls, he saw Becky Crabtree, the oldest of the five Crabtree children, walk outside the lock house holding a lantern in one hand and an empty bucket in the other.

Her long brown hair was braided into two ponytails that reached below her shoulders. She was a slender girl who was beginning to find her feminine curves. She seemed to grow prettier each time George and his family came through the locks.

When she saw George staring at her, she smiled and called out, "Hello, George." George felt his ears getting hot, though he wasn't sure why. She had said hello to him lots of times before now.

Lucas turned and saw George staring at his daughter.

He smiled and said, "Why don't you go help Becky fetch a couple buckets of spring water? She's been cooking cherry pies all day with her mother. I'm sure she's tired and thirsty. If you help her, she'll probably give you a piece of pie." He paused and eyed George. "That's all she'll give you, though." He said the last sentence loud enough so that Becky could hear it, too.

"Yes, sir!" George said quickly.

He ran across the tops of the east gates and jumped to the side of the canal. He hit his knees, but he quickly hopped to his feet and dusted the dirt off the knees of his pants. Becky smiled behind the hand she held up to her mouth.

"Becky, let me help you get the water," George called as he hurried over to her and picked up the wooden bucket.

They walked away from the canal to the spring where the Crabtrees drew their fresh water. The path was dark except for the circle of light cast by Becky's lantern.

George felt light-headed walking with her so much so that he stumbled because he wasn't looking at the ground but at her. He had known Becky ever since he had started boating on the canal. They had always been friends since they were so close in age, but last year, George had started looking at her differently. He had even started dreaming of her, which made him feel uncomfortable when he saw her.

When he had seen her for the first time in two months last

month, he had almost forgotten to breathe. They had come into the lock around noon and the sun had been beating down something fierce. It almost seemed to frame her and illuminate her as she had walked onto the porch to wave to him.

They stopped walking at the spring. The water bubbled steadily from a crack in the rocky soil and flowed downhill to fill a natural basin that was about four feet deep and ten feet wide. Becky took the bucket from George and dipped it into the basin so that it could fill.

"How was Cumberland? Mama says we can go there next month with the Twiggs," Becky told him.

Jeremiah Twigg and his family lived at the lock house on Lock 64 2/3. They often sold their produce to canawlers as they came by the lock house.

"I didn't get to see much of it last time we were there. Papa let Tony watch the mules..."

"Who's Tony?" Becky asked.

"He's an orphan who lives around the waterfront. Papa gives him odd jobs to do sometimes when we're in Cumberland. He's a good worker and Papa likes him," George explained.

"That's nice."

George shrugged. "I'd like to get Tony to take me into Shanty Town and show me around sometime. He lives there. I think if Mama ever found out, she would come into Shanty Town after me."

He bent over and lifted the bucket out of the basin for Becky.

"Shanty Town? Why would you want to go there? It's so dirty and Daddy says it's dangerous," Becky asked him.

"It can't be too dangerous. Tony's only ten and he gets around all right."

They started to walk back to the house. Becky smiled and looped the arm that wasn't carrying the lantern through George's free arm.

"Has your sister met anyone in Washington?" Becky asked.

"You know all about that?"

A canal boat wasn't the only place where privacy was lacking.

"I heard my parents talking about it. Mother thought it was a good idea. That's why she wants me to go to Cumberland with her to do the same thing."

A lump formed in George's stomach. The last thing he wanted was competition for Becky's attention. Charles Watson and Herm Towne were already turning an interested eye in her direction. He'd even seen both of them sitting with her at different times

85

when the *Freeman* had come up behind their families' boats to go through the lock. What George worried about though, was when they came through the lock and he wasn't around. Then they had Becky all to themselves.

"Don't you find the guys you already know good enough?" George asked, fearing the answer.

Becky shrugged. "I don't mind them, but almost all of you boys on the canal are pretty much the same," she told him.

He wasn't sure which part of her comment insulted him more: that he was a boy or that he was the same as other canawlers. "Boys?" He paused. "We're not the same."

"Sure you are. You're all canawlers and canawlers live in the same general area, do the same thing, dress the same, talk the same, eat the same things, so sooner or later it's no wonder you all start to look alike," she explained.

"We're not. I'm nothing like Herm Towne." Herm was at least six inches shorter and twenty pounds heavier than George was.

"Yes, you are. Where's the canawler gentleman, the canawler scientist, the canawler politician, the canawler soldier?"

George shook his head. "You're trying to group everyone together too broadly."

"How so?"

"Look at the differences between my father, and say, Ben Hawkins. They're nothing alike, but they're both canawlers."

Captain Hawkins was a rough canawler with a quick temper. The man fit in well with the river rats in Shanty Town.

"Your father is a good man," Becky agreed.

George nodded. "My sister could find a good man among the canawlers, and she could find a lout in Washington." He paused. "And you could find one among the canawlers, too."

Becky giggled and clutched his arm tighter. "Oh, I know that, but I'm not going to pass up a chance to go to Cumberland. Besides, I might get a new dress out of it."

George wasn't sure if he should be relieved or not. After all, the boys would swarm all over a pretty girl like Becky when they saw her in Cumberland. Maybe he could start looking for a girl in Washington himself. Would Becky be as worried about him as he was about her?

Becky was so pretty, though! Who could measure up to her?

George set the bucket on the stoop and straightened up. Thomas came running up holding out his cupped hands.

"Look at this, George," Thomas said excitedly as he thrust his hands at George.

George looked into his brother's hands as Becky held the lantern up high enough so that he could see. Thomas was holding large pieces of three bird shells. The pieces were pink with green specks on them.

"I'm going to put them in my treasure box," Thomas said.

Thomas's treasure box was a wooden chest their father had built last winter so that Thomas would have a place to store his many "treasures" that he accumulated during the season like turtle shells, shiny rocks, and feathers. Otherwise, their mother had a tendency to throw them out as trash.

However, George didn't want to deal with Thomas's treasures at the moment. He was more interested in trying to win his own treasure, which happened to be Becky Crabtree.

"That's great, Thomas. Why don't you go do that? I'm busy here," George said.

Thomas grinned. "Are you crazy, George? You better not try and steal a kiss from Becky right here in front of everyone."

George's eyes bulged and he felt his cheeks flush. "You'd better get, Thomas, or I swear one morning you'll wake up swimming for your life in the canal."

Thomas laughed and ran off. Becky put her hand on her mouth and started laughing, too.

"It's not funny!" George told her.

Becky lowered her hand and tried to keep a straight face. "Are you going to try and steal a kiss from me, George Fitzgerald?"

George straighted his back and looked directly at her. "I don't steal anything, but I was thinking of *giving* you a kiss."

"Where?"

"Back at the spring."

"Why didn't you then?"

George's resolve broke and he looked away. He could only stare into her eyes for so long before he felt like he was falling. He dug his toe into the soft ground. "Well, we were talking and then I started thinking that maybe you didn't want a kiss from a canawler after all those things you were saying. Maybe you wanted to be kissed by some rich Cumberland boy up on Washington Street."

Becky giggled again. She giggled at the times when George felt the most unsure of himself, which only made matters worse.

"You're jealous," she said.

"Am not," he said too quickly. He took a deep breath. "I'm just concerned about you, that's all. I like you, Becky. A lot."

She rose up on her toes and kissed George on the cheek before he could say anything. Then she giggled and hurried into the house.

George could feel himself turning bright red as he looked around to see if anyone had seen Becky kiss him, but it was too dark. They seemed to be alone.

What did that kiss mean?

Was she thanking him for his concern or reassuring him that she liked him as well?

He touched the spot on his cheek where she had kissed him. It felt warm.

"George!"

George spun around and looked down the canal. He could see the lights on the *Freeman*. His family was waiting for him just beyond the lock.

"Coming, Papa."

He sprinted for the canal boat. As he ran up to where Lucas was standing near the east end of the lock, he heard his father ask, "What do you hear about the war?"

"It's not going well for the Union. McClellan's not the man for job, especially against the likes of Lee, Stuart, and Jackson."

"How about locally?"

"There've been raiders from Paw Paw. They leave me alone, though. I'm not a target for them. They'd like to blow up the canal, though, and do it permanently. They just don't know how, but you'd best be careful, Hugh. If they can't shut down the canal, they'll try and divert the boats, most likely in the slackwater areas."

George's father lit his pipe. "I'm being careful. I've got four rifles spread out on the boat in the mule shed, hay house, family cabin, and by the tiller. That way, I'm never far from one."

Lucas nodded. "That'll be fine as long as you don't come on too large a group of Rebs."

"Come aboard, George," Hugh said to his son.

George jumped from the bank onto the canal boat and landed against the hatch covers. When he stood up, he looked back at the Crabtree house. Becky was standing on the porch, holding up a lantern so that he could see it was her. She didn't wave. She just watched.

George shook his head.

Women!

12

THE WORK ENGINES
OF THE CANAL
MAY 1862

As the *Freeman* started eastward down the canal, Hugh saw more and more boats coming up the canal to load coal at Cumberland. It always amazed Hugh that with 185 miles of canal to travel, the boats always seemed to back up at Cumberland and Georgetown. He hoped to get to Georgetown quickly enough by running around the clock to avoid the congestion at the wharves in Georgetown.

Already, boats were beginning to back up at the locks. Hugh had to wait for the *Honest Abe* to come out of Lock 58 headed toward Cumberland before he could move the *Freeman* into it. Further down, near Little Orleans, the *Freeman* passed the *Independence* also on its way west to Cumberland.

Because the *Freeman* was going east and loaded, she had the right of way on the canal. John Rowley told his son Lou to slack off on the tow ropes. Rowley let his canal boat drift to the north side of the canal while the tow ropes between his boat and mules sunk under the water to the bottom of the canal.

George walked Seamus and King Edward slowly down the towpath, walking them between Rowley's mules and the canal so that the tow ropes wouldn't tangle. Hugh kept the *Freeman* tight against the south shore so he could pass the Independence without a problem.

"How's traffic at the basin?" Hugh asked as the two boats passed.

"Crowded, but they're moving steady now that the government is letting them move," Rowley told him.

In all, the government had seized 162 canal boats from late in 1861 to March 1862. Half had been sent to the Lower Potomac, thirty one had been sent to Liverpool Point in Charles County, Maryland, to blockade the Potomac from the Confederacy and the rest had been used to transport troops to the Peninsula. All of them, except for the canal boats sent to Liverpool Point had eventually been returned to service on the canal.

The *Independence* had been one of the confiscated boats. Rowley hadn't been as lucky as Hugh had, though. Rowley had lost a month of work time while the *Independence* served as a troop transport.

"Guess I'll see you in Georgetown."

"I hope not. I intend to be gone before you get there."

Rowley waved as the boats passed. Lou started his mules walking again and in a minute, the *Independence* was back on its way to Cumberland.

Hugh took George's place when they changed mules after they went through Lock 56 at Sideling Hill. Thomas stayed behind at the lock, fishing in the canal as the *Freeman* moved on. He came running up to Hugh half an hour later, holding a large striped bass that had to weigh at least four pounds.

"Look, Papa!" Thomas called.

Hugh turned and saw the fish. "Well, I can see what we'll be eating for dinner tonight."

Thomas clutched the fish protectively to his chest. "No, Papa. I don't want to eat him. I want to keep him in a bucket."

Hugh sighed. The bass was destined to become another one of Thomas's pets, but it certainly looked like a better dinner.

"Thomas, we don't have a bucket we can set aside for you to keep a bass in."

"But I'll take good care of him, Papa."

"That's not the point, son. You probably would take good care of him, but we don't have the room. Besides, a bass as big as that one is used to having a lot of room to swim around in. How do you think he'll like being crammed in a bucket where all he can do is chase his tail all day? Would you like it?"

Thomas thought for a moment. "I guess not."

"I'll tell you what. Why don't you let that big ol' bass go in the canal, and if he really likes you, he can follow you all the way to Georgetown?"

Thomas squinted at his father. "But how can I take care of him if he's down in the canal?"

"I'm sure your mother will let you throw some bread crumbs behind the boat after dinner for him to eat," Hugh promised.

Thomas thought for a moment and nodded. He bent down next to the canal and let the bass go. It lay on its side and Hugh thought that it might have been out of the water too long and died. Then the tail flapped and the bass turned over as it dove deeper into the canal.

Too bad, Hugh thought. It would have made a good dinner.

"Come on, Thomas. Walk with me," Hugh said, putting his arm around the young boy's shoulder and walking alongside the mules.

Thomas was Hugh and Alice's youngest surviving child. There had been two other children born after Thomas. A daughter had been born dead and Sean had died shortly before his first birthday when he took sick.

Hugh and Thomas walked on towards the east with Thomas singing "Goober Peas" over and over until even Jigger and Ocean looked tired of hearing it.

As they moved on toward Tonoloway Creek, Hugh saw another boat in front of them. It didn't seem to be moving and Hugh wondered if there was traffic coming upriver from the aqueduct. The Tonoloway Creek Aqueduct was a single 110-foot stone arch that carried the canal over Tonoloway Creek near Lock 52. However, the aqueduct was only wide enough to allow one boat to pass through it at a time.

As they came up on the boat, Hugh saw it was the *River Rose*, captained by Benjamin Hawkins, a man Hugh had very little respect for because he gave canawlers a bad name. The man had a shabby looking boat, and he frequently disobeyed the rules of the canal. Hugh had seen the boat definitely moving faster than four miles per hour and ignoring the right of way of boats coming down the canal.

Hugh had heard that Hawkins almost got into a shooting match once when he entered the Paw Paw Tunnel going west, ignoring the fact that there was already an eastbound, loaded boat in the tunnel. The mule teams and boats met near the center of the three-quarters-mile-long tunnel. Because the towpath and canal were so narrow in the tunnel, neither the mules nor boats could pass.

Captain McLarty on the eastbound boat had told Hawkins to back his boat out of the tunnel, and Hawkins had told McLarty to go to hell. Hawkins had come to the front of his boat holding a loaded shotgun. He'd threatened to shoot McLarty right off his boat if he didn't back his boat out of the tunnel. Luckily, McLarty had grabbed his own rifle and the two men had stood facing each other for eight hours. Meanwhile, boats going both east and west had started backing up both inside and outside the tunnel.

It had taken the district supervisor, riding hard from Oldtown, to resolve the problem. When he'd ordered Hawkins to back out of the tunnel, Hawkins had threatened to shoot the supervisor. The district supervisor hadn't drawn a gun. He'd simply told Hawkins that he had half an hour to back out of the tunnel or he wouldn't be allowed to travel on the canal any longer. Then the supervisor had walked further east to tell the other captains to clear the tunnel until all of the loaded boats were through. Because of the inconvenience and lost day of work, the incident hadn't made Hawkins any friends.

Hugh stopped Jigger and Ocean. The *River Rose* was in the middle of the canal, effectively blocking any other boats from passing.

Then Hugh saw why Hawkins was stopped.

Hawkins himself was doing a stretch as a mule walker. However, his pair of mules weren't walking. Both of them were standing still and one of the pair was actually sitting on its hindquarters. Hugh couldn't blame the mule. Canal mules generally had a work life of about fifteen years on the canal. They worked hard pulling laden-down barges. Even if the barge did float, it was still a heavy load to pull. Because of that, Hugh had always tried to treat his mules well. He kept them well groomed and their hooves clean. He didn't beat them, and he even made sure they were taken care of during the winter months of inactivity.

So it angered Hugh when he saw Benjamin Hawkins using a stick to beat the mule that was sitting on the towpath, trying to get it to stand.

"Thomas, stop Jigger and Ocean and keep them calm."

"Yes, Papa." He was frowning at Hawkins, too. The boy had good instincts.

Hugh hurried forward and put himself between Hawkins and the mules.

"What do you think you're doin', Fitzgerald?" Hawkins yelled.

"Tryin' to keep you from killing your mule. Can't you see he's bleeding?"

Hugh could actually see more than that when he was this close to the mule. The pair of mules were thin, a sign that they hadn't been fed well during the winter, and a poorly fed mule just wasn't going to pull as strongly as well-fed lean mules, no matter how much a driver beat them. And Hugh could tell these mules had been beaten a lot. The mule that was sitting was bleeding in at least three places.

"They're my mules," Hawkins said. "I can do with them what I want."

"Not in front of me, you can't."

Hawkins raised his whip as if he was thinking about using it on Hugh.

"This is the only way to make these beasts move." Hawkins waved the whip in the air.

"You know better than that, you fool. It's only you and a handful of other fools who think a mule won't move without being beat half to death."

"Do you kiss your mules goodnight, too?" Hawkins spat off to the side of the towpath.

"You're blockin' the towpath, and I'm ready to pass. So if you'd be moving your boat and beasts, I'll be on my way."

Hawkins raised his whip again and pointed it east and west. "No one's moving up or down on this canal until I get my boat moving."

Hugh had flashes of another Paw Paw Tunnel stand-off with Hawkins whipping a dead mule, trying to make it walk. Hugh had no desire to spend most of the next day here, watching Hawkins beat the mule until it began to stumble along.

He took hold of the harness chain and gave the mule a tug. "Come on, boy. Stand up and start moving," Hugh said.

The mule shook its head, trying to shake Hugh's hand off. Still, the animal did not stand up.

Behind him, Hawkins laughed. "A sweet word and a dollop of sugar will not make the beast move."

Hugh switched over to grabbing the harness chain of the mule that was standing. He tugged on the chain.

"Come on, lad. You and your mate are holdin' up traffic," Hugh urged.

The mule took a step forward but was quickly stopped by the fact that his partner was sitting on the towpath. Hugh kept urging the one mule forward. If a pair of mules could pull a loaded canal boat, then one mule could certainly get a second mule to start walking. However, this second mule was resisting fiercely, and truthfully, given how Hawkins treated them, Hugh couldn't blame them.

Thomas came walking down the towpath. "Let me help, Papa."

"This is men's business, boy," Hawkins said.

He moved to push Thomas back down the towpath, but Hugh stepped around the mule team and grabbed Hawkins' hand.

"Don't touch my son, Hawkins," Hugh said firmly. He was ready to fight if Hawkins laid a hand on Thomas. Thomas was not one of Hawkins' mules, and Hugh wouldn't allow him to be treated as such.

Hawkins saw the fire in Hugh's eyes and hesitated. "I don't

want him spookin' my mules."

"Your mules need spooking or something if you want them to move again." Hugh turned to his son. "What do you want to do, Thomas?"

Thomas held out a slice of apple to the mule that was seated. The black mule sniffed at the apple and Thomas's hand. The mule shook its head and reached out to take the apple in its mouth. Thomas held his hand flat so that the mule couldn't bite him if it took a notion.

The mule swallowed the apple slice and brayed. Thomas stroked the mule's neck, making sure not to come close to one of the bleeding cuts.

Thomas walked half a dozen steps away from the mule and held out another piece of apple toward the mule. The mule leaned forward and brayed, wanting the apple but not wanting to move.

Thomas shook his head. "No, you come and get it."

As if he understood Thomas, the mule lumbered to its feet and walked toward the young boy. Thomas grinned and let the mule eat the piece of apple from his hand.

"Good job, Thomas," Hugh said.

Hawkins mumbled something Hugh couldn't understand.

The boy turned to Hawkins. "You just have to give him a reason to want to walk. Beating him just gives him a reason to want to sit down."

Hugh laughed and took the rest of the apple from his son. Then he tossed it at Hawkins. The other man juggled it for a moment before he was able to grab it.

"You'd better keep your mules moving, or I'll have to find the district supervisor and let him know how you're obstructing hardworking folks like me." Hawkins grumbled. "And you'd probably do better if you listened to my son's advice from now on," Hugh called out as Hawkins started his mule team working.

13

COURTING IN THE CAPITAL
JUNE 1862

The *Freeman* floated out of the tidewater lock, the first lock on the C&O Canal. Hugh kept the canal boat close to the shore as Alice walked the mules forward along the towpath. She was taking an infrequent turn as a mule driver.

It was a nice change to be able to get off the boat for a little while. She was usually too busy with work on the boat to drive the mules for a trick, but she wanted to free up Elizabeth's time so that she could get ready to go to the Sampsons' home this evening.

Alice enjoyed the time she spent alone with her thoughts walking Jigger and Ocean, though. The canal walk was generally quiet unless they were locking through, passing another boat or Thomas was collecting his treasures to save in his small, wooden box.

It was nice simply to walk along and let her thoughts wander. Mule driving wasn't much more demanding than simply walking and keeping the mules doing so for six hours, which was about as long as a trick lasted. Thinking about other things also helped to keep her from thinking about how long she had been walking.

She and Hugh had a good life along the canal. She loved Hugh and she loved her children. Even their canal life was enjoyable. She certainly didn't mind getting away from Sharpsburg, even if living conditions on the *Freeman* were cramped.

Alice had been married to Hugh for almost twenty years now. They had been together since before the canal opened to Cumberland and for the twelve years since then. That had been a day that had changed their lives. Hugh had sold their farm in 1849 and had the *Freeman* built for $1,200. They had lived on the boat year round for six years until they had enough money to buy the house in town, which was good since they had two children at that point and the family cabin was confining to children.

She stopped the pair of mules next to the line of mules that were picketed near the wharf. The line of canal boats waiting to offload looked to be a mile long, over fifty boats. Long, but certainly not the longest line she had ever seen. Some of these boats used to be towed down river to some southern ports, but that had stopped when the war broke out. Now most of them would be towed into the river and off-load their cargo to a ship in Rock Creek or onto wagons at the wharf.

George tossed the mooring lines ashore and then jumped onto the bank with his mother. He pulled on the lines to help pull the *Freeman* into shore and then tied the lines to the posts on the wharf.

Hugh locked the tiller in place and came ashore himself. Joseph Partridge, the wharf owner, walked down the trail toward Hugh. He was a tall man with a very round face, though his body was stick thin. Despite the warmth of the day, he was dressed in a fine suit.

"Good day, Fitzgerald," Partridge said, holding out his hand. He stood a whole head above Hugh when they stood together.

Hugh grumbled and Alice elbowed him in the ribs. "Be nice."

"Be nice she says when I'm being robbed. I'd bet you'd invite the fox into the hen house, too," Hugh told her.

He fished out his wallet and counted out the dock fee to the owner. Partridge smiled as he counted the money. When he had finished, he looked surprised.

"There's only two days fees here. You think you'll be out that soon?" Partridge asked as he glanced over his shoulder at the line of boats.

"I plan to be."

"If not, I'll be back."

Hugh sighed. "Of that, I have no doubt."

Partridge walked away and Hugh turned to Alice and said, "If I had half a brain, I'd sell the *Freeman* and open my own wharf here in Georgetown. I'd probably make three times as much as I'm making now."

Wharf owners in Georgetown had a thriving business. With a relatively small investment, they were able to charge canawlers twice as much to tie up at their wharves than wharf owners in Cumberland got. Plus, the canawlers generally had to stay three times longer in Georgetown until they could offload their cargo.

"Is Elizabeth getting ready?" Alice asked her husband.

"Yes."

"We'll be gone most of the afternoon. I want to do some shopping before Elizabeth and I go to the Sampsons this evening."

Hugh sighed and fished out his wallet again. He pulled out a five-dollar bill and handed it to his wife. "Is that enough?"

Alice smiled and kissed him on the cheek. "Yes, dear." She turned toward the boat and called, "Elizabeth, come out, dear. There are things we need to do yet."

Elizabeth stepped out of the family cabin and onto the race plank. She wore a light yellow dress that was hemmed with white lace around the sleeves and neck. Her hair was tied in an attractive bun on top of her head. It made her look a few years older.

"You look beautiful, darling," Hugh said.

"I feel all tied together and constricted like I'm a birthday present to someone," Elizabeth grumbled.

Hugh grinned. "Well, you certainly will be a present for some lucky man someday."

He kissed her on the forehead and held her hand to help her across the fall board and onto the shore.

When Elizabeth stopped in front of her, Alice inspected her daughter's preparations. She straightened the seams of her dress and checked to make sure that her white shoes weren't dirty or scuffed.

"Mama!" Elizabeth said, exasperated.

"I just want to make sure that you look your best," Alice said.

"She looks like an angel," Hugh called from the boat.

"Fine," Alice said, straightening up. "Let's go into town."

They started to walk away from the waterfront toward Bridge Street. Alice stopped in at some of the various shops along their route. She bought some steaks, corn meal, a new hat for Elizabeth, and new shoes for Thomas

"You need to be on your best behavior this evening," Alice said.

"I know, Mama."

"Abel Sampson is a very eligible young man, but he's also used to living in the city. He doesn't want to court a girl who runs barefoot and drives mules on the canal."

"But that's who I am. Why should I try to be someone else?" Elizabeth asked.

"Because I don't want you to be forever connected to the canal," Alice told her.

Elizabeth stopped and stared at her mother with a look of shock on her face. "Why not? You are."

"But the canal is not always going to be here."

Elizabeth's eyes widened as she gasped. "They wouldn't fill it in, not after all of the trouble they went to to build it."

Alice shook her head. "No, I mean that the canal won't always be here as a business. New ways of transportation are being developed all of the time. Better roads for the wagons and faster trains. The trains are already threatening to take our trade away from us."

"No." Elizabeth shook her head. "The railroad won't ever replace the canal."

"It already has, Elizabeth. This canal was obsolete when it opened. That's why it was never built all the way to Ohio."

The C&O Canal and the B&O Railroad both began construction on July 4, 1828; the canal from Washington and the railroad from Baltimore. In the following years, the canal was delayed by an extended legal battle at Point of Rocks, fighting for the right of way and by Mother Nature near Paw Paw, Virginia, to dig the Paw Paw Tunnel. By the time the canal reached Cumberland in 1850, the railroad had already been there and operating for eight years.

"Canawlers won't let the canal die," Elizabeth insisted.

"Canallers don't have any control over the matter. Not only does the railroad go places the canal doesn't go and won't ever go, Mother Nature takes a hand in things every once in a while and shuts the canal down with spring floods. If there's a break in the canal bank, it shuts the entire canal down because the water drains out. If a section of railroad is destroyed, it only stops traffic around that area."

Elizabeth crossed her arms over her chest and said, "If the canal is dying, why do you and Papa stay here?"

"Because it's the life we've chosen to live, and the canal will last our lifetimes. It might not last your life or George's, though. The two of you haven't committed your lives to the canal yet. I'm just trying to keep your options open. If a better life presents itself to you, why shouldn't you take advantage of it?"

Elizabeth shrugged. "I guess I should." She paused. "Mama, is Abel Sampson good looking?"

Alice laughed and hugged her daughter.

"He's a handsome lad, and according to his parents, he's smart, too."

Elizabeth shook her head slightly. "Then why hasn't some fancy Washington girl caught him? He's eighteen. There must be something wrong with him."

Alice cocked her head to the side and said, "Oh, I imagine the girls have tried for him, but I know Abel's mother. Grace and I are old friends, and she's been encouraging him to keep his options open, too."

"What if we don't like each other?"

Alice grinned. "I've got other friends with sons."

They both laughed at that.

Alice and Elizabeth walked to the Sampsons rather than riding the mules. That way, they wouldn't smell like canal animals when they arrived. Elizabeth stopped walking when she saw the Sampsons' brick house and stared at it in awe.

"It's such a beautiful house, Mama," Elizabeth said.

Alice smiled. It was a good sign that her daughter liked the house, or at least Alice would take it as one. It meant that the canal and canal boats didn't truly own her daughter yet.

Alice examined her daughter one last time. This would be an important evening for Elizabeth. Even if she and Abel didn't marry, Alice still hoped their time together would allow Elizabeth to meet other eligible young men in Georgetown and Washington who weren't connected with the canal.

Satisfied, the two women walked onto the wide porch and knocked on the oversized front door. Chess answered it.

"Hello, Chess," Alice said.

"Good afternoon, ma'am." He waved them into the foyer. "Mrs. Sampson said you would be comin' by this evening. Can I get either of you something to drink?"

"No, thank you," Alice said.

Chess led them into the sitting room.

"Alice!" Grace Sampson said, jumping to her feet. She hurried across the room to hug Alice.

Grace pulled back and turned to look at Elizabeth. "Elizabeth, you're no longer a little girl. She looks as beautiful as you do, Alice."

Blushing, Elizabeth said, "Thank you, ma'am."

Eli walked into the room with a newspaper tucked under his arm. "Good day, beautiful ladies," he said with a broad smile.

Elizabeth blushed even brighter.

"How do you do, Congressman," she said, shaking his hand.

Eli smiled. "Just Eli, please. I hear enough 'Mister Congressman' in the Capitol building."

Elizabeth let the conversation between the adults fade into the background as the turned to look at the person who had walked into the room behind Eli. He was a young man, and he dressed in the uniform of the Union Army. His light brown hair seemed unruly, though undoubtedly it was combed. He wore wire-rimmed glasses that slightly magnified his blue eyes.

"I see you've noticed Private Sampson," Eli said. "Abel, come over here and meet Miss Elizabeth Fitzgerald."

Abel Sampson stepped forward and shook Elizabeth's hand.

"Elizabeth, it's good to see you again. You're looking lovelier than ever," Abel said, smiling. They hadn't seen each other since Elizabeth was six years old.

Elizabeth felt herself blushing again. How could she be so easily swayed? Was it the uniform? Or was it how the magnification his glasses gave his eyes made them look like doe eyes?

"My mother didn't tell me you were in the army," Elizabeth said.

"I wasn't until three days ago. I assume you've heard that things haven't been going as well as they could be for the Union."

Elizabeth wasn't sure if she should be offended by Abel's assumption that she didn't know what was going on with the country. It was her country, too. Of course, she tried to find out what was happening with her country. However, Abel didn't seem to be trying to be condescending to her.

"We can judge which side is winning by which way the bullets are flying over our heads," Elizabeth said only half jokingly.

Abel thought for a moment and then smiled. "I guess you do have to ride the line, don't you?"

"We have to watch ourselves. Raiders have already made a couple of breaks in the canal. They may get tired of fighting the canal and turn their attention toward us."

"Elizabeth!" Alice said, shocked.

"Well, it's true, Mama. I've heard Papa talking about it," Elizabeth said. She watched Abel closely to see if he would react like her mother. He didn't.

Abel nodded. "With the losses the Union has experienced lately, all able-bodied men need to come to her defense. Since I'm Abel and this is my body, I'm rising to the call."

Elizabeth laughed.

Eli put his hand on his son's shoulder. "You've run that joke into the ground, son."

"But Elizabeth hadn't heard it."

"But I have—again and again and again, and it's beginning to hurt my ears."

Grace took hold of Elizabeth's and Alice's hands. "Come, dinner should be ready, and we can all get something cold to drink."

The dining table was made of cherry wood with a white lace tablecloth on it. All six of the wall sconces were lit to give the room some light. The table was set with a large pot roast that sent a wonderful aroma into the air. Eli held out chairs for Elizabeth and Alice while Abel pulled out his mother's chair for her.

"Are you going to be stationed in Washington, Abel?" Elizabeth asked.

Abel looked up as he sat down at the table. "Actually, I'm stationed in Georgetown on the canal at the aqueduct."

"On the canal? Really?" Alice said.

"I'm part of the aqueduct defense." The Alexandria Aqueduct was a half-mile long aqueduct that ran from Georgetown to Rosslyn, Virginia. It was the only connection near Washington City between the Maryland and Virginia shores, and as such, it was a likely crossover point for an invading army. At the beginning of the war, the aqueduct had been closed off and drained and protected. "I have to keep the Rebs from blowing it up or from coming across what we are calling the Aqueduct Bridge now," Abel said.

The army had taken it over in December and converted it to a bridge in January. With no access to the aqueduct, canallers could no longer get to Alexandria's deep water wharfs. It was also harder for the larger canal boats to unload at Georgetown because they had to get under the bridges over the canal.

"I'll look for you when we leave," Elizabeth said.

"That should make my friends on the bridge jealous," Abel told her, smiling.

Elizabeth blushed.

"You're a lucky man to have been posted so close to home," Alice said as Eli began to carve the roast beef.

Abel looked down at the table. "I think my father had something to do with that."

"Your posting is nothing to be ashamed of, Abel," Grace said, patting his hand.

"At least you didn't pay someone to take your place in the army. You joined voluntarily," Elizabeth added.

Men who could afford it sometimes paid someone else to take their places in the army. It was legal, but Elizabeth didn't like the way it took advantage of poor men in need of money. She was glad to see that Abel wasn't a person who would do such a thing.

Abel looked up and smiled at her. It made her blush again. Why did he keep doing things like that?

"That's right, son," Eli said. "You saw your duty and you're doing it. Protecting that bridge is important. Without protection, the Confederates could come marching across the river and into

Washington, and our forces would be endangered if we had to cross the river on ferries."

Abel nodded. "Yes, sir. I understand that. I just don't want to get what I get because of who my father is," he said quite sincerely.

Eli waved his fork in his son's direction. "Abel, I said nothing to anyone about where you should be appointed. I can't say that your name might not have influenced a decision, but I did nothing except support your decision to serve your country," Eli told him.

"Thank you, Father."

Eli seemed content and continued eating.

As the dinner continued, Elizabeth found herself enjoying the company of the Sampsons. She liked them all. Eli was funny. Mrs. Sampson knew all about the goings on in Washington City, and Abel...Abel was a gentleman.

By the end of the evening, she began to regret that she and her mother would have to leave soon. She liked Abel Sampson, and she felt that he felt the same way. Maybe her mother and Mrs. Sampson had made a good arrangement.

Elizabeth and her mother left for the boat shortly after eight o'clock. Eli offered to have a carriage take them back to the wharf, but Alice said that it was a warm evening and they would walk back to the *Freeman*.

As mother and daughter walked down Union Street, Alice asked, "Well? What did you think of Abel Sampson?"

Elizabeth felt herself blush. She was doing a lot of that this evening. "He was very nice."

"Did you like him?"

"Mama, I barely know him."

"But what are your first impressions? Do you like him?" Alice pressed.

"Yes," Elizabeth admitted, blushing. She looked away from her mother.

Alice clapped. "Wonderful!"

"Don't start planning the wedding yet, Mama," Elizabeth said, placing her hand on her mother's arm.

"Of course not, but at least your father will be happy you're not thinking about getting married to a railroader."

"Who said I'm thinking about getting married? And I don't even know any railroaders," Elizabeth said, shocked.

Alice laughed. "With Hugh Fitzgerald as your father, that's not surprising."

"Why? Is it simply because he's a canawler?"

Alice sighed and slowed her walk. "It's part of the reason, but I think your father's hatred goes quite a bit beyond that."

"Why?"

"Because when I first met your father, I was engaged to a man named Henry Danforth. He's an engineer with the B&O. At least he was. I haven't seen or heard about him for years."

Elizabeth stopped walking. It was hard imagining her mother being in love with anyone but her father. It just didn't seem right. And he had been a railroader, too!

"Oh."

"More like oh-oh." Alice paused. "I fell in love with your father, but Henry didn't give up easily. It went beyond the normal canaller-railroader feud and became personal. They got in a fist fight whenever they saw each other, whether I was around or not. It only let up when your father and I married and moved to Sharpsburg," Alice explained.

"How did you pick, Papa? How did you know that he was the one you should marry?"

Her mother thought for a moment. She smiled at a remembrance and said, "I loved his Irish accent, but I loved him because he showed that he loved me more than simply saying it."

"Showed you?"

Alice nodded. "He held my hand, shopped with me, listened when I had things to say. Things like that showed me that he meant it when he said, 'I love you.'"

Elizabeth almost laughed at the image that popped into her head of her father shopping with her mother. She imagined him burdened down with various packages and trailing around Cumberland behind her mother. It was funny because she couldn't see him doing that now.

"I never knew that about you and Papa."

Alice sighed again. "I don't talk about it because I don't want to make your father any more bitter towards the railroad. It's not good for him to have that kind of anger. It's a blind spot that he has."

"I won't say anything. I promise."

Alice patted her daughter's arm. "Good girl."

Hugh was lying on the roof of the family cabin when they reached the wharf. He had the canopy down and was laying with his hands behind his head, staring at the stars.

"The stars are lovely and bright tonight, lasses, but not nearly as bright as the two of you," he said as he pushed himself up on his elbows to stare at them.

Elizabeth giggled. Her mother rolled her eyes.

"You've been kissing the Blarney Stone again, Hugh Fitzgerald."

"And don't you love it when I do," he replied. "How was dinner?"

The stepped from the wharf onto the race plank. Alice leaned across the roof and kissed him on the cheek.

"Fine. It was good to see Grace. You should have come. I bet you and Eli Sampson would get along fine. He doesn't seem at all like a congressman," Alice said.

"I know that. I like Eli and I owe him a lot, but someone had to stay and make arrangements to get rid of this load."

Alice cocked and eyebrow. "Did you?"

Hugh nodded. "I did. Tomorrow morning we'll get towed out to the *Larkspur* and offload there. We can be on our way in the evening."

"I'll get the cabin ready then."

She walked past him and into he family cabin.

Hugh turned to Elizabeth and said, "So did your mother marry you off, darlin'?"

"Not yet, Papa."

"And what did you think of Abel Sampson?"

Elizabeth grinned. "I liked him."

Hugh shrugged and said, "That's as good a start as any."

When Alice woke in the morning, she felt the boat moving faster than it usually did. She was used to the barely noticeable four mile per hour pace, but now she felt as if she were riding in a charging carriage. She sat up in bed and looked out the small window in the stateroom.

She couldn't see the wharf.

"Hugh, are you up there?"

"Yes, I am, darlin'. Top of the morning."

"Are we being towed?"

"Yes, we're almost there."

"Where are the children?" Alice asked.

"Thomas and Elizabeth are back on the wharf tending the mules. You know how upset they get when there's too much activity around them. Besides, they'll stay cleaner that way."

"Which ones? The mules or the children?"

Hugh chuckled. "Both, I hope, but Thomas could find dirt in a desert. George is up front. He'll help me with the shoveling."

Alice pulled on a calico dress over her nightclothes and walked topside. In front of the *Freeman*, she could see a steam-powered boat pulling on the tow ropes. The Canal Company had tried steam-powered boats on the canal, but they tended to move faster than the four mile per hour speed limit, which could damage the canal bed. Plus, the steam engines took up room in the holds, cutting down on how much a steam boat could carry. Still, there were a couple of captains who preferred steam boats, and those captains you could hear coming a mile or more away. Alice just didn't like the way the steam boats made a lot of noise and destroyed the quiet peacefulness of the canal.

The odd thing was that the steam engine had been born along the canal. James Rumsey, a Cecil County, Maryland, wheelwright, blacksmith, tavern keeper, and friend of George Washington gave the first steamboat demonstration in America on December 3, 1787. The boat had traveled along the Potomac River at four miles per hour for the watching audience. That boat would have worked well on the canal and not damaged it.

The tow lines slacked as the steam boat stopped pulling. The *Freeman* continued to drift slowly forward as Hugh pushed the rudder to one side to bring the *Freeman* parallel to the *Larkspur*. The captain of the steam boat tossed the *Freeman*'s tow lines to the sailors on the *Larkspur*. George grabbed another set of hawsers attached to the stern and tossed them onto the deck of the *Larkspur*.

"You'd better cover everything that you want to keep clean, Alice," Hugh said quietly.

Alice nodded and went below. She shut the shutters on the windows in the family cabin. Around each window she wrapped a blanket to seal it from the outside as best she could. She closed the door to the cabin behind her and tacked another blanket to the wall over it.

When she had finished, she began helping George and Hugh lift the hatch covers off of the holds and set them aside. Alice spent most of the next six hours aboard the *Larkspur* watching the sailors and her husband and son shovel coal from the *Freeman*'s holds into the large wooden crates that were then lifted by crane up the side of the *Larkspur* to be dumped into the *Larkspur*'s holds.

Coal dust made a dark haze around the two boats and the dust stuck to the men's sweat-slicked bodies and clothes. It took five hours to shovel all of the coal out of the holds. They finished of-floading the coal around four o'clock, and the men all dove into the water, in their clothes, for a quick swim to wash themselves off. Unlike many of the canallers, Hugh had made sure that every-one in his family had learned how to swim.

By the time the steam boat had pulled them back to the wharf, George and his father had replaced the hatch covers over the holds. Alice opened up the family cabin to air it out and clean the thin film of coal dust that had gotten through her barrier and coated everything.

The sailors on the steam boat tossed their ends of the tow ropes onto the *Freeman*. George picked them up and began to coil them.

"All right," Hugh said. "Let's hitch up the mules and head for Cumberland."

14

UNDER FIRE
JUNE 1862

Hugh piloted the *Freeman* out of the Fifteen Mile Creek Aqueduct and felt the water that had been building up behind the canal boat give it a small push as it left the narrow channel. Steering the boat was second nature to him, and he could navigate the canal in his sleep. He could close his eyes and know just by how long he waited before he needed to turn and how far to turn. He could judge by the sound of the water moving around the boat whether he was drifting to one side of the other.

Not that piloting was boring. It gave him lots of thinking time, and Hugh Fitzgerald was a man who liked to think.

He thought about what he would buy in Cumberland with some of the money he had earned from delivering his last load of coal to Georgetown. The mules were due to be reshod, and during the wait time to take on a load of coal at the basin would be the time to do it. He wondered whether he should hire Tony and another person to work as a hands on his boat so that he could leave Alice, Elizabeth and Thomas at home in Sharpsburg. Hugh was hoping to make a final decision by the next time he passed through Sharpsburg.

In the midst of this, Hugh heard a rifle shot. Almost immediately, he heard the bullet smack one of the hatch covers with a loud "thunk."

"Everyone get down!" Hugh yelled, as he squatted down with his hand still on the tiller.

Had that been a stray shot or was someone purposely firing at him and his family?

Hugh looked around the edge of the family cabin. George was duck walking next to Ocean and King Edward on the towpath, keeping them between him and the direction from where he had heard the shot. George looked all around himself, trying to see where the shot came from, but he also kept the mules moving forward. It would be the only way they might get out of rifle range.

"Hugh, what's wrong?" Alice called from inside the cabin.

"Stay in there. Someone fired on us."

Hugh wondered if a Rebel patrol was nearby. They would have had to come across the Potomac since the shot had come from the Maryland side. The raiders had been hitting targets up and down the canal with more frequency this year than last. They had attempted to blow up some of the aqueducts unsuccessfully. Hugh took pride in the fact that the superior masonry of the aqueducts, which his Uncle John and one of his cousins had helped build, had thwarted the Rebels, but their attacks had caused delays. This year, they had already been left in a dry canal once. That breach had taken three days to repair.

Two lock houses had been burned, though, and the families had run off to the more-protected towns. The lockkeepers were living in tents until the company built them new houses. All of the lockkeepers were carrying rifles or pistols now. Some of the raiders had attempted to destroy some of the more-remote locks. They would do whatever they could to disrupt trade into Washington City.

Canawlers were carrying weapons because one canal boat had been hijacked near White's Ferry and the cargo of fruits and vegetables had been ferried across the river to the Rebels there. The Rebel army in Northern Virginia was starving because they had eaten everything they had and their supply lines weren't reliable to bring them enough food. They had taken to making raids on Union supply lines, and in desperate cases, commandeering the grain and animals of Virginians.

Hugh was beginning to have serious doubts about his choice of bringing his family with him this season. The boundary between the Union and Confederacy seemed to be slowly creeping north. No longer could it be said that the Confederacy stopped at the banks of the Potomac. The Federals didn't seem to be able to hold their own borders. Some weeks, it even seemed the canal was within the Confederacy; a thought which had given Hugh nightmares.

On their way to Cumberland, Hugh had heard a story about Boonsboro, which wasn't too far from his hometown of Sharpsburg. Being so close to the Maryland-Virginia border, the town was divided in its feelings about the war. They were united in their feelings about their town, though. When the Union Army was nearby, everyone in town flew the Union flag, but when the Confederacy was the nearest army, the town flew the Confederate flag. Supporting your nation was one thing, but supporting your town was much closer and dear to most people.

Hugh kept one hand on his rifle and his other on the boat's till-er. He held the *Freeman* on a straight path down the middle of the canal. He watched the shore, scanning the trees for signs of who-ever had fired at his boat. It must have been a lone scout. A patrol could have opened fire and killed both him and George in the opening volley.

Hugh shifted his position slightly and another shot plowed into the deck in front of him. He saw the path the bullet had cut. He let go of the tiller and quickly fired a shot into the trees on the bank.

He grabbed the tiller again and shoved it to the side to move the *Freeman* away from the shooter. On the towpath, George had switched sides so that he had the mules between him and the shooter.

"What do we do, Papa?" George called out.

"We keep moving east."

"But that's going toward him. The shot came from ahead of us."

"No use in us turning back. It would take too long. Besides, we'd have to come this way at some point. We can't let one man shut the canal down. He might kill someone on the next boat that comes along. We need to warn them," Hugh called back.

"He might kill us!"

That was true enough. Hugh now had to face the dilemma that Solomon Greenfield had posed. Someone had brought the war to him. What was he going to do? Hugh wondered if he could live with the guilt if he turned back and someone on a eastbound boat was killed.

"He might at that, son. Be ready to take these mules to a run if need be," Hugh told his son.

Hugh wondered if the mules could be made to run. For years, they had been trained to walk at a slow and steady four miles per hour pace. These mules didn't even bolt when the locomotive en-gines blew their whistles as they passed the canal boats.

He thought he saw a flash of metal in the trees. Hugh waited until he saw it again. He quickly raised up his rifle and placed two shots near the flash; one above and one to the right. Even if he didn't hit the shooter, he might at least scare him away.

What had caused the man to fire on the Fitzgeralds? If he wanted to scare the Fitzgeralds, he had accomplished that grandly. Maybe he had been hoping to cause a break in the canal bed, which a rifle shot would not do. The water still flowed gently through the canal.

The *Freeman* went around a bend in the canal and Hugh stood up. He set the rifle down on the roof of the family cabin where it was still close at hand.

George saw his father standing and said, "Are we safe, Papa?"

"For now, but keep your ears and eyes open. If we meet anymore raiders, you'll more than likely hear them before you see them."

George stood up and brushed the dirt from his pants. "Yes, sir."

Alice opened the door to the family cabin. Her green eyes were wide with fear, and her lips were pressed tightly together. She stepped outside and looked up at Hugh.

"It's all right, Alice," he said quietly.

"All right? All right! Someone was shooting at us, Hugh! We're not soldiers. We're no threat to anyone," she said excitedly.

Hugh slowly shook his head. "We are a threat to some people simply because we live north of the Potomac."

"Only to the fiercest Rebels."

"Fierce or not makes no difference to a bullet." He paused. "I made a mistake bringing you, Elizabeth and Thomas along this season. When we reach Sharpsburg on the way back, you three will be safe."

Alice began to cry. "I don't want to leave you and George out here. If it's too dangerous for us, it's too dangerous for you."

Hugh shook his head. Hadn't she been the one who had suggested back in March that she and Elizabeth might stay behind?

"We have to continue our work, else we won't be able to make it through the winter. We've got no land to farm. What would I do to support us? I'm a canawler," Hugh said.

"If you or George were killed, I wouldn't be able to make it through the winter! I don't want to lose you to a sharpshooter's bullet."

Hugh was touched by his wife's claim, but he knew that while she believed it, it was still not true. She was a strong woman; stronger than maybe she even realized.

Hugh placed his hand on his wife's cheek and wiped away her tears. How he loved this woman!

"You wouldn't die, no matter how much you love me," Hugh said.

"And how do you know that?"

"I know your heart just as you know mine. I didn't marry a hot-house flower. You endure and bloom in all seasons, harsh and mild."

"Hugh Fitzgerald, I do believe you've been kissing the Blarney

Stone to weave together a tale like that." She sounded angry, but she smiled, obviously pleased by the compliment.

Hugh put his arm around her shoulder. "Aye, probably. I just don't like hearing you talking the way you were."

"I'd better go tell Thomas not to wander off anymore along the towpath," Alice said as she pulled away.

"That's a good idea. He was feeding his pets in the hay house when I last saw him."

So far this season, Thomas had captured a box turtle, a rabbit, a chipmunk, and a sparrow with a broken wing. He kept them all in homemade cages in the hay house and fed them twice a day. Hugh had doubted his son would care for the animals, but Thomas had risen to the responsibility. Even so, Hugh had had to draw the line when Thomas caught a fawn in one of his snare traps.

As they approached the Paw Paw Tunnel, Hugh hesitated. The near-total darkness at the center of the three-quarters-mile-long tunnel would make a fine place for an ambush, or Rebels could hide on top of the stone entrance behind the parapet.

"On your toes, George," he called to his son.

"Yes, sir." George wasn't dumb. He understood the danger the tunnel presented.

Hugh picked up his rifle and held it at his side as Elizabeth went aft and lit the headlight. He kept an eye on the top of the stone arch as the *Freeman* moved into the tunnel. Then he watched behind the boat for any man-shaped silhouettes entering behind him.

It seemed they were alone for now.

Hugh worked a longer shift at the tiller than usual. He felt as if someone was still watching him. He didn't want to go below only to have the sniper shoot at Alice or the children. No, his place was at the tiller and near his rifle.

Alice came out of the family cabin around midnight. She passed a cup of coffee to Hugh. He took it and sipped at it. It was hot, rich, and helped wake him up.

"You can't keep steering the boat all day and all night, too, dear," Alice said.

"I know. I just want to take the boat through to morning."

"And then what? Will we be any safer in the morning than we are now?"

He sighed and raised his eyebrows. "I don't know."

She put a hand on his arm. "Yes, you do. We'll still be on the canal, and the canal will still be the border between the North and the South."

Hugh nodded numbly. His eyes ached from trying to see in the dark.

"I know. I don't know what to do. It doesn't feel right leaving you in Sharpsburg, either," he admitted.

Alice hugged him. "I'm sure you'll figure out what's best."

"Do you know?"

"No, but I trust your judgment." She kissed him on the cheek.

As she turned to walk away, the boat suddenly jerked to a halt throwing Alice against the corner of the cabin. She yelled in pain.

Hot coffee splashed over the edge of the cup and burned Hugh's hand. He dropped the tin cup and reached out for Alice.

"I'm all right," she said. "What happened?"

Hugh couldn't answer her because he wasn't sure himself. He hadn't run into the bank or another boat.

"Papa, the water's dropping," George called from the shore.

Hugh picked up a lantern and held it over the side. He could tell by how high the water reached on the boat that the *Freeman* was resting on the bottom of the canal. The water level was about a plank too low to float an empty boat.

He slapped his hand against the wall of the cabin. "There must be a break somewhere down the canal."

"How long will we be left here this time, do you think?"

It wasn't the first time there had been a breach in the canal. In fact, the Rebs had been trying repeatedly to destroy some of the aqueducts rather than simply damage them.

"Not seeing the break, I couldn't say," Hugh told her.

He wasn't thrilled with the thought of sitting in one place for a couple of days until the Canal Company could get a repair team to fix the breech temporarily. The sniper was still out there.

"Where are we at?" Alice asked.

"About a half mile west of Lock 66. In the morning, we'll go see if the Crabtrees would like some company until we're floating again."

15

UNWANTED BEAR HUGS

JUNE 1862

George tapped his fingers against his thighs as if counting off the seconds his family was wasting. It frustrated him that he had to wait for them as they rode the canal mules down the towpath to the Crabtree lock house. He wanted to get to the lock house quickly and see Becky before Josh VanMeter sweet-talked her into taking a walk with him in the forest.

He waved to his family for them to catch up with him. King Edward with Hugh atop him came plodding up next to Ocean.

"There's no rush, son. The Crabtrees aren't going anywhere," George's father said.

But Becky might be.

He had seen the *Low Mountain* heading toward Lock 66 as the *Freeman* came out of the lock. The Low Mountain had been heading east when it grounded, which meant that Josh had already had time with Becky when the canal boat locked through and would be wanting more.

"I'm going to go on ahead and let them know we're coming," George said anxiously.

His father shook his head. "You're going to stay right here with us. After what happened yesterday, we can't be sure who's out there or what caused him to take a shot at us."

George sighed as a vision of Becky kissing Josh flashed through his mind. "Yes, sir." It was nearly a moan when he said it.

Even so, as soon as George saw the lock house, he kicked Ocean into a trot. The east gates of Lock 66 were closed so he jumped off the mule onto the swing arm and started to walk across the temporary bridge.

"Who's that up there?" George almost stumbled and fell into the canal. "George Fitzgerald, what are you doing up there?"

George looked down and saw Lucas Crabtree and Cyrus VanMeter standing in the bottom of the lock. Lucas was pointing to something on the lock door. When the canal was empty, the locks were sixteen-feet deep to allow for raising and lowering boats from one level to another.

"The *Freeman* grounded near the tunnel, sir. We thought we'd come and visit for awhile. The rest of my family should be along in a bit," he said.

Lucas just laughed.

"What's so funny, sir?"

"I just have a feeling that things are going to be interesting around here until the canal floods again," Lucas said. Cyrus VanMeter chuckled and grinned.

"I don't understand," George said. He felt like he was the butt of a joke, but he couldn't figure out what it was.

"You wouldn't, son. Not until you're an old man with children, like me." Then he laughed again, slapping Cyrus on the shoulder.

George looked away over the canal. "There's the rest of my family now."

Hugh walked up to the edge of the lock and looked over the lock doors and down into the canal. He grinned down at the two men.

"Hello, Lucas. I thought we'd visit until the company fixes this breach. I hope you don't mind," Hugh said.

"Are you willing to help out?" Lucas shot back.

Hugh tipped his head toward them. "Always. What do you need?"

"Cyrus and I could use some help rebalancing this door. Josh is out checking my trap line for some fresh meat to feed all of us, and Pauline's going to need help cooking enough food to feed this crew," Lucas said.

George felt his spirits lift. Josh was off checking trap lines and hunting. That meant he wouldn't be with Becky, at least right now. George still had time to establish his place with her before Josh showed up.

"Fine then," Hugh told Lucas. "We'll fit ourselves in where we can. What about your gardens?"

"Becky's out there weeding it now."

"I'll go help her," George offered.

Before either his father or Lucas Crabtree could say anything, George jumped from the lock door and took off running toward the garden. The garden was on an acre of land that had been cleared behind the canal house. The Crabtrees sold a lot of their surplus to canawlers during the late summer and fall.

Becky was squatting down in one corner pulling weeds from

between rows of pea plants. Her reddish-blond hair was tied back to keep it out of her face. Her face was sweaty and her arms were covered with dirt. She looked up as George approached and smiled. George felt himself stop and stare at her.

"You got stranded, too," she said.

She wiped her face against the sleeve of her dress to clean the sweat from her forehead.

He jerked a thumb over his shoulder. "Near the tunnel."

"The VanMeters were just finished locking through the last lock when their boat stopped. I guess it's a good thing that they weren't caught in the lock when it happened."

"I told your father I'd help you with the weeding," George said.

"Then come over here and start on the next row." The next row in the garden was carrots.

George obediently took his place. As he worked alongside Becky, he found himself having to resist the urge to reach out and touch her. He wanted to hold her hand. He wanted to stroke her cheek.

"How was Cumberland?" he asked.

Becky looked over and smiled at him. "Wonderful. I got material for two new dresses and even some chocolate candy."

"I can see why you wanted to go."

"I don't get to go often and it's usually in the winter so I save up my money for when we do go. We even went to see a show at the theater on Baltimore Street."

"I wish I could have gone with you," George said.

Becky laughed. "I would have liked to have seen you helping me pick out fabric for a new dress."

"I would have done it," George said defiantly.

"I don't believe you."

George straightened up and said, "I would have done it because I would have been with you."

Becky blushed and looked away. "Thank you."

They worked for awhile in silence, occasionally stealing glances at each other. There was so much George wanted to tell her, but the words seemed to dry up in his throat. He was surprised he had been able to tell her what he had. He was a fool when it came to Becky Crabtree, and he was certainly no match for smooth-talking Josh VanMeter.

By the time they had finished weeding the garden, George was dirty and slick with sweat. He wished the canal was full so he could take a swim and clean up.

He stripped out of his shirt and wiped his face on a clean spot, probably the last one on his shirt. Behind him, he heard Becky gasp. He turned around and saw her staring at him. She quickly looked away.

George grinned at her embarrassment. "I'm going to walk down to the river and wash up." He thought that it was hot enough that he could rinse out his shirt and wear it until it dried. "Do you want to come?"

"I'll have to see if my mother needs any help in the kitchen."

"She'll have more than enough help while my mother, Elizabeth, and Mrs. VanMeter are around." He wanted Becky to walk with him somewhere where they could be alone.

George tucked the end of his shirt into his waistband and walked back to the house with Becky. Thomas was sitting on the swing arm of the canal door, dangling his legs as he watched the men working below.

"Where ya going, George?" Thomas asked.

"Down to the river...swimming."

Thomas hopped off the swing arm and ran up to George. "Can I go? Please!"

"Take him with you, George!" his father called from below. "He keeps trying to climb down into the canal and get in our way."

George rolled his eyes. Taking his little brother swimming was the last thing that George wanted to do. How would he get another kiss from Becky with Thomas around?

George sighed as he walked across the top of the lock doors. "Yes, sir. Come on, Thomas."

His little brother cheered and started to follow him across the doors.

"What's wrong, George?" Thomas asked.

"I was hoping Becky would come with me, not you."

"George is sweet on Becky! George is sweet on Becky!" Thomas started to chant, but George quickly pushed him into the weeds off the side of the towpath. Then he started to run down the path that led to the Potomac River.

He jumped off the low ledge into the shallow water with a loud splash. Then he waded deeper into the river. Luckily, the current wasn't swift here like it was in other areas along the river.

George dove under the cold water, rolled over, and surfaced. Just as he did, Thomas ran down the path and jumped into the water.

"Becky's coming! Becky's coming," he yelled.

George stood up. The water came up to the middle of his chest. He ran his hands through his hair to push it back off his face.

Becky came walking down the trail with Josh VanMeter. George's smile fell. Josh seemed to have grown a foot taller since George had last seen him. He was taller than George was now, and he had thick black hair that Becky had commented on before. George did not like him.

"Hi there, Fitzgerald," Josh said, waving.

"He showed up from hunting after you had already left for here," Becky said. "He offered to walk me down."

George puffed out his chest to make it appear larger. "How was hunting, Josh?" George asked, not really caring.

"Nothing in the traps, but I shot two rabbits."

"You'd better be careful shooting around here. Someone might think the South is invading," George warned him.

"That might not be such a bad thing." Josh's expression said he was serious.

"It would be if they start shooting back. Besides, someone took a couple of shots at my family while we were on the canal yesterday."

Josh nodded. "I'll watch out. If I had known you and your family were going to be here, I would have stayed out until I shot something bigger."

George smiled and said, "Maybe you should have, Josh."

Before Josh could reply, George felt himself being pushed under the water. As his head slipped under the water, he heard Thomas yelling, "George is sweet on Becky! George is sweet on Becky!"

George let himself drop to the bottom of the river so that he fell away from Thomas's grip. Then he launched himself off the bottom.

As he broke the surface, he yelled, "Thomas! Where are you, you little brat!"

He regained his footing and looked around. Thomas was scrambling back onto dry land while Josh and Becky laughed at George. George felt his face flush from embarrassment. He stalked back to the shore amid their laughs, knowing his face was bright red.

"Dunked by his little brother!" Josh yelled.

George sloshed out of the river, not even pausing when Becky called for him to wait. He didn't want to hear Josh make fun of him. He didn't want to see Becky looking at him. Anything but that!

When he reached the towpath, he stopped to catch his breath.

"Did you hear what they did in Boonsboro to keep from being burned out during the war?" George heard Lucas Crabtree ask.

"What? That's the way we'll be heading. Maybe we can use the same idea," George's father said.

"Boonsboro's pretty evenly split between Rebs and Yanks. They argue amongst themselves, but none of them want to lose their homes. So when the Union Army is nearby, everybody, even the Rebs, wave the stars and stripes."

"And if it's the Rebs, they switch flags," Hugh guessed. He'd told the story before.

"Right on the button. No one says anything to betray the other because they're neighbors. Heaven forbid, both armies get nearby. Which flag would they fly?"

"If both armies were that close, they'd have much larger problems to worry about. There might not even be a town left by the time the armies left."

Hugh climbed up the braces of the canal door to get out of the canal. Though the canal itself was only six-feet deep, the canal locks were sixteen-feet deep from the top of the high level to the bottom of the lower canal section. His father was shirtless and covered with sweat. The three men hadn't wasted time getting to work at rebalancing the doors.

Hugh saw George and said, "Hello, son. Back so soon?"

George nodded. "I was feeling tired. I thought I'd walk on back to the boat and clean up a bit."

"Be careful." His father paused. "Are you taking one of the mules?"

George shook his head. "No, I'm in a walking mood. I'll be back for supper."

Hugh stared at him for a moment and then said, "Best check with your mama before you go. See if she needs you to bring anything back with you," Hugh suggested.

"Yes, sir," George mumbled.

He started to walk away, but his father called to him. "George, there's more than one woman in the world that you can love and more than one woman that can love you. The trick is finding one of those women that love you and being able to love her back. It'll happen, son, if not with this one, then with someone else."

George turned back. How had his father known what was bothering him? "What if she's the one?"

"Then you two are dancing around the subject like a pair of skittish colts."

George sighed and shrugged.

He calmed down as he walked along the towpath. He thought about what his father had said to him. Did he need to treat his relationship with Becky differently?

How differently?

As he walked, he saw a thick, sturdy branch. He picked it up to use as a walking stick. It took him almost half an hour to walk to the *Freeman*. He found the fall board lying in the brush off to the side of the towpath and laid it across the canal to the boat.

George started to throw his walking stick aside but stopped himself. He studied the stick again. Maybe he could make use of this. He broke the thinner end off over his knee and tossed the scrap aside. The other piece he held onto as he crossed the fall board.

He walked into the hay house to lay down on the straw tick that served as his mattress. A warm breeze blew through the two open doors and felt comfortable. George took his penknife out of his pocket and opened it. He studied the piece of wood, looking at it from different angles. He ran the knife lightly along the edge of the branch, shaving the bark from the outer edges. George started whistling as the knife bit deeper into the wood.

He wasn't sure how long he worked. He lost track of the time as he worked on his project. It was talking on the canal that broke his concentration.

"C'mere, little guy. I'm not going to hurt you."

Thomas was talking, but to whom was he talking?

George stood up and put aside his carving. It didn't look like much now, but it would soon enough. Thomas was the last person he wanted to see it right now, especially after what his little brother had done to him earlier. If there had been water in the canal, George would have dunked Thomas and held him underwater for awhile.

George crawled out of the hay house window and onto the race plank. He stood up and looked out onto the towpath. Thomas was tossing bits of cornbread to a black bear cub. As the cub gobbled up the chunks of bread, Thomas moved closer.

"Do you like that, boy?" Thomas asked. "How would you like to take a ride on a canal boat?"

Thomas tossed out some more cornbread. He was only a couple of feet from the cub.

"Thomas, no!" George yelled.

Ignoring him, Thomas lunged out and grabbed the cub, hugging its neck. The cub bellowed as it tried to pull away.

"Thomas, let it go!" George yelled.

Then George heard a sound that chilled him: the answering roar of the mother bear. The huge black bear burst out of the woods on the land side of the canal about twenty yards west of the boat. She hesitated only momentarily when she saw Thomas wrestling with her cub. She jumped into the canal and galloped across to the canal bed, roaring as she did.

George ran across the fall board as the she bear scrambled up the side of the canal bed. He grabbed Thomas by the arm and pulled him off the cub.

"I want to keep it," Thomas said.

"She won't let you!" George yelled, pointing at the she bear.

He tugged Thomas along with him back across the fall board. The she bear was on the towpath side of the canal and charging toward George and Thomas. As the she bear reached the end of the fall board, George kicked his end off of the boat. The board crashed into the bottom of the canal and the black bear rolled down along the cleated side and crashed against the hull of the *Freeman*.

"Get Papa's rifle!" George told his brother.

Thomas ran along the race plank toward the family cabin.

The she bear reared up on its hind legs. Its claws were able to reach over the side of the boat so that George had to jump back on the hatch covers to keep from getting clawed. He looked for something he could use to hit the bear and knock it from the side of the boat. There was nothing close by, though, and the bear was beginning to pull itself up the side of the boat.

George wondered if the door of the family cabin was strong enough to hold back an angry she bear. He doubted it.

"Thomas, get ready to jump over the side when I tell you to!"

Thomas ran back with the rifle. George grabbed it and pointed the barrel at the bear's head. He couldn't bring himself to pull the trigger, though. He couldn't fault the she bear for wanting to defend her cub.

The bear cub bellowed again from the towpath.

The she bear stopped and released her grip on the boat. She fell back to the ground and then scrambled up the side of the canal to join the cub.

On the towpath, she turned back and bellowed once more at Thomas and George as if to warn them not to let it happen again.

George held up his rifle and shouted, "Go on, before I change my mind and shoot you."

The she bear used her nose to drive the cub into the woods toward the river.

Thomas hugged his brother tightly around the waist. "Thank you, George."

George patted him on the shoulder and said, "You're lucky. You know that, don't you? You could have been killed. You've got to stop doing things like that, Thomas."

Thomas nodded, still not letting go of his brother. George could feel him trembling. Thomas was more scared than he let on.

"Why didn't you shoot her?" Thomas asked.

"Because she was just a mama trying to protect her baby." George sat down on the edge of the hatch covers. Thomas sat down with him. "You've got to be more careful about the pets you try and collect, Thomas. One of them might take exception to it like that she bear did."

"But it was so cute."

George just sighed and lay back on the wooden covers.

16

AMBUSH

JUNE 1862

David Windover settled himself into the V of the maple tree branches and laid his rifle across his legs as he was observed the Union patrol movement from hiding. The C&O Canal towpath was twenty feet below him and to his right. Somewhere off to his left he could hear the Potomac rushing around some rocks, but he couldn't see the water from his position.

He was comfortable in the spot, but he knew that he couldn't relax. He was in enemy territory. If he let himself forget that, he would be captured, or worse yet, killed.

He looked further down the path, trying to see McLaughlin or Thelen. He couldn't. They were well hidden in the high branches and leaves. David wondered if he were hidden from their sight. Probably not.

He still doubted whether this was a good idea, but they needed to find out how the Union patrols were deployed around the river. So far, judging by what they had seen along their observation posts, there weren't a great number of troops, especially not with most of the fighting going on in Virginia. It seemed that each patrol was responsible for about three miles of river, probably on the assumption that a large army coming across the river would be easy to spot. That could be useful. If the Confederate Army came across in small companies, they could regroup on the Maryland side of the river and capture a couple of Union patrols, which would open up a large hole in their patrol line. Then the entire Confederate Army could come across the river relatively unseen.

He would have to send that suggestion back with Thelen when David sent him back with another report for Colonel Collins.

David heard talking and knew it wasn't from McLaughlin or Thelen. They weren't that careless or loud. He began to see patches of blue through the leaves and knew that a patrol was coming from the east.

"Are we going to be back in time? I wanted to go into town tonight," one of the soldiers asked.

"Tonight's not your night," came the reply.

"I traded with Porter. I met a girl at the general store last week, and I wanted to see her again."

David saw six soldiers in the patrol. All, except for one, were young men who barely looked old enough to shave. The sixth man wore a short beard and looked to be as old as David.

The patrol walked beneath David's perch as if they were only on a summer walk. They weren't walking in formation and they didn't seem too concerned about what was going on around them. It was one of the sloppier patrols he had seen during the past few months.

That would be something worth noting in the report to the colonel.

David heard a shot and one of the soldiers was flung back against a tree beside the canal. It was quickly followed by a second shot. Another soldier dropped to his knees holding his stomach.

The patrol scattered and began to run. The shots had to have come from Thelen and McLaughlin, but why? They weren't here to engage the enemy. They were supposed to be observing and reporting back to Colonel Collins.

Why did those two feel the need to kill when it was unnecessary?

"Don't let them get away!" McLaughlin called. "They'll go for help and bring another patrol back after us!"

Thelen answered with a screeching rebel yell.

McLaughlin was right. Now that they had stirred up the hornet's nest, the soldiers would all have to be killed or David and the others would have a company of Federals chasing after them.

David braced himself in the V of the tree and raised his rifle. His shot hit a soldier who had kneeled down to try and get a shot at McLaughlin and Thelen.

The patrol, or at least what was left of it, disappeared around a bend in the canal. Four soldiers were on the ground. Two were on the run.

David dropped to the ground. Thelen and McLaughlin followed him and dropped from their perches, ready to fight.

"What do you think you're doing?" David yelled at them.

"Killing the enemy," McLaughlin said.

"We're supposed to find a way for the army to come across the river not to try and take on the Union by ourselves."

Thelen chuckled. "We could. They are sitting ducks."

David looked at the bodies of the four dead soldiers on the ground. Two of them were sprawled across each other like two carelessly discarded logs. Another soldier's face was masked in blood.

David shuddered.

Was this how he would wind up? Dead on some narrow path shot full of holes by Union soldiers? The soldiers would be looking for David's detaill now.

David pointed to the west. "It's time to move upriver."

"Upriver?" McLaughlin repeated. "The patrol went east."

"And where do you think those two who ran are going? Do you want to face those two and a patrol when they'll be ready for you?"

"We could catch 'em!"

"Sooner or later, the Union is going to realize we're here. Thanks to what you started here today, it will be sooner. Now let's go!"

Thelen glanced at McLaughlin. David bit back a sharp response. He was in charge of this patrol, not Corporal McLaughlin.

McLaughlin nodded and started walking to the west.

They had walked less than a mile when a shot broke the natural quiet of the canal. Thelen fell onto his back and lay still. McLaughlin spun around and dove onto David so that they both fell into the brush alongside of the towpath.

"Who was it?" David asked in a slight panic.

"I saw a flash of blue just before Thelen fell. Another patrol must have heard our attack and come to see what was happening."

David looked at Thelen. The private wasn't moving. He was dead. Blood pooled around his torso.

"We'd better move before they come after us," McLaughlin said.

McLaughlin slipped quietly into the forest. David followed him, though not as quietly.

"Are we going to go back to get the body?" David asked him.

"And do what with it?" McLaughlin snapped.

"Bury him," David said.

David was amazed that McLaughlin could feel so unfeeling about someone he had treated like a friend. Jonas Thelen deserved a good Christian burial. David wouldn't want to have been left lying on the towpath if it had been him instead of Thelen.

"The Yanks will do that," McLaughlin said.

"It doesn't seem right."

McLaughlin spun around and poked a finger in David's chest. David backed off a step. "Do you want to go back there? Do you think they will simply arrest you after they find what's left of the patrol we ambushed?"

David shook his head and tried to rein in his fear. "No, but we could go back later."

McLaughlin snorted. "What do you care if he's buried or not? Thelen meant nothing to you. He means nothing to no one. He was just a backwoods boy whose father and brother have already died in this war. Now the devil's got all three of them," he shouted.

"He was a soldier under my command."

McLaughlin snorted. "He wasn't under your command. Why do you think he was sent north by Colonel Collins?"

"He was good in the woods."

"He is, but so are many others. He was sent north because he wouldn't take orders." McLaughlin grinned. "He was a real rebel."

"And you?" David asked, dreading the answer.

"I don't take orders well, either, especially not from a spoiled city boy who don't understand the woods," McLaughlin snapped.

David bit back a reply when he saw the hard stare in McLaughlin's eyes. The corporal was right. David had never been in command of this patrol. They had all been misfits who had been sent away to sink or swim.

And now it looked as if they would probably sink.

LOOKING FOR A FUTURE
JUNE 1862

Tony wound up his fishing twine into a ball. His last worm was gone and he hadn't been able to catch one single fish that was big enough for him to eat. They had all been runts like him.

He was hungry and had been hoping for something more to eat than bread and cold vegetable soup. Whenever he and his mother had money for meat, his mother ate it. She said that she had to keep her strength up since she was working to support the both of them.

Tony stowed the line and the straight branch that he used for a fishing pole under a bush. It was a good hiding place, and he knew that his pole and line would be there the next time he returned to fish. No one ever bothered to walk this far away from the basin to fish.

Tony lifted the edge of a large flat rock. In a shallow hole underneath was his cash can. He didn't need to look inside the can. Tony knew how much was in there. He just needed to see it and remind himself of his future. Actually seeing the coins and bills told him that he had a future.

His future was growing as the can filled. Tony knew that, but where was it going? He was still stuck in Cumberland under his mother's bed. The money wasn't doing him any good right now.

Tony let the rock drop back to the ground. As he walked back toward Shanty Town, he crossed a walking bridge over the canal.

Tony stopped on top of the bridge and looked eastward. A light boat—one with empty holds—approached the basin. He squinted to try and make out something familiar about the boat or crew. He sighed. It wasn't the *Freeman*.

Tony always kept an eye out for the Fitzgeralds. Mr. Fitzgerald was always willing to hire him for an odd job or two. Tony never let his mother know about his extra work and his coins went into his cash can. He had learned a lot doing the odd jobs Hugh Fitzgerald gave him. Tony could pick a mule's hoof, coil lines and harness a mule. All of those jobs were harder than they looked, but Mr. Fitzgerald was patient with him and taught Tony what he needed to know.

Tony wished that the Fitzgeralds would hire him to work with them on the canal instead when they were in the canal basin. Tony wanted to see Washington City. It might be where he wanted to go when he left Cumberland for good.

Tony waved to the mule driver as the teenage boy led the two mules pulling the *Sarah Girl* under the bridge.

I could do that job, Tony thought. It doesn't look that hard and I would do it well. He would pull the canal boat himself if it would get him out of Cumberland.

Tony didn't even mind working for Hugh Fitzgerald. It wasn't like working for his mother. For one thing, Mr. Fitzgerald paid him. Besides that, Tony didn't mind the odd jobs. The Fitzgeralds were nice. Even their mules were nice, though Thomas had warned him to stay out from behind them.

Tony sighed and started walking again. It was getting late. The railroaders and canallers would start their drinking soon in Shanty Town's many taverns. If his mother got lucky, she would meet someone this evening. If Tony got lucky, she wouldn't.

McKenney's Tavern, his mother's current home, had an out-side staircase along one side. It wasn't the most-stable staircase, being made of scrap lumber, but it allowed the four people who rented rooms above the tavern to get to their rooms without having to walk through the tavern. Some men didn't want to be seen with the women they met.

The hallway between the rooms was dark without even a lantern to break the darkness. The noises of another woman engaged in his mother's business came from one of the rooms. Tony took six steps forward and stopped. When he held out his hand, he felt the door frame.

Tony tapped on the door to his mother's room. He never would call it his room. It was simply a place that he chose to stay because he had nowhere else to go.

His mother flung the door open and pulled him inside by the arm. Tony tried not to wince at her tight grip.

"Where have you been? Do you know what time it is?" she squawked as she shook him. Her fingernails bit into his arm.

He didn't answer her.

"Anyone who's willing and has money will be gone before I get downstairs."

Tony stared at his mother quietly. He had once thought that

she was beautiful. She must have been beautiful if so many men wanted to be with her. That was before Tony had realized what went on on the bed above him when he was hidden underneath.

Now he could see his mother as she really was. Her dark hair was still lustrous, but it framed the face of a tired, used-up woman who couldn't hide her fatigue behind powders and cremes. Only the shadows of night helped hide her faults.

"Now get under the bed so you'll be ready when I come back," his mother said as she pressed down on his shoulders.

"Can't I just wait until I hear you coming?" Tony asked.

"No!" his mother snapped. "The last time you stayed out, the man heard you moving around to get under the bed. I had to tell him that it was probably a rat." Tony wondered if his mother thought he really was a rat. "Now get under there and be ready when I come back."

Tony reluctantly got down on his belly and slid under the bed, careful not to get any splinters in his belly. That had happened once and he had cried silently for half an hour until his mother's friend had left.

His mother slid the bedspread down a little further than usual to hide Tony from view. Then she must have blown out the lantern flame because the room got dark. Tony heard the door open and close.

He would be alone for however long it would take for his mother to lure a man up to her room.

He closed his eyes, crossed his arms on the floor in front of him, and rested his head. He could feel the vibrations from conversations and music through the floor.

He must have fallen asleep. Either that, or his mother had been awfully quick in finding a man to bring to her room. The slamming of the door and loud laughter woke him from his nap.

Tony wiped his eyes and waited.

He heard moans and wet kisses from outside of his hiding place. He could see dark shadows beyond the bedspread. His mother never turned up the lantern wick when she was working. She liked to give Tony darkness to work in, or so she said.

His mother said, "I need the money."

"Can't that wait until later?" the man asked.

"Later, there will be no way to get back what I give you if you don't pay. Not that you would, mind you. I just have to be consistent," she said in a husky whisper that she used with men.

The man grumbled, but he didn't leave so Tony guessed that

he must have fished out his wallet and a few dollars.

"That's a generous man," his mother said.

"Let's see how generous you are," the man said in a low voice.

The bed above Tony squeaked as his mother and her man fell onto it. Tony shifted position so the sagging mattress wouldn't pin him to the floor.

"Why don't you get out of those pants so you can move around," his mother said.

The man laughed and a few moments later, Tony heard the heavy pants drop to the floor beside the bed. Tony peeked under the edge of the bedspread. He saw the dirty pants laying in a heap near him.

The bed began to jiggle and Tony heard his mother grunted. That was the signal.

Tony lifted the edge of the bedspread and reached out for the man's pants. He fished out the wallet and pulled it under the bed with him. The man had twenty-six dollars in the wallet. Tony took two one-dollar bills. Then he closed the wallet and slid it back in the pocket. With luck, the man would think that he had bought a few more drinks than he could remember.

Next, Tony fished his hands into the man's front pocket, searching for a few coins that he could add to his cash can.

"What's that?" the man asked.

Tony jerked his hand back. He hadn't gotten a coin, but he wasn't sure why the man had spoken.

His mother said, "Nothing. Keep going. You can't be finished yet, are you?"

"Let go of me. I think I saw something."

Tony heard the man's feet hit the floor. He pushed himself as far away as he could and still be under the bed. Had the man heard coins jingling above the sound of the noises Tony's mother was making?

"It's just a rat. This place has dozens of them."

"What I caught a flash of didn't look like a rat!"

Had the man seen him? Tony didn't think so. His mother had given the signal. That meant the man wasn't near the edge of the bed. How had the man seen him?

What could he do?

"Come back to bed. You're breaking the mood," his mother said.

"I'm sure you can get back in the mood since I haven't got my money's worth yet," the man told her.

A rough hand threw back the bedspread and Tony saw a bearded face peer in at him. The man frowned.

He reached under the bed with one hand and pulled Tony out by the scruff of his neck. Tony didn't resist. What good would it have done? The man was much bigger than he was and Tony had no place to run.

The man had on a dirty white shirt but no pants. Tony's mother was sitting on the bed with the bed sheet drawn up around her.

"What do we have here? A very big rat, I see," the man said.

Tony watched his mother's expression change from fear to confusion and then to anger.

"What's a boy doing under my bed?" she said.

"Getting an earful of more than a boy his age should be hearing, I think." The man glanced at his pants. "And probably a handful of more than he should, too." The man glared a Tony, showing his tobacco-stained teeth. "Give it over, boy."

"What?" Tony said, trying to sound innocent, which was ridiculous given his situation.

The man backhanded Tony across the mouth. Tony's head rang from the pain in his jaw.

"Do you give it over or do I take it out of your hide?" the man asked again.

Tony fished the two dollars from his pockets and gave it to the man. His mother gasped.

She waved a finger at Tony. "He's a thief. Call the sheriff."

The man laughed. "Oh, I'm sure you want me to bring the sheriff here. Now I want my money back," the man said to Tony's mother.

He let go of Tony. Tony backed away from him and stood near the door in case he needed to run.

"I do not owe you money," his mother said indignantly. "You're the one who stopped, not me."

"You're the one who hid a thief under your bed." The man pointed at Tony.

"I did not. I've never seen this boy."

The man grinned. "You must think me a total fool. This boy is your spittin' image. He's your son if you ever had or ever will have one." The man paused. "And if you don't give me my money back, I will get the sheriff and bring him over here. I'll show him this little operation you have running here."

His mother's expression matched the man's. She opened her

small purse and took out the man's money and threw it at him. He caught it before it hit the floor.

"There's your money. Now take it and get out of my room," his mother said, nearly yelling.

The man picked the money up off the bed and shoved it into his shirt pocket. Then he pulled his pants on, all the while watching Tony's mother. He slid the suspenders over his shoulders, turned around and walked out of the room. He slammed the door behind him.

As soon as he had gone, Tony's mother spun around and slapped Tony.

"You careless piece of trash! You've cost me a night's work and he'll probably warn all of his friends to watch out for me! I'll probably have to move again, and I just found this room."

She slapped Tony again. He fell back against the bed.

"It wasn't my fault!" Tony said.

"He saw you."

"But you gave the signal," Tony said.

She began pulling her clothes on. Tony sat up on the bed

"Where are we going?" Tony asked.

"We are going nowhere. I'm leaving here alone. If I can't trust you to do one simple thing to earn your keep…"

Tony didn't say anything. He let the sentence hang unfinished. Arguing wouldn't have helped. His mother would have gotten angrier and hit him again, and Tony had been hit enough tonight.

He rubbed his cheek and wondered if it would bruise.

Maybe his mother was right this time. Maybe he no longer had the stomach to lay hidden under her bed just to steal a few coins. Tony still had his cash can. There was enough money in it to get him somewhere.

It was time that he find out just where.

18

CHOOSING LIFE
JUNE 1862

David stood back and watched McLaughlin tamp the black powder into the hole in side of the aqueduct. He couldn't help but marvel at the man's ability to destroy things.

The corporal had spent an hour creating a hole deep enough in the stonework so the explosion would do significant damage. It hadn't been easy. The stones were so tightly packed that even when the little bit of mortar was removed the stones wouldn't give, and David and McLaughlin didn't have the proper tools to chip the stone away.

Not that David could tell McLaughlin that. The Tennessean had worked at it until he broke a knife blade and nearly sliced a finger off. Then he had continued to work at the stones with a stump of the blade.

"Damn those Mick stone masons!" McLaughlin muttered as he wiped the sweat from his brow with a grimy sleeve. It wasn't the first time he had uttered the oath either.

"Aren't you Irish?" David asked.

"I'm Tennessean," McLaughlin shot back.

He used a thick stick with a smooth end to tamp down the powder. This went much quicker and easier than creating the hole had gone.

The aqueduct was a 110-foot arch over Sideling Hill Creek. He could see the pride that had gone into the stone work. Granite stones were cut so precisely and laid so tightly that the canal bed that passed over top the arch held water. David wished that he could have been there to watch it being built. It would have been a wonder to witness.

David had seen five aqueducts during his travels along the canal and each one was unique in size and structure. Antietam Creek Aqueduct was 140-feet long with three unequal arches. The Conocheaque Creek Aqueduct was 210-feet long with three arches. Licking Creek Aqueduct was a long, single ninety-foot arch.

Tonoloway Creek Aqueduct was a 110-foot single arch, similar but not identical to the Sideling Hill Creek Aqueduct.

It would be a shame to destroy this aqueduct, but McLaughlin was anxious to strike at the Union for killing Jonas Thelen, or so he said. David thought the man just wanted to fight, and he wasn't too concerned who he fought. David had very little control over him.

McLaughlin said that he wanted to destroy the aqueduct to stop the coal traffic going into Washington City.

"Why not simply blow up the berm? It would be much easier to blow apart," David asked him.

"It would be easier to destroy, but it would also be easier for the Yankees to fix. Destroying the berm will delay them. Destroying the aqueduct will stop them," McLaughlin had told him.

McLaughlin shoved his homemade fuse into the hole and ran it down the side of the aqueduct wall until it reached the ground. The other end he stuck into a small pile of black powder.

He began pouring out a thin line of black powder toward the river.

"Why are you doing that?" David asked. "Why not light the fuse?"

"Because we've got to have enough time to find cover, otherwise when the aqueduct blows, those rocks will act like bullets and they'll be coming right at us." He pointed to the bank near the river. "I want to be behind there when it does blow."

McLaughlin stared at the bank and then the aqueduct. He nodded and capped the small barrel of powder. David was still wondering where the backwoodsman had found the powder and if he had killed anyone to get it. He decided that he really didn't want to know.

McLaughlin took a match out of his pocket. He lit it with a flick of his thumb and tossed it on the powder. The black powder sizzled and then flared up around the end of the powder line. Then the sparkling flame began to eat up the powder and creep toward the aqueduct.

"Don't stand there gawking, City Boy, or you'll be dead," McLaughlin warned him.

The corporal was walking fast toward the river. David sighed and started after him.

David saw movement out of the corner of his eye and turned back.

He saw a young boy leading two black mules toward the aqueduct. The canal boat that the mules pulled would be close behind.

David glanced at the powder line. It had reached the fuse and was beginning to start up the wall. The boy and the mules might make it across the aqueduct, but the canal boat would be right on top of the explosion when it happened. What would happen to the crew then? Would they be hurt or killed in the collapse?

"Stop!" David called to the boy. "Stop!"

The boy looked down at him. David ran forward a few steps, waving his arms.

"What are you doing?" McLaughlin called from behind them.

David ignored him. He couldn't allow innocent people to be killed. He had family that lived in the north. His war was against the military and the government, not against Union citizens.

The boy stopped the mules, but to David's dismay, the canal boat continued to drift forward into the aqueduct.

David glanced at the fuse. It was working its way up the side of the aqueduct. He ran forward and jumped up into the air. He grabbed hold of the fuse and pulled it from the aqueduct wall. He dropped it onto the ground as it fizzled to the end and went out.

Behind him, McLaughlin screamed in anger.

"Mr. Geoffreys, it's a Rebel!" the boy shouted.

David looked up and saw the boy who had been walking the mules looking over the side of the aqueduct and down at him.

David heard a shot and rock shards sprayed the top of his head as the bullet ricocheted off the granite blocks.

David ducked and ran toward the river. McLaughlin drew his pistol and started firing back at the canal boat captain.

"You are a fool. You went to all that trouble to save their hides and they tried to kill you!" he yelled at David.

"It was the right thing to do," David said.

"It was the stupid thing to do!"

David looked over the edge of the bank and saw a man peering over the side of the aqueduct. He held a rifle and was searching for movement in the trees.

"Mr. Geoffreys, it looks like that Rebel was trying slow us down to blow up the aqueduct. He warned us off, but I saw him pull a fuse out and throw it to the ground," the boy said.

The man shook his head. "He wasn't warning us. He was trying to make sure that we were on top when it blew up."

David sighed and slid back down the bank and sat down. He shook his head slowly. So much for his good deeds.

"Don't get comfortable. The Yankee patrols will be looking for us around here once they hear about this," McLaughlin told him.

David stood up slowly. He suddenly felt very tired. He wanted to go home. When would it all end?

19

AMBUSH ON THE CANAL
JUNE 1862

George sat on his bunk carving on a chunk of wood when Elizabeth poked her head in the window of the hay house. She climbed in and sat down on a bale of hay across from George. The room smelled strongly of hay since George had had the shutters closed. Elizabeth wrinkled her nose at the smell.

George kept his head down, concentrating on how his knife moved around the piece of wood, shaping, poking and cutting.

His father had come back to the *Freeman* about two hours ago to change his shirt and wash off. Mrs. Crabtree wanted to have a nice dinner tonight outside the lock house so Hugh had thought he should look presentable. He had said that his family should do their best to be good guests since they were imposing on the Crabtrees' hospitality.

"Papa told me about what you did this afternoon for Thomas. He's very proud of you," Elizabeth said as she leaned forward to see what her brother was doing.

Thomas had run back to the lock house about a half an hour after the bear had gone back into the woods. It had taken him that long to work up his courage to leave George.

George shrugged and didn't look up. "I didn't do much. It was the cub that saved its mama. If she'd come over the side, I would have shot her."

"I'm not talking about saving the mama. I'm talking about saving Thomas."

George snorted. "He wanted to keep the cub as a pet."

The boy didn't have a lick of sense. George hoped that he hadn't been so stupid when he had been Thomas's age.

Elizabeth rolled her eyes. "That's Thomas."

George nodded.

"What's that?" Elizabeth asked, pointing to the carving in George's hand.

George stopped his carving and stared at the wood. It was taking shape, but he still needed to work in the details. "It's something I'm working on for Becky to give to her to remember me."

Elizabeth's eyebrows arched. "You see her once a week or so. Do you think she'll forget you? You can't be here everyday."

"I...I want her to know how much she means to me." George couldn't bring himself to look up at Elizabeth. He was afraid she might laugh at him.

"You've never made stuff for other girls along the canal."

George shifted uncomfortably on his straw mattress. "I know, but Becky's different."

Elizabeth leaned forward. "How so?"

George didn't say anything, and she probably thought he wasn't going to answer. He just sat on his bunk and turned the carving over and over in his hands, staring at it. He tried to imagine how it would look when it was finished.

"She just makes me feel different inside. I can talk to her about anything...when I'm not getting tongue-tied. She's full of...of energy, of life. She makes something dull like weeding the garden seem exciting. And she's pretty, definitely pretty, whether she's dressed up or muddy from dust and sweat."

"Do you love her?" Elizabeth asked.

"I suppose I do." George nodded as if agreeing with himself.

She leaned forward anxiously. "How do you know?"

"By the way I feel when I'm around her or when I think about her."

"But you've acted foolish over other girls before."

George frowned as he blushed with embarrassment. "It's like you said earlier, never quite like this. I feel different about her."

"How do you know that sometime later on you won't act even more stupid over a different girl?" Elizabeth asked without a trace of sarcasm.

George sat up straight. "Elizabeth!"

"I'm serious."

She might be serious, but she didn't have to be so blunt!

George paused and thought. How did he know? He didn't.

He finally said, "I might act...a bit overanxious again, but at some point, I've got to be willing to accept the responsibility of a wife. So whoever I'm in love with at that time will probably be the one I ask to marry me."

"You make it sound so simple and so permanent," Elizabeth said.

George laughed. "If it was that easy, I wouldn't be here. I'd be with Becky, but she's with Josh VanMeter."

"If it makes you feel any better, Mr. VanMeter put Josh to work on the lock doors and Becky is helping prepare dinner. They haven't been able to talk, except when Thomas gathered everyone together to tell them what had happened to him and how you saved him."

"How did Becky react to that?"

Elizabeth smirked. "You mean does she think that you're a hero?"

George blushed and looked down. "No. Yes." He frowned. "Did she say anything?"

"No, but I think that she was impressed."

"Why?" George pressed, anxious to hear.

"Everybody was impressed, except Josh. He looked angry."

George lay back on his bed and smiled. "Serves him right."

His father poked his head into the hay house. "George, why don't you see if you can hunt up some meat for the Crabtrees? They're using a lot of their own food to feed us until the canal's got water in it again. Josh's hunting didn't yield much this morning. Now that the sun's getting low, you should be able to find some game out and about."

George sat up. "Yes, sir."

He relished the chance of bringing down a big buck and showing up Josh. He slung his cartridge bag over his shoulder and belted on his hunting knife. Then he picked up his rifle and climbed outside.

Thomas was lying on top of the family cabin playing with a box turtle under the shade of the awning. When he saw George ready to hunt, he quickly sat up.

"Are you going hunting, George? Can I come? Please?" Thomas pleaded.

Hugh cleared his throat and said, "I don't think so, Thomas. Hunting's a man's job, son, and you're not quite old enough yet. I wouldn't want you getting in George's way while he's tracking game."

Thomas stopped jumping around. "Oh."

"It's all right, Papa," George said when he saw the disappointment in Thomas's face. He was surprised that his brother had given in so easily.

Hugh looked between his two sons. "Are you sure?"

"I think Thomas has learned to listen me. I don't think he'll be a problem if he comes with me. Will you, Thomas?" George said.

Thomas shook his head vigorously. He turned to his father and said, "Gosh no, Papa. Without George, I would have been bear breakfast."

Hugh chuckled. "All right. Go along with the both of you then."

Thomas ran toward the fall board. "Yea!"

George and Thomas crossed the empty canal bed and walked into the forest. George had an excellent sense of direction so he wasn't worried about getting lost. Besides, he knew that even if he did get lost, he knew all he had to do was walk southwest until he reached the canal. At that point, he would know exactly where he was. He knew every foot of the canal by memory. He certainly wouldn't walk beyond the canal's boundaries. Even the Rebs and Yanks had to cross the canal going from Virginia to Maryland. There was no avoiding the 185-mile long canal. It was almost as if the government, by digging the canal, had drawn a line in the country and dared the South to cross it.

About half an hour of walking yielded nothing, but George did find a likely watering spot so he settled down to wait and see if a deer would show up to take a drink.

"George, there's sassafras roots here. Can I dig some up with your knife so Mama can make sassafras tea?" Thomas asked.

George handed his brother his hunting knife. "Go ahead. If you see any worms, grab them, too, we can go fishing on the river tomorrow."

Thomas smiled and started to dig in the ground while George watched the clearing near a shallow creek. He heard the sound of branches breaking. At first, he thought it would be deer would be coming to drink, but deer wouldn't be so noisy.

He put his hand on his brother's back. "Thomas, be still and be quiet," he said softly.

Thomas was good to his word to listen to his brother and was immediately still.

George watched and waited and heard more branches crack. Then he heard someone curse and another person laughed.

"Who is it?" Thomas whispered.

George waved his brother to be quiet.

Two men walked into view. They were Union soldiers patrolling the river area or perhaps hunting for game like he and Thomas were.

"You think we gonna find General Jackson hiding in the woods, Charlie?" one of the soldiers, a dark-haired man with a long mustache, asked.

"I'm trying to find my way back to the river so we can find the camp," the other soldier asked. This one was a tall man who was very thin.

"And whose fault is it that we're lost?"

Charlie said, "I didn't hear you complaining none when we left our route to go to Long Jack's." Long Jack ran a tavern in Little Orleans.

"That was before you got us too drunk to know where we're going."

Soldiers.

So the Union Army was close by. George wondered if this was part of a small river patrol or a larger army massing. Was another portion of the Union Army heading south across the river to fight?

One thing for sure was that George wasn't going to introduce himself to the soldiers. His father had been telling him since last year that where there were soldiers, there was fighting, and where there was fighting, there was death. George wasn't anxious to be involved in it.

George stayed quiet and let the soldiers walk by no further away than two yards from George and Thomas.

When they were gone, George nudged his brother. "Let's go."

"Why?"

"There won't be any game along the trail, not with the noise those two were making. We'd best find another place to hunt."

George and Thomas started to move back the way they had come when he heard a shot. Someone screamed. There was another shot. The same person screamed again. Then George heard a third shot.

And silence.

George froze and waited. He pressed his hand down on Thomas's shoulder to stop him.

What did he expect to hear? What had happened?

"George, were they hunting, too?" Thomas whispered.

George shook his head. "I don't think so."

More than likely, they had been hunted. If there had been a fight, it hadn't been much of one. Three shots, that was all.

What should he do? Suppose one of those soldiers was hurt and needed help?

George grabbed his brother's hand. "Come on, Thomas, and be quiet."

They crept along within the trees and brush and moved parallel to the game trail the soldiers had been walking along. George wanted to stay off the trail in case he came across whoever had been doing the shooting.

About fifty yards away from where George had first seen the soldiers, he saw them again. They were lying on the ground. One was lying on his face, but the second one was lying on his back and his eyes were wide open, staring right into the setting sun.

"What's wrong with them?" Thomas asked.

George felt a chill run through him when he realized he was looking at corpses. He had never seen a dead man.

"They're dead," he whispered.

George stood still as he searched the trees. He couldn't be sure that whoever killed these soldiers wasn't still around. He lifted his rifle and held it at ready. He hoped that he wouldn't have to shoot someone.

Was the person who shot those soldiers still around? Was he aiming at George and Thomas even now? George felt the small hairs on the back of his neck begin to stand up.

"George, let's get out of here," Thomas said.

George nodded. "That's a good idea. Let's get Papa and bring him back here. He'll know what to do about these soldiers."

They backtracked their trail as quietly as possible. When George felt they were far enough away, he broke into a trot and kept it up until he and Thomas reached the *Freeman*.

They ran to their boat, yelling for their father. When Hugh appeared out of the family cabin, George explained everything that had happened with Thomas interjecting his theories on occasion.

"War is bad enough without raiders entering into it," Hugh said when George finished talking.

"What's a raider?" Thomas asked.

Hugh frowned. "Someone who sneaks around to do his fighting. They won't face you head on like a man would do. They'll burn your crops so you can't feed your army and shoot you in the back. Winning at all costs is what they do and they don't care who gets hurt to do it."

"What do we do about them?" George asked.

"We stay alert and armed. It might be the same person who shot at us. We also need to warn the VanMeters and Crabtrees, especially the Crabtrees, since they won't be moving on when the canal fills again. If the raiders stay in the area, the Crabtrees might be in danger."

"Do you think the person who shot those soldiers is the same person who shot at us earlier?"

Hugh nodded. "I hope so. I'd hate to think there's more than one of them around."

Hugh picked up his rifle, which leaned against the side of the family cabin where it could be easily reached.

"Thomas, you go inside and tell your mother that George and I are going back to bury those soldiers and collect their identification and personal things," Hugh said.

Alice poked her head out of the window. "He doesn't have to come in to tell me. I heard you. I don't think you should go, Hugh. The killer could still be waiting there."

Hugh shook his head. "I don't think so. Part of a raider's ability to survive depends on him staying on the move. He won't stay near those bodies and chance that a larger group of soldiers would show up and start searching for him."

"Are you sure?"

He shrugged. "If you were married to one of those soldiers, wouldn't you want to know what happened to him and that he was buried?"

Alice sighed. "Just be careful. I don't want to be a wife wondering what happened to her husband and son."

"We'll be careful."

Thomas said, "Can I come too, Papa?"

Hugh shook his head. "No, I need you to stay here with your mama and sister."

"But I can help dig the grave," Thomas insisted.

Hugh scratched his ear. "But who would watch your Mama and sister if you came along? They'll be afraid and need the calming influence of a man," he asked Thomas.

Thomas thought for a moment and then said in a serious tone, "I guess I had better stay here since the women need protecting."

Hugh grinned and Alice had to put her hand over her mouth to keep from laughing. Hugh clapped Thomas on the shoulder and said, "Thank you, son. I feel a lot better knowing you're watching them."

George led his father back to the clearing. The bodies were still there in the same positions they had fallen. Hugh frowned and took the rifle from George.

"Let's move in closer. Go slow and be quiet," Hugh told his son.

They walked slowly and Hugh held the rifle at ready. He stood near the bodies and turned in a slow circle, searching the trees. Nothing caught his attention.

"Start digging, son. Set aside any rocks you find. We'll use them to cover the graves when we're finished burying them."

George started digging with the shovel while his father stood guard over him. When George tired, they switched places until they had a large hole about two feet deep.

Hugh stuck the shovel in the pile of dirt and bent over the bodies. They were cool and their eyes stared forward, unfocused. He searched the bodies until he found their wallets in the jackets. He also checked to see if they had any letters on their bodies that he might be able to forward with their wallets to their next of kin. He only found the wallets.

When he was through, he placed the bodies side by side in the shallow grave and buried them. Then he and George placed rocks on the mound.

George finished and looked at his father. "What do we do now?"

Hugh passed the rifle to George. He searched the brush and found a couple of dead branches. He broke them up and tied them up with twine to form two crosses, which he placed in the dirt at the head of the grave. Then he kneeled down and offered up a prayer that God would grant the soldiers the peace for which they had fought and died.

The dinner that night at the Crabtrees was subdued because of the news Hugh brought with him as he had handed Lucas Crabtree the pair of wallets. More than once, a stray sound sent the men rushing for their rifles. Everyone stayed close to the house and said very little. It was as if they were staying quiet so that they could listen to the night.

It was almost a relief when the meal was finished and the families separated to go into the house and to their boats. What should have been a joyous party turned into a funereal occasion.

"This war is going to suck every last one of us into it before it's through," Cyrus VanMeter predicted. "Mark my words."

"We do what we have to do," Lucas added.

"I don't have to let my family be shot at by Rebs. We're not soldiers."

"But we are Americans and this war is about what kind of Americans we'll be," Hugh chimed in.

Cyrus spat a huge wad of chewing tobacco into the canal.

"Well, I want to be a live one," Cyrus said.

Hugh nodded. "Aye, that we all want." He waved to them. "I'll see you in the morning."

The moon was full as George and his family crossed the swing arms to go across the canal to the towpath. He looked down to watch where he was stepping and he saw the moonlight shimmering on something in the canal.

"Papa," George said.

"Is something wrong?" Hugh's voice was tense.

"There is something in the canal."

"A person?"

George realized with those two words that the empty canal provided a path to move troops without being easily seen.

"I don't think so."

Hugh lowered his lantern down the side of the lock gate. George clearly saw that there was a layer of water covering the bottom of the canal. It was only a few inches deep, but it would be deep enough to float a canal boat soon enough.

"They must have repaired the breach and opened the guard locks," Hugh said.

"Already? That was fast," George said. His present for Becky wasn't ready yet.

"Go on to the boat. I'm going to tell the Crabtrees that we'll be moving on in the morning. Lucas will want to open the gates after we're on the towpath."

"No, we'll wait," Alice said. "I don't want to be separated now."

Hugh disappeared into the darkness, leaving the lantern with his wife. He was back a minute later.

"Let's move on," he said.

Back at the *Freeman*, George closed himself up in the hay house. It was hot without the breeze circulating through the open windows, but it was the only way he could keep the lantern lit without his mother complaining. He sat on a bale of hay carving his present. It took a long time and his hands started to cramp with the effort of holding the knife and guiding it through the wood. He wished he could paint it, but even if he had the time, he didn't have the paint to decorate it.

George did as much work as he could with the time given. The finished product was acceptable, but it wasn't as beautiful as he had hoped. His vision of it had exceeded his skill.

It would have to do, though.

His father threw open the shutters to the hay house window way too early or so it seemed.

"Time to go," Hugh announced, shaking him on the shoulder.

George struggled to his feet. "Yes, sir."

"You all right, George? Didn't you sleep?"

George shook his head. "I had something to do before I went to bed."

"Are you going to be all right walking the mules? I don't want one of them kicking you because you're drowsy and not paying attention."

George stretched. "Just let me splash some cold water on my face and drink a cup of coffee. I'll ride them if I have to."

His father nodded. "Go ahead. Elizabeth's got breakfast ready."

"Elizabeth?"

"Your Mama couldn't sleep a wink last night. She was too worried that a Rebel sniper would sneak up on us. She only fell asleep an hour ago, so be quiet and don't wake her."

George nodded. He walked across the hatches to the family cabin. It was still dark out but there was hint of red in the trees to mark the coming dawn. He smelled Elizabeth's cooking the moment that he stepped out of the hay house.

In the family cabin, she had biscuits and bacon ready to eat, as well as eggs from the Crabtrees' chickens. George sliced the biscuits open and stuffed them with the fried eggs and crisp bacon. Then he shoved half of one of the sandwiches in his mouth.

"George!" Elizabeth whispered. "You know if Mama was awake, she wouldn't let you do that."

George shrugged and filled his cup with coffee. Then he was headed out the door with his breakfast. He needed to hitch up the mules for the morning shift. They would be well rested and ready for a little work.

He took a swig of the hot coffee to wash the biscuit down and stuffed another biscuit into his mouth.

George sat his coffee and biscuit on the window sill of the mule house and grabbed the harnesses off their pegs. He began to get King Edward and Ocean ready to work. By the time he was finished, the activity and coffee had him fully awake, though his carving hand still ached a bit from his night's work.

He attached Ocean and King Edward to the tow line once they were on the towpath. When his father signaled he was ready, George tapped Ocean on the flank and said, "Gee-haw."

The mules started forward. The slack came out of the tow line and it rose from the water, dripping wet. Then the mules were leaning into their harnesses, straining to move the barge. They took one step forward, then another, and the barge began to move very slowly.

Once they were moving at a steady pace, George heard his father blow, "Lock ready! Lock ready! Lock ready!" on the tin horn.

George walked beside Ocean, looking at the canal. It looked to be back up to its normal level. It had to be. Between the bottom of the canal and the bottom of a loaded barge was only a few inches of clearance, even when the canal was full.

The season usually had a dry span or two because of weather-related breaks in the canal. How many would there be this season with the Rebels hoping to shut down the canal, and hence, the supply of coal into Washington?

A vision of the two dead soldiers flashed through George's mind. He shuddered.

There were worse things than being left high and dry.

Once his father had maneuvered the barge into the lock at the Crabtrees' house, George called to his brother who was sitting under the canopy. "Thomas, can you watch the mules for me?"

"Why?" his brother asked, coming to the edge of the barge. He chewed on a biscuit lathered with butter.

"I've got to give Becky something before we go."

"What?"

"It's private."

Thomas smiled. "I bet I know what you're going to give her...a kiss."

"Thomas, either you help me, or..." He searched for the right threat. "Or the next time you get a bear mad at you, I may just let her play with you for awhile before I help you."

He didn't like threatening his brother, but he didn't have long to give Becky her present, either. He just wanted some privacy with her.

Thomas's mouth dropped open. "Criminy! Can't you take a joke, George? I'll help you."

He hopped onto the canal wall before the boat got too low as it was being lowered. He walked over to the mules and petted them. George immediately dashed across the boat to the other side of the lock.

He found Becky behind the lock house, tying drooping tomato plants to sticks in the ground so they would stay upright. She stopped working when she saw George.

"I guess that's the *Freeman* locking through," she said with a smile.

George nodded. For a moment, he couldn't find the words that he wanted to say. "I can't be away for too long, but I wanted to give you something. I've been working on it since we grounded," he finally managed to say.

He took the figure from his shirt pocket. It was a galloping unicorn carved from wood.

Becky put her hand to her mouth. "It's beautiful, George," she said.

"Then you like it?"

Becky smiled and George felt his breath catch. "I love it. It's the prettiest present I've ever received."

"I carved it myself," George said proudly.

"George!" his father called from the canal.

"I've got to go," George said. "I'll see you in a week or so."

He turned and ran back to the canal. As he was running across the west end swing arms, he heard Becky call to him. He stopped running and turned back toward the house.

Becky stepped up on the swing arms and walked up to him.

"I forgot to say thank you." She stood on her toes and kissed him on the lips. Then she turned and quickly ran off.

When George opened his eyes and saw that he was alone, he thought he might have imagined it all. But then why did his lips still tingle?

"George!" his father called again.

The barge was moving out of the lock. Forgetting where he was, George turned to walk to the towpath. He lost his balance on the swing arms. He pinwheeled his arms, trying to stay upright.

Instead, he fell into the canal on the west side of the swing arms.

Now he was awake!

He touched his lips as he surfaced from under the water.

Boy! Was he ever awake!

20

DEATH COMES TOO QUICKLY
JULY 1862

Alice wrung the dirty wash water out of one of Hugh's shirts. At least she thought it was Hugh's. It could easily have been George's. Her oldest son was nearly as big as his father was.

She used a wooden clothespin to hold the shirt on the line she had strung from the canopy to the hay house. It was a warm day out so the clothes should dry quickly.

Thomas climbed out of the window of the hay house and looked around. He walked slowly toward the mule shed looking at his feet. It seemed like strange behavior even for Thomas. She thought he would have been asleep now after having walked the mules during the night.

"What's the matter, Thomas?" Alice asked.

The young boy stopped an looked at her. "Oh, nothing."

Alice raised an eyebrow. "Nothing?"

Thomas nodded vigorously. "Nothing's wrong, Mama. At least I don't think so."

That stopped Alice. "Why don't you think so?" she asked.

"My turtle went for a walk."

Alice had to admit that that did sound fairly innocent. "Your turtle? What turtle?"

"I found a good-sized snapping turtle last night on the towpath. So I put him in a bucket in the mule shed when we were locking through last time," Thomas explained.

Alice rolled her eyes. Would Thomas ever stop collecting his pets?

"So why isn't it still in the bucket?" she asked.

Thomas shrugged. "I don't know. One of the mules in the shed must have kicked it over. I went to take him a biscuit left over from breakfast and saw the bucket, but the turtle was gone."

"Well, maybe he crawled over the side of the boat and went back into the water where he belongs," Alice suggested.

Thomas glanced into the canal. "I hope not. I was going to

teach him to do tricks."

Elizabeth screamed from the mule shed. Alice and Thomas ran along to race plank to starboard window. Elizabeth climbed out of the window and let her feet hang in the water. Since the boat was loaded, it sat low in the water and the water was only a foot below the race plank. Tears ran down her cheeks.

"Elizabeth, what's wrong?" Elizabeth asked.

"A snapping turtle's in the mule shed. It bit my foot while I was rubbing down Ocean. I thought that it was going to take my toe off."

"Thomas!" Alice said.

Thomas looked like he wanted to slink off somewhere and hide, but where could he have hidden on the canal boat? He looked at his feet and shuffled nervously.

"Look at what your turtle has done to your sister," Alice said.

"I didn't tell it to bite her," Thomas defended himself.

"His turtle?" Elizabeth asked.

"How many times have I told you not to bring dangerous animals on board?" Alice told him.

Thomas shrugged. "I don't know, but a snapping turtle's not dangerous. They're not poisonous and they can't move all that fast. All Elizabeth had to do was not step on it."

Elizabeth shouted, "I couldn't see it. Not with two mules in there and all of the shadows."

"That's not my fault," her brother told her.

Elizabeth scowled at him. "It won't be my fault when you wake up with a snapping turtle in your bed, either, which I'm sure will happen if I find the turtle first."

Thomas paled. He realized that his sister was probably angry enough to carry out the threat.

"I'll find the turtle," he said as he stared at his feet.

"You do that and then you throw it overboard," Alice told him.

Thomas sighed and climbed into the mule shed.

Once he was inside, Alice turned to her daughter. "And you shouldn't threaten you brother. The skin on your foot isn't even broken. I've seen you hurt worse and complain less."

"It scared me. The turtle shouldn't have been in with the mules. What if it had been one of them that was bit?" Elizabeth asked.

Alice patted the top of her daughter's head. "Do I need to start dressing you in long dresses again so that you can be my little girl?"

Elizabeth frowned and turned away. "No, Mama."

"Good. I expect Thomas to act like a little boy. I expect you to act like a young lady."

"Hello, *Freeman*."

Alice looked down the canal. The *Glorious* was approaching. The Ruhls were another boating family from Sharpsburg. Alice waved to them. Paul Ruhl was at the tiller. His son, Vincent, was leading the mules. They both waved to her.

"How are things ahead?" Hugh called from the other end of the boat. He was at the tiller on their boat.

"Quiet, which is the way I like it," Paul said.

"Aye, I can agree to that," Hugh said.

Alice heard a rumble and squeal of metal against metal that interrupted the two men's conversation. She looked beyond the *Glorious* and saw a line of dark smoke rising above the trees. It told her that a train was coming before she even saw it.

So much for quiet.

The black-metal engine came into view a few moments later, quickly gaining on the *Glorious*. The railroad track ran parallel to the canal along this stretch and was so close that an engineer could spit into the canal, which they often did when passing one of the canal boats. It showed their contempt of the canal business.

The train chuffed along, moving steadily west. As it passed the *Glorious* and *Freeman*, the whistle blew high and shrill.

On the towpath, the mules danced around, startled by the unexpected sound. King Edward surged forward in the harness while Jigger abruptly sat down. The two Ruhl mules leapt into the air, kicking out at anything around them.

George grabbed the lead chains and spoke calmly to King Edward and Jigger while alternately stroking their necks. Vincent Ruhl dropped to the ground trying to avoid the kicking mules.

As the engine passed by Alice, she thought that she heard the engineer and coal man laughing. Hugh shook his fist at the train and probably shouted a few choice words that Alice was glad she couldn't hear over the train noises.

Railroaders were notorious for scaring canal mules whenever they had the opportunity. It wasn't bad enough that canallers had to fight nature and avoid the war, they had to still deal with the railroad, which wanted all of the coal trade from Western Maryland. The railroad had already managed to steal most of the flour and produce trade so that coal transport was the only thing that kept the canal turning a dollar.

"George, are you all right?" Alice called.

"Yes, Mama. King Edward and Jigger worked against each other so not too much happened," George told her.

Hugh yelled, "If I knew who that was, I'd find him and give him a good thrashing."

"Where's Vincent!" Amanda Ruhl yelled from aboard the *Glorious*.

Alice looked beyond where George was standing on the towpath and saw that the two Ruhl mules had calmed down, but Vincent was nowhere to be seen.

"Mama, I saw Vincent fall into the water after one of his mules kicked," Thomas said from the window of the mule shed.

He tossed the snapping turtle overboard. It landed in the water with a loud splash. Elizabeth yelped and quickly stood up to get her feet out of the water.

"Vincent's in the water," Alice called over to the *Glorious*.

Amanda screamed. "He doesn't know how to swim."

Paul Ruhl dove over the side of the canal boat and into the water. George quickly followed him into the water. Hugh ran along the race plank and dove into the water when he was beyond the mule shed.

Alice hurriedly climbed up on top of the mule shed and scanned the water, looking for the young boy. She couldn't see anything in the water other than the thrashing around caused by the men.

"Elizabeth, Thomas, come up here and help me look for Vincent," Alice said.

Her children quickly climbed onto the roof and stood next to her. They didn't see anything. Alice put her knuckles in her mouth and bit down lightly.

Paul surfaced and shouted, "Do you see him?"

"No!" everyone answered, including Amanda Ruhl and her daughters who were standing on the roof of the mule shed on their boat.

"Damnation!" Paul shouted.

He dove under again just as George came up for air.

"I found him," George shouted.

George swam to the side of the canal, towing the young boy beside him. Alice couldn't see Vincent moving around. George pushed Vincent onto the towpath and climbed out after him. Hugh and Paul saw what he was doing and swam over to the towpath.

George laid out the body and put his head on the boy's chest. He looked at Paul and shook his head.

Paul scurried out of the water and rushed over to Vincent. He put his ear to Vincent's chest and listened for himself. Then he turned the boy on his side and began to pound Vincent on the back, trying to force the water out of his lungs.

"Come on, son. Breathe! Breathe, boy!" Paul said.

A little bit of water spilled out of Vincent's mouth, but it came from Vincent being turned on his side, not coughing.

Even from the boat, Alice could tell that the boy was dead.

Hugh, George and Paul spend most of the afternoon digging the grave for Vincent's body. Paul insisted that it be in sight of the canal so that he could visit it often during the season. He didn't want to take the body back to Sharpsburg because he didn't want to have to carry the body on the boat. It would have upset his three daughters too much, not to mention Amanda.

Alice sat in the family cabin of the *Glorious* with Amanda Ruhl, trying to console her. Alice remembered the babies that she had lost and how inconsolable she had been. How did it feel to lose a child Vincent's age, one who had grown and developed and who people had known and loved?

She sat with Amanda at the small table in the middle of the cabin, neither of them speaking. After awhile, Alice felt the need to move around so she began to clean the cabin. Amanda watched her and Alice frequently touched her as she passed by.

Amanda wept at odd intervals and Alice let her cry, knowing that the emotion couldn't be held in if Amanda was to recover.

A knock came at the door as the sun was setting. Amanda wasn't crying at the moment, but she also made no move to stand and open the door.

Alice walked to the door and opened it. George was standing outside, dirty and sweaty from digging all day.

"We're finished digging the..." He looked over his mother's shoulder at Amanda. "We're finished. Papa and I are going to wash up. Mr. Ruhl is still with the ...with Vincent. Mr. Ruhl wants to bury him now, so Papa said that I should tell you so you could get Mrs. Ruhl ready."

Alice nodded and patted his arm. "That's fine, son."

George turned away, but stopped and turned back. He looked

at Alice. She saw confusion and fear in his expression. He might have been sixteen, but he looked like a little boy to her right then, nervous at having gotten into trouble.

"Mama, that could have been me," he said.

She didn't have to ask what he was talking about because she had been thinking the same thing.

"It's not you, though." And that was what was important, she thought but didn't say because Amanda was near.

"But why did it have to happen?" George asked.

Alice stepped outside and shut the door behind her.

"I can't tell you that. I don't know," she told her son.

"I know how to swim, but if one of the mules had kicked me, I could have drowned. We saw blood on Vincent's head. That's what happened to him."

Alice shook her head. "Don't worry about what didn't happen, George. Be thankful for it."

"But Vincent was only two years younger than me." He seemed on the verge of tears.

Alice nodded and hugged him briefly. "Then be glad you still are alive and enjoy it."

George stared at her for a moment and then turned and climbed the three stairs to the race plank. Alice sighed and went back inside to help Amanda. The next couple of hours would be very hard on her.

Alice was almost embarrassed because she found herself quietly thanking God that it was Vincent who had been killed and not George.

"Amanda, it's almost time for the funeral. Do you want to change into something else?" Alice asked her, laying a calming hand on the woman's shoulder.

Amanda shook her head. "No, I want to see my son."

"I'll take you there then. Paul is there now." Amanda should be able to have a few final moments alone with her son.

Alice wasn't so sure that Amanda would walk if Alice didn't lead her. The grieving woman seemed numb to everything around her.

Alice took Amanda by the arm and led her up to the race plank and across the fall board to the towpath.

Elizabeth and the Ruhl girls had all of the mules picketed off to the side of the towpath and were feeding them by hand. Four-year-old Ellie Ruhl was chasing a butterfly along the towpath.

When Paul saw Amanda approaching, he stood out and held

out his arms to her. She rushed to him and cried in his shoulder. Then she dropped to her knees beside her son and clutched him to her chest as she cried over Vincent's body.

Alice turned away and left them in peace.

The funeral was short.

Vincent's body was wrapped up in two blankets and lowered respectfully into the deep hole that the men had dug.

The Fitzgeralds stood around the grave in their Sunday clothes. The Ruhls wore clean outfits, but they didn't have Sunday clothes. The only reason that the Fitzgeralds had such outfits was because Alice had known that they would be attending church on Sundays and packed appropriately.

Paul and Amanda stood together holding hands at one side of the grave. George stood across from them still looking confused and scared. Thomas looked uncomfortable in his dark suit as he watched robins fly overhead. Elizabeth was holding Ellie's hand. Ruby and Emma, the other two Ruhl girls, stood quietly next to their parents.

Hugh stood at one end of the grave. He opened the family Bible and read a handful of verses from the New Testament that showed how much Jesus had loved children and their sweet spirits.

When he finished reading, Hugh closed the Bible and said, "Vincent, you were a good boy, and I know that you will be welcomed into Heaven and be happy there. We will miss you here, but we are glad at your happiness and hope that we will meet you again one day. Amen."

Paul looked over at Hugh and said, "Thank you, Fitzgerald."

Hugh nodded and walked over and put his arm around Alice.

"I'll change and come back to bury him," Hugh said to Paul.

Paul shook his head. "No, I'll do it on my own."

Hugh nodded again. He and Alice turned and walked back toward the *Freeman*. The children followed silently.

Hugh stopped on the towpath and stared across the canal.

"Do you see something?" Alice asked.

"Just iron death."

"What?"

"I've been saying for years that the railroad wanted to kill the canal and now it's gone and killed a canawler," Hugh explained.

"It was an accident, Hugh," Alice said, not liking the hatred that she heard in her husband's voice. He had no tolerance for either the railroad or the Confederacy.

Hugh shook his head. "It wasn't an accident. The engineer knew what would happen when he blew that whistle. He knew that it would spook the mules. That's why he did it."

"He didn't know that a boy would die."

"Would he have cared? I don't think so. Those railroaders are hateful people."

For all the good and love in Hugh, he had a blind spot when it came to the railroad. He didn't even hate the Confederacy nearly as much as he hated the railroad. The war was a matter of loyalty to his country, but his anger at the railroad was personal.

Alice hugged his arm and led him across the fall board and onto the boat.

Screams and cries woke Alice up from a sound sleep. She sat up in the bed. Hugh was snoring softly beside her. It hadn't been him who woke her.

She listened for the noise again. She heard soft sobs. They sounded like they were coming from Thomas.

She reached across Hugh and grabbed her housecoat. Then, rather than crawl over him, she parted the curtains and crawled out the window onto the race plank.

As she stood up, she saw Thomas sitting on the roof of the family cabin. He usually preferred to sleep out here on warm nights. He wasn't sleeping now, though. He was sitting up with his blanket around his shoulders and crying.

Alice climbed up beside him and put her arms around his shoulders.

"What's wrong, Thomas?" she asked softly so as not to wake anyone.

He wiped his eyes with his hands and said, "I had a bad dream."

"Do you remember what it was about?"

She felt him nod.

"I dreamed I was the one that got killed, not Vincent. 'Cept I wasn't really dead. I just couldn't move or talk or anything. And Papa, he put me in that hole and began throwing dirt on me. It got so dark. I woke up, but when I woke up, all I could see was dark."

Alice hugged him tighter and felt him snuggle against her. She hadn't realized that Thomas had been so upset by the funeral. He had barely seemed to notice it. George had been the one who she would have thought would have been having nightmares.

"It's all right now," she whispered. "You're alive, Thomas."

"I know, but Vincent's not."

What could she say to that? "No, he's not."

There was a loud splash that sounded behind them. Alice turned to see what it was. The moonlight wasn't bright, but she could see two large shadows moving across the canal.

"What is it, Mama?" Thomas asked.

"Shhh!"

The last thing she wanted to do was attract attention.

She watched the shadows climb out of the canal and disappear into the forest between the canal and the river.

Smugglers or spies. She wasn't sure which, not that it mattered much.

No matter where they went the war was always near the edges of their lives. Sooner or later, they were going to run into each other.

21

THE BLOODIEST DAY
OF THE WAR
SEPTEMBER 1862

David and McLaughlin approached the picket slowly so as not to startle any of the guards. The guards had just come through a long day of fighting on South Mountain to the east and they were nervous as well as exhausted. The two scouts wore their uniforms, but that wouldn't ensure their safety. David didn't want to be shot dead by his own side in this crazy war.

They stopped their horses in the middle of the road as the sergeant approached them, holding his rifle up so the barrel was pointed at David.

"Sergeant, I'm looking for General Lee," David said.

The middle-aged sergeant squinted, trying to make out David's features in the twilight. "And you are?"

"Lieutenant David Windover of the 21st Virginia and Corporal Tim McLaughlin of the 18th Tennessee. We're scouts for Colonel Collins under the command of General Jackson."

"General Jackson's not here."

David nodded. "We know that, but the information we have is more pertinent to General Lee rather than General Jackson."

The sergeant snorted, but he lowered his rifle barrel. "The men are resting. Tomorrow, it looks like we march into Hell. I suppose the general is asleep, too. I'd be if I had the chance," the guard said.

"We have information about the position of the Army of the Potomac that I am sure he will want to hear. If you're going to march into Hell, you need to know where the demons are waiting," David insisted.

General Robert E. Lee had brought his army across the Potomac at the fords around Leesburg, which was about twenty miles east of Sharpsburg where they were now. They had crossed on the fourth of September, just a week after their second victory at Bull Run. General Lee had wanted to keep the Federals on the defensive and relieve Virginia of some of the burden of feeding his army. He also wanted to win over Maryland to the cause of the South. If he could accomplish that, Washington City would be in enemy territory. Its capture could break the Union and secure independence for the Confederacy.

Most importantly, a victory in the north would allow Britain and France to recognize the legitimacy of the Confederacy and send them their much-needed aid. It would also weaken Lincoln's position with his own government.

Some of the information that David and McLaughlin had forwarded to the colonel had helped General Lee plan where to cross his army. They had told Colonel Collins where the least-defended fords were located and how heavy the harvests were on the north side of the river. When the two scouts had reported in to Colonel Collins while the army was in Frederick, the colonel had given them new orders, which were to watch the Army of the Potomac and keep the colonel updated on the Union Army position.

Colonel Collins had then returned to General Stonewall Jackson who took his army to Harpers Ferry where he used his artillery to pound the Union depot at Harpers Ferry from the high hills surrounding the town. It was a quick, decisive battle. Jackson left General Ambrose Powell Hill in charge of the occupation of the town and depot.

"I'll have someone take you to the general," the sergeant said as he waved to another man.

A private walked up and saluted.

"Take these two men to General Lee and make sure they don't get into trouble along the way. If the colonel says he doesn't know them, shoot them," the sergeant said.

"Yes, sir." The private's voice cracked, showing his nervousness.

As they rode through the various camps, David noticed how tired the soldiers looked. No wonder. They had just fought and lost a battle on South Mountain. It was more than simply being tired, though. The soldiers were undernourished and lacking equipment. Some of them were even barefoot. The Confederacy just hadn't had the manpower to hold the mountain passes west of here. It was surprising that they had held out on the mountain for as long as they had. Now General Lee had concentrated most of his forces around Sharpsburg to keep his army from being divided by McClellan's Army of the Potomac.

The private rapped on the pole of a tent. "General Lee, two

men to see you, sir. They say they are scouts."

"Come in," the general said from within the tent.

The private pulled back the tent flap and ushered them inside. David saluted the general. McLaughlin took off his hat.

"Thank you, Private. It's all right," General Lee said.

The private saluted and ducked out of the tent.

The commander of the Confederate forces was sitting at a small table looking at a map lit by a lantern. He looked tired, but then so did everyone. When he looked up, David saw dark shadows under the man's eyes. General Lee rubbed his eyes and drew his shoulders back.

When the private had gone, General Lee asked, "What news do you have, Lieutenant?"

"South Mountain weakened the Federals, but not enough, sir. From what we can tell, McClellan still has about 60,000 men," David said.

"Still?"

David nodded.

"That's more than twice as many as we've got," McLaughlin added.

"How do you know that?" General Lee asked.

"I may not be able to read, but I can count, sir. If I can look over our encampments and make that guess so can McClellan and his spies. He's got to be feeling confident right now. He drove us out of the mountains and while he can't beat us with skill, he'll overwhelm us with numbers. Everyone of our boys is twice as good as their soldiers, but like I said, they've got more than twice as many men as we do. Out here in the open, they can simply outrun us."

Lee sighed and shook his head. "It's going to be a bloodbath tomorrow. Good men will die, and in the end, I fear we cannot prevail."

David leaned over the map and pointed at the bluff on the eastern side of Antietam Creek. "The Union artillery is here." Then he pointed to Nicodemus Heights and the bluffs by Lower Bridge. "Our cannon are here." He ran his finger along the line that represented Antietam Creek on the map. "And here is where the men will die. The cannon will tear them up. They will slow down here in order to cross the creek. That means they will cluster around the bank. The shrapnel will find plenty of bodies."

"What does their artillery look like?" Lee asked.

"It was hard to get close enough to tell the types, but it looks as if there are about 250 pieces, and maybe only 100 are smoothbore," David explained. David looked at McLaughlin for confirmation and the corporal nodded.

Lee's army only had about 150 pieces with fifty being smoothbore. The smoothbore cannon were less accurate than the newer rifled cannons, which meant the Union not only had more artillery pieces, they had more better ones.

"You do not bring me good news, Lieutenant," Lee said.

David nodded. "No, sir, but it's accurate. You are a better strategist than McClellan is. If anyone can figure out a way to overcome a greater force, it will be you, sir."

Lee bowed his head slowly in David's direction. "I thank you for your faith in me, Lieutenant. I pray that it is not misplaced."

"We should pull back into Sharpsburg," McLaughlin said. "It would still be a bloody fight, but the Union wouldn't shell their own people. It would provide some relief."

The sudden silence made David nervous. General Lee just stared at McLaughlin. David wondered how close the general was to calling the Tennessean a coward or something worse.

"We are not here to cause the destruction of towns and innocent people, Corporal. These people were our countrymen until last year. They are still our family. We want to force President Lincoln into recognizing the Confederacy not lay waste to the North."

He shrugged, unconcerned. "Well, the Yankees have pretty much done just that where they could in the South. I don't see why we shouldn't give them back a taste of it."

General Lee eyes narrowed as he stared at McLaughlin. "Because we are gentlemen and soldiers not mercenaries. If we lose our souls in the process of winning a battle, then we have surely lost the war."

David was glad to hear the colonel give voice to his own feelings. Maybe it would silence McLaughlin.

Lee clasped his hands in front of his mouth and studied the map for a few moments. He closed his eyes, and it looked like he was praying.

When he opened them, he said, "I'll consider this with my other generals. Get some sleep, gentlemen. In the morning, I want you two with me to carry messages between the commanders."

David saluted. "Yes, sir."

As he turned away, he wondered if tomorrow he would die.

David awoke in the morning to the sound of thunder. Then he

realized it was artillery exploding and jumped to his feet. Because it had been a warm night, he hadn't bothered to pitch a tent. He had laid out his bedroll under the open sky. The first hint of morning was just appearing over South Mountain and the fighting had already started. It was going to be a long day.

General Lee was standing outside his tent looking over the battlefield through his sailor's glass. He lowered the brass tube and closed it.

"They're shelling Jackson's men over on Nicodemus Heights," he said as calmly as if he was noting the weather.

David didn't need a sailor's glass to tell him that. He could see the explosions of fire and dirt from his position. Men were already dying. He almost hoped that they had died in their sleep so they wouldn't have to suffer.

"Jackson's going to need help because as soon as that artillery fire lightens up, the infantry will move in. Corporal McLaughlin go tell Major VanDorn to move his men to reinforce Jackson when the artillery barrage lightens up," Collins said.

McLaughlin saluted and hurried away.

The Federal infantry began moving in across a large cornfield to the north of Sharpsburg until the Confederates rose up and fired on them driving them back. That only caused McClellan to train his artillery on the cornfields. VanDorn took his men to reinforce Jackson and they held off the Federals trying to take the hill. David winced as the lines of men fired into each other at less than 200 yards apart.

There was no strategy here. It was an all-out fight until the last man was left standing.

This was worse than his nightmares!

A rider came in with a dispatch from General Ambrose Burnside. General Lee read it and frowned.

"Go see how the men are doing in the West Wood and bring me word. I don't want the Union to flank us," Lee told David.

David saluted. "Yes, sir."

He mounted his horse and galloped off toward the forest. He kept himself hunched over his horse's neck to make a smaller target for anyone thinking of disrupting the Confederate communications.

David arrived in time to see a division of Union soldiers coming through the forest only to be met by a withering barrage of rifle fire at point-blank range. He took up a position on the line and added his own fire. It wasn't that he thought his one rifle would turn the tide, but his rifle fire might keep one more Confederate soldier from dying and one more ghost from haunting his dreams.

David fired blindly. He pointed his rifle and pulled the trigger. The Union soldiers were clustered so close together because of the trees that he couldn't help but hit them.

By the time David returned to General Lee two hours later, he had news to report.

"The Federals tried to reinforce the division in the West Wood, but they passed near General Hill's men." The men were hidden in an 800-yard trench that had been worn down by heavy wagons taking grain to a mill. Though five brigades had started out in that position, a messenger had ordered three brigades to reinforce Jackson in the East Woods. "The bodies of dead soldiers are piling up in front of the lane and serving as breastworks for General Hill's men," David told the colonel.

Lee nodded, but didn't say anything. He looked at his map and then out on the battlefield. Then he re-read the dispatches gathered around the map.

Suddenly, the general said, "What are they doing?"

David looked where he was pointing. Some of the Union soldiers had flanked the road and were firing straight down it. The Rebels were fleeing over the edge of the road to avoid being slaughtered.

"Get down there and tell them to hold the trench. It's too good a position to surrender," Lee said.

David was on his horse again riding towards the fleeing Rebels.

"Get back!" David called to the fleeing men. "The general said to hold the trench."

The men ignored him and swarmed around as they ran toward the Sharpsburg. A bullet hit David in the arm, spinning him off his horse to the ground. When he stood up, most of the Confederate soldiers had passed him by and he saw a wave of blue heading in his direction.

David knew fear then like he had never known it as thousands of muskets and rifles were pointed in his general direction. He turned and ran with the Confederate soldiers.

For all General Lee's talk about not wanting to harm towns or civilians, Sharpsburg was in flames. Stray shells had exploded in the streets and houses, sparking fires. Wounded soldiers wandered back and forth looking for horses and food or simply comfort. Gunpowder smoke stung his eyes.

The civilians were nowhere to be seen, probably hiding in their cellars. David wondered if they would have room for him. He settled for finding a shady spot under an oak tree in someone's yard that kept the heat of the noon day sun off of him. David sat near a well so that he could wash out his wound and bandage it with a linen napkin he found in one of the houses that had been scavenged.

The fighting continued for another five hours. Not that David cared much as long as the Union didn't come marching into town. Confederate companies had been in retreat through the town for three hours. It was obvious that the South had lost this battle. It had been inevitable as General Lee had predicted last night. Now they just wanted to get across the Potomac to the relative safety of Shepherdstown.

The question that nagged at David was why General Lee hadn't retreated last night. He had known that he would be leading men into a losing battle today. Had he fought simply to give the Union a bloody nose before he ran? What had been the sense in fighting this battle?

A small group of Georgia sharpshooters had held thousands of Union soldiers at bay keeping them from crossing a bridge over Antietam Creek and adding their strength to the main battle, but even the Georgians had given way to the sheer number of Union soldiers and were in retreat.

David ate some dried beef and fresh bread that he had found in the house and watched the remains of the Confederate Army come through town. If they were indicative of the state of the Confederacy, then the Confederacy was on the verge of collapse. The house had either been abandoned or the residents were hiding in the basement.

Many men, like David, were wounded or so exhausted that they lay down to sleep or die. David had rested through the afternoon and the food had returned some of his strength. He was ready to move on.

As the sun started to sink low, he finally stood up and went in search of General Lee. He headed north toward the edge of town, but was stopped by what he saw. In the waning light, what he had at first thought were small hills in the land were piles of bodies.

He stopped walking when he passed near the sunken lane where General Hill's men had made their stand. The trench was filled to almost ground level with dead Confederate soldiers. The men had been making their stand in their grave.

David felt as if he would throw up.

"A man could walk from here to Boonsboro and never have to set foot on the ground."

David turned around and saw McLaughlin behind him. It didn't surprise him that the Tennessean had survived the battle. McLaughlin was a survivor more than he was a soldier.

"The South has lost," David said as he scanned the field.

"No, we haven't. The Union could have ended the war right here. We were too weak to stop them. They could have taken General Lee and destroyed he Rebel army, but McClellan didn't have the stomach to press his advantage. It was a standstill."

David shook his head. "That is not a standstill. I have never seen so many dead bodies."

"The colonel figured you were among them, City Boy."

David lifted his bandaged arm. "I got shot off my horse and joined up with the nearest company." He failed to mention that the nearest company had been in retreat, but McLaughlin didn't need to know that.

"The general wants to collect the wounded off the field and then we're leaving Maryland," McLaughlin said.

"What about the dead?"

"What about them?" McLaughlin turned away. "There's probably one dead man for every two living. Should you and I carry a body over the river just so it can be buried on Southern soil?"

If McLaughlin hadn't cared about whether Jonas Thelen had been buried or not, why should he care about thousands of Confederate soldiers?

David shrugged. "I guess not."

"The Union thinks they won this battle. Let them clean up the mess. We've had to do it when we whupped them on our land."

David looked back over the battlefield. How could there be anyone left alive when so many men were dead?

How could either army claim it had won this battle?

22

AFTERMATH
SEPTEMBER 1862

Hugh took off his hat and wiped the sweat from his forehead with his sleeve. It felt too hot for a September day. Maybe that would mean they would have a longer season this year before the company would drain the canal. A few more runs in the season would certainly bring in some welcome money to carry them through the winter.

He glanced nervously around. He had heard distant thunder yesterday and there hadn't even been a cloud in the sky. He wasn't so big a fool that he didn't realize what that meant, though he hadn't said anything to upset the children.

As the *Freeman* came into view of Harpers Ferry across the Potomac, Hugh gasped. Now he knew where the thunder sounds had come from. Harpers Ferry was in shambles. The damage was quite obvious even from across the river. Buildings were splintered. Craters marked the roads. Fires burned in some fields and buildings.

"Elizabeth, hold up," Hugh called to his daughter. She was taking a turn at walking the mules this morning.

Elizabeth stopped the two mules and Hugh steered the boat over to the towpath where it bumped against the side and then stopped.

"Alice, come up here, please." Hugh made an effort to keep his voice calm. He didn't want to panic his family, and he certainly didn't want them to know how scared he was.

Alice opened the door to the family cabin and stepped out. She couldn't see over the top of the family cabin, though.

"What is it?" she asked.

Hugh waved her up. "Can you come up here?"

She walked up the stairs and as she turned toward him, her eyes widened when she saw Harpers Ferry. Crowds of people wandered the streets. Many of them would be without homes now. Others would be searching out friends and relatives to see if they had survived. Hugh also saw a lot of gray uniforms among them and the Confederate flag waved proudly at the top of the hill.

"They must have shelled it yesterday. I heard artillery exploding," Hugh said.

"They? They who?"

"The Rebels. The Union had this town the last time we passed here. Now the Rebels do. They must have driven our boys out," Hugh explained.

Alice put her hand to her mouth. "But they would have been shelling their own people."

Hugh nodded slowly. It didn't really surprise him. "We need to decide if we should go on to Cumberland."

Confused, Alice stared at him. "Where else would we go? Anywhere along the canal will be dangerous. We've already seen that."

He looked westward. "There may be more trouble ahead, more than we've seen so far. I'm not so sure it's safe for you and Elizabeth to be traveling with us. It might not have been such a fine idea I had to bring you along this season; not if it gets you or Elizabeth hurt."

"We been all right so far and we've been together."

Hugh pointed to Harpers Ferry. "But that's not a minor skirmish that went on over there. That was a siege of a town."

"But it was on the Virginia side of the river," Alice said.

Hugh knew what she was getting at. "We don't know if the Rebels stayed on that side of the river."

"The South is fighting a defensive war. They wouldn't have crossed. Everyone knows that. You even told me that," Alice argued.

Hugh didn't answer at first. He didn't know how to answer. With the success on the battlefield that the Rebels had had, they might feel confident enough to cross into Maryland. Hadn't he seen evidence of an army crossing down near Leesburg? At the time, he had thought it was the Army of the Potomac heading south, but what if it had been Lee's army heading north?

"Let's keep going for now until we know what's happening," Hugh said.

He had Elizabeth start the mules walking again, and for once, he didn't think they were moving too slowly. Instead of going back into the cabin, Alice stayed at the tiller with him.

Three hours later, they tied up next to Lock 37 because no one had answered their "Lock ready!" call.

Hugh hopped off the boat onto the berm side of the canal where the lock house was. It was a small, white, clapboard home, just like most of the other lock houses along the canal. Only this one looked empty.

He rapped on the door. "Prado!" he called.

The door opened slightly and Hugh saw Adam Prado. The man looked tired, as if he hadn't slept in days, but he also looked afraid.

"Didn't you hear me calling?" Hugh asked.

"I heard you, but I'll be damned if I go out in the open," Adam told him.

"Why not?"

"Because all Hell opened up here yesterday, you dumb Mick!" Adam nearly shouted. He kept his voice down as if he was afraid he would attract attention.

"Yesterday, we were forty miles east of here, so pardon me for not knowing what is happening," Hugh shot back angrily.

"The Union and Confederacy had one big battle up around Antietam Creek and South Mountain before that. Must have been near 100,000 men fighting," Adam said.

One-hundred thousand men? That was enough to fill a large city and they had all been hell-bent to kill each other.

Antietam Creek was just east of Sharpsburg. A vision of the destruction at Harpers Ferry flashed in Hugh's mind.

"Who won?"

"Anyone who was left alive. Solomon Greenfield said that Lee has been moving his men across the river up near Shepherdstown."

Hugh leaned closer. "What about Sharpsburg?"

Adam shook his head. "It's a mess from what I hear."

"You mean you haven't been there to check and see if anyone needs help?"

Adam snorted, "They're not my responsibility."

Hugh shook his head.

"No, they're not your responsibility. This lock is your responsibility and you don't seem to be taking care of it, either."

Hugh turned and stomped away. He had no desire to argue with Adam. A major battle had been fought near Sharpsburg. What did a minor argument mean compared to that? His concern was for his friends and neighbors in Sharpsburg. How had the town fared?

Alice was waiting for him when he got back to the boat.

He told her, "There was fighting around Antietam Creek. I'm going to ride into town and see if there's anything I can do."

"What if there's still fighting going on?"

"Adam says the Rebels have been moving back across the river near Sharpsburg."

"Then the South did try to invade Maryland."

Hugh nodded. "It looks like."

Alice went into the mule shed and led King Edward and Ocean out. Hugh looked at the mules, then at his wife.

"I only need King Edward," Hugh said.

"I'm going, too."

Hugh shook his head. He had known she was going to say that. The armies might not be fighting anymore, but Hugh wasn't sure he wanted his wife to see what the battle had left behind.

"I want to check our house. There are supplies there that might be needed," Alice said.

"No, Alice. I can do that alone. It's too dangerous. We don't know what we'll find there. There might be looters or snipers in town or along the way," Hugh warned her.

"I want to make sure that our friends and neighbors are all right. They may need help," Alice said.

Hugh gritted his teeth. His wife was as mule-headed as him sometimes.

Hugh sighed. "Fine, but go wake up George to have him sit watch with a rifle. I don't want any deserters trying to get aboard the *Freeman*."

Alice looked a bit worried. "Do you think that would happen?"

"With everything else that has happened on the canal, I don't want to take any chances."

Alice went into the family cabin and roused George. A few minutes later she came out. George stuck his head out of the window.

"He's getting ready," Alice said.

"I'm up," George said. "What's wrong?"

"Your mother and I have to go into town. I want you to keep a rifle with you. There's been trouble in town and we want to check on the house. I want you to take care of the boat," Hugh said.

"I let Thomas sleep," Alice told Hugh.

Hugh nodded. "That's probably better. I wouldn't want him wandering off down the canal right now. George, if he does wake up, keep him close to the boat."

Hugh was quiet as he and Alice rode into town. He wanted to brace himself for what he would see. One-hundred thousand men? Even if one in 100 had died that would mean 1,000 men were dead. Hugh couldn't imagine that many dead men, let alone if more had died.

They came across signs that an army, or at least part of an army had passed through: trampled grass, broken brush, and discarded bones from meals.

Hugh smelled the smoke and gunpowder before he even saw Sharpsburg. That surprised him. He thought that the smell would have dissipated before now. There must have been a lot of shots fired for the smell to linger so long.

As they came out from under cover of the trees, Hugh noticed all of the birds in the air.

"Crows," he muttered.

They approached the town from the south. At least it wasn't still smoldering like Harpers Ferry. There were a few familiar houses missing, though, and others that showed fire damage. Hugh also saw a few artillery craters, but nearly as many as he had seen checkering the streets of Harpers Ferry. This town hadn't been the target of the attack; Harpers Ferry had.

Alice grabbed Hugh's arm. "Oh, Hugh, look!"

She pointed at something in town or rather where something was not. Their house was just a handful of black embers.

As they rode up Main Street, they saw soldiers trudging out on the Shepherdstown Road. Townspeople stood in the street, taking stock of the damage. Some stared around with blank expressions in their faces and no hope in their eyes. Others looked at the damage and slowly shook their head. Hugh didn't see as many people as he would have liked. He wondered if many of them were still hiding in their homes like Adam Prado.

Marty Laws stood in the porch of his store, which was undamaged, and raised a hand to Hugh and Alice as they passed.

"I'm sorry about your house, Hugh, but I'm glad you weren't here," Marty said.

"What happened?" Hugh asked.

"Everyone was running around, trying to make sure their own homes were safe. Yours just wasn't a high priority."

Hugh nodded and continued on.

As he and Alice rode up to the lot, Alice began crying. "There's nothing left."

Their home was just a few blackened timbers on top of the stone foundation. Alice walked up the edge of the foundation and looked down into the basement where so many slaves had been hidden. The shelves were still intact against the walls, but that was all. Their home was gone.

Hugh sighed and put his arm around her. "I'm just glad you and Elizabeth didn't stay behind this season. We can rebuild the house. We can live on the canal boat until we do. We've done it before. It's not that important."

He wished that he felt as confident as he sounded.

"We've got nothing to come back to now."

"We always had everything that was important with us anyway."

They walked the mules back into town, and Hugh turned to go up the Hagerstown Road.

"I want to see where they fought. Why don't you go get the children and we'll see how we can help out around here," Hugh told Alice.

Alice hugged herself as if she were cold. "No, I want to stay with you. I don't want to be alone right now," she said quietly.

They rode north. He was expecting to see smashed artillery pieces and small craters all throughout Miller's cornfields and the surrounding area. What he found were rows upon rows of bodies and pieces of bodies.

It was worse than Hugh had imagined.

Much worse.

Small clusters of people loaded the bodies onto wagons to be carted off for burial. So this was where most of the people in town were.

What really amazed Hugh was that clusters of Union and Rebel soldiers were gathering the bodies rather than shooting at each other. If they could get along now, why couldn't they get along before all of the shooting started?

"There are so many dead," Alice said from beside him.

"The ground has been washed in blood. God has cursed this ground," Hugh said quietly.

Alice sobbed quietly. "It's so senseless. They died and the fighting will continue, if not today, then tomorrow or the next." She paused. "What did they die for?"

"Freedom. They died for freedom."

"What good does that do now?" Alice asked. "Think of all the mothers and wives who must be crying today."

Hugh hugged Alice to his chest. "We all die, Alice. There's no avoiding that. What's important is how we live the time God gives us. The Union is fighting for freedom."

Alice raised her head and said, "So is the South, Hugh. They want freedom to make their own choices and live how they see fit.

Isn't that the same thing we're fighting for the slaves? The Union is fighting it for others. The South is fighting for themselves. For God to let so many men die, can he be granting either side's cause?"

23

SHANTY TOWN
SEPTEMBER 1862

When the *Freeman* tied up at the wharf in Cumberland, Tony was fishing nearby in the Potomac River. That always seemed to be where George found him, sitting on the bank of the canal with his fishing line in the water. George wondered if the boy ever went home. Tony was always at the waterfront when the *Freeman* came into the basin, and he was always ready to work. He never talked about his parents or if he needed to let anyone know where he was.

Did Tony even have a home?

The young boy raised his hand as George jumped onto the pier to tie the boat up to the wharf.

George returned the wave. "Hi, Tony."

"Any work for me?" Tony asked.

"Papa's sleeping, but since he usually has you take care of the mules while we're here, I'd say go ahead and do it again. You can unharness and picket Seamus and Jigger first. Then come aboard and lead King Edward and Ocean out."

Tony smiled. He pulled in his fishing line and laid it aside. Then he jumped the small gap between the boat and the pier and landed on the race plank.

"Hope you're not going to make the mules jump," George said.

"No, sir. I'll lay out the fall board first." It wasn't really needed when they were tied to the wharf, but it did make it easier to get the mules ashore because they were used to using the cleated walkway.

George nodded. Tony was picking up the canal terminology quickly enough. He was a hard worker, too. George wondered how long it would be before one of the canal boat captains who hired his hands asked Tony to work for him as a mule driver.

Tony detached the mules from the tow ropes as George began to haul in the rope and coil it on the dock in front of the mules shed. Tony undid the harnesses and pulled the gear off. Then he placed a bridle on each mule and led them off to the side. He spoke to them as he walked and made sure they were picketed before coming back to get the harnesses. He shoved his arms through the gear, lifted it and carried it into the mule shed.

George watched Tony drop the fall board from the mule shed to the pier. The younger boy disappeared into the mule shed. A few moments later, he led Ocean and King Edward out of the mule shed and onto the bank with the other mules.

George looked down and saw his mother step out of the family cabin with Elizabeth.

"George, your sister and I are going into town for some food. Let your father sleep. He's been worried since Sharpsburg and hasn't slept much."

His father had turned oddly silent after viewing the carnage at Sharpsburg. It was very much unlike him. George was curious how bad it had been, but his father wouldn't let him leave the *Freeman* while they were near Sharpsburg.

George nodded. "That's fine. I can make the arrangements with the basin master to take on a load of coal when he comes around."

"I know you can." She kissed him on the cheek. "We should be back soon. Make sure that Thomas doesn't get himself into trouble."

George rolled his eyes. Keeping Thomas out of trouble was like trying to keep the wet out of water.

He looked around and saw Thomas sitting with the mules and Tony pouring a bucket of grain into the portable feed trough.

George watched his mother and sister walk away, heading into Cumberland. Thomas and Tony waved to the women as they walked by on their way into town.

George climbed up on top of the family cabin and sat under the canopy. He counted the boats waiting to take on coal. Seeing as how the basin closed up for the day, it would be sometime tomorrow before they were able to get moving again.

Captain Tanner of the *Union Belle* walked over to the *Freeman* from his boat, which was tied up two boats ahead of the *Freeman*.

"Where's your father, George?" Captain Tanner asked.

"Sleeping, sir. He had the night shift," George told him.

Tanner scratched his whisker-stubbled chin. "I heard about what happened in Sharpsburg. Anyone you know killed in the fighting?"

George shook his head. "Most of the fighting was outside of town. I didn't hear about anybody in town getting killed, but our house and some others burned down. The town's a mess right now."

"That's a shame, but at least our boys sent the Rebels running back across the river. I was going to take your father for a drink in the Waterman's Tavern."

"In Shanty Town?"

Captain Tanner nodded.

"He wouldn't go there, sir. He never goes into Shanty Town," George said.

Captain Tanner laughed. "Never say never, George. Your father and I have shared a drink or two in Shanty Town. He's Irish, like yourself, George. Whiskey is like mother's milk to him."

Mother's milk? George had never seen his father take a drink.

"Tell him his old friend Jimmy Tanner was by to see him."

George nodded. "I will, sir."

Captain Tanner walked away. George watched him go, feeling confused. Captain Tanner had been talking about a man George didn't know. It certainly hadn't been his father who Captain Tanner was talking about. His father had told him that he never went into Shanty Town. It was too dangerous and rough and no place for a decent man, his father had said.

George walked across the fall board to where Tony and Thomas were talking.

"Tony, you live in Shanty Town, don't you?" George asked.

Tony squirmed. "I guess you could say that."

"What's it like?"

"Mean," Tony said quickly. He frowned at the thought of it.

"Mean? How can a place be mean?"

"It's not the place. It's the people who live there and come there. I'll be glad to leave it one of these days," Tony said.

"If you want to leave it, why don't you sign up to crew on one of the canal boats?" George asked.

Many of the canal boats were actually owned by the boatyards that built them since the boats were too expensive for many people to purchase. The boatyard owners also hired crews to run their boats.

Tony shook his head. "When I leave here, I don't want to come back. I'm saving money to go to California. I heard that they found gold there a few years back. I don't need much to live on. I figure to buy me a train ticket and go out there with a couple of big sacks."

"Train?" George shook his head. "You'd better not tell that to

Papa. He hates the railroad. He'd give you a long talking to about travelling by train."

Tony blushed. "I'll remember that."

George looked around. Across the river was Virginia, a place that was supposed to be filled with enemies. They had come across the river and destroyed his home. Men had died by Antietam Creek, Dunker's Church and Miller's cornfields; thousands of men, according to his father.

But his father had lied to him. He had been to Shanty Town.

His father had gone to drink in Shanty Town and nothing bad had happened to him. Why shouldn't George be able to go there as well?

George had heard the stories from other boys about the whiskey, taverns, and women in Shanty Town. A lot of people went there. Why shouldn't he? He had seventeen years old for two months now. He was a man and should be allowed to make his own decisions.

He was old enough to fight, kill, and die in this war. Why wasn't he old enough to decide about Shanty Town for himself?

"Thomas, Papa's asleep. Mama said to let him sleep because he needs the rest," George told his younger brother. "You stay here with the boat. Mama and Elizabeth should be back in a couple hours. I'm going into town. I'll be back before too long."

George turned and started to walk away.

"George, Cumberland's that way," Thomas said, pointing north.

"I know," George said and he kept walking toward the southwest.

Hugh awoke feeling refreshed. The first thing he noticed was that the boat wasn't moving. They must have reached Cumberland. He was surprised that he had slept through the morning but not disappointed.

He sat up and stretched. It felt good to finally sleep without seeing all of those dead men in his dreams. He'd had the same dream the last three times he had slept. He'd kept seeing visions of the killing field as he had seen it at sunset with the red glow of the setting sun reminding him of blood as it fell across the corpses.

Last night he had slept, though, and what a glorious, grand feeling it was!

Hugh parted the curtain and looked outside. It was early afternoon. He wondered how long the *Freeman* had been tied up at the wharf. He had gone to bed after they had gone through the lock at Oldtown.

"Alice?" he called. When there was no answer, he called, "George?"

Still no answer.

Someone scurried across the hatch covers. Thomas dropped down so suddenly in front of him. Startled, Hugh jumped back.

"Hi, Papa," Thomas said cheerily. He sat down on the race plank and looked in the window.

"Afternoon, son," Hugh said, grinning.

"Papa, it's not fair that I have to wait around while everyone else gets to go into town," Thomas said, frowning.

"I'm not in town."

"But you were asleep. That doesn't count."

Hugh ran his hands through his light brown hair and scratched his head.

"Are you by yourself?" Hugh asked.

Thomas shook his head. "No. Tony's with me. We're fishing in the canal."

"Then why do you want to go into town? Fishing's a fine way to pass the time. It certainly beats shopping in a dress shop."

"Fishing's great, and I don't want to go into town. I just don't think it's fair that I can't," Thomas explained.

Hugh closed his eyes and slowly shook his head.

"Go fish, Thomas," he said.

Hugh walked out of the stateroom. Alice had left a pot of coffee on the warm stove. Hugh threw some more coal on the fire to get the fire going and heat up the coffee. Then he poured himself a hot cup of coffee. He took a sip. It was strong.

He took the cup of coffee outside with him and sat down on the top of the family cabin.

He watched Tony and Thomas fishing in the canal basin. They didn't seem to be having much luck, but they were smiling. They looked so much alike that they could have been brothers.

"Fitzgerald!"

Hugh looked around and saw Jimmy Tanner standing on the mule shed of his boat, waving his arms at him. Hugh hesitantly waved back.

What did Jimmy want? The man was a drunkard who was a bigger gossip than a woman at a church quilting bee. It was amazing that the man could even steer a canal boat. He was probably one of the reasons that the Canal Company forbid drinking on the canal.

Jimmy hopped off the mule shed and limped across the fall

board to the pier. Then he hobbled over to the *Freeman*. Years ago, a canal mule had kicked Jimmy in the knee while he was in a drunken stupor. Jimmy had been so drunk that he hadn't even felt pain, though the kick had broken his knee.

"Your boy told me you were asleep," Jimmy said.

"I just got up," Hugh told him.

"I heard about your house. Sorry situation." Jimmy clucked his tongue and shook his head.

"Thank you."

"I thought we might go over to the Waterman's Tavern and share a few tales over a whiskey," Jimmy suggested.

So that's what Jimmy was after. He wanted gossip fodder. Not that not having facts would stop Jimmy. Even if the man had the facts, he was known to overlook them if they didn't work well with his stories.

"I don't go into Shanty Town, Jimmy," Hugh said.

"Of course you do. I've been with you a time or two in the Waterman's Tavern."

"Jimmy, if I ever went into Shanty Town, Alice would skin me alive."

Jimmy scratched his head. "Well, I thought for sure that it was you, Fitzgerald. Are you sure? You're getting older, you know. Maybe your memory is not what it was."

"I'm only thirty-four, Jimmy. You're seven years older than me. If anyone's memory is going, it's yours," Hugh told him.

Jimmy slowly shook his head. "You do live in Sharpsburg, don't you?"

Hugh chuckled. "Not anymore, but I will again. We'll rebuild the house as we get the money."

Jimmy scratched his chin. "Well, I've got to think on this. I believe I'll go to the Waterman and drink...think things over."

And most people thought that the Irish were drunks!

Hugh sipped his coffee and watched Jimmy limp away toward Shanty Town. He was sure that the canawlers in the Waterman's Tavern would soon be hearing tales of Antietam from Hugh Fitzgerald as told by Jimmy Tanner. Of course, the tales would only last as long as the whiskey would.

Hugh leaned back and took another sip of coffee.

Elizabeth and Alice returned just about the time Hugh finished his coffee. Elizabeth rushed onto the boat to show him some cloth and ribbons she had bought for a dress that she wanted to sew, undoubtedly to impress Abel Sampson.

So much for Elizabeth becoming a canawler. She was growing up and becoming a woman. Not that Hugh would be any less proud of her, but he would miss the tomboyishness of his only daughter. By next season, she and Alice would no longer would want to travel on the canal because it wouldn't be fitting for a lady. That would mean that she and Alice would both start staying at wherever they would be living next year. Hugh would miss them. He would miss them desperately.

Hugh slid off the roof and kissed Alice on the cheek as she came aboard.

"What are you doing?" she asked.

"Just enjoying the day...and life." Seeing all of the dead men at Sharpsburg had scared him. How many of them had expected to die that day? Hugh had decided he wasn't going to take any day for granted, especially while this country tried to hold itself together.

"Where's George?" Hugh asked.

Alice shrugged. "I left him here. He said that he would make the arrangements with the basin master for a load of coal."

"I thought he went into town with you." Alice shook her head.

Hugh turned toward Thomas. "Thomas, didn't you tell me that George went into town with your mother and sister?"

Thomas shook his head. "No, Papa. I told you that he went into town, but he left after Mama and Elizabeth. He was going toward Shanty Town."

"Shanty Town?"

Thomas nodded.

"Why would George go into Shanty Town?" Hugh asked.

Tony stood up and said, "He was asking me about Shanty Town right after Captain Tanner left."

Tanner. Hugh sighed. Jimmy must have said something that reawakened George's curiosity about Shanty Town and its taverns.

"How long ago did George leave?" Hugh asked.

Tony thought for a moment. "About half an hour after Elizabeth and Mrs. Fitzgerald left."

"That would have been about an hour ago," Alice added.

"Then I'd better go fetch him before he gets himself into trouble," Hugh said.

Hugh set his coffee cup on a hatch cover and started across the field to Wineow Street. He had no idea where to start looking. He wanted to find him quickly, though. Shanty Town was no place for a young boy. River rats and railroad riff-raff frequented the small collection of shops and taverns. This was where the men and women who were unacceptable in Cumberland called home, and it wasn't unusual to find a dead body lying in an alley in the morning.

There were a few stores in town that catered to canawlers and railroaders. Hugh had been to them on occasion for fittings or equipment, but he doubted that was where George would be. No, George would want the thrill of being in a tavern and those were the places that were the most dangerous.

The first tavern he came to was the Rail and the River. Hugh stepped inside and let his eyes adjust to the dim light inside. When they had, he scanned the crowd, looking for George. There was an argument going on over a card game at one of the tables. However, Hugh didn't see his son.

Hugh ducked outside and moved onto the next saloon. He had no luck there or at the next one either.

In the fourth tavern, the Queen's Crown, Hugh almost didn't see George. The crowd was loud and rowdy and was primarily railroaders. Hugh saw his son surrounded by a crowd of men who were making the most noise in the tavern. They were laughing and slapping George on the back. Four empty whiskey bottles sat on the bar in front of the crowd. As Hugh watched, the bartender brought another bottle and George paid for it. Now Hugh knew why the crowd was surrounding his son. They were sucking the money out of him.

Hugh pushed his way between the six men surrounding George and grabbed his son by the arm.

George turned. He saw his father and he barely registered his presence. When he opened his mouth to say something, Hugh smelled whiskey on his breath.

"Hi, Papa!" His words were slurred.

"Let's go back to the boat, George," Hugh said.

He tugged at George to get him started moving.

"Don't leave us, Georgie Boy," one of the men said, pulling him back to the bar.

"He has to get ready to work," Hugh said diplomatically. Most of the men surrounding George were railroaders and Hugh didn't want to anger them unnecessarily.

A flurry of voices objected to George leaving or at least his money.

"We don't want him to leave yet. I've only had two drinks,"

another man said.

"I'm sorry," Hugh said, his voice tightly controlled.

"How about he goes and you stay," one of the men said. "The boy was running out of money anyway. You can take his place."

Hugh tried to separate himself from the crowd but they were keeping tight around him.

"I'm sorry. His mother is waiting for us," Hugh said. He tried to keep the anger from his voice. He wanted to lash out at these railroaders, but they outnumbered him. It was more important to get George out of the tavern and back to the safety of the boat.

The men laughed, which only made Hugh angrier.

"Let's go, George," Hugh said to his son.

Hugh wished he knew these men, but they were railroaders not canawlers. Not only were these men generally hostile to canawlers, they had found a young boy to fleece.

It was just one more reason for Hugh to hate railroaders.

Hugh pushed toward the door, but the crowd wasn't parting for him. So Hugh pushed harder. The bearded man he pushed stumbled and fell back into a table. The table tipped over, dumping the man on the floor.

Hugh pulled George through the opening and headed for the door. The bearded man got back on his feet. He seemed a bit unsteady. He was probably just as drunk as George was.

The bearded man spun Hugh around and punched him in the face. Hugh staggered backward and grabbed his nose. It was bloody but not broken. It throbbed painfully, though.

"If that's your best, you'd better go home. My son could hit better than that," Hugh said before his better sense could stop him.

The bearded man yelled and charged Hugh, swinging his fist wildly. Hugh leaned to the side. He hooked his arm with the man's swinging arm and with his free arm, Hugh began pounding the man in the side. Then Hugh pushed the bearded man back into the crowd.

"Take your friend!" Hugh shouted.

The crowd yelled and began to charge at him. It helped that they were half a dozen drunken men trying to converge on one man. They ran into one another as they neared him.

A blow landed on Hugh's shoulder and another on his chin. The shoulder punch didn't hurt so much, but the one on his chin slammed his teeth together painfully. Hugh struck out at the closest face and hit the man in the ear.

Hugh tried to back away, but the men were pressing in on him. It wouldn't take long before they organized themselves enough that they would wear him down and then beat holy hell out of him.

Hugh felt a table behind him and tried to move around it. He could use it to keep a couple of these men off of him.

A man leaned in close. Hugh's hands were occupied fending off other blows and so he head butted the man in the nose.

Hugh felt a sharp pain in his stomach and side. He kicked out at whoever was nearest.

Then, surprisingly, the crowd backed away from him. Hugh drew himself up straight and stared at the group of railroaders.

"Did you cowards decide to try a fair fight for a change?" Hugh asked, between heavy breaths.

"No need," one of the men said and Hugh noticed the bloody knife in his hand.

Hugh looked down and saw blood all over his stomach. He'd been stabbed. Something appeared to be pressing through a four-inch slash across his stomach. The amazing thing was that Hugh didn't feel any pain, at least not yet. He did feel weak, though.

What would these cowards do if Hugh faltered now?

Hugh turned toward the door. George was still there. Even in his drunken stupor, George looked scared at what he saw.

"Get help," Hugh told his son.

The room wavered in front of him and Hugh fell to his knees.

"Go!" Hugh ordered his son.

The last thing Hugh saw before he blacked out was George running out of the tavern.

24

THE END OF A DREAM
SEPTEMBER 1862

George staggered out of the Queen's Crown and into the middle of Wineow Street. He slipped in a mud puddle and nearly went sprawling into the street. He had to run forward to keep his balance until he was able to stand again. He was breathing hard, though he hadn't run anywhere.

He turned back to the tavern, tempted to go back inside.

What could he do, though?

He hadn't even been able to help himself when he had gone into the tavern earlier. The railroaders had zeroed in on him and surrounded him. They had pretended to be his friends only as long as he had bought them drinks. When he had tried to leave, they had gotten angry and begun pushing him around. His money had been running out when his father had come to his aid.

If his father hadn't come in, would the railroaders have attacked him like they had his father?

They had stabbed his father!

George shook his head, trying to clear the fog that his four drinks had cast over his mind.

He had to get help for his father!

What should he do? He couldn't think clearly!

He needed to get back to the canal boat. He mother would be there and she would know what to do. She could get help for his father.

George staggered through the street, heading for the river. He saw the *Freeman* and he saw Tony sitting on the ground near where the mules were grazing.

"Tony! Go get the sheriff!" George called.

Tony jumped to his feet. "What's wrong?"

"Railroaders in the tavern stabbed Papa. Get the sheriff!"

"Is your father dead?"

George shook his head. "Not yet, but he's hurt!"

Tony grabbed George's arm. "Then they'll be long gone,

George. Even if you could get the sheriff, the men wouldn't be there when he came. We need to get your father to a doctor."

George saw his mother come out of the family cabin. "What are you yelling about, George?"

"Papa's hurt!"

"Where is he?"

"He's in Shanty Town."

Tony spoke up. "George and I will get him, Mrs. Fitzgerald. We'll bring him back here, but Mr. Fitzgerald's going to need a doctor. Can you find one in town who will come to the boat?"

"Yes," she said without hesitation.

"Then hurry up and get him while George and I get Mr. Fitzgerald," Tony said. His stern expression showed how serious the situation was.

Tony grabbed George by the arm. "Can you take me back to the tavern where your father is?"

George and Tony ran back into Shanty Town. As they neared the Queen's Crown, George saw his father lying in the street. The two boys hurried over to him. George rolled him over. He was unconscious.

"Grab him under the arm and let's get out of here!" Tony said.

George leaned over, his head swimming and grabbed his father under the arm. He saw the gaping wounds in his father's stomach. The wound was filthy with mud. George almost gagged.

He looked over at the tavern instead, but he couldn't see anyone beyond the dark doorway.

His father looked so pale and his stomach and legs were covered with blood. It seemed too much blood for a person to have lost.

Tony knew as soon as he saw Hugh that there wasn't hope for him, not unless the doctor was better than Tony thought he would be.

Tony and George half dragged/half carried Hugh to the *Freeman*. As they drew closer to the canal boat, Tony called out, "Elizabeth!"

His sister came out of the mule shed, shading her eyes to see George and Tony.

"Lay out some blankets on the hatch covers!" Tony said.

The doctor was going to need room to work and cabin on the canal boat was too cramped.

Elizabeth ran across the race plank and into the family cabin. She came back out with her arms filled with blankets. She quickly spread them out on the hatch covers in a thick pallet.

Tony and George carried Hugh across the fall board and laid him on the hatch covers. Tony thought that Mr. Fitzgerald looked unnaturally pale.

"We're going to need some clean sheets for bandages," Tony said.

"I'll get them," Elizabeth volunteered.

"Is he alive?" George asked. Tears were in his eyes.

Tony watched Hugh's chest move up and down as he breathed. "Yes." Only Tony wasn't sure how much longer he would be alive.

"What happened to Papa?" Thomas asked.

"Railroaders stabbed him," George answered sharply.

"Why?"

"Because they're bad men."

Tony saw Alice pull up in front of the boat in a carriage. She climbed out quickly and led the doctor onto the *Freeman*.

The middle-aged doctor rolled up his sleeves and began to examine Hugh's wounds, moving the loose pieces of flesh and organs around.

"I need a bucket of clean fresh water," he said.

Elizabeth rushed off to get it. The doctor ripped open Hugh's white shirt exposing his chest and stomach. His hands moved quickly over Hugh's body, probing for additional wounds. When Elizabeth came back, the doctor wetted a cloth in the water and washed off Hugh's wound.

The hole began to fill with blood again, but not as quickly as Tony thought that it should. He thought that was a bad sign.

"I'm going to have to stitch him closed. It doesn't look like any of his organs were damaged, but he's lost a lot of blood," the doctor said.

"Will he live?" Alice asked.

The doctor shrugged. "I don't know. He's lost a lot of blood already. I wish I'd been able to get to him here quicker."

The doctor opened his bag and took out a needle and thread. He was threading the needle when he stopped and leaned down next to Hugh and sniffed. Tony could smell it, too. Hugh had voided himself. Tony also knew what that meant. He had seen it happen to other men who had run afoul of Shanty Town.

The doctor lifted Hugh's hand and felt for a pulse.

He set Hugh's hand down and looked at Alice and shook his head.

"No!"

She bent down and grabbed Hugh's face in her hands. "Hugh Fitzgerald, don't you die on me. Not now! Hugh!"

There was no response.

"Is Papa dead?" Thomas asked.

Elizabeth wiped away her tears and took her brother by the hand. She tried to lead him away, but Thomas resisted, dragging his feet.

"I don't want to go," he complained.

"Come with me, Thomas. You can have a piece of apple pie, but only if you stay in the cabin," Elizabeth promised.

"But what happened to Papa?"

Elizabeth's voice hitched as she tried to keep from crying anymore. She led Thomas away without saying anything.

"I'm sorry, Mrs. Fitzgerald," the doctor said.

Alice was sitting next to Hugh with her head on his chest.

George stood off to the side staring at his father's body. He seemed to be in a daze. Tony wondered if it was because he had been drinking.

Tony also stared at the body. He had seen dead men before. You didn't live in Shanty Town and not see dead men, but looking at Hugh was different. Hugh Fitzgerald had been his friend. He had been a man who cared for Tony in a way no one, including his mother, had cared for him.

Tony shook his head. It wasn't right.

Tony wanted to scream at George and call him a fool. If he hadn't gone into Shanty Town to try and prove something to himself, his father would still be alive. Tony stared at George and wondered if he realized that.

Even more to blame were the railroaders. Tony wished he knew who they were. Then he realized that even though he didn't know who they were, he knew where they drank and they would return there eventually when they were sure the sheriff wouldn't come after them.

"I'll send an undertaker over to collect the body," the doctor said as he closed his bag.

Alice finally looked up and nodded.

"Is there a reverend you would like me to contact?" the doctor asked.

Alice shook her head. "We're canallers...canawlers. We never went to any one church."

"I'll find someone," George said.

185

"Who?" his mother asked.

"Reverend Jackson is on Washington Street. His son is a can-awler. He would help out." Tony thought that George's voice sounded too calm for a boy who had just lost his father.

Before his mother could say anything, George turned and slowly walked away. Tony watched him go and wondered if George even realized where he was.

"Is there anything I can do for you, Mrs. Fitzgerald?" Tony asked.

Alice looked at him as if seeing him for the first time.

"No, Tony. Thank you, but I guess you'd better go home," she said.

What home? Tony thought. He was living in a lean-to next to the river. It wasn't a bad place to be during the summer, but he didn't know what he would do when the weather changed.

"I could sit with you so you won't be alone," Tony offered.

Alice shook her head. "I'm not alone. My Hugh is here and it will be the last time I get to spend with him for awhile."

Tony turned and walked back across the fall board. He had intended to go back to his lean-to, but as he crossed Wineow Street, he stopped.

Tony spun around and ran back to the *Freeman*. Alice didn't even look up as he ran to the family cabin. Inside, Elizabeth was crying softly while Thomas ate his apple pie and stared at her.

"Can I have some lantern oil?" Tony asked.

Elizabeth looked up. "I suppose. We keep a small barrel in the hay house."

Tony went back outside and walked reverently behind Alice and Hugh. He climbed into the hay house window and saw the barrel. Tony opened the barrel and dipped an empty bucket into it. Then he resealed the barrel and left.

He wondered if he would be suspicious walking down Wineow Street with a bucket of oil. It was getting late, though, and men were more interested in getting their drinks or women than in paying attention to one small boy.

Tony saw the Queen's Crown and peeked inside the door. The railroaders were back. They knew the law couldn't reach them here. Tony moved to the side. He splashed some of the lantern oil in front of the doors. He hesitated to see in anyone noticed. No one did. He then splashed the rest of the oil on the walls and under the windows until the bucket was empty.

He stepped back off the boardwalk and stared at the tavern.

Should he do this?

The men inside had killed Hugh Fitzgerald for nothing, but did they deserve to die? Was he the one who should be doing this?

Who else would do anything about it?

The sheriff didn't come into Shanty Town and the Fitzgeralds had other things on their minds. How would justice be served?

He listened to the laughter and loud voices the railroad from inside the tavern. Didn't they care what they had done to a good man?

Tony reached into his pocket and pulled out a box of matches that he used to light his campfires at night. He struck one and tossed it under a window.

The flame caught and spread quickly along the front of the tavern. Now people began to notice the flames and stop and point. The voices in the tavern changed from happiness to fear.

One drunk man staggered through the doors and the flames. His clothes caught fire, but the man didn't even notice that he was on fire at first. When he finally did, he began to scream and run wildly down the street. People dodged away from him, not wanting to be caught in the flames.

A few people on the street tried to throw water on the flames around the tavern, but most of the building had caught fire and it was spreading to the rest of the tavern quickly.

Tony backed away.

He was satisfied. The Queen's Crown would be in ashes. If the men inside died, then it was justice. If they got out, then it was God's will.

Tony turned and walked away.

Alice sat next to Hugh's body holding his hand. She barely noticed the sun setting and didn't even bother to light a lantern.

She had stopped crying. She was out of tears.

"Hugh," she whispered.

She didn't expect an answer, but saying his name helped her hold onto him.

She watched the undertaker stop his wagon in front of the boat. The old man hopped from the wagon and walked slowly onto the boat. He stopped in front of her and removed his hat.

"Mrs. Fitzgerald, my name is Charles Howard. Dr. Vance sent me to you," the old man said.

Alice took a deep breath and nodded.

"Where will you take him?" she asked.

"My parlor is on Decatur Street just past the intersection with Baltimore Street. You can return with me if you choose," Howard offered.

Did she want to see Hugh prepared for burial?

"He doesn't have a suit," Alice said.

Howard nodded slowly. "Arrangements can be made."

"My son went to find a reverend. When they return, we'll come to your parlor."

That way, at least, she would have some support if she couldn't stand.

Again, Howard nodded. "May I take the body then?"

Alice stood up and smoothed out her dress. "Yes."

Howard walked forward and folded the blankets over Hugh. Then, with a slight grunt, he lifted Hugh up in his arms and carried him back across the fall board. Alice was surprised that the old man was still so strong. Howard gently laid Hugh in the wagon bed and drove off.

She watched the wagon until it turned a corner and went behind a building.

Alice sat down, shaking her head.

Hugh was gone. She couldn't believe it. This couldn't be happening! It had to be a bad dream.

What was she going to do now?

She was a thirty-four year old widow with three children. Her home was gone. Her husband was dead and she had little savings. She could sell the boat, but she wasn't sure it would bring in enough money for her and the children to live on and she still wouldn't have a home.

Alice shuddered. There was so much that she needed to do yet.

How would she do it without Hugh?

25

THE TRADITION CONTINUES
SEPTEMBER 1862

Alice, Elizabeth and Thomas wept openly as their husband and father's coffin was lowered into the ground of the church cemetery. George stood silently next to them, silently looking into the grave.

Alice barely noticed the crowd of canawlers attending the funeral. Most of the families who were in Cumberland had attended. A few people, mostly those captains who worked for others, had taken advantage of the absence to jump ahead in the line to get a load of coal and be off for Georgetown.

She listened to the reverend's words and realized that she didn't even know which church he represented. She hoped that his words would bring her some comfort from God. She didn't find it. Hugh shouldn't be dead. He had only gone to collect George from Shanty Town. He'd been doing what a father should do. How could someone die from doing a good deed?

Someone had told her that the tavern where Hugh had been stabbed, the Queen's Crown, had burned to the ground the night that Hugh had died. The fire had killed four men, four railroaders, before it was put out. She could almost imagine that the fire had been caused by Hugh's anger at the railroad striking the first spark. Alice didn't consider herself a hateful woman, but she couldn't mourn the deaths of the railroaders. If the dead men hadn't been men who had killed Hugh, they had been men who had been at the tavern and done nothing to help Hugh once he was stabbed. The railroaders had thrown Hugh's body out into the street as if he had been nothing more than a piece of trash.

Reverend Jackson finished his service and people began to move around. Some left for their boats. Many of them came by and offered their condolences to her. She accepted their words without comment.

Morgan Taft approached her dressed in an expensive black suit and took her hands in his.

"Mrs. Fitzgerald, you have my sympathies at this distressful time," Taft said.

"Thank you."

"I know this is a terrible time for you. I would like to offer my assistance," the older man said in a voice heavy with sorrow.

"How so?"

Taft smiled behind his bushy beard and mustache. "Well, my dear woman, I can imagine that with the loss of your husband, your source of income is gone. In addition, the cost of this funeral will certainly have hurt any savings the two of you might have had."

He paused, expected Alice to say something. She didn't, although he was accurate. She wanted to hear what else he would say. She was also trying to rein in her building anger at this man.

"I would like to buy your canal boat. It would strap my own cash reserves to be sure, but it is the Christian thing to do for you."

"Why?" It was the only word she could trust herself to say without losing control.

Taft drew back a bit. "Why? I just said…"

"You barely know me, Mr. Taft. Why should you want to endanger your own cash reserves to help me?" Alice asked sharply.

"Because it's the…"

"Profitable is the word I think you want to use." Taft already owned five boats on the canal and he was looking to purchase more from war widows. Doing the Christian thing was the last thing that he wanted to do for the widows. He typically paid an owner half of what a boat was worth, if that.

Alice said, "I've decided to run the boat myself. My children and I have lived on the *Freeman*. It has been our second home. Now it is our only home. We are going to continue working on the canal as we always have. We are canawlers."

Taft looked shocked. "I admire your courage, Mrs. Fitzgerald, but you are a woman with three children and you will be traveling along the border between the Union and the Confederacy during a time of war. That seems quite foolish to me."

"How foolish would it be to sell our best chance of earning a living? With the *Freeman*, I will have an income from hauling coal and I'll have a home on the boat. As for the war, having a man aboard, no matter how good a man, would not stop the war." She paused to catch her breath. "If you'll excuse me, I have to leave now to change and get ready to work."

Alice turned and walked away. Elizabeth, Thomas, and George followed her.

George paused in front of Taft and said, "My mother won't be without a man on the canal, Mr. Taft. I'll be with her."

Taft chuckled. "You're not much more than a boy, George."

"I'm old enough to fight in this war."

Taft cocked his head to the side and said, "But you're not, are you?" Then he walked past George.

Alice put a hand on her son's arm. "Come along, George. Mr. Taft is just angry because he can't get the *Freeman*."

As she turned to continue walking, she saw, Tony standing near the grave. He was dressed in a clean white shirt and a pair of worn black pants. She had never seen him dressed so nicely.

"Tony?"

Tony looked up. She saw tears in his gray eyes. "Yes, ma'am."

"Thank you for coming, I'm sure my husband would be glad to know you remembered him," Alice told him.

"I'll always remember him, ma'am. He was a good man and I liked him a lot."

"I'm going to be taking the *Freeman* to Georgetown."

Tony nodded. "I guess I'll see you in a week or so then."

"Would you like to come with us?" she asked.

Tony's eyes widened and she knew she had asked the right question. She was going to need help and Tony had already learned what he needed to know to work on the canal. He would be a good hand. Hugh would have been proud to see him working on the canal, particularly on the *Freeman*.

"Why?" Tony asked.

"I could really use some help from someone I can trust." Tony smiled. "I can't pay you much, but you'll have room and board."

Tony nodded quickly. "I'd like that very much."

26

THE UNDERGROUND RAILROAD MEETS THE C&O CANAL
SEPTEMBER 1862

Tony adjusted quickly to life as a canawler. He had been watching the canawlers for months and studying what they did. It was as if he had been preparing for this time. Working for Mrs. Fitzgerald on the canal wasn't much different than the work he'd done for Mr. Fitzgerald in Cumberland. He only wished that Mr. Fitzgerald could see how well he was doing on the job.

Surprisingly, what Tony had the most trouble getting used to was the relative quiet of the canal. Oh, he heard birds singing and the river running at times and conversations aboard the boat. But where were the thousands of voices that he was used to hearing in the background? Where was the clang of the church bells ringing out the hours? Where were the sounds of clopping hooves and creaking wagons?

Having a soft bed in the family cabin on the canal boat was a big advantage to sleeping on the ground or under his mother's bed. He slept on the top bunk in the family cabin above Thomas. His bunk was his own space. He kept his cash can, the holder of his future, stowed under one corner of the straw tick in his bunk.

Mrs. Fitzgerald fed him well, too. Tony had grown to like turtle soup. At first, he had only eaten it so as not to offend Mrs. Fitzgerald. Now, he looked forward to her or Elizabeth serving it with cornbread.

He put a thick slice of ham between two pieces of bread and went outside to see the setting sun. George was steering the boat while Elizabeth drove the mules on the towpath. Tony climbed onto the roof of the family cabin and sat to eat.

He watched another boat approach them going west. The mules passed each other first on the towpath. The other boats' mules stopped and gave Elizabeth, King Edward, and Jigger the right of way since it would be easier to restart an unloaded boat than a boat sitting low in the water with 120 tons of coals in its holds.

The Cumberland-bound boat drifted toward the north side of the canal as the *Freeman* began to pass. Then the boat suddenly changed direction and headed right toward the *Freeman*! It looked like the corner of the boat would smash into the side of *Freeman*.

"They're going to hit us!" Tony yelled, pointing to the boat.

George pushed the tiller to the side so that the *Freeman* actually turned into the other boat. Tony thought that he was crazy. Did he want to crash?

The boats hit, the boards creaked and cracked, and the *Freeman* shuddered. The impact sent Tony rolling off the roof. He landed on his backside on the cargo hatches.

The boats slid apart and passed each other.

Alice ran out of the family cabin. "What happened?"

"The *Jaybird* hit us. They would have sunk us, too, but I turned the *Freeman* so we only hit broadside," George said.

"Why did they hit us at all? We have the right of way!"

"I'd like to know that, too." George turned around and yelled, "Why did you hit us? Are you crazy? You could have sunk us!"

There was a young boy at the tiller talking to Harv Tomlinson, the captain of the *Jaybird*.

"Sorry, George. It wasn't part of the plan. Billy's still pretty new to this. He was trying to give you a wide berth, but there's a deadfall in the water that he was trying to miss, too. I guess he couldn't miss both of them. Are you taking on water?" Tomlinson called.

"I can't tell until we either sink or offload. I think we're fine."

Tomlinson nodded. "Good. Good. I'll be more careful about how Billy gets his experience. He'll be much better the next time we pass."

Tony hoped that wouldn't be for quite some time.

When the *Freeman* stopped in Williamsport for the evening, a man came to visit Alice. Tony thought the man looked like a gentleman. He was well groomed and dressed in a suit. Tony wondered if Mrs. Fitzgerald was courting someone less than a week after her husband had been killed. After talking for a short while, the two of them walked away.

Now where are they going? he wondered.

Tony was asleep in his bunk when Mrs. Fitzgerald returned to the boat. Thomas was asleep in the bunk below him and Elizabeth was sleeping in her mother's room where she now shared the bed with her mother since Tony slept in her former bunk.

Because Tony was so uneasy in the silence along the canal, the sound of the door to the family cabin opening woke him.

Mrs. Fitzgerald came into the family cabin and looked around as her eyes adjusted to the dark. Then she opened the doors to the pantry that opened into the space under the cockpit.

Tony was about to say something to her when two men quietly entered the cabin. He kept his mouth shut and watched from the bunk instead. He felt oddly like he was under his mother's bed watching her entertain her men friends again. He hoped that the same thing wasn't about to happen.

Mrs. Fitzgerald began handing items off the bottom pantry shelf to one of the men, who gently sat them on the table in the middle of the room. When the shelf was empty, the man helped Mrs. Fitzgerald lift the shelf out of the pantry. She pushed away the back wall of the pantry. The man who had been helping her motioned to the other man who crawled into the opening and behind the false wall that his the space behind the shelves.

"I know it's cramped, but my children don't know about this," Mrs. Fitzgerald whispered.

"I understand, good lady. He has experienced worse," the man who was still visible said.

"Are you sure you don't want me to take him to Hancock?"

The man shook his head. "No, the Confederate sentiment there was stirred up by the recent battle near Sharpsburg. It would be too dangerous for the young man. Besides, someone is waiting at Weaverton to help the young man on his way."

"Well then, Weaverton it is."

Tony watched Mrs. Fitzgerald and the remaining man replace the shelf and the food items. Then she closed the doors on the pantry.

The man stood and tipped his hat to her. "God be with you, Mrs. Fitzgerald."

"Not with me, but hopefully with the young man in the pantry. He's the one who needs God's assistance," Alice said quietly.

The stranger left and Alice stood alone in the dark. She looked over at Tony. For a moment, he thought that she knew he was awake. She said nothing and walked into her room.

In the morning, Tony noticed how Mrs. Fitzgerald kept glancing at the pantry, especially when Elizabeth opened the doors to get out something she needed, such as flour.

Tony kept trying to find a chance to talk to Mrs. Fitzgerald alone, but it always seemed as if someone else was around. Since she had said Thomas, George and Elizabeth didn't know what she did, he didn't want to expose her. What he did want was an explanation.

Finally, he saw her hanging laundry on the line between the family cabin and the hay house in the early afternoon. Thomas was brushing and feeding Seamus and Ocean in the mule shed. Elizabeth was walking the mules and George was at the tiller.

"Mrs. Fitzgerald?" Tony said.

She smiled at him. "Hello, Tony."

It made him so happy to see her smile once again that he almost forgot what he wanted to talk to her about. He didn't want to see that smile leave her face, especially if he was the cause of it leaving.

"Mrs. Fitzgerald, I need to talk to you about something," he said after a moment.

"What's that?"

"First, I'd like you to promise that you won't be mad at me."

Alice stopped hanging up the laundry. "Now that sounds like something Thomas would say right before he tells me something that deserves punishment. Is there a reason that I might be mad at you?"

Tony shrugged. "I'm not sure, but I like being on the canal with you and your family. I don't want you to leave me in Cumberland when we get back there."

She reached out and brushed his hair out of his face. "I wouldn't do that, Tony. You've been a big help on the boat."

"But I saw something last night, something you don't want George, Elizabeth, and Thomas to know about," Tony admitted.

In that moment, he saw the realization of what he was talking about dawn in her eyes.

"So you were awake?" Tony nodded. "I was afraid that might happen sometime, but I always thought it would be Thomas. When Michael asked for my help, I couldn't say no."

Tony didn't know Michael, but he assumed that it was one of the two men he had seen last night.

"I wasn't sure what I was seeing last night, but I've been thinking about it this morning. Is the man in the pantry a slave?" he asked.

"Not anymore," Alice said quickly.

"If you get caught..."

Mrs. Fitzgerald nodded. "I know. That's why it's important not to say anything about what you saw last night to anyone."

"But why would you want to risk your boat and your freedom to help a nigger?" Tony asked.

"Tony!" Alice scolded.

"Well, he is."

"That's a crude term. He's a negro."

Tony rolled his eyes. "He's a slave, ma'am, an escaped slave, and his being on board could get you arrested," Tony warned her.

She gave him a sideways glance. "I'm not going to say anything to cause that. Are you?"

The answer didn't require Tony to think much. "No."

"And why is that?"

"Because I don't want to get you in trouble."

"Why?"

"Why?" That was an unexpected question and gave him pause. "Because I like you. You and Mr. Fitzgerald helped me out when I needed to get away from Cumberland."

Alice patted him on the cheek and smiled. Then she said, "Just like Hugh and I helped you because you needed it, I am helping the young man in the pantry because he needs my help."

"But he's not a person. He's property."

Alice looked surprised. "Not a person? Have you ever seen a slave, Tony?"

"Not close up." Certainly no one in Shanty Town had owned one.

Alice nodded her head toward the family cabin. "Follow me."

They walked into the room and Alice closed the door behind her to give them some privacy. She opened the doors to the pantry and reached between the shelves and knocked on the false wall. The panel swung back and Tony found himself staring at the blackest face he had ever seen.

The slave scuttled backward as far as he could.

"It's all right," Alice reassured him.

She passed him a plate of food left over from breakfast. The slave moved toward the shelves and took it from her hands.

"Are you all right?" Alice asked.

"Yes, ma'am," the man whispered as he gobbled down the food.

"Just make sure that when you dump your waste bucket out the window that there's no other boat nearby," Alice told him.

The slave nodded. "Yes, ma'am."

He passed the clean plate back to her. She took it and backed away from the pantry.

"We should be to Weaverton in another day," she said.

Then she stepped back and shut the pantry doors.

Alice looked at Tony and asked, "Did you get a good look at him?"

"Yes, ma'am."

"Did he have two eyes, a nose, and a mouth?" Tony nodded. "Hair on his head? Ten fingers and toes? Does he walk on two feet?" Tony nodded again. "Then how does he differ from you?"

Tony's eyes widened in amazement. How was the slave different? Was she blind? "He's black as the night, ma'am."

"So the color of his skin makes him different inside?" Mrs. Fitzgerald asked him.

"Uh-huh."

"Then what happens when my children turn brown under the summer sun? Do they become different? Or what about Thomas, who usually turns red from sunburn? Are they slaves because their skins become darker?" Alice questioned.

Tony looked at his feet. "No, ma'am."

"That's right. And when Thomas's red skin peels off, he's still the same boy. It's not what's outside that makes a person, Tony. It's a man's soul, their connection to God, that makes us what we are."

Tony nodded. "Yes, ma'am."

He wasn't sure that he agreed with her, but he knew Mrs. Fitzgerald was a good woman so he considered what she said. He certainly understood the need to be free. How long has be saved his money and planned on leaving Cumberland to be free from his mother?

And now he had. At least for awhile.

Alice seemed satisfied with his agreement. She bent over and kissed him on the cheek. Tony blushed.

She left to finish hanging her laundry, leaving Tony in the cabin. Tony sat at the table and cut himself a slice of blueberry pie. He started to eat it and then stopped. He cut a second piece and laid it on a plate.

Tony opened the doors to the pantry.

"Hey, you in there," he called softly. "Do you want a piece of pie?"

The false wall slid back and Tony saw the black face staring eagerly back at him. The man's eyes danced back and forth between looking at Tony and at the pie.

"Yes, sir."

"I'm not a sir. I'm just a kid," Tony told him.

He passed the soon-to-be ex-slave the pie. The man quickly ate it and smiled. Tony studied him as he ate. The slave was a man, and if he was, didn't that mean that he had a soul?

"That was good," the black man said, licking his fingers.

Tony smiled. "I'm glad that you liked it. Mrs. Fitzgerald made it."

"She's a good woman. Yes, she is."

"She is," Tony agreed.

Tony took back the plate and closed the doors. He frowned as he thought about what it meant to be a slave and how dangerous a journey the man had made.

Could Tony have done it? He doubted it.

Did that mean his will to be free wasn't as strong as this man's? His mother hadn't held him in chains and yet Tony had remained obediently under her bed as if he had been chained there.

Tony heard the brass horn blow the notes for "Lock ready. Lock ready. Lock ready."

He walked out onto the race plank.

"We're coming into a lock," George said. "Do you want to help with the lock doors?"

"Yes."

Tony walked toward the hay house to check the hawsers and throw them ashore as they neared the lock. Throwing the heavy ropes was going to put muscle on him by the end of the season that was sure.

The funny thing was that Tony didn't want the season to end.

Tony slept lightly. He opened his eyes occasionally to make sure he wasn't missing anything.

Alice slipped out of her room sometime after midnight. She went outside to check on something and then came back into the cabin.

She opened the pantry doors and began taking items off the shelf.

Tony slipped out of his bunk and squatted down next to Alice. She looked at him and smiled. Tony didn't say anything. He took a jar of flour from her hands and set it quietly on the table.

Together, they emptied the shelf and pulled it free.

"Come on out. It's time to move on," Alice whispered.

The black man slid under the remaining shelves and sat up. He smiled at Tony and Alice.

Alice moved to put the shelf back, but Tony shook his head.

"I'll put this away, ma'am. You go ahead and get him where he needs to go," he said.

Alice smiled. "Thank you."

The slave reached out and shook Tony's hand. Both of the man's big hands swallowed Tony's hands in the clasp.

"Thank you, boy who thinks he's too young to be called sir."

"My name's Tony."

"Thank you, Tony."

"What's your name?"

"Walter."

"Good luck, Walter."

Walter stepped back and went out the door.

"I won't be long," Alice told Tony. "I saw the lantern marking where I need to go. I need to escort Walter to him."

She left the cabin and Tony replaced the items back on the pantry shelf and closed the doors. About the time he was finishing, Mrs. Fitzgerald returned.

She sat down and whispered, "It's a relief that that's over with."

"If it's such a relief, why do you do it?" Tony asked.

"Because it's the right thing to do."

He sat down in a chair beside her. "Is Walter going to be all right?"

Alice sighed. "He should be if he gets to Canada."

"Canada?"

Alice nodded. "If he's caught in the United States, he's subject to the Fugitive Slave Law, even if he's in a free state."

"But we're at war with the South," Tony reminded her.

"There's that to consider, but would you want to risk your freedom on that chance?"

Tony shook his head. "No, ma'am. I guess not."

She reached out and patted his hand. "You did well, Tony. I'm proud of you."

Tony beamed at the compliment. "Thank you, ma'am."

27

BECOMING A MAN

SEPTEMBER 1862

By the time the *Freeman* left Georgetown, riding high in the water, Tony had had his first chance to tour Washington City. He'd found it exciting and larger than Cumberland. It was filled with more people than Cumberland and many of them were soldiers. It seemed as if it was the center of the world with all its hustle and bustle.

He had visited some places with the Fitzgeralds. Other times, he took off by himself and explored to those places less frequented by respectable people. Still, even with the city's grand buildings and crowds ripe for the picking, Tony hadn't wanted to call the city home.

He had been tempted at times to abandon the Fitzgeralds altogether and strike out on his own. One afternoon while they were still waiting to offload their coal and the Fitzgeralds had gone to visit Congressman Sampson, Tony had even packed up some supplies with the intention of leaving.

He barely got a mile from the wharf before he noticed a family—two boys and their parents—walking along the street. He stopped and watched them. Although they looked nothing like the Fitzgeralds, the family reminded Tony of the canawlers.

It was the family bonds he was seeing, not the physical similarities. These were people who cared about each other; people who had committed themselves to each other.

Tony suddenly felt a longing within him. At first, he thought that it was hunger pains. He was used to those. These feelings were in his chest, though. He wanted, not food, but to see Mrs. Fitzgerald smile at him, to hear George compliment him on his work coiling a line, to eat a delicious apple pie that Elizabeth had cooked and to run and play with Thomas.

He turned back to the wharf. He had already found a home.

A day out of Washington City, the Fitzgeralds stopped for the night at the Great Falls Lock because they had gotten a late start in the day getting out of Georgetown.

They tied the *Freeman* up next to the lock house, which also served as a tavern. Once they were ashore, Thomas led Tony down a well-worn path out onto the rocks to look at the falls.

Tony watched the Potomac River rush over the ledge and pound the rocks below. He had never seen such power in water. If he had been standing on those rocks, he would have been crushed as flat as a piece of paper. It amazed him.

"It's a good thing you don't try to use the river to travel," Tony said when he saw the powerful falls.

"Couldn't even if the falls weren't there," Thomas said.

"Why not?"

"Well, the river flows east. We'd certainly get here quick enough, but how would we get back? It would be the mules fighting against the river current," Thomas asked.

"Canal boats could be paddle wheelers," Tony suggested.

"That would burn the coal we're supposed to be moving and it couldn't get past spots on the river like this. A canal boat wouldn't work on the river either because it's not built to navigate a river."

Tony was surprised that Thomas sounded so knowledgeable about what types of transportation would work on the river.

"Why not?" Tony asked.

Thomas shrugged. "I'm not sure. Papa…" Thomas paused and almost cried at the mention of his father's name. "Papa used to tell me that. I think it has something to do with how canal boats are built. Because they are built to move a lot of coal, they can't move around in a river quickly. George would know better."

Tony nodded.

Thomas pointed to something across the falls.

"Do you see that?" he asked.

Tony looked. He thought that he could see some cut stone and timber walls near the river.

"Is there a canal on the other side of the river?" he asked.

Thomas nodded. "Part of one. George Washington tried to build a way for boats to go upstream and around the falls. He built locks on the Virginia side to skirt the falls."

"So why aren't there any boats going through that way?"

"Because the Potomac's too hard to navigate like I told you. There are too many rocks and shallows to use it for travel."

They stared at the water rushing over the rocks for a little while longer and then made their way back to the canal. As they walked across the lock doors, Thomas eyed the pigs in the pen near the tavern. He grinned.

"Want to do something fun?" Thomas asked.

Tony looked around. "That depends on what you call fun."

"Just watch what I do and be ready to grab a ride!"

Thomas walked over to the shed and scooped a handful of grain from the feed bin and dropped it in a small pile outside of the pig pen. He opened the gate and waited. The half a dozen pigs inside milled around until a large one noticed the open gate and the grain. It walked out and began eating.

Thomas quietly closed the gate. He moved up beside the pig and suddenly jumped on its back and grabbed its ears.

The pig squealed and took off running with Thomas bouncing on its back.

"Thomas, what are you doing?" Tony yelled.

"Pig riding," the boy yelled gleefully.

The pig swerved back and forth, running wildly and squealing. Some of the tavern patrons began to come outside to see what was going on and causing the pig to squeal. As they saw Thomas hanging onto the pig's back, they laughed and pointed at him. Thomas bounced up and down, barely maintaining his balance on the frightened pig.

Alice walked out of the tavern where she had been buying some fresh milk from Roberta Thompson, the wife of the lockkeeper. She saw Thomas and yelled, "Thomas Jefferson Fitzgerald, you get off that animal right now!"

"I can't let go, Mama!" Thomas yelled back.

"You will or I'll make you run like you're making that pig run. I'll make you squeal louder than him, too!" Alice threatened him.

Some of the spectators laughed at that.

Thomas let go of the pig's ears. The pig made a sharp turn and sent Thomas tumbling in the dirt. He rolled into a sitting position and sat up, grinning. Some of the spectators applauded.

"Thomas, what were you doing?" Alice asked as she ran to him.

"I was showing Tony how to ride a pig."

Alice turned to look at Tony. "You're not going to try that now, are you?" It was more of a threat than a question.

Tony shook his head as he blushed. "No, ma'am."

"Are you all right?" Alice asked her son as she brushed dirt off of his clothes.

"I'm fine. You should have let me stay on, Mama. I could have tamed him," Tony complained.

"You could have also broken your head wide open if you had fallen on the ground wrong," she scolded.

"But I only fell because you told me to let go."

Behind Alice, George laughed. "You should have let him ride, Mama. I've seen lots of kids in Georgetown do it. None of them got hurt."

Alice spun around and faced George, her eyes wide. "Excuse me, I am the mother here."

"But I'm the captain..." George started to say.

"Captain? Captain of what? Certainly not the *Freeman*," Alice snapped.

George looked worried. "Well,..."

"When your father died, the *Freeman* became my boat and I know how to steer the boat as well as you. I am the captain of the *Freeman*."

"But you're a woman," George said.

"Yes, I am, and there are women captains on the canal or hadn't you noticed that?" Alice nearly shouted at him.

She glared at all three of the boys. "All of you get back on the boat."

Thomas, Tony and George trudged back to the canal boat. Tony wondered what would happen now. He had never seen Mrs. Fitzgerald angry before. What would she do to them?

"Your mother is very mad," Tony whispered.

"She gets that way sometimes," Thomas told him.

Thomas certainly didn't seem very worried, but George was trudging along as if he knew he was going to be beaten when he got back on the boat. That's what Tony would have expected if his mother had been as angry as Mrs. Fitzgerald was.

But nothing happened when they arrived back inside the family cabin.

When Alice came into the family cabin, she took the stew off the small pot-belly stove and began filling the bowls on the table.

"Sit down, all of you. It's time to eat." She paused. "No, don't sit down. First, all of you go wash your hands, especially you, Thomas. You were holding onto that animal's ears."

"But Mama, it's my mouth that will touch the food. Not my hands," Thomas complained.

"Thomas..." she said sternly.

Thomas quickly stood up from the table. He trudged over the

small table by the wall as if he had just received the worst punish-ment in the world and washed his hands. Tony and George did the same thing once Thomas had finished.

George felt himself getting more anxious the further west they moved. They were moving closer to the Crabtrees' lock. They hadn't been able to stop at the lock on their way east because it had still been early in the day and his mother had been rushing to get the load of coal to Georgetown.

Now, though, it was late in the day and they could easily push on and get close to the Crabtree lock house. His mother didn't run the *Freeman* all night any longer, which meant if they stopped close enough to the lock, George would be able to visit Becky.

He wouldn't suggest to his mother that they stop, though. He wouldn't want her to do the opposite just to prove to him that she was captain of the *Freeman*.

He still couldn't believe how she had embarrassed him at the Great Falls Tavern! She had treated him just like he was a boy like Thomas or Tony.

His father wouldn't have done that.

But his father was dead and that was his fault. Everyone knew it, though no one said it. They said the railroaders had killed him, but if it hadn't been for George being so childish, his father wouldn't have gone into Shanty Town. So maybe his mother was right to treat him like a baby.

His mother came out of the family cabin, wiping her hands on her apron. She looked to the west to see how low the sun was and then at the land around her.

"We're about six miles from the Crabtree lock, aren't we?" Alice asked George.

"Yes, ma'am," he said stiffly.

"Let's push onto the Crabtrees' house and tie up beyond the lock. Then we'll be able to get started right away in the morning."

"Whatever you say."

He wanted to cheer, but he didn't want his mother to think that she was doing any favors. It didn't really matter, though. He was going to see Becky again. Maybe she would make him feel better.

Alice looked at him and sighed.

"I thought that you would be happy to hear that," she said.

"I am."

"You'd better show it better when you see her."

His mother was trying to show how clever she was at guessing what he wanted. Did she know that he would trade having Becky's love if he could have his father back?

"Is that an order, Captain?" George asked sarcastically.

"No, it's a suggestion, son." She frowned. "George, when you're an adult, you can make your own choices. Right now, though, you are still a young man and my responsibility. As for contradicting something I told your brother, well, Thomas is definitely a child and I am his mother. You are his brother. It is my responsibility to decide what is best for him, not yours."

"I'm a man, Mama." George couldn't even convince himself when he said that.

She held up a finger. "You're a young man, George. There's a difference."

"Not much. I could fight in this war or take on a man's job like steering this boat."

His mother put her hands on her hips and stared at him. "It doesn't take a man to get into a fight; it takes a man to walk away from a fight. As for your job making you a man, I can also steer this boat, but I am certainly not a man," she told him.

George looked away from her. "You don't understand."

"I do. You're anxious to grow up and you feel like I won't let you."

"Yes," George groused.

"Perhaps that's part of the reason, but another part is certainly that your own actions have shown that you are not grown up yet," Alice told him.

She went back into the family cabin.

George wanted to yell something back at her, but he felt it would just support what she had said about him. How could he prove to her that he was a man? How could he prove it to himself?

As they moved through the lock an hour and a half later, George noticed Union soldiers standing around the lock with Mr. Crabtree.

What did they want?

"Are you going to tie up here tonight, Alice?" Lucas Crabtree asked his mother. Mr. Crabtree had addressed her as the captain of the boat.

The comment caused George to wince since he was at the tiller and not his mother.

"I planned on it, but it looks like you might be crowded around here tonight," she said, nodding toward the soldiers.

"They're one of the Union patrols watching the river and canal. We usually give them a good home-cooked meal when they come by. It helps encourage them to check up on us and make sure that we're all right." Lucas grinned as if he was knew something he wasn't saying.

"Maybe I should help your wife do some cooking then," Alice offered. "She must have her hands full to feed everyone."

"She's got Becky helping, but if you and yours want to stay, I guess a couple extra hands won't hurt. The soldiers brought a deer with them so I've got some venison roasting out back, too."

The west lock doors opened and Elizabeth had the mules pull the boat out of the narrow lock. George steered the boat over to the towpath. Tony and Thomas were quick to lay out the fall board and they each took one of the remaining mules in the mule shed ashore.

Alice said to George, "I'm going over to help Mrs. Crabtree with supper. I'll take Elizabeth with me, too. You boys can join us when you've got everything taken care of here."

George nodded. His mother crossed the fall board and called to Elizabeth. Together they walked down the towpath and crossed over to the Crabtree lock house on the closed lock doors.

Tony was unhitching Jigger and Ocean while Thomas picketed the other two mules in a place that would be out of the way if another canal boat came along.

George set up the portable feed bin, jabbing the pointed post into the ground. Thomas ran back on board to get the feed for the mules.

"Hurry up," George told him. "I want to see Becky."

"Don't worry, George," Thomas told him. "If you're not around, I'm sure one of these soldier boys will be happy to fill in for you with her."

George picked up a rock off they towpath and heaved it at his brother. Thomas dove into the hay house and the rock banged harmlessly against the boards.

Becky wouldn't do that to him!

She knew how George felt about her. She had accepted his carving. She had kissed him!

Still, the soldiers didn't know that he and Becky were nearly engaged. They might have other thoughts about the matter.

"When Thomas decides to show his face, have him fill the feed bin. Then you two can come over to the lock house," George told Tony.

Tony nodded. "Can I go fishing instead?"

"Why? Don't you like venison?"

Tony shrugged. "I've never had it."

"It doesn't taste gamey, not the way Mr. Crabtree cooks it. He likes to use lots of spices like they did in the taverns in Baltimore when he lived there."

Tony shrugged again. "I just like to fish."

"Well, don't be late for supper. Mama will be mad."

Tony grinned. "I'm never late for a meal."

George chuckled and walked away. He nearly skipped across the lock doors in anticipation of seeing Becky again.

Would she greet him with a kiss? He hoped so. He'd been looking forward to another kiss from her for weeks.

She probably wouldn't with all the soldiers around. She would smile at him. He was sure of that. She could do that and it would be enough.

He walked into the lock house since the front door was open. Two soldiers were in the front room talking as they relaxed on chairs. George walked to the kitchen at the back of the first floor. His mother, Elizabeth, and Mrs. Crabtree were cutting vegetables and preparing some meat.

"Is the boat set?" his mother asked.

"Yes, ma'am." He looked around. "Where's Becky?"

"I'm not sure. She was here just a moment ago."

"She's out back setting the big table since we have such a crowd for supper this evening," Mrs. Crabtree said.

"I think Private Conason went with her," his mother added.

George hurried out the back door. Becky was laying out plates on the large wooden table that Mr. Crabtree had made years ago. A young soldier was holding the stack of plates and handing each one to her as she laid them out on the table.

"Becky?" George said.

The looked up and smiled. "Hi, George. It's going to be like a party around here tonight with everyone that's here."

"We're on our way to Cumberland."

Becky turned to the soldier. "Jeff, this is George Fitzgerald. He and his family are canawlers. George, this is Private Jeff Conason from New York. He's part of the border patrols along the river."

George stared at the soldier. He looked to be about George's age. He was a couple inches taller than George was, but he was as skinny as a rail.

"How long have you been here?" George asked.

"We walked in about an hour or so ago," Conason said.

"Not here at the lock house; here in the area."

"Oh, my company is stationed in Oldtown. We've been here since late last year."

"Jeff was at the battle of Sharpsburg," Becky said. "George lost his home in the battle, Jeff."

Conason frowned. "I'm sorry. It was a very bad day for everyone on both sides."

Becky finished with the plates and began laying out the utensils. Thomas came walking around the side of the lock house.

"When do we eat? I'm hungry," he asked.

"Soon. Everything is just about ready." Becky turned to Conason. "Can you finish setting the table while I go get the bread?"

"Sure."

The soldier began laying out the utensils and Becky went into the lock house.

George watched the soldier for a few moments and then asked, "How old are you?"

"Seventeen."

"Have you really seen a lot of fighting?"

Conason shrugged. "Sharpsburg was the worst. A lot of my friends died. Most of the rest of my fighting has been trying to keep smugglers from crossing the river."

"I found a couple dead soldiers not far from here back in the summer," George said.

Conason nodded. "That would have been Richards and Tooley. Snipers got them. Mr. Crabtree gave us their wallets. There's been at least one Reb group of spies on this side of the river. We shot one of them a couple months back, but there were at least two more with that spy. That's who we're mainly on the lookout for; spies and watching out to see if General Lee tries to come back north."

Becky came back out with two fresh-baked loaves of bread. She set them on the table next to the unicorn that George had carved for her. He hadn't noticed it on the table before now.

"Oh, that smells good," Conason said.

"I see you still have your unicorn," George said.

Becky looked at it and then at George. "Yes, I like to keep it out where people can see it."

"That's a cute toy," Conason noted.

"It's not a toy," George said defensively.

Conason picked it up and turned it around in his hand.

"Of course, it is. It's something like a father would carve for a kid to play with. I thought it was for a little brother or sister of Becky's."

Or something that a boy would carve for a girl he loved, George thought.

"I have a younger sister," Becky said.

That was her defense? Why didn't she say that George had carved it for her? Did she expect George to say something? It was her gift and her place to defend it.

Instead, she simply took the unicorn and shoved it into her pocket, looking embarrassed as she did it. She knew she was hurting George. She had to know. She just didn't care.

"I'm going to start bringing out the food. Why don't you go collect everyone back here?" Becky said to Conason.

When the soldier left, George said, "Why didn't you tell him that I carved the unicorn for you?"

"I didn't want to embarrass you."

"It wouldn't have embarrassed me. It would have made me proud to hear you say that I had made it for you," George told her.

Becky shrugged. "I'm sorry, George, but it is just a toy."

George blinked without saying anything. He stared at her. He couldn't believe what she had just said, but she had said it. She considered his gift of love nothing but a toy.

He shook his head and turned and walked away.

"George!" Becky said from behind him.

He ignored her. He certainly didn't want to hear her make up an excuse. She had told him the truth. She didn't know how special he had considered that unicorn. She didn't care.

He considered going back onto the boat, but he thought that she might follow him there. He walked to the river instead. Tony was sitting on the bank, fishing. He seemed quite content being alone. George wished that he felt the same way.

"Hi, George," Tony said, waving his hand. "Is it time for dinner?"

"Yea, they're getting it ready now ," George told him.

Tony pulled in his line and wrapped it in a ball. "I wasn't having much luck anyway. I guess I will have to try venison. I hope that Mr. Crabtree prepares it as good as you said."

George sat down on the bank and stared out onto the water.

"Aren't you going to eat?" Tony asked.

George shook his head. "Not hungry."

"I heard you say you were starving."

"Well then, I lost my appetite."

Tony walked over and stood next to George. "Did something happen?"

George just wanted Tony to leave. He wanted to be by himself.

"Not to you, Tony. Everything's fine for you," George said.

"But for you things are miserable," Tony suggested.

George nodded. "That's right."

"I admit you've had it tough this summer, losing your father and your home, but you haven't had to go through it alone. Your family has been here to help you."

"They can't help with this."

"That's only because you probably won't let them. I've had to live on my own, George, and you were right when you said things aren't bad for me. They aren't bad for me because I've got people around me like your mother and you to help me."

"Go away, Tony," George said, waving the younger boy off.

Tony sat down and pushed a worm onto the hook of his fishing line.

"I think I'll just sit here and fish for awhile."

"Supper's ready," George reminded him.

Tony shrugged and tossed his line into the water. The line slapped the water and then sunk. "I'll catch us a big bass and we'll have us a tasty dinner, just the two of us."

George tried to ignore him, but when Tony got a bite on his line a few minutes later, George couldn't ignore him.

"Whoa!" Tony said as he started pulling back on the line.

"Hurry up and land him," George told him.

"I'm trying. I could use some help."

George reached out and grabbed the twine and began pulling it in. A bass jumped out of the water and George pulled it onto the bank. He ran forward and grabbed it before it could flip itself back into the water and swim away.

"It's a beauty," Tony said proudly.

"Sure is," George said, smiling.

"Now we just need to get a fire going."

"I'll do that," George said. "Why don't you go back to the boat and get some fruit and vegetables, pepper and butter to go with this?"

Tony nodded. "I'll do that."

George suddenly realized that he wasn't thinking about Becky any longer. Tony had tricked him. No, not tricked him. Tony had just directed George's attention elsewhere.

As Tony started to walk away, George said, "Tony."

Tony turned around. "Do I need to get something else?"

George shook his head. "I just wanted to say thanks."

Tony smiled. "I'm glad I could help. Fishing gives a person time to think and decide what's important."

28

THE FORTUNES OF WAR
OCTOBER 1862

David and McLaughlin stood at the edge of the woods staring at the barn about fifty yards away. David couldn't see any movement around either the barn or the wooden farm house beyond the barn.

"I think they're gone," David said.

"It doesn't matter if they're gone or not as long as they don't see us, City Boy," McLaughlin said.

David winced but didn't say anything. His relationship with McLaughlin was fragile. The corporal obeyed him only when it followed McLaughlin's interests. Colonel Collins hadn't given him another man in their detail and had refused to switch McLaughlin for anyone else.

Of course, after Sharpsburg, David was surprised that he and McLaughlin had still been sent back into enemy territory to spy on the Union.

The colonel had showed no sympathy for David's predicament.

"Corporal McLaughlin's a soldier of this army, Lieutenant. He will obey an officer," Colonel Collins had told him.

"But he doesn't, sir."

"Then perhaps you had better learn to command."

David started across the field, keeping the barn between him and the house so that it would be harder for anyone in the house to see them. They reached the barn without any sort of alarm being raised. McLaughlin grinned widely.

"I want a chicken," he said.

"I would be happy for half a dozen eggs," David said.

"Well, when I get my chicken, I'll squeeze the eggs out of it for you." McLaughlin made a strangling motion, clenching his fists as if he was squeezing a chicken's neck.

They moved around the corner of the barn, parted the doors, and slipped inside. There were two horses in stalls, but the stalls that held the cows and goats were empty.

"The wagon and horses are still here," David said. That meant that the owners were home more than likely.

"Then we'll be quiet."

They moved through the barn to the other side. The chicken coop was next to the house with about ten yards of space between them.

"That's too close," David said. "They'll see us for sure."

"I want to eat roasted chicken tonight," McLaughlin insisted.

Their diet this past week had been dried beef and coffee. They had had some hardtack early on, but that was long gone. David would have had them go into Williamsport and buy food, but each of them only had Confederate scrip, which wasn't likely to the welcomed there.

"What's going on here?"

David and McLaughlin spun around. A man, probably the farmer, was standing at the doors where David and McLaughlin had entered. He was holding his rifle and staring at them.

McLaughlin, who was already holding his pistol out, raised it and shot the man in the chest. The farmer groaned and fell to the ground.

"What are you doing?" David yelled. He looked back and forth between the dead man and McLaughlin.

"He was going to shoot me," McLaughlin said simply.

"He was protecting his farm."

"I was protecting us."

A young boy about twelve years old came running into the barn. "I heard a shot, Pa. Was it..."

He saw David and McLaughlin and slid to a halt. Then he saw his father lying on the ground. McLaughlin calmly raised his pistol and shot the boy through the head.

David nearly screamed as the sound of the shot echoed through his head.

David turned and wrestled the pistol away from McLaughlin. McLaughlin pushed him away and shoved the pistol into its holster.

"He was just a boy," David yelled.

"They are the enemy, City Boy. We must kill the enemy if we are to win this war," McLaughlin said. David could tell that the man felt no remorse at all for the two murders.

"Go get your chickens," David told him. "I want to leave here as soon as possible."

"What are you going to do?"

"Bury these two. They deserve that at least."

McLaughlin shrugged and walked out of the barn. David

looked around among the tools and found a spade leaning against the wall. He took it and went out back of the barn and began digging a hole.

What had they become? They had started out as soldiers. Then they had become spies for their country. Now they were thieves and murderers. This was not how the war was supposed to be. This was not part of what his father had told him that a soldier should be. It was certainly not a part of any of the stories his grandfather had told him when he was a boy. George Washington had not been a thief and murderer.

The least he could do was to make sure that this father and son had a decent Christian burial. He could show that much humanity. He would leave a marker and a note about what had happened.

He found his rhythm and the shoveling became easy. It also kept his mind off of why he was digging the hole.

A woman's scream brought him out of his thoughts. David dropped the shovel and looked around. Then he realized who it was he had heard. Father and son were inside the barn. Where was the mother? She had still been in the house!

David ran onto the porch of the house and through the front door. The room was empty. He ran through the other rooms on the ground floor and found them empty as well.

He heard another yell and headed upstairs. As he stepped through the doorway of one of the bedrooms, he saw McLaughlin. The Tennessean was lying on top of the farmer's wife. David couldn't see her face. All he saw was her dark-haired head shaking back and forth. McLaughlin's pants were down around his knees and the woman's skirt had been ripped off and was lying on the floor. She was struggling to push the larger man off her.

In his anger, David drew his pistol and put it against the back of McLaughlin's head. Then he pulled back the hammer.

McLaughlin stopped moving immediately.

"What are you going to do? Are you going to kill me, City Boy?" McLaughlin asked.

"If I have to." His voice was steady. He was surprised that he felt no fear at shooting his companion. "Now get off her."

"She's seen us. She'll give the Northerners a description of us."

"They already know that we're around or have you forgotten Sharpsburg?"

David stepped back, keeping his pistol pointed at McLaughlin. The Tennessean rolled off the woman and stood up. He bent down and pulled his trousers up and slipped the suspenders over his shoulders. The woman wrapped herself in the blanket on the bed and sobbed. David kept his attention off her and on McLaughlin.

"I was done anyway," McLaughlin said.

At that moment, David wanted to smash the man's teeth in and make that smile disappear.

"Let's go," David said, nodding his head toward the door.

"What about her?"

"What about her? It doesn't matter that she's seen us, so have the patrols. Even if they know what we look like, they have to catch us, which they haven't been able to do," David said.

McLaughlin grinned. "That's because of me, City Boy. You need me."

David nodded. "That's right. I need Corporal McLaughlin of the Confederate Army. What I see is a rapist who General Lee would have shot dead already."

McLaughlin still had enough shame to look at the floor when David mentioned General Lee. The Confederate Army loved their commander, but Robert E. Lee was also known as the ultimate Southern gentleman. He would not have held to this type of behavior.

"So what are you going to do?" McLaughlin asked.

"We're going to leave here and you're going to start acting like a soldier. If you want to start acting like a soldier again, then I'll treat you like one. If you can't act like a soldier who would make General Lee proud, I'll kill you."

McLaughlin glared at him. "No. I'll kill you," he said calmly.

David believed him, but he didn't care. David shrugged. He had already realized that was a strong possibility.

"Perhaps. Or perhaps you'll remember your duty to your state. Either way you're going to leave here now. You decide how," David said.

McLaughlin smiled and David wondered if he had slipped up somehow.

"I didn't think you had it in you, Lieutenant."

"If we are going to be independent from the North, we have to show that we're worthy of governing ourselves."

McLaughlin raised an eyebrow. "By not having women?"

"Not the way you were treating her. Act like General Lee would. That's the way a Southerner should act," David told him.

McLaughlin walked by him and out the door.

David looked back at the sobbing woman. He was ashamed to

be here, ashamed not to be doing more, and ashamed to have been a part of all of this. She was lying on the bed with a blanket drawn up to her neck. She probably didn't even know her husband and son were dead yet. They had just destroyed this woman's life.

"We'll be going soon, ma'am," David said before he left. He paused and added, "I'm sorry about everything that's happened."

The two soldiers walked downstairs and outside the farm house. David ushered McLaughlin toward the barn.

"You're going to bury the men you shot before we leave," David told the corporal.

They walked behind the barn. McLaughlin picked up the spade and began shoveling out the hole that David had started digging. As McLaughlin threw dirt to the side, David stepped back so that he could watch the farm house in case the woman came out.

He didn't want to have rescued her only to have her come after them with a loaded rifle.

He saw an odd movement out of the corner of his eye. He didn't try to figure out what it was. He dropped to the ground and rolled to the side. When he looked up, he saw McLaughlin raising the shovel to hit him on the head.

David jumped to his feet and dove forward. He hit McLaughlin in the stomach and pushed him back against that barn wall. In a moment, David's pistol was out of its holster and in McLaughlin's face.

"This is twice. You don't get another chance," David threatened.

"The Good Book says to turn the other cheek," McLaughlin said.

David grinned wickedly. "I did that, but I've only got two cheeks and you've slapped them both. You may not respect me, but I don't rightly respect you either. Don't tempt me, mister. I will live or die by my word. I'm giving you a chance at life. Why don't you take it?"

"Now I see why they made you a lieutenant," McLaughlin said, grinning.

"No, they made me a lieutenant because I'd gone to the University of Virginia. My father made me this mean," David corrected him.

McLaughlin laughed despite the fact that he had a pistol pointed at him.

"You ain't seen mean. My father made mean, too. I wonder if I'd gone to college if they'd have made me a lieutenant,"

McLaughlin said.

"They still might. I'm not a soldier, and I don't particularly want to be one."

"Neither did I."

"Nor do I want to be a dead man."

"Nor do I." McLaughlin laughed. "Listen to me saying 'nor'. You might think I was a gentleman." He got control of himself. "It's fine, Lieutenant. Maybe you're interesting enough to keep around for a bit."

David looked at him and slowly back away giving McLaughlin some room to continue his digging.

"Maybe then you're useful enough to keep around for a little bit," David said.

29

DECISIONS
OCTOBER 1862

By the time the *Freeman* reached Georgetown in early October, George was in a sour mood. He knew he was in a bad mood, but he didn't care, much less try to change his attitude. He growled at Tony and Thomas and muttered around Elizabeth and his mother.

He still hurt from the way Becky Crabtree had treated him around the soldiers, especially Private Conason. She had swooned over the soldier like...like a little girl. George hadn't even looked for her when the *Freeman* went through the Crabtree lock on their way to Georgetown. He had stayed in the hay house and hadn't even come out to help lock through the canal boat.

He didn't want to see Becky. George didn't want to talk to her. Let Becky come and apologize him to him for the way she had acted.

She hadn't. She still considered him a boy.

At least his mother had reason to think of him as a boy. It had been George's foolishness that had led to his father's death. George still had dreams about how his father had looked when he turned to tell George to get help. His father's shirt had been bloody around the belly and his father held in his own entrails with one hand. George has seen fear in his father's eyes. George had never seen his father afraid before then, and it had been the last time that he had seen his father alive.

George was at the tiller when the *Freeman* came into the tidewater at Georgetown to offload.

"Just because we're off the canal doesn't mean you can run the mules!" George snapped at his brother who was walking the mules.

Thomas ignored him. The mules weren't moving any faster so Thomas had nothing to worry about. He knew his job and was doing it.

"There's no need to yell," Elizabeth said. She was sitting on the roof of the family cabin reading her school lessons.

"I'm at the tiller right now, so I'm the one who decides how things run on this boat," George told her.

Elizabeth simply rolled her eyes and went back to her lessons.

They tied up at the wharf and George felt at a loss for what he should do now. His mother would make the arrangements with the wharf owner and the Canal Company. All he had to do now was wait until it was time to offload their shipment of coal.

He thought about taking a nap, but if he slept, he would dream about his father and Shanty Town. He didn't want to do that.

He walked along the wharf for awhile, not talking to anyone. Most of the crews were gathering into the family cabins for dinner. He could see the lanterns were already lit now that the days were getting shorter. He sat down on a wall and looked down river. He could see a large ship out in the river. He couldn't tell whether it was a warship protecting the city or a freighter waiting to take on coal.

He walked back to the *Freeman* about half an hour later. He could see the lantern light on in the family cabin and assumed everyone was on the boat eating supper. George didn't feel hungry and he certainly didn't feel like hearing their conversations, so he went to his bunk in the hay house.

He had barely climbed inside when Elizabeth opened the shutters and climbed inside with him. She sat down across from him and closed the shutters.

"What do you want?" George snapped.

"I wanted to talk with you," she said quietly as she leaned back against the wall and looked at him.

George stared back at her without saying anything.

Finally, he stood up and said, "Well, it's been great talking to you, but I've got to go." He opened the shutters behind him, making ready to go out the window.

"Sit down, George."

"Don't you understand? I want to be alone," he said over his shoulder.

"You've wanted to be alone since you saw Becky flirting with the soldiers."

"So?"

"She's just a girl, George. I should know because I'm one. She's probably forgotten all about him," Elizabeth told him.

George shook his head. "No. They come by every couple days for dinner. Those soldiers get to spend a lot more time with her than me." He slammed his hand against the wall. "And I was worried about Josh VanMeter."

219

"It's not like there aren't any other girls around here. How many do you know?"

"A lot, but Becky's the one I like."

"You're too young to be thinking like that."

George began to stomp around the hay house. Not that there was much room to move around in. "Too young? You sound like Mama! I'm not a boy, Elizabeth. I'm a man. I'm the same age Papa and Mama were when they got married. I don't need anyone standing around worrying about my feelings and patting my hand to reassure me that everything's all right."

"You act like you do."

He stopped and glared at her. "Well, I don't."

"Then if you want to be considered a man, you had better start acting like one. As long as you act like a pouting little boy, that's how everyone is going to treat you."

George felt his face flush with anger and embarrassment. He pushed past his sister and stepped through the window. Then he walked down the race plank until he could jump on the wharf. He wasn't going to stay on the boat just so everyone could taunt him.

They all blamed him for his father's death. George couldn't help what had happened. He hadn't even been able to protect himself from the railroaders let alone his father. He hadn't been able to do it because ... because he was a boy.

Canawlers were finishing their meals and coming outside for the warm night. Some of the younger boys were ashore grooming their mules and checking their shoes. The farrier in Georgetown usually did a good business in shoeing mules while the canal boats were tied up at the wharves waiting to be offloaded.

George looked at the canawlers. Most of the captains were older men. A lot of the younger captains had gone off to war and their wives were now the captains of their boats until they returned. A lot of the crews were boys Tony's age.

Where were the men George's age? They were fighting in the war.

Dying, his mother would say. Either way, those men were doing what was expected of them. They were defending their country and trying to hold it together. They were being forced to become men.

What was George doing? He was steering a canal boat back and forth between the two armies. He was in the middle of a war and trying not to be part of it.

George shook his head. He walked back to the canal boat. Elizabeth had gone. George closed himself up in the hay house. He reached under his bunk and slid out the wooden crate where he kept his personal things. He took out a piece of paper, jar of ink, and pen. He was supposed to use these for his lessons, but he had another use for them now. He laid the paper on a board and began to write.

Alice and Elizabeth walked through Georgetown to the Sampsons' home. Alice wasn't sure she wanted to leave the boat, but George certainly wasn't willing to talk about all the things that were bothering him, and Elizabeth was anxious to see Abel.

He was growing up and thought no one could understand what he was going through. He needed his father to help him through all this, but that wasn't going to happen. Alice hoped that Eli might have some advice about what she could do to help her son. She had a feeling that he had gone through the same thing when Abel had joined the army.

Alice stopped as she rounded the corner and came in sight of the Sampsons' house. The windows and doors were draped in black.

Someone had died.

"Mama, what's wrong?" Elizabeth asked when she saw the house.

"I don't know. Everyone seemed healthy enough when we were here last," Alice told her.

They hurried their pace to the house. Alice knocked on the door and waited anxiously.

Chess answered the door. He tried to smile, but couldn't manage it. He looked tired.

"Hello, Mrs. Fitzgerald," Chess said.

"What's wrong, Chess?"

"It's Master Sampson. He was killed." Chess's eyes welled up with unshed tears.

Beside her, Alice heard Elizabeth gasp. Alice knew her daughter had been looking forward to seeing Abel. She made a point of visiting him either at the house or at his post on the Alexandria Bridge whenever they came into Georgetown.

"What happened to him, Chess?" Alice asked.

"I think Mr. and Mrs. Sampson tell you. Won't you come in?"

Elizabeth and Alice came inside as Chess shut the door. He led them into the sitting room. Grace was sitting in a chair reading a

Bible. She looked up when she saw Alice.

"Oh, Alice," she said, as tears started running down her cheeks. She closed the Bible and rushed over to hug Alice.

When Grace pulled back, she said, "Please sit down. Chess, could you make us some tea, please?"

"Yes, ma'am."

He left the room and Alice and Elizabeth sat down on the sofa.

"Chess told us that Abel had died. What happened?" Alice asked.

"He was shot."

"Shot? He wasn't in a fighting unit. He was guarding the bridge. Was there fighting that close to Georgetown?"

Grace nodded. "There's been a lot more incidents since the second battle of Bull Run. A sniper shot Abel four days ago. The army thinks a group of Southern smugglers was trying to sneak into Washington City to get supplies for folks in Alexandria."

Alice shook her head and reached over to pat her friend's arm. "Oh, Grace, I'm so sorry."

"We buried him yesterday. Eli is out at the cemetery now."

Alice's pain at losing Hugh was still fresh so she could sympathize quite easily with what her friend was going through right now.

"Is there anything we can do?" Alice asked.

Grace shook her head. "Not unless you can remove the pain."

"If I knew, I would have done it for myself."

Alice and Elizabeth stayed with Grace for two hours. They said very little. They simply tried to share each other's grief. Their tears ran freely. When they finally left, it was just growing dark. Alice promised she would return tomorrow and go out to the cemetery with Grace.

"It's not right, Mama," Elizabeth said as they were walking back to the canal boat.

"No, it's not, but life doesn't have rules," Alice agreed.

"I liked Abel. He was such a nice boy."

Alice nodded. "He was, but nice boys die as easily as bad ones."

When they returned to the boat, Alice saw Tony and Thomas fishing off the wharf. George was nowhere to be seen. He was probably still sulking in the hay house.

In the family cabin, she closed the door and lit a lantern. As the light spread throughout the room, she saw a letter propped up in the middle of the table. Alice picked it up and recognized

George's awkward handwriting. A chill went through her. Why would George be writing her a letter?

She opened the letter and read it quickly. It slipped through her fingers as she realized what it was saying. This couldn't be happening. Not now!

"Thomas!" she yelled.

Alice ran out onto the race plank.

"Thomas, where's George?"

"He went walking into town," Thomas said, unconcerned.

"Where?"

"He didn't say."

Now Thomas was beginning to look nervous, wondering if he had done something wrong.

"What's wrong, Mama?" Elizabeth asked.

"George wrote a letter that said he was joining the army," Alice told her.

Elizabeth took the letter and read it. "No! Why would he do that?"

"He thinks it's what a man needs to do."

From the wharf, Tony said, "He had a sack with him when he left, Mrs. Fitzgerald. I thought it was odd, but then George has been acting odd lately."

Alice shook her head and tried to keep from crying. She had to do something. She had to stop George. She didn't want him to wind up like Abel Sampson.

"When did George leave?" Alice asked.

Thomas shrugged. "Not too long ago."

"Elizabeth, you stay here. I'm going to try and find your brother."

"But you don't know where he went," Elizabeth said.

"I'll find him," Alice said, determinedly.

Alice walked down the street away from the wharf, not sure of where she was going. George would be looking for the nearest recruiting station. Where would it be? She looked for soldiers, but there weren't any on the streets. She shook her head and continued walking. Then she saw a sign calling for recruits in front of a small storefront.

She went into the building. Inside, one man was sitting behind a table. He was a captain in the army. He was signing up a young man, but the young man wasn't George. He looked as young as George, though.

Alice sighed. She hoped that she wasn't too late.

She walked up to the table.

"Excuse me."

The captain looked up and frowned. "Yes."

"I'm looking for my son."

The captain looked at the boy's signature on the form. "Fine, son. You go through that door and there's a man back there who'll outfit and make arrangements for you to be trained. Congratulations for your decision to support your country in her need."

The young man stepped back and gave the captain an earnest, if awkward, salute. The captain returned the salute and the youth went through the side door.

"Now, ma'am, how can I help you?" the captain said to Alice.

Alice leaned over the table. "My son. I'm searching for my son."

"And you believe he joined the army?"

"Yes, he said he was going to."

The captain's brow furrowed. "At this recruiting station?"

Alice shook his head. "No, he didn't say where he was going."

"Was your son of age, ma'am?"

"No he was not," Alice said firmly.

The captain nodded. "Ah, we have a lot of youth like that. God bless them. They want to serve their country."

"And you allow them to join?" Alice said, shocked.

"They don't tell me they are underage when they sign up, ma'am. They list themselves as being older," the captain said, unconcerned.

Alice sighed. This wasn't going to be easy.

"Has a George Fitzgerald signed up with the army then?"

"No, ma'am."

"Aren't you going to look through your papers?"

The captain shook his head. "I don't have to. I've only had four young men sign up today and none of them was George Fitzgerald."

Alice sighed. "Where is the next-closest recruiting station?"

"On K street." He paused. "Do you plan on visiting each recruiting station in Georgetown?"

"If I have to. My son has joined the army when he is underage. If the army won't do something about it, I will."

"Let me ask you this, ma'am. If your son lied about false age, isn't it a good guess that he might have lied about his name?"

Alice stopped and began to cry. She knew the captain was right.

"What am I going to do?" Alice asked.

"There's not much you can do. I have never seen a mother or father find a son who had joined under another name. I've searched through bigger piles of recruits than this and talked to many a recruiter who has also. A boy who wants to serve his country will, ma'am. We lost over 12,000 men at Sharpsburg in just one day. The Union needs all of the men we can get because I have a feeling that this war is going to be lost by the side that runs out of men first."

Alice turned away from the captain and left without saying anything. What was she going to do? Should she look at all the recruiting stations anyway? She didn't think the captain was lying to her. George would have to lie about his age and if he did that, what would stop him from lying about his name?

She cried all the way back to the boat.

When Elizabeth saw her coming, she ran out and helped her find her way to the family cabin. Elizabeth had some water heating up and she made Alice some tea.

"I guess you didn't find him?" Elizabeth said.

Alice shook her head as she took the cup of tea.

"Why did he go?"

"He thinks he needed to prove himself," Alice told her.

"This isn't the way to do it."

Alice nodded. "No, but he thinks it is."

She finished the tea quickly then walked into her room. She laid down on the bed she had shared with her husband only a month ago. How she wished Hugh were here! He would have been able to keep George from running off, but everything Alice had done only seemed to push George toward leaving. She hadn't been able to make him see that maturity did not come with being able to kill another person.

Alice turned into the pillow and cried herself to sleep.

When she awoke in the morning, Alice decided that if George had left to prove himself to her, she had to prove herself to her family. George might be gone, but she still had three children who were depending on her. She had to keep the *Freeman* running. Since their house was gone, they would need as much money as they could get to make it through the winter.

George's leaving caused a problem for her being able to run the boat. She was short her strongest hand. She couldn't afford to hire a hand so she and the children would have to manage as the crew. It would be hard work for them, but they could do it. She could do it.

She shook her head slowly as she sat up in bed. She had wanted Elizabeth to be a lady for so long, and now Alice needed her daughter to act like a man.

Alice dressed in a clean dress and went out in the family cabin. Elizabeth had left warm biscuits and cold ham on the table. Alice slathered a biscuit with honey and went out onto the race plank.

Elizabeth was on the roof of the family cabin reading her lessons.

"How are you feeling this morning, Mama?" Elizabeth asked.

Alice patted her hand. "I'm feeling better. Thank you for asking. Where are the boys?"

"Tony's fishing and Thomas is visiting boys on the other boats."

Joe Norman, the wharf master who coordinated which boats would offload where, stopped in front of the *Freeman*. "Hello, the *Freeman*."

"What can I do for you, Mr. Norman?" Alice asked.

"I came to make the arrangements for you to offload today. Where's George?"

"He joined the army."

"The army? That's surprising. I would have figured George for a navy man myself."

Navy? Alice hadn't even considered the navy, though it would have made little difference. His letter had said he had gone to fight for his country, but he could have joined the navy. Either way, he still would have had to lie about his age and more than likely, his name.

Even if she could find George and bring him home, how could she keep him from leaving again? Would she tie him with a leash to the roof of the family cabin like she would a three-year old? The captain has been right about one thing: a boy who wanted to serve would find a way to serve.

Norman asked, "Are you going to be able to offload your coal, Mrs. Fitzgerald?"

Alice straightened up. "How can you even ask? We know our job. Just tell us when and where. We'll be ready. We're canawlers!"

30

PIRATES
OCTOBER 1862

The trip back to Cumberland was quiet. At least it seemed so to Tony. Everyone was feeling George's absence and trying to deal with it. It wasn't that George had made a lot of noise when he was with the *Freeman*. His running away to join the army or navy had wounded his family and left a hole in their lives that they hadn't filled yet and might never be able to do.

The silence reminded him of how the Fitzgeralds had been just after Mr. Fitzgerald had been killed last month. They hadn't had time to get over that loss and now they were faced with what George had done.

Tony hoped he had a chance to tell George how stupid he was. He had runaway because he wanted to prove he was a man, but his actions only showed that he was more of a child than Thomas was. George had abandoned his family when they needed him.

Tony also knew that George's absence meant more work for everyone else. He did his best to fill in the gaps where he saw them, but he knew he was no replacement for George or Mr. Fitzgerald. Mrs. Fitzgerald has lost her husband and son within a month of each other and still she kept the *Freeman* working. She refused to surrender to grief or pain or fatigue.

On their way back to Georgetown with a load of coal in their holds, things began to brighten a bit. Thomas began to wander along the canal more, looking for animals to adopt. Elizabeth smiled occasionally and once on a warm day, Tony even heard her singing to herself.

The good mood lasted until they neared Hancock where Maryland was less than a mile wide.

The sun was beginning to set and Tony began to look forward to dinner. He was lying on his bunk and smelling the delicious aroma coming from the stew Elizabeth was cooking. She had even let him taste the stew as it had cooked.

Tony heard Thomas yell and jumped from his bunk.

"Thomas!" Mrs. Fitzgerald yelled.

Tony grabbed the rifle that hung on the wall and ran into the stateroom. He parted the curtains and saw a group of Rebel soldiers had stopped Thomas and the mules on the towpath. Tony raised his rifle to his shoulder and fired. The shot took one of the soldiers out of the saddle and the kick from the rifle knocked Tony off the bed.

"Get out of here now or we'll shoot the boy!" one of the soldiers demanded.

"Tony. Elizabeth. Come on up here," Mrs. Fitzgerald said.

"Is there a pistol?" Tony asked Elizabeth as he stepped out of the stateroom.

Elizabeth shook her head. "What's happening?"

"Rebels."

They walked onto the race plank together and stood next to Alice. The soldier Tony had shot was sitting on the towpath while another soldier tried to staunch the flow of blood from the man's shoulder. Another half a dozen soldiers were sitting on their horses near Thomas. One of the men had Thomas sitting in front of him with his pistol next to Thomas's head.

"Where's the captain!" the soldier holding Thomas demanded.

"I'm the captain," Alice said.

"You're a woman."

Alice stood up straighter. "I am. My husband was killed last month in Cumberland."

"If you're lying, the boy is dead."

Alice sneered at him. "Don't you think I realize that? I'm not lying."

The soldier turned to the soldier next to him. "Check it out."

The second soldier dismounted his horse and jumped from the towpath to the canal boat. He walked past Tony on his way into the family cabin and Tony's eyes watered from the odor. The soldier obviously hadn't bathed in a long time.

The soldier came out holding both his rifle and Mr. Fitzgerald's rifle in one hand and Elizabeth's pot of stew in the other hand.

"No one's inside, but I've got us another rifle and some dinner!" the soldier yelled, holding up the pot of stew.

The soldier holding Thomas sat him down on the ground, then dismounted. He hopped onto the canal boat and approached Mrs. Fitzgerald. He tipped his gray hat to her.

"I'm Major Samuel Parkinson of the 7th Virginia," the soldier said.

"I'm Alice Fitzgerald."

"Mrs. Fitzgerald, this boat is now the property of the Confederate States of America."

"Why do you want a boat that carries coal? Are you that desperate for fuel?" Alice asked.

Parkinson's eyebrows arched. "Coal?" Alice nodded. "We expected this boat to be full of corn or flour. That's what we were told."

"The *Freeman* has never hauled fruit or grain. It was never profitable for us, especially when the railroad moves it quicker. We're not even carrying coal right now." Parkinson looked skeptical and Alice pointed to the holds. "Feel free to check under the hatch covers. You obviously don't take my word for it."

Parkinson walked to one of the nearby covers and lifted the edge of the cover. He peered underneath at the shadows, then pulled back and let the cover drop.

"They're empty," he called to his men on the towpath.

"So much for trusting Shaffer's source of information," one of the men muttered loudly.

Parkinson turned back to the Fitzgeralds and Tony. "You all had better go ashore."

"Why?" Alice asked.

"We're going to burn this boat and sink it in the canal."

Alice ran forward and grabbed the major's arm. "No! Don't do that. Please, sir. This is our only home. Our house in Sharpsburg was burned during the battle last month."

"Sharpsburg? We were there. It was hell, if you pardon my language." He paused. "Still, we need to block the canal and sinking this boat will delay things for awhile."

"But it's not a permanent solution."

Parkinson shook his head. "I'm sorry, ma'am, but we need to do our duty."

"Your duty is to fight other soldiers not women and children."

Parkinson winced at that.

A horse came galloping down the towpath. The soldiers all raised their rifles in the rider's direction. The rider didn't slow.

"It's Shaffer. It's Shaffer," the rider yelled.

The soldiers relaxed.

"What are you doing here, Shaffer?" Parkinson asked.

229

"Major, the Union patrols are only a mile or so behind me and heading this way."

"I thought you said they were heading west."

"They were, but they changed direction when they heard the shot." Shaffer looked around and saw the wounded soldier sitting on the towpath.

Tony grinned. It was his shot that was going to bring help for the Fitzgeralds. The Union would drive these men off before they could do any damage here.

"Do we take Hoskins?" one of the soldiers asked. "I don't think he can set ahorse. He's losing a lot of blood."

"I can take care of him," Alice offered.

Parkinson turned to her and said, "Thank you, ma'am, but he would not want to be caught on this side of the river when the Union gets here. We'll take our chances and so will he."

"Do we take the women?" one of the soldiers asked.

Alice shuddered. She didn't like the way the soldier who has asked the question was staring at Elizabeth. Alice would never allow Elizabeth to go with these men.

"Of course not. We're gentlemen. We are not guerillas," Parkinson said.

Parkinson grabbed the lantern that was hanging above the family cabin and threw it onto the hatch covers. The lantern shattered and the oil caught fire. Then he ran into the family cabin and threw down the lantern inside, catching the family cabin on fire.

"No!" Elizabeth screamed.

Parkinson ran out of the family cabin and jumped ashore. "Let's get away from here."

As soon as they were moving away, Tony ran to the hay house. He jumped through the window and threw a bucket from inside the hay house out onto the towpath.

"Thomas! Start filling buckets! Quick!"

Thomas ran over and grabbed the bucket. He dipped it into the canal and passed it up to his mother's outstretched hand. Alice ran into the family cabin and threw water on the flames.

Tony ran down to the mule shed and threw out another bucket that was stored there. Thomas filled it and passed it to Tony. Tony took the bucket and threw the water on the flames that were on the hatch covers. The water didn't spread the oil because the oil had already soaked into the wood.

Elizabeth danced around on the covers, trying to stamp out the flames and beat them out with her shawl.

Tony tossed his bucket back to Thomas. Thomas filled it and passed it back to Tony. Tony threw the water onto the hatch covers.

"Mrs. Fitzgerald, how are things inside?" Tony called.

"They're under control, but things are still on fire," Alice called from inside the cabin.

When Tony got his next bucket of water from Thomas, he threw the water on the open window of the family cabin where he saw flames beginning to eat at the curtains.

Their firefighting efforts went on for almost fifteen minutes before everyone stopped to look around.

"Does anyone see any flames?" Tony asked.

No one did.

"Check under the hatch covers, Elizabeth," Tony said.

She lifted the edge of each hatch covers and looked under where the flames had been. "It doesn't look like there's any fire down here."

"Mrs. Fitzgerald, is it all right to wet down the holds just to be safe?"

Alice walked out of the family cabin. Her face and clothes were smeared with soot. Her hair was in disarray. She looked exhausted.

"Fine. Do that."

"We're lucky that they didn't shoot the mules or we would have been stranded for awhile," Elizabeth said.

"We are lucky that they didn't shoot us," Tony added.

"How is the cabin, Mama?" Elizabeth asked.

"There's some minor damage and scorched wood, but we'll be able to use it. We'll have to replace the bedding, though. It caught fire too quickly."

"Here come the soldiers," Thomas announced.

Everyone looked to the west. A patrol of half a dozen soldiers came marching down the towpath. The patrol stopped in front of the *Freeman*.

The soldier in the lead said, "It looks like you had some trouble, ma'am."

"You could say that. We were attacked by a Confederate patrol and they tried to burn our boat," Alice said as she brushed her hair out of her eyes.

The soldier suddenly stood up straighter. His eyes darted around searching for possible threats. "Rebels? Where did they go?

"They talked about going back across the river. One of them is wounded. They thought that we were carrying food."

The soldier nodded. "Between our army and the Rebels, we've eaten just about everything in sight in Northern Virginia. They'll have to move either further south or north again or risk starvation. If they move north again, we'll be ready for them," the soldier promised.

"They knew you were moving this way. That's why they left," Elizabeth said.

"It would have been nice if you had gotten here earlier. You could have either captured them or helped us put out the fire," Tony added.

"We didn't know they were here, young man," the soldier said defensively. He turned to Alice and said, "Is there anything we can do now?"

Alice shrugged. "I guess not."

The soldier nodded sharply. "Then we'll be moving on. Maybe we'll catch up with the Rebels."

"Not walking you won't," Tony said.

The soldiers started marching again. When they were out of sight, Alice walked over and hugged Tony. Tony felt himself blushing.

"You did an excellent job defending this boat and helping put out the fire. Thank you. I'm so glad you're part of my family now," Alice said.

Tony smiled. Part of my family. He was unsure of what he should say so he simply hugged her back.

31

THE END OF THOMAS'S HOBBY
OCTOBER 1862

Tony watched the sun rise in the east as he sat on the mule shed. He was serving his shift on watch while the Fitzgeralds slept in the family cabin. They hadn't left the area after putting out the fire, though they had moved onto the next lock where they could add the safety of the Bittinger family to their own numbers. Mrs. Fitzgerald and Jonathan Bittinger, the lockkeeper, had also set out watches to keep an eye out for any further Confederate patrols that might have ideas about sinking the *Freeman*. Tony had drawn the last watch before they would start east again.

He would be glad to leave the area, too. He was worried that the Rebel patrol would come back to finish what they had started this afternoon. Tony had shot one of their men, after all. He understood the need for revenge.

He would have to convince Mrs. Fitzgerald to allow him to buy a new rifle in the next town. It was too dangerous to travel on the canal nowadays without some sort of protection. The Rebels had taken all of the weapons and Thomas's slingshot just didn't do the job of protecting the family.

Thomas was the first one awake. He came out of the family cabin and stretched. Then he saw Tony and waved. Thomas was the only one in the family who hadn't had to take a watch since Mrs. Fitzgerald considered him too young to stay up that late at night and still pay attention.

Elizabeth opened the door to the family cabin a few minutes later and stepped outside. She still looked exhausted. She hadn't slept easily if she had slept at all.

"Good morning," Tony said cheerily.

"I hope so."

"Did you sleep at all?" Tony asked.

Elizabeth shook her head. "I kept listening for horses or voices."

"Think we'll get to Georgetown today?" Tony asked.

Elizabeth shook her head. "Maybe, we're still about forty or fifty miles away."

Tony sighed. "That means forty or fifty miles of worrying about Rebels."

"You can't worry about them," Elizabeth said. "They're part of the canal now like the railroaders who blow their whistles to taunt the mules. You just have to get used to them and be cautious."

Tony arched his eyebrows, surprised to hear her say that. "Then why are you worried?"

Elizabeth smiled. "Because I don't believe what I just told you."

Tony chuckled.

Elizabeth ran her hand through her hair to brush it out of her face. "I'm going to start breakfast."

"Is Mrs. Fitzgerald awake?"

Elizabeth shook her head. "No, she finally fell asleep near morning. She kept tossing and turning worse than me."

"I'll tell Thomas to be quiet then."

Elizabeth grinned and glanced over at Thomas. "That will be like telling a river not to run."

She went back inside to start cooking.

Tony had to thank the Rebels for one thing. They had shaken the Fitzgeralds out of their depression that had hung over them since George had run away.

Tony wondered if fear was a good trade-off for depression.

Tony slept after breakfast. He fell asleep in his bunk with the lingering smell of bacon in the family cabin. Thomas was walking a trick with the mules and Elizabeth stood at the tiller steering the boat. Tony woke up sometime in mid-afternoon and saw Mrs. Fitzgerald cutting up vegetables for a stew at the table. Her back was toward him.

"What time is it?" Tony asked as he stretched.

"Just after three o'clock. You slept well. Even the horn blowing at the locks didn't wake you up," Alice said.

That surprised Tony. He was usually a light sleeper. All of the work he was taking on lately must be wearing him out more than thieving in Cumberland had.

"Guess I was tired," Tony said.

Alice nodded. "I guess. Do you want something to eat now? You and I will have to relieve Elizabeth and Thomas before the turtle stew is finished."

Thomas rubbed his eyes. He hopped out of his bunk and

walked over and sat down across the table from Mrs. Fitzgerald. He cut himself a piece of cheese and ate it with a chunk of soft bread covered with butter. The stew was beginning to smell good. Maybe he would be able to snatch a bowl when the *Freeman* went through a lock.

"How are you?" Tony asked.

Alice stopped her work and looked at him. "I'm fine. Thank you for the bravery you showed yesterday in saving the boat."

Tony shrugged. "This is my home now."

She reached over and patted his hand. "I'm glad to hear you say that, and I'm glad that you are here with us."

Tony felt himself blushing so he kept his head down.

Tony finished his meal and went outside. The warm sun felt good on his face. There wouldn't be very many warm days left this year. They were already well into October.

"I'm ready to drive the mules whenever you want to switch," he told Elizabeth.

She didn't look as tired now as she had this morning. The further they went without meeting a Rebel patrol, the more relaxed she must become.

"There's a lock in about two miles. You can take over for Thomas then," Elizabeth told him.

About half an hour later, the *Freeman* tucked itself into the lock and Tony laid out the fall board to walk the fresh team of mules onto the towpath. Thomas unharnessed King Edward and Ocean he was walking and brought them back on board the canal boat. While Tony was harnessing Jigger and Seamus, the *Freeman* was lowered to the next level.

As Tony had the mules pull the boat out of the lock, Thomas came out of the mule shed. He ran to the edge of the boat and jumped ashore, dropping to the ground and rolling in the dirt.

"What are you doing?" Tony asked.

"I'm not hungry so I'm going critter hunting and see what I can find," Thomas said as he stood up.

He dusted himself off and ran off ahead of Tony. Tony walked alongside the mules, watching Thomas dart in and out of the trees next to the towpath, looking for an animal he could capture.

Suddenly Thomas screamed. He ran out onto the towpath.

"Cottonmouth!" he yelled.

Tony halted the mules. "What's wrong?"

"A cottonmouth bit me."

Tony felt a moment of fear and then he jumped on Thomas, pulling him to the ground. Thomas tried to struggle, but Tony lay on top of him forcing him to be still.

"Be still! Do you want to die quick?" Tony told him.

Thomas froze.

"What are doing?" Thomas asked.

"I'm going to try and get the poison out before it gets too far into your body. Hopefully, all your running didn't send it dashing away to your heart."

Tony could feel Thomas's heart hammering away in his chest and he worried that it was already too late. He pulled his knife out if its sheath.

"Where did you get bit?" he asked.

Thomas sat up and pulled up one of his pants legs. "Down around my ankle."

It didn't take Tony long to find the puncture wounds on the outside of Thomas' right leg just above the ankle. He turned Thomas's foot to the side and poised the knife over it.

"This is going to hurt, but I've got to get the poison out," Tony warned him.

Thomas clenched his teeth together and nodded. Tony cut two parallel lines, each about a half inch long on Thomas's leg. A line ran through each puncture mark. Thomas moaned slightly, but he didn't yell out. Tony was proud of him.

Then he bent over Thomas's leg and sucked blood from the wound. When he got a mouthful of blood, he quickly spit it off to the side. He kept repeating the procedure and forcing himself not to gag at the taste of the blood.

Elizabeth and Mrs. Fitzgerald brought the *Freeman* close to the towpath and came ashore. Mrs. Fitzgerald hurried over and held on-to Thomas while Tony continued his slow and steady sucking.

"I'm sorry, Mama," Thomas said weakly.

"I've warned you about collecting snakes," his mother told him gently.

"I wasn't trying to collect him. I know better than to grab a cottonmouth. He was just there when I went into the woods, look-ing for something to catch," Thomas explained.

After spitting out ten mouthfuls of blood, Tony thought it was enough. If poison was still in Thomas's body after all that, Tony wouldn't be able to get it out now. It would have circulated too far away from the bite site. Hopefully, there wasn't enough poison left to kill Thomas now.

Tony sat up. "He'll need to be cleaned up and bandaged."

Alice said, "Thank you."

She closed her eyes and sighed.

Tony crawled over to the canal and scooped out handfuls of water to rinse the taste of blood out of his mouth. He didn't want to leave any of the poison in his mouth to hurt him.

Alice ripped off a piece of one of her petticoats and wrapped up Thomas's leg tightly to stop the bleeding. A small area of the bandage turned red, but it didn't spread far.

"Help me get him on the boat, Elizabeth," Alice said.

Together, the two women lifted the boy and carried him back across the fall board. They laid him on the roof of the family cabin underneath the canopy and then disappeared inside the cabin. Elizabeth came back out with pillows and a blanket and Alice came out with a basin of water and soap.

Alice lifted his pants leg and removed the bandage. She wet a rag and wiped it on the soap. Then she began scrubbing the wound. Thomas winced and began to cry.

"It's got to be clean so it doesn't get infected," Alice said.

Tony walked aboard slowly. He felt tired, but he had barely done any work. Elizabeth turned to him and said, "Let me make you some tea with honey to get the taste of blood out of your mouth."

"That would be nice. Thank you," Tony said, nodded. His mouth still had the coppery taste of blood in it.

Tony walked over next to Mrs. Fitzgerald and looked over her shoulder. She appeared worried as she finished rewrapping Thomas's leg.

"What's wrong?" Tony asked.

"He's got a fever already."

Tony sighed. "Then I didn't get enough."

Alice put a calming hand on Tony's arm. "Whatever you got will help. Right now, his body's got to fight what's left."

She went into the family cabin to get a clean rag. Tony moved up next to Thomas. Sweat beaded on the boy's brow, though the day wasn't that hot.

"Thomas, you'd better get better so I can hit you for making me suck on your foot," Tony said to him softly.

"It was my leg," Thomas whispered.

"Well then, it smelled like your foot."

Thomas smiled and closed his eyes.

Alice came back out holding a rag. She climbed up on the roof next to her son. Then she soaked the rag and bathed Thomas's forehead. Thomas smiled.

Elizabeth brought out Tony's tea and handed it to him. She stood on the race plank and stared at her brother with worried expression on her face. Tony sipped the tea and it did sweeten the taste in his mouth. He was glad to get the coppery tang of Thomas's blood and the filthy taste of canal water out of his mouth.

Alice cried softly as she bathed Thomas's forehead. Tony didn't even have to ask why she was crying. He knew. She was worried that Thomas would die. She was afraid that she would lose another member of her family, and Tony couldn't tell her that she wouldn't.

First, Mr. Fitzgerald had died. Then George had run off to join the army, which could very easily mean the he would die in the war. How would she react if Thomas died on top of all that?

Why were so many bad things happening to them so quickly?

"I did what I could, ma'am," Tony said to Alice.

Alice looked up, her eyes red with tears, and patted his hand. She even smiled at him.

"I know, Tony, and he's alive now because of what you did," Alice told him.

Tony turned to Elizabeth and said, "We'd better get going. Maybe we can get to a doctor in the next town. I can walk the mules if you'll take the tiller. That will allow your mother to be with Thomas."

Elizabeth nodded. "That's a good idea."

Tony drained the rest of his tea and then put the cup inside the family cabin. He paused as he came back out to look at Thomas and Mrs. Fitzgerald. He hoped Thomas lived, not only because he was beginning to consider Thomas his younger brother, but also he didn't want to see Mrs. Fitzgerald hurt anymore. She was a good person who deserved happiness not misery.

He ran across the fall board and then flipped it aboard the *Freeman*. It landed with a loud clatter on the hatch covers. Then Tony walked over to the mules and started them moving after first making sure there were no stray snakes on the towpath.

Tony wasn't going to help Thomas any by sitting around, and Thomas wasn't going to get better any faster if the canal boat sat still. But if Thomas needed a doctor, the Fitzgeralds would need money. The only way to get money would be to deliver a load of coal.

Mrs. Fitzgerald moved Thomas into her room later in the afternoon. She slept with him in the bed while Elizabeth slept in Thomas's bunk.

In the morning, Tony awoke to hear Mrs. Fitzgerald sobbing loudly. He knew what had happened. He climbed out of his bunk and walked over to the curtain that separated the Mrs. Fitzgerald's room from the family cabin.

"May I come in?" he asked.

After a moment, she said, "Yes."

Tony parted the curtain with his hand and looked inside. Thomas was lying on his back with his eyes closed and Mrs. Fitzgerald was sitting next to him, crying.

"Did he..." Tony started to say, but he didn't want to give voice to the word.

Mrs. Fitzgerald shook her head.

"I just told her that I think I'm going to stop collecting snakes," Thomas said.

Tony laughed with relief.

32

WOUNDED IN ACTION
OCTOBER 1862

David watched McLaughlin insert the fuse into the wall of the Monocacy River Aqueduct west of White's Ford. The gunpowder-coated twine just barely reached the ground about fifteen feet below.

"That fuse is shorter than the one before. Will we have enough time to find cover?" David asked as McLaughlin climbed down the side of aqueduct wall.

McLaughlin stared at him and spit out a wad of chewing tobacco. It landed near David's feet.

"We'll have time. I just want to make sure that you don't have time to change your mind like you did the last time," McLaughlin said.

David did not regret pulling the fuse before, although it had ended badly for him. If he hadn't done anything, the crew of that canal boat would most likely have died. That was something that he couldn't have lived with.

"I didn't want innocent people to die," David said simply.

McLaughlin shook his head. "You just don't understand, Lieutenant. That's why you have those bad dreams every night. There are no innocents in war. If those innocent people are on the canal, they know the dangers. They are giving aid to those politicians in Washington who want to control the South. We are trying to free all of the South, not just the southern slaves," said McLaughlin. He was referring to Lincoln's proclamation after the Battle of Antietam, which said that all of the slaves in the Confederacy would be free on January 1 unless the states rejoined the Union. It was a political maneuver, full of more bluster than power since the South didn't recognize the Union government's power over them.

David heard the crack of a rifle and McLaughlin suddenly spun around. His shoulder quickly turned red from the bullet wound.

David looked around and saw a Union patrol charging across the towpath toward them. McLaughlin struggled to get a match out and light the fuse. Another shot ricocheted off the rocks above their heads.

David grabbed the corporal and pulled him under the aqueduct arch. The stone would shield them for a few moments. It would also hide them long enough so they could get out of sight.

"We've got to get out of here," David said.

"No! I want to blow the aqueduct up! That will stop them!" McLaughlin insisted.

"If we stay any longer, they'll capture us."

David tugged at McLaughlin's arm. The corporal hesitated. Then he grunted and reluctantly followed David. They stayed near the side of the arch that rose over the river. The water at the edge of the arch was shallow so it didn't slow them down greatly as they slogged through the water. They rounded the other side and waited.

"Watch above," David told McLaughlin. "I'll watch under the aqueduct."

David looked around the corner of the aqueduct wall. He saw one of the Union soldiers slide down the hill to the river. David fired his pistol at the man. The boom echoed loudly under the arch. It almost sounded as if the aqueduct had exploded. The soldier dropped to the ground and disappeared back behind the wall. David wasn't sure if he had hit the man or not, but he had delayed the patrol chasing him.

"They'll try and surround us," McLaughlin muttered. He stuffed a kerchief into his wound. It was filthy but it stopped the blood flow.

David nodded. "I know. I just wanted to make sure they have to send at least part of the patrol back up on top of the canal. It will give us a few moments more."

"For what?"

"To get ahead of them."

"I say we stay and fight it out," McLaughlin said, almost snarling.

"It's ten to two against us, and I have no desire to spend the rest of this war in a northern prison camp," David snapped.

David headed north into the woods, trying to put as much distance between him and the patrol as possible. He was hoping he would be able to find some place to hide until the patrol had given up hunting him and McLaughlin.

He heard McLaughlin running behind him. At this point, he no longer cared if the corporal stayed with him or not. Their usefulness north of the Potomac was coming to an end. The patrols along the river were growing numerous as the North realized that the South was willing to come across the river and wage an offensive war.

Further behind, David heard a series of rifle shots. McLaughlin grunted and fell in a heap on the ground. Then David felt something slam into his thigh. The shot staggered him but he wouldn't let himself fall. If he fell, the Yankees would be on top of him. He grabbed McLaughlin under the arm and lifted him to his feet.

David turned west and McLaughlin followed. The corporal had been shot in the side and was losing a lot of blood. He held one hand to his wound, but blood was seeping between his fingers.

"They don't have to rush. We're leaving a trail plain enough for them to follow," McLaughlin said, holding up his bloody hand.

McLaughlin was right, but David wanted to at least get out of eyesight of the patrol. If Union soldiers couldn't see David and McLaughlin, they would worry about an ambush. They would move slower and be more cautious in their pursuit. That would allow David and McLaughlin even more time to get away and hide.

David took his kerchief from around his neck and stuffed an end in either end of McLaughlin's side wound. Then he ripped the sleeve off of his shirt and tied it around his own leg.

"They won't hold for long," McLaughlin said, eyeing the bandages.

"It doesn't have to. It just has to hold for long enough for us to hide that trail you were talking about," David explained quickly.

Once their wounds were bound, David began running again in a different direction. He pulled McLaughlin with him. McLaughlin gave David support because of the wound in his leg and McLaughlin kept himself standing by leaning on David.

"Where are you going?" McLaughlin laughed.

"I saw a place we can hide earlier, but only if we don't lead the patrol to it with a blood trail."

They came to the canal and David slid into the water as quietly as he could. Since the canal was six feet deep, they had to swim across. David hoped that the water would wash off any blood long enough for them to hide somewhere. If they could get out of the canal without bleeding again immediately, it would delay the patrol finding them.

David was worried about McLaughlin, though. The man was losing blood fast. He needed to rest and have someone stitch him up. He couldn't do either with a Union patrol on their heels.

David pulled himself out of the canal. He thought he heard the Union patrol calling out to each other as they searched for them to the north. David pulled McLaughlin out of the water.

They stood up again and half ran/half slid down the hill on the other side of the towpath. Then David began to look around for the landmarks he had noticed yesterday when they had camped near here.

He saw the outcropping of granite. He hurried to it and looked behind the brush. A deep hole was beneath the stone.

"Here! Get in here!" David told McLaughlin.

"That could be a critter's burrow," McLaughlin said.

David grabbed a stick and poked in the hole. Nothing came out.

"Nothing in there's now. Get in. We won't stay that long hopefully," David said frantically.

McLaughlin slid into the hole feet first. Once he was in the hole, he rolled onto his back and sighed. Then he closed his eyes as if he were going to sleep.

"Move over," David said.

McLaughlin scooted to the side. David slid in backwards on his belly. The hole was just wide enough to hold the both of them if they didn't breathe deeply.

Once they were both in the hole, David pulled the brush back in front of them. It was too dense to see through, but that would mean the Union soldiers also wouldn't be able to see through it to where they were hiding. David had only found the hole by accident this morning when he was searching for firewood.

He drew his pistol and waited.

If they were found now, they would have no choice but to fight. There was no retreating.

About ten minutes later, he heard the patrol. They were up on the towpath still searching for David and McLaughlin.

"I can see where they slid down the bank here," one of the soldiers said. He sounded nearby.

"But do you see any sign of the Rebels?"

"No, sir."

"How could they have gotten away? We hit the one at least twice. He's in no shape to run. We saw his blood trail. Look for it."

"I don't see any blood. My guess would be that they went into the Potomac and crossed over to Virginia," the first soldier said.

"If that's so, hopefully, they won't come back. Let's get moving."

David waited anxiously, hoping that they would leave. He listened and heard nothing, but the sounds of birds. When he was sure they had gone, he closed his eyes and sighed.

"Not bad, Lieutenant," McLaughlin said. "You've got the makings of a mountain boy."

David simply shook his head.

33

A MEETING OF THE WAYS

OCTOBER 1862

Alice stood at the tiller guiding the *Freeman* along the canal. She had never done much piloting when Hugh has been alive, but now she was forced to do many of the jobs required to run a canal boat. Steering wasn't particularly difficult, except at the locks, but it still took up her time. She didn't mind steering, though. When she stood with her hand on the tiller, she felt close to Hugh.

Now that the nights were getting cold, Alice was beginning to wonder how much longer they could make runs on the canal. Sooner or later, the decision would be made to drain the canal for the winter and she would have to have the *Freeman* where she wanted to spend the winter.

Maybe she and the children would spend the winter in Cumberland. There would certainly be more opportunity for her to take on work through the winter months in the Queen City. She could sew, cook, or keep house for one of the wealthy families in town. They would also be able to get an early start on next year's season if the *Freeman* was already in Cumberland when the canal opened. It might allow her an extra run next season, and an extra run would mean extra money.

"Mrs. Fitzgerald!" Tony called.

Alice looked up over to the towpath. Tony was riding on the back of one of the mules and pointing further down the towpath.

Alice followed where he was pointing down the canal. She saw two men limping along the canal in the same direction the *Freeman* was traveling. The men were supporting each other. It almost looked like they had fallen against each other to remain standing. Their clothes were dirty and they looked as if they were about to collapse.

The men stopped and turned to face Tony when he spoke. They moved to the side of the towpath. Alice noted that they were armed, but their pistols were still holstered. They certainly didn't seem threatening, but she was still cautious. They would still have to pass them.

"Keep walking until you get to them," Alice told Tony.

The boy did as he was told. As the boat began to drift to a stop, Alice steered the boat over to the towpath where it settled to a stop against the bank.

"Hello," Alice told the men.

"Hello, ma'am," said one of the men said as he tipped his cap to her. Alice recognized his accent as Virginian.

He was the older of the two men, though probably a few years younger than Alice was. It was hard to tell through the dirt and whiskers on his face. The other man was barely out of his teens. Both of the men had wounds that were wrapped in dirty cloths.

"You're hurt. If you come aboard, I can make sure your wounds are cleaned and wrap them in some fresh bandages," Alice told them.

The second man shook his head, but the first smiled at Alice. He had a warm smile that hid the pain his wound was probably causing him.

"That's mighty generous of you, ma'am, but do you think it's wise to take two strangers on board?" he said as he glanced at his companion.

"What are your names?"

The man hesitated and said, "I'm David Windover and this is Tim McLaughlin."

Alice smiled. "Well, that's the first step to not being strangers. My name is Alice Fitzgerald. The young man there with the mules is Tony." She paused. "Thomas!"

Thomas climbed out of the hay house.

"Lay out the fall board. We've got some visitors coming aboard," Alice said.

Thomas hurried across the race plank to the mule house. He climbed in the window and a few moments later shoved the plank out across the gap between the boat and the towpath.

"Mrs. Fitzgerald, your offer is very kind, and very much appreciated, but I don't think you understand the situation," David said.

McLaughlin whispered something in David's ear that Alice couldn't hear. David shook his head.

"Mrs. Fitzgerald, your offer is generous, but I don't think you realize who we are. I'm a lieutenant in the Confederate Army. McLaughlin is a corporal," David admitted.

Alice nodded. "And unless I miss my guess, you are from Virginia, Lieutenant."

David grinned and scratched his chin. "I take it if we had tried to fool you, it wouldn't have worked."

She liked his smile. It was genuine and not forced.

"Not completely," Alice said.

"And you're still willing to help us?"

Alice waved them aboard. "You and the corporal are hurt and need help. I am a Christian woman who believes in the Bible and the lessons it teaches. I believe this situation compares to the parable of the Good Samaritan."

David nodded knowingly. "Well, ma'am, seeing as how everything is up front between us, I guess Corporal McLaughlin and I will accept your kind offer because it's certain we're not going to get a better one on this side of the river."

They staggered across the towpath and David helped McLaughlin across the fall board. Alice opened the shutters on the window of the hay house. She waved the two men inside.

"You two can stay in here while you're with us. I'll have Elizabeth heat some water. We'll wash your wounds and then stitch them up," Alice told them.

As McLaughlin started through the window, he said, "This is right kindly of you, ma'am." Alice placed his accent further south, either Tennessee or Kentucky.

"You're quite welcome, Corporal." She turned to Thomas who was staring at the soldiers and said, "Go tell your sister to heat a basin full of water. When it's hot, bring the water, some bandages, and needle and thread. We have some work to do on these men."

"Are they really soldiers?" Thomas asked skeptically.

"I think so."

"They don't look like soldiers. They're filthy."

"When they are better, you can ask them about it before they leave. Now go, Thomas," Alice insisted, shooing him away.

Thomas ran toward the family cabin and jumped through the open window instead of going through the door. Alice rolled her eyes.

When they had gone inside, Alice turned and saw Tony staring at her.

"What's wrong?" she asked him.

"I don't understand you," Tony said.

"What's there to understand?"

Tony pointed to the hay house. "They're Rebels. How can you help them when they are going to be fighting against George?

246

They keep the slaves that you are trying to free." Tony shook his head. "No, I just don't understand it."

Alice put her hands on Tony's shoulders and looked him in the eyes. "Tony, if George were hurt in the South, I would hope that someone would treat him like this. As for these men being slave owners, number one, I don't know that they are and number two, I am fighting against an ideal and a form of government not against individuals."

Tony shrugged. "I don't see the difference."

"Sometimes, you help a person not because of who they are or what they did but because of who you would become if you didn't help them. Do you think Hugh needed a boy to watch the mules when he first met you in Cumberland?"

Tony's eyes widened. "He didn't?"

"No, he allowed you to help because you needed help, but you were too proud to admit it. He helped you in a way that you could accept, and when I finally came to really need your help, I knew I could trust you and that you could do the job that I needed done. I knew you would treat me as Hugh had treated you. No act of kindness is ever lost even if you don't know where it goes," Alice explained.

"Maybe, but I think you'd have a hard time convincing the brawlers in Shanty Town of that, ma'am," Tony told her.

Alice sighed and gave him a quick hug. "Why don't you go help Thomas get what I need?"

Tony shook his head. "I'm going to stand outside here."

"I need someone to walk the mules and take the tiller," Alice said.

"Thomas can walk the mules and Elizabeth can take the tiller. I'll stay here."

Alice tried to keep from smiling at Tony's defiant stance with his arms crossed over his chest. Even if these two men did turn out to be dangerous, what could one young boy do against them? Not that she thought that they would be dangerous. Lt. Windover had been frank with her and acted the part of the gentleman. McLaughlin hadn't said much, but she suspected that if the lieutenant was helping him, he couldn't be that bad.

She nodded in agreement to Tony's terms. "If you think it's best, then that's what we'll do. I appreciate your concern for me."

"Thank you."

When Elizabeth came out with the hot water and bandages, Alice told Elizabeth and Thomas to start the boat moving.

Alice put the thread and needle in her pocket and draped the rags over her arm. Then she took the basin of hot water from Elizabeth and went into the hay house.

McLaughlin lay on the far bunk with one arm across his eyes. David sat on the hay bales under the window that Alice had entered. He reached forward to take her arm and help her into the hay house.

"I can't tell you how much I appreciate this, ma'am. We're about done in. I think we must have been walking for three hours," David said.

She set the basin on the opposite end of the bunk and laid the rags next to it. She dipped one of the rags into the water and wrung it out.

"You'll need to expose your leg wound," Alice told David.

He pointed to the corporal. "You'd better see to McLaughlin first. He was hit twice and needs to have those wounds closed up."

"I take it that it wasn't your own men who shot you?" Alice said, testing Lieutenant Windover's honesty.

David shook his head. "No, ma'am." He paused and stared at her. "Does it make a difference? Do you want us to leave?"

Alice was seriously considering it when the boat gave a small lurch to mark that it was moving again. She had promised these men safety. Would she go back on her word now?

"No, you are both hurt badly. I've tried to stay out of the war, and as long as you are on my boat, you are also out of the war. Do you understand?"

David nodded. "Yes, ma'am. We'll keep the peace."

"That's all I ask. Now I need to take a look at Corporal McLaughlin's wounds. You'll have to take off your shirt and lay on your stomach, Corporal," Alice said.

She pulled off the dirty kerchief from the side wound. The blood was crusty and so she pulled it away from the wound gently. The bullet hole started to ooze blood. She laid the rag on the wound and heard McLaughlin suck in air because of pain.

"I'm sorry," she said.

McLaughlin smiled. "That's all right, ma'am. It hurts a little, but your touch will do me a lot better than all that dirt."

Alice wiped at the wound to clean it. Then she stitched up the hole as if she was sewing closed a tear in a shirt.

When she finished with that wound, she moved on to work on his shoulder wound. She couldn't find an exit wound for the shoulder wound, so she poked her finger gently into the hole, hoping she would find the bullet. She did. She dug out the bullet with a loud sigh from McLaughlin. She sewed close the wound.

He needed to see a doctor, but she doubted that that would happen any time soon.

Finally, she closed the exit wound on McLaughlin's side.

When she was finished, she said, "Go ahead and rest, Corporal. I'll bring in some blankets later with something for the both of you to eat."

"Do you have any fresh bread, ma'am?" McLaughlin asked.

Alice nodded. "It's baking now."

McLaughlin closed his eyes and moaned in pleasure. "I thought that I smelled it."

Alice turned to David. "And now it's your turn, Lieutenant."

David nodded and unwrapped the bandage from around his leg. "I'm going to take out a knife now to cut off my pants leg. Don't be afraid."

"Thank you for warning me."

David grinned and pulled out his knife. His teeth gleamed white against the dirty face. David cut a ragged line around his thigh and pushed his pants leg down around his ankle.

Alice repeated the process of cleaning the wound. She hoped that she was doing enough to help them and the wounds wouldn't get infected.

As she stitched the hole on the front of his thigh closed, she told him, "A doctor really should look at these wounds. I'm not used to working with bullet holes."

"You can understand that we can't exactly trust the doctors around here, ma'am. We'll have to take our chances," David said.

Alice nodded. "Can't you return to your army?"

"Eventually. It would take a bit to find them. We were sent north to look things over and send reports back."

"You're spies."

"Yes, ma'am," David said without hesitation. He had come to accept the label.

Alice said nothing while she gathered up her dirty rags and sewing materials. What was she thinking by bringing two Confederate spies aboard her boat? Tony was right. She had to get rid of them as soon as possible. This could turn out worse than what happened with the Confederates who had tried to burn the *Freeman*.

"I'll get you both something to eat. Why don't you wash your hands? I'll be back shortly," Alice told the two of them.

She stepped past Lieutenant Windover and went out the window.

David rinsed his hands in the basin and then lay back on the hay. The room smelled of hay, but it was clean. He felt his body relaxing for the first time in days.

On the other side of the room, McLaughlin chuckled and spit a wad of tobacco onto the floor.

David looked at the mess and said, "You'd better clean that up."

"Why?"

David propped himself up on one elbow. His leg was throbbing, but at least it wasn't bleeding anymore. Mrs. Fitzgerald had done a good job of patching him up.

"Haven't you got eyes? This is not a filthy tavern. It's a clean boat."

"It can't be too clean if they carry coal," McLaughlin noted.

David sighed. "Look where you are, McLaughlin. Now ask yourself if you want to be walking the towpath and hiding from patrols when Mrs. Fitzgerald comes back because this woman won't put up with rudeness or filthiness."

McLaughlin rolled his eyes. He sat up in the bunk and picked up the basin. Then he dumped it on the floor to rinse away the tobacco stains.

"Happy now?" he asked.

David nodded.

"I still think we'll be out on the towpath before dark," the corporal said.

David thought for a moment. He didn't know this woman or her family, but he trusted them. Mrs. Fitzgerald could have turned them away or refused them aid, but she did neither even after learning who they were. That said much for her character.

"I believe her. When she says we can mend here as long as we keep the peace, she means it," David said.

McLaughlin laughed. "You just like the way she looks."

"What do you mean?"

He grinned evilly. At least it appeared evil to David. It reminded David of how McLaughlin had looked at the farmer's wife near Williamsport. The grin chilled David. He wanted to grab his pistol and shoot the man in the face.

"I mean she's a fine-looking woman whose husband is probably off fighting in the war. She's probably looking for a man to help keep her warm what with winter coming on and all."

David shook his head and lay back. "McLaughlin, we've got a good offer here. Don't make a mistake like you did before."

McLaughlin arched his eyebrows. "And if I do?"

David turned his head to look at the younger man. "Then I'll have to kill you," he said flatly and he meant every word. McLaughlin was dangerous not only to others but also to David, but he had given the corporal a chance to redeem himself. If McLaughlin ignored the opportunity, then it would be his fault. David would not let what happened at the farm house happen again.

From outside, David heard the boy with the mules yell, "Mrs. Fitzgerald! Soldiers coming!"

David sat up quickly and looked out the window. Coming toward the boat on the towpath was a Union patrol of six men, probably the same one that had shot holy hell out of him and McLaughlin earlier in the morning.

David pulled back and slowly closed the shutters. Then he drew his pistol and laid it on his lap. McLaughlin sat down beside him with his pistol. He peered between the crack in the shutters.

"What do we do, Lieutenant?"

"We wait quietly and see what these people do," David told him.

"She'll turn us in."

David shook his head. "No, she won't. She gave her word." He was taking a risk, he knew, but if Alice Fitzgerald had done this much for them, she wouldn't turn them in now.

"That was before the boys in blue came walking up. Do you think she wants to be caught with two Johnny Rebs on her boat?"

"She'll stand by her word," David insisted.

"And if she doesn't?"

"Do you want to charge out of here with your pistol firing at those soldiers? How far do you think you'll get?" David asked.

"You just want to wait here?"

David nodded. "We can watch from in here. If she tells them we're in here, then we can do something about it."

"I just hope it's not too late then," McLaughlin said.

Alice shaded her eyes and watched the six-man patrol approach. One of the men patted Thomas on the back as he passed.

Thomas smiled at him. The men were walking casually, but their rifle barrels were up.

They stopped in front of Alice.

"Good afternoon, ma'am," the lieutenant said.

"Hello, Lieutenant."

"We're searching for some Rebels that might be nearby. We had a run in with them a couple hours back and shot at least one of them."

Alice sighed and shook her head. "I'm sorry I can't help you."

It wasn't actually a lie. She couldn't help them because she had given her word to Lieutenant Windover and Corporal McLaughlin that they could remain on the boat.

"Can we come aboard and take a look around, ma'am?" the lieutenant asked.

Alice raised her eyebrows. What made them suspect that there was a reason to search the boat?

"Excuse me?" she asked.

"We'd like to search your boat."

Alice drew she shoulders back. "I take offense at your insinuation, Lieutenant. I'm a Marylander."

The lieutenant gave her a flat stare, unfazed by her reaction. "So are some Southern sympathizers."

"I am not a Southern sympathizer. I believe in a whole Union and I'm against slavery. I also believe in my right to own property." She said it so forcefully that there should have been no doubt in the lieutenant's mind where her loyalties lay.

"Yes, ma'am."

"And as this is my property, I will be making the decisions on who does and doesn't come aboard. If you want to act like a ruffian, do it somewhere else."

The lieutenant sighed and looked around. "I can force my way aboard, ma'am."

Alice nodded. "You can, but you would be a private before the month is out. I would make a report to Congressman Eli Sampson of Pennsylvania when I get to Georgetown. He and his wife are dear friends of mine. I'm sure he would look poorly on your abuse of power. In fact, I can show you a letter with his signature that freed our boat when the government was confiscating canal boats earlier this year."

The comment stopped the lieutenant and he had the good sense to blush.

"I'm only doing my job."

Alice shook her finger in his direction. "No, you're not. You have no reason to search this boat. You just want to do it because you can." She waved them aboard. "Well, come on over, gentlemen. Only it won't be gentlemen who come aboard."

The lieutenant frowned and shook his head. "Fine, ma'am. Have it your way, but I remind you that we are only here to protect you. Things would be easier for us if you cooperate."

"I do cooperate with reasonable requests, and I do thank you for the efforts that you make on behalf of the canawlers. I don't dislike soldiers. My son is a soldier."

The lieutenant waved the patrol forward and they continued down the towpath. Alice watched until they were gone and then let out a big sigh. She put a hand on the tiller as she felt her knees weaken.

She walked to the hay house and knocked on the shutter. Lieutenant Windover opened it.

"Thank you for lying for us," he said.

"I didn't lie. Everything that I say is completely true," Alice said more defensively than she had intended. She knew that she hadn't lied, but she also knew that she had danced around the truth so much that it made her dizzy.

Windover smiled at her. "Yes, ma'am. I would expect nothing less from a lady."

Lieutenant Windover and Corporal McLaughlin remained in the hay house. They slept a lot as they tried to recover from their wounds. At least Corporal McLaughlin did. Lieutenant Windover kept crying out in his sleep from nightmares. The two soldiers stayed completely out of sight whenever another boat neared or went through a lock. Alice didn't want to have to answer unnecessary questions about her two passengers.

When they reached the wharf at Georgetown, Windover and McLaughlin had to stay in the hay house with the shutters closed. Tony or Elizabeth generally took them their meals.

It seemed odd to Alice that this was much the same way that she and Hugh had transported slaves in the past. Only these two weren't slaves. They were slave owners.

What would Hugh think about her aiding those who enslaved others?

The two men impressed her. They kept their word and kept the peace aboard her boat. That is, until they got outside of Georgetown and beyond Great Falls.

Alice sent Elizabeth out with some dinner for the lieutenant and corporal. Her daughter had only been gone for a little while when Alice heard her scream.

She rushed out of the family cabin. At the other end of the boat, she saw Lieutenant Windover come out of the mule shed. He had been brushing the mules to help with the chores on board. He still had the brush in his hand.

"Where's Elizabeth?" Alice asked Tony who was at the tiller.

"She went into the hay house with food."

Alice rushed down the race plank and looked inside the hay house. Elizabeth was wrestling with Corporal McLaughlin as he groped at her and tried to pull her skirt up and get on top of her. She reached out for her mother and Alice grabbed her hands.

"Mama!" she called.

McLaughlin only laughed.

Then Lieutenant Windover appeared in the window behind McLaughlin. He didn't even hesitate. He grabbed hold of the top of the sill. Holding onto it, he swung himself into the cabin and kicked McLaughlin in the head. McLaughlin yelled and let go of Elizabeth. Alice quickly pulled her out of the hay house.

Elizabeth hugged her and sobbed into her shoulder.

"What are you doing? We gave our word," Windover said.

"You gave your word," McLaughlin said.

McLaughlin scrambled to grab his pistol. Windover let go of the window sill, trying to reach the pistol first. They rolled back and forth on the floor punching at each other.

Alice yelled for Elizabeth to get the rifle. The girl climbed out of the hay house and ran into the family cabin while Alice watched the two men fight.

Windover punched at McLaughlin and hit him in the nose. Blood splattered over the deck. He grabbed McLaughlin by the hair and smashed his head into the deck.

"You'll kill him!" Alice yelled.

Windover smashed the corporal's head into the planking again and again until McLaughlin stopped fighting. Only then, did Windover stop. He kneeled over McLaughlin's body, panting heavily.

"You killed him," Alice said.

Windover shook his head. "No, ma'am. He's alive, but he deserves to be dead. I warned him about acting like this."

Then Windover looked down at his leg. His wound had torn open and was bleeding.

"Looks like I didn't do myself any favors," he said and then he passed out.

When David awoke, he was laying in the bunk in the hay house. He looked over and saw that McLaughlin was also in the room. The corporal's hands and legs had been tied tightly together. He was also still unconscious.

David was surprised that he wasn't similarly trussed up.

"You're awake."

David looked through the window next to him and saw Tony standing on the race plank with the rifle. The young boy looked angry.

"I'm surprised I'm still here," David said.

"I am, too. I would have left you on the towpath for the Union to pick up." Tony paused. "I'll go get Mrs. Fitzgerald."

He left and David lay back on the bunk and closed his eyes. He should have killed McLaughlin. The man deserved no less.

"Lieutenant."

David opened his eyes and saw Mrs. Fitzgerald looking in the window at him. She had a lovely face, but she was glaring at him right now.

"Are you going to turn us over to that patrol now, ma'am?" David asked.

She frowned. "And why shouldn't I?"

David shook his head. "No reason. No reason in the world. We broke the peace. I would do it if I were you. You have to think about the safety of your family."

"You say that, and yet, you were the one who rushed in to save Elizabeth."

David shrugged and glanced over at McLaughlin. "But I knew McLaughlin could be like that. I should have been more careful or at least warned you about him. Is your daughter all right?"

Alice nodded, watching him. "She will be."

She seemed to be searching for something, but David didn't know what to tell her.

"I don't know how to begin to apologize for abusing your kindness," he said.

"You opened your wound."

"I deserve worse."

"I'm not sure if Corporal McLaughlin will regain consciousness. I think his skull is fractured from the pounding that you gave him," Alice told him. She didn't sound all that disappointed.

David looked over at his companion again and found that he didn't care whether McLaughlin lived or died. He had no feeling whatsoever for the man.

"If there is a God in heaven, he won't regain consciousness," David said.

"What should we do with him?"

David thought for a minute. McLaughlin was helpless. They couldn't very well kill him in cold blood, but the Fitzgeralds couldn't risk leaving McLaughlin on board in case he should regain consciousness and cause trouble for them.

"Leave us on the towpath for the patrol to find. They'll get us medical attention and you won't have to worry about him harming you or your family. He is no true Southerner," David admitted.

Alice cocked her head to the side and stared at the lieutenant. "And are you a true Southerner, David Windover?"

David nodded. "Yes, ma'am, I believe I am."

"Then you will want to be leaving and going back to join your statesmen."

David was surprised at the way she phrased the statement. She didn't say "I want you to go" but "You'll be wanting to go."

"I believe you'll want me to go," he said.

"Must you fight to prove yourself a Southerner?" Alice asked him.

"That is what I want least to do, ma'am. I've seen so much death that it haunts me in my dreams. I would prefer never to meet death again until it is my turn to answer to my maker."

Alice nodded. "Then stay here. We need help. If you want to cleanse your honor for the corporal's actions, then help me run this boat."

Lieutenant Windover's eyebrows raised. "Do you know what you're asking? I'm an enemy soldier. Even if I wasn't a soldier, I still have no experience working on a canal boat."

"You've shown me that you're not my enemy, and I need the help if I want to keep this boat moving. What if that patrol had forced their way onto the boat because I'm a woman? If my husband had been here, that wouldn't have happened."

"That is probably true," David answered.

Alice smiled. "Then will you come to the aid of a woman like you came to my daughter's aid? A true gentleman would."

David stared at her in amazement. She was trying to make him feel guilty for wanting to make sure she and her family were safe!

"You speak like a lawyer, trying to twist words and logic," David said.

"Do I? You don't want to fight. I am offering you an alternative to fighting that will benefit both of us," Alice said innocently.

David sighed.

"What will your children say?" he asked.

"I am the captain of this boat, not them. They will listen to me."

"And what will your husband say?"

She crossed her arms over her chest. "My husband is dead, but if he were alive, I think he would accept a true gentleman's word."

David smirked and shook his head.

"I guess we had better set McLaughlin on the towpath. It's a long way to Cumberland and we've got a long way to go yet."

34

HISTORY REPEATS
OCTOBER 1862

David threw himself into his work on the canal boat. Because of the wounds in his leg and side, he couldn't walk with the mules, but he did brush and feed them once they were on board. He was used to working with horses on his father's plantation so it wasn't that much different. The mules weren't as sleek as his father's horses, but his father's horses weren't as powerful or hard-working as these mules.

Occasionally, when Alice was at the tiller and Elizabeth driving the mules, David would fix a meal in the family cabin. He didn't serve anything fancy, but he had learned to do a little cooking while he was in the army. He put that skill to use.

He dressed in Alice's dead husband's clothes so that it wasn't apparent he was actually a Confederate deserter, though his accent would certainly make people suspect.

He would have to buy his own clothes as soon as he could, though. He had caught Alice staring at him sometimes with tears in his eyes. She never said anything, but he knew at those times she was thinking of her husband. He hated to be a sad reminder of that to her.

At night, he slept alone in the hay house. Many times, he would simply lay awake wondering what he would do when he was healed fully.

He worked hard because it took his mind off what he had done.

Was he a traitor? He had left a fellow soldier for the enemy and was giving aid to the enemy.

But if he was a traitor, why had his nightmares stopped? He was sleeping better than he had in over a year. His soul was telling him this was right for him while his mind called him a traitor. Would he never know peace?

David sat up when he heard a knock on the closed shudder of the hay house.

"Lieutenant Windover?"

"Come in, Thomas."

The shutters opened and Thomas slipped inside. He closed the shutters behind him and held his hands over the lantern to warm them. The weather was noticeably cooler.

"It's cold out tonight," Thomas said.

"What do you do when the water in the canal freezes?" David asked.

"Oh, they'll drain the canal before it freezes too hard. When you start seeing a morning crust on the water, then you know it will only be a couple of weeks before they drain it."

"What happens to the boat then?"

"It will stay wherever it is when the water is drained. We can't float without water. We usually stop near Sharpsburg, but I'm not sure if we'll do it this year."

"Why not?"

"Our house burned down in the battle there last month. I heard Mama talking to Elizabeth about staying in Cumberland this winter so she could take in odd work like sewing, cooking, and cleaning for the rich people there," Thomas explained.

David nodded. He lay back on his bunk and put his hands behind his head. He wondered what would happen to him this winter. Would he return to the army? Could he bring himself to do it?

He wasn't needed at Grand Vista. His brother was the heir so there was no place for David there, especially if he was branded a deserter.

"Are you really a soldier?" Thomas asked.

David rolled his head to look at the young boy. "Don't I look like one?"

"No. You looked like a bum when I saw you on the canal."

"That's because I'd run into some trouble."

"My brother's a soldier."

"Really? Where is he serving?"

Thomas shrugged. "We don't know. He ran away to join the army because he thought it would impress a girl and he felt guilty about Papa dying."

"Guilty?"

"Papa was killed by railroaders while he was trying to get George out of Shanty Town. I heard Mama tell Tony that George's letter kept talking about how George wanted to be a man so he could take care of himself and wouldn't get anyone else killed."

"The army won't help him there. It's all about killing," David told the younger boy.

Thomas nodded. "Mama says killing's no way to solve a problem."

"You seem to listen in on a lot of people's conversations."

Thomas grinned. "That's the only way I learn anything good."

"Well, your brother chose the wrong reason to fight. He's not going to impress the girl if he gets himself killed," David told him.

"Why did you join the army, Lieutenant Windover?"

"Just call me David, Thomas." He paused. "And I guess I joined because my father wanted me to join. He expected it of me. Besides, I wasn't going to inherit."

"Inherit?"

"When my father dies, my older brother will get our plantation."

"Are those good reasons to fight?" Thomas asked.

His question was innocent enough, but it hit David hard. Fighting because his father expected him to fight was no reason to be in the army. David believed in the Confederate cause, but he was no soldier. He knew that. He was the son of a plantation owner. That was how he had been raised. He hadn't learned to fight. He had learned to ride and govern a plantation not that he ever would.

"No, Thomas, I guess it's not a right reason to fight," David said.

"Then why do you do it?"

David shrugged. "Probably for the same reason that your brother did. It seemed like the right answer at the time."

"But you're not a soldier now."

"No, I guess I'm not."

"Will you be when you get better?"

David shrugged. "I don't know."

"I think I want to be a soldier when I get bigger."

"Why would you want to do that? I would hope that this war would be long over before you're old enough to fight in it."

Tony straightened up as if standing at attention. "I used to play soldier with the boys back home. I was very good."

David smiled and shook his head. "Why did you come in here, Thomas?"

The boy shrugged. "I thought you might be lonely. Everyone else has a bed in the family cabin. Besides, Tony dared me. He didn't think I'd be brave enough to be in here alone with a Reb after what your friend tried to do to Elizabeth."

"McLaughlin was no friend of mine," David said quickly.

Thomas nodded. "Oh, I know that, but Tony thinks all Rebels are alike. He doesn't like them because we're at war."

David had gotten that feeling from the way the Tony treated him.

"Are we at war?"

"Not you and me. I like you. Mama says you are a gentleman and Elizabeth says you rescued her," Thomas told him.

David was glad to hear that. He didn't want to be hated.

"Well, you can go back now and tell Tony you won the bet. Tell him you faced down the mean Rebel and that I cowered in fear of your great strength."

Thomas laughed. "Oh, I will. Don't worry. He'll owe me a penny."

David liked the work on the canal. It wasn't demanding. The hardest part was steering the boat into a lock without crashing it into the walls. It took a steady hand and a sense of timing. He supposed that unloading coal was back breaking, but he hadn't had to do that yet.

When they arrived in Cumberland, David was tempted to stay on the boat while everyone else went into town.

"You can't hide out forever," Alice told him.

"Don't you think it might be somewhat obvious that I'm a soldier with all the bullet holes in me?" David asked a bit sarcastically.

"Only if you limp around and show them off. You haven't been limping much since yesterday, and I don't think you're going to go around showing your scars off to anyone you would meet."

David shook his head. "I have no desire to go into town. I just want to rest and recuperate so I can be of some use to you. I'm hoping to be able to drive the mules on the way back to Georgetown."

Alice smiled at him. "Well, I have to admit that would be a help. My feet certainly do get tired and swell up from six hours of walking."

"You and the children go on into town and get what you need. I'll watch the boat. We're not even close to being near the front of the line for coal."

Alice finally agreed because she needed to fill the pantry with some winter supplies. She also wanted to get some heavier clothes for Thomas who had outgrown much of his things during the summer. His winter clothes from last year would no longer fit him. Tony would need winter clothes as well.

After they had gone, David went into the family cabin to drink a cup of coffee while he read a copy of the *Alleghenian*. He was hoping to read news about how the war was going, but with winter coming on there was little activity concerning the war. The armies were worried about feeding themselves and staying warm through the winter.

Tony walked in just as David was finishing his cup of coffee.

"Didn't you go with the others?" David asked.

Tony shook his head.

David watched the young boy cut himself a piece of bread and cheese. He sat down on his bunk to eat it while David watched.

"You don't trust me, do you?" David asked him, deciding to take the bull by the horns.

"No."

"Why not?"

"You're a Rebel," Tony said as he ate.

"I'm fighting for what I believe in."

"But you're not fighting, are you? So I guess you don't believe in it too much. You gave it up when it suited your purpose. You betrayed your country to become a Rebel. You betrayed your state when you stayed here. So when will you betray us?"

So Tony thought that David was a traitor, too.

The boy hopped from his bunk and stomped out of the family cabin. David followed him.

"I didn't betray anyone," David said, though Tony's words came dangerously close to some of David's own thoughts.

"That's what you say. I see something different."

Tony jumped from the race plank onto the dock.

"Where are you going?" David asked.

"I'm going to see my mother."

David blinked. "Your mother? I thought you were an orphan."

Tony shrugged. "Not really. My mother just doesn't want me. She betrayed me so I know how it feels. I don't want the Fitzgeralds to feel like that. They don't deserve it."

"If she betrayed you, why are you going to visit her?"

"I just want to make sure she's all right. She's still my mother."

Then he turned and walked away.

Alice, Elizabeth, and Thomas came back about half an hour later. David helped her fill the pantry with the items she had purchased.

When they had finished, she asked, "Where's Tony? I bought him a new pair of shoes. Otherwise, he's going to have cold feet this winter."

"He said he was going to visit his mother," David told her.

Alice froze. David lowered the newspaper he was reading and stared at her. "What's wrong?" he asked.

"He went into Shanty Town," she said.

"Is that where his mother lives?"

Alice nodded.

"Then I guess that is where he went," David said.

"How could he be so foolish?"

Elizabeth said, "Tony's not foolish, Mama. He was raised there. He knows how to get along. He'll be all right."

"What's the problem?" David asked.

"Shanty Town's very dangerous," Elizabeth told him.

"It's deadly," Alice added. "Hugh was killed there when he went to fetch George. Tony's just a boy. That's no place for him."

David saw fear in Alice's eyes. It was the same fear he had seen when he had been fighting McLaughlin to help Elizabeth.

"Then I'll go get him," David said.

Alice grabbed his arm. "No, David. Don't you understand? You'll get killed if you go. It's filled with men like Corporal McLaughlin."

"Well, someone has to fetch Tony and since I'm the one who let him leave, I'm the one who should get him."

Alice shook her head. "You couldn't control what Tony did."

"Maybe not, but just the same, someone needs to go get him, and I'm the most likely one. I'll be fine. I know how to take care of myself," David reassured her.

Alice looked doubtful.

He walked outside to the hay house and fished his pistol out from where he had rolled it up in his bedroll. He shoved the .36 Navy Colt into his waistband and then put his coat on over it. If Shanty Town was as dangerous as Alice thought, then he needed to be prepared.

"Do you think that will help you against a dozen men?"

David turned around and saw Alice staring at him. She had followed him out of the family cabin. She was staring at his waist where he had tucked the pistol.

"I don't intend to use it if I don't have to. No man wants to die. If they see this, it may discourage them from doing something foolish."

"I wasn't trying to shame you into going after Tony," Alice said.

David nodded. "I know that. It's something that Tony said that's making me go after him."

"What was it?"

David wasn't a traitor. Not to these people who had shown him kindness when they should have hated him.

"That's between me and him."

David climbed onto the race plank and then hopped onto the dock.

"We'll be back soon." He waved to her and then walked away in the direction that he had seen Tony go.

Tony climbed the old rickety staircase on the side of McKenney's Tavern and opened the door into the hallway for the four rooms that Carter McKenney rented out. The hallway was still dark as usual.

Tony walked to the familiar room and stood in front of the door.

He still wasn't sure why he was here. He didn't want his mother to take him back. Did he want to show her that he could survive better than she had? He didn't know. He felt the need to see her again.

Tony knocked on the door.

A woman who was not his mother opened it. She was a few years younger than Tony's mother and had darker hair. She also looked as if life hadn't been as hard on her as it had been on Tony's mother.

"What do you want?" the woman snapped.

"I'm looking for Carol," Tony said. Carol was the last name his mother had used.

"Well, I'm not her. Now get away from here. I'm expecting someone." She waved him away.

The woman started to close the door, but Tony wedged his foot in between the door and the frame to keep it open.

"This is her room," Tony insisted.

"This is my room. I've had it for over a month. Now get."

Tony withdrew his foot and the woman slammed the door in his face. His mother was gone. Where had she gone? Was he going to have to knock on every door in Shanty Town to find someone who knew where his mother was living?

He walked down the interior staircase to the tavern. Carter

McKenney tended bar. Tony walked through the crowd to the bar. McKenney was overweight and some of the buttons on his shirt were missing.

"Mr. McKenney?" Tony called.

The bartender came over and stood in front of him. "What do you want?"

"I'm looking for my mother."

"I don't know where she is and I don't care, other than the fact that she owes me her last month's rent for leaving town," the tavern owner said.

"You haven't heard where she went?"

"If I had, I would have gone there myself and collected my rent. Now get out of here, boy."

Someone grabbed Tony by the neck and pulled him back from the bar. A man spun him around to look at him. The bearded man looked familiar, but Tony couldn't remember where he had seen him before.

"Hey, boys, this is the brat I told you about. The one that tried to rob me while I was enjoying myself," the man called out loudly.

Rob him? Then Tony remembered where he had seen this man. This was the man who had caught Tony under his mother's bed. He was the man who had finally forced Tony to leave his mother.

"This brat and his ma have been running a side business robbing her customers. You don't want to take your pants off around her."

"Then how are you going to have any fun?" another man asked.

"Well, you might have your fun, but it will cost you more than you want." The man turned to stare at Tony. "Where is your mother, boy?"

"I don't know. I'm looking for her."

Tony struggled to get away, but the man's grip was too tight. He was very drunk and very angry.

"Who have you robbed lately?" the man said as he shook Tony.

The boy winced in pain.

"No one! I've been working on the canal," Tony told him.

The man grinned. "That gives me all the more reason to not like you. You're a wet canaller."

The man slapped him across the face and the room began to spin in front of Tony. He tried not to cry, but his eyes were watering regardless. He was scared and he was hurting.

Then he saw David walk into the room, smiling. The Rebel officer walked over to the group of men and Tony and leaned one arm on the back of a chair. Tony wondered if David would help him. He'd certainly given David no cause to like him.

"I'd heard that Shanty Town was tough, but I guess the people who told me that were wrong," David said nonchalantly.

"What are you talking about, Mister?" one of the men asked.

"I don't consider it 'tough' for a group of men to beat up a child."

"This brat's a thief!" the man holding Tony yelled as he shook Tony.

"I am not!" Tony insisted.

The man slapped him again. "You are, too. I caught you at it. Remember?"

"That was before. I'm working for wages now. I've got a job." Tony looked at David and said, "Tell them, Mr. Windover."

The man looked at David. "You know this brat?"

David nodded. "I do, but I don't know what sort of deal he's got worked out with Mrs. Fitzgerald. I guess she might be paying him."

The man holding Tony growled. "I thought as much."

"However," David added. "Seeing as how I've found him to be honest and since I trust Mrs. Fitzgerald, I would have to say the boy's not lying."

The man holding Tony loosened his grip a bit. He stared at Tony for a moment and then said, "Well, it's good to hear that the boy has a paying job, because I would say that he owes each of us here who had the experience of paying double for a two-bit whore a drink."

The man reached his hand into Tony's pocket searching for money. Tony tried to scoot away, but the man kept him close and fumbled around in his pocket. Tony didn't know what to do. He was only one boy against seven men, but he wouldn't allow himself to be bullied.

Tony kicked the man in the shin. He grunted and pulled his hand out of Tony's pocket and slapped him harder than he had before.

David said, "You know, that still doesn't seem quite fair. After all, what is the boy going to do if he doesn't want to buy you all drinks? You are all so much bigger than he is. It just doesn't seem right to watch you all picking on this boy."

"Well what are you going to do about it?" the man holding

Tony asked. He bent over and rubbed his sore shin.

David straightened up. "I guess I'll have to even the odds up."

As he spoke, David grabbed the chair he had been leaning on and swung it up to poke one of the men in the chest with the chair legs. The man staggered back and fell into some of the others. Then David swung the chair backhanded into the head of the man who was holding Tony. The man dropped unconscious to the floor.

David dropped the chair and grabbed Tony's wrist to pull him to him. Tony didn't need any urging to hurry over behind David.

As the stunned men began to regroup, David backed away and pulled his pistol from his waistband.

"Now, boys, I think you need to ask yourselves just how badly you want that free drink, especially if it would just run right out of the holes this pistol would put in you," David warned them.

The group stopped. Some of the men grumbled, but none of them moved toward David.

"I thought that might be the case. I'm sorry to interrupt you boys and your fun, but Tony here has a job to do and I aim to see that he does it."

Still holding the gun on the men, David backed away toward the door. Tony stayed close to him, not sure of what would happen.

As they moved into the street, a few of the men came to the door to watch them go, but most of them must have gone back to their drinking. Tony only saw three men in the doorway.

David turned away and put a hand on Tony's back to hurry him down the street.

"Let's get going before they drink in more courage," David said.

He shoved his gun back into his pants and buttoned his coat.

"That was great, Lieutenant!" Tony said, looking back over his shoulder at the tavern.

"Don't call me, Lieutenant," David said, looking back over his shoulder.

"Fine, but it was still great."

David shook his head. "It was risky is what it was. If they'd been smart, I wouldn't have gotten away with that."

"Then why'd you do it?"

"Because if I was smart, I would have thought of something better. I couldn't, so I did the only thing I could think of. I just had to hope that they were dumber than I was. They were."

Tony chuckled.

"What are you going to tell, Mrs. Fitzgerald?" Tony asked.

David thought for a moment and then said, "I'll tell her I found you with some old acquaintances and brought you back."

Tony didn't want to lie to Mrs. Fitzgerald. She deserved more after everything she had done for him. What Mr. Windover was suggesting wasn't actually a lie, though, was it?

"You're not lying to her, are you?"

David nodded. "I'm just being a bit vague. I won't lie to her if that what you're wondering. She deserves the truth, but in this case, I think the all-out truth would just upset her."

Tony nodded his agreement. "It would."

When they got back to the boat, Alice was waiting outside for them. She rushed over and hugged Tony when she saw that he was all right. Tears were in her eyes. Tony wiped them off her cheeks.

"What were you thinking going into Shanty Town?" she asked him.

He felt his face turn red. "I guess I wasn't thinking too smart, ma'am. No one has ever worried about me before."

Alice looked at David. "He wasn't in trouble?"

David hesitated and said, "He had met up with some old acquaintances. I had to drag him away from them."

Alice eyed David suspiciously. "And that's all?"

"That's all I'm willing to say," David said. He looked at Thomas.

"I was in trouble, ma'am. Some men who knew me before caught me and were shoving me around. Mr. Windover came in and got me away from them."

"And neither one of you were hurt?" Alice asked.

David shook his head.

Tony said, "I was slapped around a couple times, but other than a sore face, I'm all right." He rubbed his sore cheek.

Alice sighed. "Well, I'm just happy that both of you are back safe and sound, but Tony don't you do anything that foolish again."

Tony was surprised to find he felt warm inside, though the air around him was cold. He wasn't sure what he was feeling, but it felt good.

"I think I've learned better, ma'am. I won't do it again," Tony said.

Alice nodded. "Good. Then both of you get into the family cabin. Elizabeth is cooking up some chicken soup."

"Yes, ma'am," David and Tony said together.

35

STORMY WEATHER
OCTOBER 1862

The *Freeman* left Cumberland early the next morning heading for Georgetown with 121 tons of coal in its holds. As the Fitzgerald crew worked their way down the canal, David took his turn as a mule driver. He liked being able to move around without worrying about being shot.

He found himself walking lightly with a spring in his step, at least for the first few hours. Then his wounded thigh began to throb and he started to limp.

Since the mules knew the path, all David had to do was walk with them. It allowed him time to think about what he would do when the season ended. Would he return to the army or the plantation? He had no future with either. Maybe he should just go west to California.

At Lock 74, he noticed calluses on his palms as he wrapped the hawser around the snubbing post. Would he work on the canal long enough for them to harden? He held onto the hawser, slowly letting it out as the canal boat dropped lower into the canal.

When the east end lock gates opened, David started the mules walking again. As soon as the *Freeman* was clear, another boat slid into the lock to be raised to the next level.

"Do you want something to eat?" Elizabeth called to David.

"No," he answered, waving to her. "I'm fine."

They had been walking for another hour when David saw another boat coming toward them.

"What do I do?" David called to Thomas.

"You have the right of way. Just stay inside her mules. She'll stop the mules and let the rope get some slack in it," Thomas explained.

David did as he was told, but as he neared the boat, a train whistle blew loudly. The mules David was leading stomped nervously at the sound. The mules the young girl was leading weren't as calm, though.

The lead mule reared up and tried to turn away from the canal.

The girl pulled on the lead rope to pull the mule back and wound up getting kicked in the head.

David let go of his lead rope and ran to the girl to help her. She was bleeding badly from a wound on her head, but she was still standing and trying to calm the mules. As David grabbed the lead rope, the girl fell to the ground. David quickly turned the mules away from her.

"Doris!" a man on the boat yelled.

David saw the man jump to the shore. He ran up to David and the girl. David stood up and let the man get next to the girl.

Alice and the children came running up beside David.

"Those damn railroaders," the man muttered.

Alice squatted down next to the girl and looked at Doris's wound.

"Elizabeth, hand me those bandages I brought," Alice said.

Elizabeth came forward and gave her mother the torn cloth that served as bandages. Alice must have seen the wound from the boat and come prepared to help. Alice wrapped the girl's head.

David passed control of the mules to Thomas. Then David stood over Alice as she tended the girl.

Alice patted the girl's cheek. "Doris. Doris, can you hear me?"

The girl turned away and began crying.

"Is she going to be all right?" the man asked.

"I think so, Lou. The wound wasn't deep. It just knocked her a little senseless."

"But all that blood."

David agreed. He had never seen a child wounded like this. It angered him.

"You know head wounds bleed a lot," Alice said, hoping to calm the man.

"But I'm not used to seeing that blood on my daughter," Lou said sharply.

"Give her some time to rest. She should probably be fine tomorrow except for a sore head. I don't even think she needs to have the wound stitched up."

Lou smiled. "Thank you, Alice." He paused and looked across the canal. "Someone needs to do something about those irresponsible railroaders."

Yes, thought David. The railroaders were responsible. They had spooked the mules. How could they do something like that?

"What's the problem with the railroad?" David asked Tony.

"Railroaders and canawlers hate each other. They fight for business. When some railroaders see the opportunity, they spook the mules with their whistles," Tony told him.

Now David knew why the mule drivers were needed. If the mules got spooked, someone needed to keep them calm.

"Don't railroaders know what happens when they blow their whistles?" David asked.

"Sure they do. They just don't care," Tony said.

David shook his head. It wasn't right. With so many soldiers dying in the war, people should treasure lives that didn't have to be wasted.

Lou scooped up the young girl in his arms. Two boys on his boat had lowered a fall board to the towpath. Lou walked across the fall board onto the boat. One of the boys came onto the towpath and walked over to the mules.

"Let's get back on board," Alice said to everyone. "We've got a load of coal to deliver."

When everyone was aboard, David started the mules moving again, but he couldn't get the image of the young girl being kicked by a mule out of her mind.

With all of the killing that was going on in the war, why did people have to bring the violence off the battlefield? Everyone seemed to accept the railroaders' actions as part of life on the canal. It didn't make sense to David. Why should he accept what was wrong?

David was so quiet that Alice noticed. "What is wrong?" she asked.

David shook his head.

"You seem very...pensive," she said.

He looked away from her gaze and saw Tony staring at him. David had thought he was finished with the boy's suspicions but apparently not.

"I thought I was done with that," David said.

"Done with what?" Alice asked.

"With having to watch people die."

"Dying is just the end of a life. If you live, you have to die."

"You can't believe that," David said, suddenly looking at her. "Not after what happened to your husband."

"Oh, I believe it. I don't like it, but I've had to face it too many times not to believe it."

The *Freeman* stopped for the day near the Oldtown Lock. Af-

271

ter everyone had gone to bed, David walked back to the hay house with the intention of going inside. Instead of going inside, he went to the mule shed and rooted through the tools until he found a hammer and pry bar. He grabbed them both and jumped ashore.

It was time for justice to come to the railroad.

He took a lantern with him as he walked through the night. He crossed the Potomac at a ford the Oldtown lockkeeper had told him about. He came to the railroad tracks and set down the lantern between the ties.

"Now the question is why are you about to destroy the track," a voice asked from behind him.

David spun around and saw Tony standing there. Somehow, he wasn't surprised that the boy had followed him. He was surprised that Tony had been able to sneak up on him. After living half a year in the wilderness, he had hoped his woodsman skills were greatly improved. Apparently not.

"Call it revenge if you want," David admitted. "Maybe it's time the railroaders know a little bit of the misery they've brought on the canallers."

Tony came forward. "I know that feeling. I felt the same way after Mr. Fitzgerald was killed in Shanty Town. The trouble was that after I had my revenge, it didn't change anything. Mr. Fitzgerald was still dead and another tavern sprung up where the one I had burned down had been. In the end, I changed nothing. I didn't even feel better."

Tony had burned down a tavern?

"Maybe so, but I can't let what they did to that girl go unanswered. She could have been killed," David said.

"But will you hurt who you want to hurt? Will tearing up track stop one more person from being hurt by the railroaders? I don't think so."

Tony was probably right, but David felt that he had to do something. The railroaders were like McLaughlin. If they were allowed to get away with their dangerous tricks, the tricks would simply become more dangerous.

"So you're saying I shouldn't do this."

Tony shrugged. "I'm not saying do one thing or the other. I'm just a kid, but being with the Fitzgeralds has made me think things through more than I used to. I've seen how rash decisions affect the people around you in ways you don't think of."

David squatted down and stared at Tony. "I don't suppose Alice would approve of me doing this, would she?"

Tony shook his head. "Not likely."

"I don't suppose that she knows you burned a tavern down?"

Even in the lamplight, David could see Tony blush. "She knows that it burned, but she doesn't know that I did it. I hope she doesn't find out, either," Tony said, shooting David a glance of concern.

"Your secret's safe with me." David stared at the iron rails. "Then I guess I'd better not do this."

"I won't say otherwise if you do do it because I can't say it would be wrong or at least I can't say I wouldn't do it."

"But we'll both know what I did even if you don't say anything."

"I've lived with worse," Tony said.

David shook his head. "No, I won't do anything. There's got to be another way."

He picked up the lantern and tools. Then he and Tony started walking back to the boat. Tony seemed to slide between branches rather than pushing them aside. How did he do that?

"You want Mrs. Fitzgerald to like you, don't you?" Tony asked as they walked.

"Yes. She's a woman who a person just seems to want to please. I know I do. She went out of her way to help me."

Tony nodded. "I know. The problem is that I just never know if I'm doing the right thing."

"Has she told you otherwise?"

Tony shook his head. "No, but..."

"She's a truthful person, Tony. She'd tell you if you were in the wrong."

Tony nodded. "I sure hope so."

Five days later, they offloaded their coal without much of a wait at Georgetown. There were plenty of ships ready to take on coal and carry it up the coast where winter weather had already settled in. People needed to stay warm so there was a growing demand for coal for their stoves.

On the way back to Cumberland, the weather turned ominous about three miles past Great Falls. The clouds darkened as they quickly moved in from the east.

David saw them and said to Alice, "I'd say we're going to have rain in another hour."

"Better rain than snow. I'd like to get a couple more loads of coal in before winter shuts the canal down," Alice said.

"Can we keep going in the rain?"

Alice nodded. "We've got a light boat. The mules don't need as much traction so the mud shouldn't bother them. Tony has a slicker he can wear and so do I. As long as we can see, we'll be all right."

The winds came first, which seemed to surprise Alice. It was strong and cold.

"It's going to be worse than I thought," she said. "We'd better stop and wait it out."

Then the rain started; soft at first, but it quickly picked up. It began to fall hard enough to sting when it hit skin.

"Lay out the fall board, David," Alice told him. "Tony, bring the mules aboard. We're going to wait this storm out."

Lightning lit up the sky, followed a few moments later by a clap of thunder. The rain was cold and smacking hard against exposed flesh.

David laid out the fall board and then helped Tony lead Jigger and Ocean into the mule shed. It would be cramped inside the shed with all four mules at one time, but they would fit. They would endure the confinement better than they would the stinging rain.

Thomas ran down the race plank making sure all of the hatch covers were snug to keep the holds from flooding. He also closed the shutters on the windows.

The boat began to move a little up and down as David closed the shutters to the mule shed. He was unused to feeling such motion on the canal. He and Tony made their way quickly up to the family cabin where Elizabeth would be cooking something warm and delicious.

"How long do you think this will last?" he asked Alice as he came inside.

"Hopefully, no longer than an hour. Any longer than that and they may have to open the dams and locks to keep the water flowing through so the canal doesn't flood."

David sat down to drink a cup of warm apple juice that Elizabeth had poured for him. He sipped at it as he watched Alice cook ham on the stove. Off to one side, Thomas was trying to show Tony the lessons in his school books. David sighed and felt himself at peace.

Then it thundered. The boat rocked and lurched, although it was moored to a tree.

Alice paused to listen to the rain thrumming on the roof.

"It's going to be hard running against the current tomorrow," she said to no one in particular.

"Why?" David asked.

"With this much rain, the guard locks might not be able to hold back the water. That means that there will be a current pushing against us in areas. Going through the locks should be faster, though, but rough," Alice explained to him.

The boat floated to the side and David thought he could hear the mooring lines creaking as the current tried to pull the boat to the east. Thunder boomed right on top of them. Elizabeth winced at the sound.

Then suddenly Alice was falling backwards as the boat went up on one side. David reached out to catch her, but only wound up falling as the chair he was sitting in tipped back. Tony and Elizabeth yelled as they were thrown to the ground. Thomas only laughed as he rolled across the floor.

Instead of coming back down, the boat stayed upended. The family cabin was tilting at a forty five degree angle.

Alice climbed unsteadily to her feet. She quickly put out the fire in the stove before the ashes fell out onto the boat and started a fire.

"Thomas, Elizabeth, Tony, go get the mules onto the towpath, but be careful. They will be upset," Alice said.

"What happened?" David asked. He rubbed the back of his head where he had hit it against the boat.

They opened the lock gates upriver and the current shoved us up onto the side of the canal."

He was surprised to hear how calm she sounded. The motion had scared him. She sounded as calm as if this happened everyday, but David couldn't imagine that.

"You mean we're grounded?" David asked.

"For now. There's no use in getting ourselves off the bank until the weather calms down some, else we might get thrown right back up."

With the family cabin tilted at a forty-five degree angle, the floor was now the wall and the wall the floor. They had to climb up the floor and into the Alice's room. There, they could stand on the stateroom wall and hoist themselves through the window of the family cabin.

Outside in the rain, David saw that Alice had been right. It was the only thing that made sense, but he had hoped that she was wrong. He didn't think it would be easy to get the boat off the bank without harming the hull and destroying the canal berm.

David saw the children struggling to keep control of the scared mules. The children were half pulling/half leading the mules out of the mule shed. He and Alice went to help them. The mules were shaken and scared, but they hadn't been hurt when they were thrown against each other. It was more dangerous trying to move them out of the mule shed because they kept trying to step on each other to get out.

When everyone and the mules were on the towpath, Alice gathered them under the trees at the edge of the towpath.

"Now, we just wait for the rain to stop," she said.

She drew her rain slicker tighter around her.

The water in the canal was running hard and lapping over the edge of the bank. It hadn't been hard to ground the boat since it had been floating near the top of the canal anyway.

"If the water rises any higher, we can push the boat back into the canal because it will be floating," David said hopefully.

"If the water rises any higher, it will damage the canal that could cause a break," Alice told him. "That fast water will wear away at the berm. We'd still be grounded, but then so would everyone else."

The rain began to slack off after an hour. Another half an hour brought it to an end. The storm had been hard but also fast moving.

Alice motioned to the mules. "Get them harnessed. We've got to get the boat back into the water while the ground is still wet."

David quickly realized what she was doing. With slick grass and mud and the high water, the boat would hopefully slide into the canal with little damage to the canal itself.

For all of her lady-like appearances, Alice was truly a canaller and she knew her job.

Thomas and Tony brought the extra harnesses out of the mule shed and harnessed all four of the mules to the boat. As Thomas had the mules pull downriver, David and Tony pushed against the side of the boat helping nudge it toward the canal. The current also helped edge the boat into the water. Alice and Elizabeth kept the snubbing ropes around trees so that once the *Freeman* was in the water, it wouldn't race wildly down the canal with the current.

It took nearly an hour to get the boat back into the water. With every few feet the boat moved forward, it might move toward the water an inch. When the leverage was finally favorable, the *Free-*

man picked up speed. It pulled away from David and Tony and slid into the water.

David dropped to the ground, unable to tell the difference between his sweat and the rain water.

Tony walked up and slapped him on the back. "Good job."

David nodded, not saying anything because he was trying to catch his breath. He looked over and saw Alice coiling the snubbing line. When she got close to the edge of the boat, she heaved it over the side.

"I'd not like to have to do that often," she said.

"Nor would I. So much for recuperating quietly," David said.

"Very little has been quiet about this season," Alice noted as she hopped on board the *Freeman*.

David detected a note of sadness in the comment, but then why shouldn't she be sad? Her husband was dead. Her son was missing. Her home had been destroyed.

The boat had been tied between two trees to keep it relatively stable in the current. Thomas and Tony kept the mules on the towpath, though. They had been spooked and they weren't going to want to go back on board anytime soon.

David hopped onto the race plank. Alice was lifting one of the cargo hatches up.

"What are you doing to do?" David asked.

"I've got to check the hull. We hit the berm pretty hard when we were grounded. We could be taking on water."

"I'll check it if you'll hold the lantern," David offered.

He slid over the edge of the race plank and dropped down into the holds. They smelled of coal and the dust nearly choked him.

First, he listened for water dripping that would mark a leak in the hull. Hearing none, he called for the lantern. Alice passed it down to him. He walked the length of the hold examining the walls and then he double-checked. The hull walls were dry.

He walked back to the open hold and said, "No leaks. I guess we got lucky."

"That would be the first time this season," Alice replied.

36

RUMORS

OCTOBER 1862

At Lock 25, Alice first heard the rumors. David and Tony were helping John Shaw lock the *Freeman* through while she bought some fresh bread from Sadie Shaw.

Sadie passed her the loaf of wheat bread and another of white. Alice put them in a basket and covered them with a cloth.

"So have you given up hope that the Union will hold?" Sadie asked.

Alice shook her head. "No. Why do you ask?"

Sadie gave her a hurt look. "Do I look the fool, girl? I can hear a Southerner talking when I listen to your hand."

"So? Maryland borders Virginia. Many a Marylander got his start across the river and vice versa," Alice said without hesitation.

Sadie rolled her eyes. "Alice, it's obvious he's not a canawler. Do you think you were hiding it?"

Alice looked over her shoulder at David as he struggled to let out the snubbing line. He might not be a canawler, but he was trying his best. He never shirked his work and he was willing to learn. He would soon be a canawler.

"What should I have done, Sadie? Turn away a wounded man?" Alice asked.

She shrugged. "Why not? He's killing our men. I've got two boys fighting the Rebs. Your pet Reb won't get sympathy from me," the older woman said angrily.

"David's killing no one. He is helping my family when we need it."

Sadie snorted and waved a finger at Alice. "Could it be that you're just too willing to fill your bed now that your husband's gone?"

Alice reacted with more anger than she had felt in a long time. She slapped Sadie so hard that it stung her hand and brought tears to Sadie's eyes. Sadie didn't cry, though. She chuckled as if somehow Alice had proved her right.

"I love Hugh and that will never change. David does not fill my bed. Nor does he try. He doesn't even sleep in the family cabin."

Sadie grinned wickedly. "I wasn't talking about sleeping."

"You're cruel."

"I'm just saying what many others are saying. Talk of your pet Reb is going up and down the canal with every canal boat. He's a good-looking man and you're a recent widow. You wouldn't be the first to give up something less than her sympathies in a situation like that."

"Just because they talk like that doesn't mean they're right," Alice snapped.

She turned and left before Sadie could make anymore comments. She had never been friends with Sadie Shaw, but she had never known the woman to be hateful either.

She climbed aboard and took the tiller as Thomas had the mules start walking. When they were out of sight of the lock house, Tony came out of the family cabin and sat down on the family cabin roof near her.

"People can say things that can hurt you more than if they simply hauled off and punched you in the gut," Tony said after a few moments.

Alice stared at the young boy in amazement. "You know?"

Tony held his hand out and wiggled it back and forth. "Some. I caught a bit of the whispers and what some of the lockkeepers have been saying behind Mr. Windover's back. They don't mind so much saying it in front of me, but they wouldn't dare say it in front of him."

"Why's that?"

"He'd step in to defend you like he defended Elizabeth when the corporal attacked her."

"You know what they've been saying isn't true," Alice said. She asked it more as a need for confirmation that she was right.

Tony nodded slowly. "I know it's a lie, but to them who says it, it's true."

Now that confused Alice. "Why would that be?"

"Because they want to believe the worst in people. Not just you, but everyone. I used to hear the same sort of things about my mother and me when we lived in Shanty Town. They weren't true then...well, at least not completely. Still, I used to believe every bad word I heard for awhile. Then I realized how stupid that was. I knew those people weren't telling the truth because it was me that they was talking about. Who knew better what I was doing and what I thought than me? If I knew I wasn't so bad, then I had to believe that with all my heart because if I didn't believe it, then why should they?

"I can't see why they would think such a thing. I've given them no reason to believe a lie like that," Alice said. It hurt her to know that people she called her friends were spreading untrue rumors about her.

Tony shrugged. "If it wasn't that, it would be something else they would talk about. You have to believe in yourself. You know you've done no wrong. Don't act like you have."

Alice ran her hand through his hair and then kissed him on the cheek. "I'm so glad that you're a part of my family now, Tony."

The boy blushed.

"So am I," he said proudly.

37

CAPTURE
OCTOBER 1862

The Union patrol blocked the towpath and showed no signs of stepping aside for Jigger and Ocean. Thomas stopped walking the mules when he couldn't pass. Alice let the *Freeman* drift to a stop near the soldiers.

"You're blocking our way," Alice said.

"We can see that, ma'am," the lieutenant in charge said.

"Then please move. I've only got time for one or two more runs before they close the canal for the season, and I'd rather be able to winter in Cumberland than Weaverton or Hancock," Alice said, acting calmer than she felt.

What did these men want? Why were they being so much more defiant than the other patrols had been? Were they stopping all boats or just this one?

"If you'll set out your plank, ma'am, we'll come aboard and finish our business and be gone so you can be about yours," the lieutenant said.

"And what would your business be that would require you to invade my home like a thief?" Alice asked.

The lieutenant jumped from the bank onto the race plank. Two other members of his patrol quickly followed him. The lieutenant walked forward and stopped in front of Alice.

"We're here to arrest a Southern spy," the lieutenant said.

He waved his two men into the family cabin.

"You can't do that!" Alice shouted. "I'm an American citizen."

David walked out of the cabin, followed by the two soldiers. He climbed the steps and stood in front of the lieutenant.

"What do you want with my hand?" Alice asked.

"We have information that your hand is a Southern spy."

"Who would tell you such nonsense?" Alice tried to be defiant, but she was afraid. Someone had told the soldiers about David!

The lieutenant shook his head. "I'm not at liberty to say."

He nodded his head toward the shore and the two soldiers led

David off the boat. He didn't try to fight them. He went peacefully, although Alice knew he was giving up his freedom.

"What gives you cause to think this man a spy other than one person's word over another person's?" Alice asked. She was frantic to stop them from taking David. She had heard stories of what prison camps were like. David didn't deserve that.

"We have no evidence if that's what your asking, ma'am. We're going to take this man here to our headquarters in Frederick so he can be questioned. If he's innocent, he'll be released to return to work with you," the lieutenant explained.

"Frederick? That's two days away."

The lieutenant shrugged. "That's where the general is for the time being."

"Release David now. He's innocent."

The lieutenant shook his head. "I'm sorry, ma'am. I can't do that. I have my duty to do."

From the shore, David said, "It's all right, Alice. It couldn't have lasted much longer. This is better for you, anyway."

"Who are you to say what's best for me, Mr. Windover?" Alice snapped.

David just grinned. How could he smile at a time like this?

"I wouldn't presume such a thing, Mrs. Fitzgerald."

Why wasn't he upset that he was being led away to prison? Didn't he care about keeping his freedom? Why didn't he do something to help himself?

The lieutenant tipped his hat to Alice and then jumped ashore. The patrol walked past the boat, leading David. He waved to her, but he didn't stop walking.

Alice leaned on the tiller as she watched them walk out of sight. She thought about trying to forget about David as he had suggested, but she couldn't. It wasn't right that he should be taken away as a prisoner. He hadn't done harm to anyone. He wasn't a part of the fighting any longer.

What could she do to help David, though? She didn't know anyone in Frederick who could help her win David's freedom and Eli Sampson was too far away to help.

She had risked her life to help slaves win their freedom. Shouldn't she be as willing to risk as much to help a friend as she was to help a stranger?

But what could she do?

Tony came out of the family cabin and said, "I thought Mr.

Windover would betray us, and instead, we betrayed him."

Alice spun around. "What do you mean? We did not betray him!"

"We let him think that his past could be forgotten; that he could avoid the war by taking up a new life on the canal, and it just wasn't true. I thought he would abandon us, but I was wrong. He became a part of the crew; a part of the family," Tony explained.

"Like you," Alice said, ruffling his hair.

Tony nodded. "Then the family should do something to help him. Isn't that part of what family members do for one another?"

"What can we do?" She was more than willing to listen to any new ideas since she didn't have any.

"You know some of my background," Tony said.

Alice nodded.

"I'm a thief, or at least I was when I lived in Shanty Town. I can steal just about anything and I'm pretty good at it," he said quietly.

Alice suddenly realized what he was getting at. "Like people?"

Tony nodded.

David was surprised that when the Union patrol stopped for the night he wasn't tired. He had been walking so much in the past few months both on the canal and while he was serving in the army that walking a few hours was nothing for him.

The Union soldiers didn't try to question him and they didn't abuse him. They did keep their rifles pointed in his general direction, though. They thought that he was going to run if he got the chance.

They were wrong.

David just didn't care anymore. He knew that he couldn't stay with the Fitzgeralds no matter how much he might want to remain. The canal, though long, was an area where everyone seemed to know everyone else. They knew he was not a part of the canal, and they had guessed where he was from. How could he remain on the canal when most of the people considered him an enemy? Besides, winter would eventually come and the canal would be drained, leaving him with no place to go.

The patrol set up their tents and David went inside the one he had been given and lay down. Most of the patrol laid down to sleep also, but David heard two men talking. They were probably the first watch guards for the night.

He closed his eyes, wondering if he would have nightmares

again tonight. He hadn't had them while he was with the Fitzgeralds, but now he was under arrest.

What would the Union soldiers do when they found out that he was a Confederate deserter? Would they put him in a Union prison?

After a while, the two soldiers stopped talking. David knew they weren't asleep, but they were getting tired. He was, too. Maybe he would be able to sleep about the same time they switched shifts.

David did fall asleep at some point, only to be shaken gently awake a short time later. He opened his eyes and started to say something, but the shadow of the person who had awakened him put a hand over his mouth to quiet him.

The person leaned close to David and whispered in his ear, "Be quiet, Mr. Windover, unless you want to get me into a lot of trouble."

David nodded.

Tony removed his hand.

"How did you get in here?" David whispered.

Tony pointed to the split back of the tent.

"The guards didn't see you?"

"No, and they won't see you either if you do what I tell you to," Tony whispered.

Tony went to the hole he had cut and stuck his head outside. Then he parted the edges of the tent and waved David through. As David neared Tony, the boy put a hand on David's shoulder and pointed out the direction he wanted David to go.

"Stay low and don't rush," Tony told him.

They worked their way out of the camp. In a few moments, they were out of range of the light from the campfire. They blended into the shadows of the forest and moved south.

"How did you get into the camp without being seen?" David asked when he judged that they were sufficiently far away.

"I used to be a thief. These soldiers aren't used to thieves. I waited until about two o'clock when they were getting sluggish. One of the guards was even asleep, but the other one didn't bother to wake him. They were overconfident. They probably don't think you are able to get away from them."

"Does Alice know you're here?"

"Who do you think sent me?" Tony said, grinning.

"But I can't go back to the boat. That's the first place the soldiers will look for me when they realize I'm gone," David argued.

"Who says they'll find you? Mrs. Fitzgerald has a place where she can hide you," Tony explained.

"Why is she doing this? It puts her in danger."

Tony looked at him in surprise. "She believes in you, Mr. Windover. She believes in you and what you want to be and not what others are trying to make you out to be."

Tony led them through the forest, avoiding the roads that the patrol had traveled. They moved quickly, at times jogging along stretches of road until they found cover among more trees.

Thomas was the first person David saw on the canal. The young boy was standing with two of the mules on the towpath. The mules were harnessed and ready to work. Thomas waved to David as he and Tony passed him to get onto the boat.

"I'm glad you're back, Mr. Windover," Thomas said.

Elizabeth stood at the tiller. When she saw David and Tony were aboard, she waved to her brother and Thomas started walking the mules.

Alice came out of the family cabin as the boat started to move. When she saw David and Tony, she hugged them both.

"I was worried about you both. It took so long," she said.

"I had to wait until the right time to go in after him," Tony said.

"Thank you for what you're doing for me," David said.

"Right now, we need to get as far from this area as we can. I know we can't outrun the patrol when they come after us, but the further away we can get from the them, the better off we'll be. Maybe they'll even let us go without following," Alice said.

She smiled as if she was joking. However, they both knew the patrol would find them the next day.

The patrol showed up the next afternoon, moving along the towpath at double time. Thomas had been instructed not to panic at the sight of the soldiers.

Alice was at the tiller and saw them coming toward her as they approached the boat. She took a deep breath.

"Stop this boat!" the lieutenant ordered.

"What are you going to do now? Arrest my son as a spy?" Alice said, feigning innocence.

She waved to Thomas and he stopped the mules. The boat drifted to a rest next to the towpath.

"Your hand escaped from his tent last night," the lieutenant said.

"Now how could one man escape from a patrol of eight soldiers?" Alice asked.

The lieutenant's back straightened. "It would take a skilled spy to do it. I guess that proves that a spy is just what he was."

Alice nearly laughed.

"It only proves that he didn't want to be forced to go where you were taking him."

"If you don't mind, we'll search your boat now, Mrs. Fitzgerald, just to make sure your hand didn't come back," the lieutenant said.

"Well, I do mind."

The lieutenant nodded. "Then you have my apologies."

He waved his men aboard. They jumped from the towpath onto the race plank and spread out across the boat. They went into the three cabins and even jumped into the holds to search for David. In the family cabin, they opened the pantry doors and looked into the stateroom. Other men checked the holds, hay house and mule shed.

The search didn't take too long. When the soldiers came out, Alice had her arms crossed over her chest as she stared at the men.

"Did you find him, Lieutenant?" she asked.

The lieutenant sighed and shook his head. "No, ma'am."

"Then I would have you get off my boat so I can get back to work. You've already made my job harder by arresting my hand. Now you're trying to delay me further. You can be sure I'll be writing to your commanding officer this winter when I have more time."

The soldiers hopped ashore. Alice waved to Thomas and he started the mules walking. The soldiers watched the boat start to move. Alice pointedly looked away from them.

When they had been moving for about an hour, Alice had Elizabeth take over the tiller for her. Then Alice went into the family cabin and opened the pantry doors.

"It's all right, David. They're gone," she said.

David removed the false wall and stared at Alice.

"This is a convenient hiding place," he said.

"It has proved useful from time to time," she told him.

"I won't ask for what."

Alice nodded. "That's probably for the best."

David handed her some of the items off the bottom shelf. Then he removed the shelf and slid out under the remaining shelves.

"Thank you for everything you've done," he said.

"You make it sound like you're leaving."

He sighed and said, "I can't stay. That should be obvious. Someone along the way will see that I'm still on board and tell another patrol."

Alice shook her head. "You don't have to leave. The season will be over soon. You can grow a beard and mustache and change your name. No one will know."

David looked skeptical. "That's a lot to hope for."

Alice stepped back from him. "It's your choice, David, but do you really want to go back to fighting when you are needed here?"

David shook his head. "No, but…"

"Then stay."

"I can't. Staying will hurt you and the children. Those patrols are going to be searching this boat every time they see it for awhile. Even if they weren't a problem, what about the rumors that people are spreading about you? I've got to leave. Maybe I'll go to California."

Alice laid out a large pillowcase on the table. Then she began stuffing food into it.

"What are you doing?" David asked.

"If you're going to leave, at least I want to make sure you won't go hungry. Consider it your wages for the work you've done while you were here. I'll give you enough to get you halfway to California."

"You don't have to do that. What you've already done, sending Tony to get me and patching my wounds, was more than enough," David said.

"You had better get your things," Alice told him.

David walked to the hay house and packed his few things. He didn't want to leave the boat, but he didn't want to endanger Alice and the children either. He had to do what was right, which in this case, was not what was convenient or what he wanted to do.

David hefted his bedroll onto his shoulder and crawled through the window onto the race plank. Alice was standing at the tiller with Tony and Elizabeth. David walked up to them.

"I'll miss you all," David said.

"Where are you going to go?" Tony asked.

David shrugged. "I'll go back across the river, for starters. I can't bring myself to fight again, but if I'm not going to fight, I owe it to my commanders to let them know they can't depend on me. Then I will head out west to see the rest of the country."

287

"What will your commander do when you tell him?" Elizabeth asked.

David shrugged and then grinned. "Maybe I'll just send him a letter." Elizabeth smiled. "Goodbye, Elizabeth. I guess the next time I see you, you'll be a full-grown woman. You may even be married."

Elizabeth blushed.

"Will we see you again?" Alice asked.

David turned to face her. "I hope so. This war won't last forever. When it's over, I'll be able to come back and see you," David said.

"Can we come see you in California? I thought about going there at one time," Tony asked.

"You can spend the winters with me and I'll spend summers with you," David promised with more cheer than he felt. California was a long way away to make such a pie-crust promise.

David shook Tony's hand. "You'll have to watch out for these ladies now," he said.

"I will," Tony promised.

David looked at Alice. She had tears in her eyes. He leaned over and kissed her on the cheek.

"I owe you more than you'll ever know," he said.

"Then stay," she whispered.

David closed his eyes. How he wanted to say yes!

He walked down the stairs from the pilot's deck to the race plank. He hopped across the water and onto the towpath. He looked up at Alice, Tony, and Elizabeth. He willed his memory to remember their faces. Then he turned and began walking away.

He ruffled Thomas's hair as he walked by and shook the boy's hand and then he veered off the towpath toward the river.

38

WAR ON THE CANAL
NOVEMBER 1862

No one seemed to want to speak as the *Freeman* headed toward Cumberland. Alice thought about stopping in Cumberland and finding work for winter. She could get a head start on some of the other women who would be looking for winter work once the canal was drained. She had lost some of her desire to continue working on the canal, at least for this season. This year had been too draining on her emotions.

She had thought that David would stay. She had seen in his expression that he wanted to stay. Yet, he had left.

Was it so unexpected, though? What could be permanent in a time of war?

As they prepared to go into the Potomac River for a short stretch at the river lock near Dam 4, Alice perked up to pay attention. The river was still running high from the recent rain so she needed to maintain control over the boat.

Thomas rounded the curve of the canal first, driving the mules. He disappeared out of sight from Alice.

She heard a sudden volley of shots ahead of her.

"Thomas!" she yelled. She imagined him being shot at by soldiers. The image frightened her.

The tow ropes went slack, but the boat kept moving and came around the curve. Alice could see the mules stopped on the towpath ahead. Thomas was crouched beside them.

Ahead of them, she saw puffs of smoke rising from the brush and trees, marking the positions of soldiers. Other men were on the towpath, crouching and firing at the hidden ambushers. Other soldiers lay sprawled across the towpath. The Union patrol had been ambushed. Alice couldn't help but wonder if it was the same patrol that had arrested David.

The mules began jumping nervously at the shots.

"Thomas, get them back away from there!" Alice called.

Thomas grabbed the harness chains and began to turn the mules around. Ocean suddenly screamed and collapsed from a stray shot in his head. At least Alice hoped that it was a stray shot. King Edward began kicking out and rearing from the smell of blood.

"Thomas, forget the mules and get away from there!" Alice yelled.

Thomas ran. Tony went to the front of the boat and held out his hand for Thomas to catch hold of as he jumped aboard.

With the mules stopped, the boat began to drift away from the towpath. Alice had to try and hold it to the side while squatting down so she was less of a target for bullets.

The river current began to push the *Freeman* further out into the river. The tiller wasn't powerful enough to hold the boat to the side of the towpath for long.

On the shore, King Edward was struggling to run, but chained to Ocean, he wasn't able to go far. His weight and King Edward's weight were keeping the boat from drifting uncontrollably down the river. However, as the river current took greater hold on the boat, the *Freeman*'s weight began to drag the two mules toward the river, which only made King Edward panic more.

Elizabeth noticed the mule losing ground first and pointed it out to her mother. "Mama, King Edward will drown if he is caught in the river."

Elizabeth was right, but the mules combined weight was helping her control the boat. If she cut the mules free, then the current would definitely take hold of the boat. Still, if the current pulled both the *Freeman* and the mules into the river, their weight would then hinder her efforts to control the boat and keep it off the rocks.

"Tony, cut the tow rope!" Alice shouted as she made her decision.

Tony pulled his knife from its sheath and began to saw at the rope. Alice knew immediately when Tony had cut through the rope because the *Freeman* picked up speed as it headed downstream.

Unfortunately, the boat was turned in the wrong direction as it moved downriver. The boat bounced hard up and down as the waves crashed around them. It was worse than it had been on the boat during the heavy storm that had grounded the *Freeman*.

"Grab hold of something!" Alice warned the children. She didn't want any of them being washed overboard from the waves.

Alice tried to steer the boat to the shore, but she couldn't tell if she was making progress. Then when it seemed she was, she had to turn the boat back out into the river to avoid a patch of rocks.

The *Freeman* was not built for open water and she was quickly losing control over it.

From the corner of her eye, she saw someone dive into the water from the shore. She tried to see who it was, but she had to keep her attention on the river ahead.

"It's David!" Elizabeth shouted.

David? What was he doing here? He was supposed to be back across the river. He was supposed to be on his way to California.

"What's he doing in the river? Throw him a rope," Alice said.

Tony grabbed the coiled spare tow rope and heaved it into the river. It landed to David's right. David saw the splash and swam toward the rope. The current tried to push him further downriver, so that he was swimming further upriver than across it.

To grab hold of the rope forced David to stop swimming as hard. The current carried him away and slammed him against one of the rocks that Alice had been steering the *Freeman* away from. David slipped under the water for a few moments in a stunned daze, but then he came back to the surface, coughing and spitting water.

With the rope wrapped around his waist, David swam for the shore. It was easier than swimming toward the boat had been. He simply let the current carry him downriver as he worked his way toward the shore.

Once David was on the shore, he carried the line to the nearest thick-trunked tree. He threw the rope around the tree as if the tree was a snubbing post.

Alice was still struggling to keep the boat as close to the shore as possible without going onto the rocks. It was a losing battle. She was either going to have to brave the river or crash the boat and risk sinking it.

The *Freeman* passed David's position and a few yards further on, the slack in the rope ran out. The line snapped taut. David braced his foot against the tree to try and hold the rope tight.

The *Freeman* swung in toward the shore and began to hold its position against the current.

Alice sighed.

"It's working," Tony yelled from the boat.

It was working, but only temporarily. The line was slipping away under David's fingers. He hadn't had time to tie off the line to a tree and the weight of the boat and the power of the current were stronger than he could resist.

Alice leaned on the tiller to turn the *Freeman* out of the fast current and toward the shore.

"Hurry up!" David yelled. "The line's slipping!"

"I'm trying, David, but the boat will only move as fast as the water," Alice yelled back.

David leaned back, trying to hold the rope. The canal boat swung further toward the shore. Then it wedged itself between two large rocks and held tight.

David sighed as he felt the pressure against the tree lessen. He took the opportunity to tie the rope tightly around the tree.

On the boat, Tony retied the second snubbing line to the boat. Then he jumped from the boat to the rocks to make his way to shore carrying the rest of the line. Thomas quickly ran after him to help. The two of them followed David's lead and tied the snubbing line to a tree further upriver from the boat.

Between the two ropes, the boat would be secure in the river. When everything had calmed down, Alice could figure out how to get the boat back into the canal.

David retraced Tony's path across the rocks to get onto the boat. He ran up to Alice and grabbed her by the shoulders.

"Are you all right?" he asked.

She nodded. "Yes! Where did you come from?"

"I took my own advice and sent a letter to my father, telling him I was resigning from the army and I sent a letter to the army telling them I was resigning my commission." He paused. "I don't want to fight anymore, Alice. I'm not a killer."

"What will you do if you can't go home?" Alice asked him.

David grinned. "I was hoping that your offer for me to stay on as your hand was still available. I heard that you needed some help."

Alice laughed. "I do," she said.

"Then I'd like to be that hand."

"What about not wanting to live a life that isn't yours?"

David stepped back and shrugged. "The life I've been living isn't mine. It's been the army's life and before that, it was my father's life to live. Now, for the first time, I think it will be mine."

Alice hugged him once more, and this time, she had tears in her eyes.

ABOUT THE AUTHOR

James Rada, Jr. is the author of historical fiction and non-fiction history. They include the popular books *Saving Shallmar: Christmas Spirit in a Coal Town, Canawlers* and *Battlefield Angels: The Daughters of Charity Work as Civil War Nurses.*

He lives in Gettysburg, Pa., where he works as a freelance writer. Jim has received numerous awards from the Maryland-Delaware-DC Press Association, Associated Press, Maryland State Teachers Association and Community Newspapers Holdings, Inc. for his newspaper writing.

If you would like to be kept up to date on new books being published by James or ask him questions, he can be reached by e-mail at *jimrada@yahoo.com.*

To see James' other books or to order copies on-line, go to *www.jamesrada.com.*

If you liked
CANAWLERS,
you can find more stories at these FREE sites from James Rada, Jr.

JAMES RADA, JR.'S WEB SITE
www.jamesrada.com
The official web site for James Rada, Jr.'s books and news including a complete catalog of all his books (including eBooks) with ordering links. You'll also find free history articles, news and special offers.

TIME WILL TELL
historyarchive.wordpress.com
Read history articles by James Rada, Jr. plus other history news, pictures and trivia.

WHISPERS IN THE WIND
jimrada.wordpress.com
Discover more about the writing life and keep up to date on news about James Rada, Jr.